BOOKS BY KRISTIE COOK

SOUL SAVERS

Recommended Reading Order:

A Demon's Promise

An Angel's Purpose

Genesis: A Soul Savers Novella

Dangerous Devotion

Dark Power

Sacred Wrath

Unholy Torment

Fractured Faith

Age of Angels Part I: Awakened

Age of Angels Part II: Lost

Age of Angels Part III: Marked

Prophecy of the Wolves: (A Soul Savers Tie-In Novella)

Wonder: A Soul Savers Collection of Holiday Short Stories & Recipes

HAVENWOOD FALLS

Recommended Reading Order:

Forget You Not

Lose You Not

Break Me Not

The Collector: Awakening

Savage Salvation (Sin & Silk)

Sun & Moon Academy Book One: Fall Semester

Sun & Moon Academy Book Two: Fall Semester

The Winged & the Wicked (with T.V. Hahn)

Havenwood Falls Short Story Anthology 2018

Havenwood Falls Short Story Anthology 2019

Havenwood Falls Short Story Anthology 2020

BOOK OF PHOENIX

The Space Between

The Space Beyond

The Space Within

SOUL SAVERS BOOK 7

FRACTURED FAITH

KRISTIE COOK

Ang'dora
PRODUCTIONS

For Everyone

because we can all use a little faith and a lot of love

$\mathcal{A}$s the world destructed upon itself, the last thing I wanted to be doing was staring into the black abyss of a Demon's eye. Yet, here I was, standing on the marble steps of the Thomas Jefferson Memorial doing just that, while bombs exploded throughout the city and chunks of black ice crashed into the ground, transporting more Demons into this realm. Along with the ice came a rain of fire. It ignited the dry, autumn landscape, creating an orange glow in the night sky that added to the imagery of Hell on Earth.

The only thing I *did* want to be doing at this moment was to be holding my wife and son, or better yet, sweeping them off to safety. But first, I had to finish off this last son of a bitch who blocked my way to the rotunda above. The first few Demons had given me quite the beating, but I learned with each one, and had sent six, so far, chasing after their heads.

Seven had always been my lucky number. If I believed in such a thing.

I watched the Demon's horned head as its membranous wings beat at the air and its barbed tail swished to and fro, while I calculated its next move. Its green and yellow dappled skin seemed to undulate like a separate being with each movement, creating a distraction for the inexperienced. But I focused on its obsidian eyes. And when it glanced to my left, I knew it would actually go right, so I feigned that way too. Then I ducked and weaved to its left and swung my foot up. My boot slammed into its lizard-like nose, shoving its face into its head with a squishing, spurting sound as if it were made out of gelatin.

Its thick neck twisted, and a fang jutting out of its jaw hooked into my boot. When it gave a shake of its head, as though trying to throw its face back into place, it jerked me off the ground. I flew into the air, bits of black matter from its head flying with me. I flipped in midair and landed on my feet three steps above the Demon. At least I headed in the right direction.

The Demon let out a screeching, wheezing sound through its smashed nose and mouth, and then it dove at me. Its sharp claws lashed out at my face, and I arched backward out of its reach. Then I sprang back on my hands and launched myself upward, feet first. My thick-soled boots plowed into its barrel chest. The force should have sent it tumbling away, but the powerful beast barely budged a few feet before its wings caught the air. It hung there for a moment, screaming evil curses in the old language as its eyes bulged from the pressure of its crushed nose.

I glanced at the portico only a dozen steps above me now, straining to listen for heartbeats while trying not to draw the Demon's attention toward that direction. I'd heard Alexis screaming what must have been hours ago, but she'd been quiet since, and I hoped she'd been hiding somewhere safe with Dorian. Hiding wasn't like her, not for this long, but I had to hope. I could hear nothing, though, over the squawk of the Demon.

Almost there, my love. Almost there. Her telepathy had become unreliable, so I prayed that she even heard my thoughts.

While sliding a shuriken from a hidden pocket inside my jacket's sleeve, I refocused on the shrieking Demon, analyzing it again so I could seize the perfect opportunity. Since they had no hearts—their bodies weren't permanently physical—my killing power had no effect on these creatures straight from the depths of Hell. Every time I tried to paralyze them, they broke free in seconds with powerful black magic. The Ancients had once divulged to me, during my previous life when I was their pet, that most Demons were too simpleminded to use the powers they possessed. They preferred the thrill of a physical brawl.

Which was fortunate for me.

Because there was only one way to decommission a Demon: decapitate it. It wouldn't die permanently, of course. It was a spirit of the Otherworld. But it would have to return to that other realm, to Hell specifically, to heal before it could take a physical form again. And decapitation required a closeness their magic would never allow if they chose to use it.

Shaking its deformed head again, the Demon batted its wings, lifting it higher in the air so it was once again above me. And that was its mistake. It probably thought it had gained a vantage point, but instead, it exposed its vulnerable throat. At the same moment it twitched to lunge at me, I flicked my wrist, sending the shuriken across its neck. It grinned for a moment, likely believing I'd tried another of my powers on it. But the grin faded along with the inky shine in its eyes. A moment later, the head fell from the body, and then both parts disappeared.

My legs pumped up the steps toward the rotunda as I shouted for my family. "Alexis! Dorian!"

I continued calling for them, but no answer came. Where the hell were they? Why weren't they responding? Panic rose and filled my voice as I yelled their names. My heart pounded with the unfamiliar feeling of fear as I reached the center of the portico. Only broken pillars remained, the roof and walls gone. The statue of Thomas Jefferson, where Noah had been magically bound, lay on its side. On a broken piece of wall, written in what appeared to be dried blood and taking the form of Dorian's handwriting, were the words, "We don't belong with you. I have to do this. Don't try to follow."

Fuck! Dorian had taken Noah and left, possibly for the Daemoni. That must have been what had Alexis screaming earlier. But where was she now?

My pulse raced even faster as my eyes swept over the piles of jagged marble and stone until they caught on something a few yards in front of me. My heart came to a screeching halt. Locks of dark coppery hair. A pale hand. A pool of crimson. And I could see nothing else of her under the rubble.

"Oh, no." A string of profanities poured out of my mouth as I heaved a large chunk of marble to the side. I lifted another, making my way to her still body, my stomach dropping further with each stone I moved. "God, no. Please no."

I couldn't lose her. I couldn't fucking lose her, damn it!

When I cleared another boulder from the pile, my worst nightmare became reality.

The word ripped out of my chest, taking my heart with it. "NO!"

I tossed the last two chunks away and lurched forward, still refusing to believe what I saw. My boots splashed in the blood and slid on the wet marble until I crashed down next to her. My fingers automatically darted for her wrist, but I felt no pulse. No breath warmed my fingertips against her pale lips.

No, Lexi, no. Damn it, no!

I carefully lifted her broken body and pulled her into my lap. My arms wrapped tightly around her, probably crushing her further as I held her against my chest. But it didn't matter.

Because she remained so still. So cold. So . . . lifeless.

The horrific feeling that exploded within me was unbearable. Unimaginable. Unlike anything I'd ever felt before. I knew physical pain. From all of the wars I'd been in, all of the suffering at the hands of Lucas and the Daemoni Ancients, all of the times they'd tried to take my heart but couldn't, I knew physical pain very well. I knew emotional pain. I knew misery and regret when my son had been taken. I knew grief and sorrow from others' deaths, especially Rina's and Sophia's, because I'd come to love them. But this . . .

This unfathomable sensation inside me . . .

This agony of my heart being bludgeoned by a dull machete with each beat it made that hers did not echo . . .

This torture of my soul clawing and scrabbling, tearing itself apart as it searched for hers . . .

I did not know this kind of internal mutilation. I didn't know how to handle it, what to do with it.

Senseless words blubbered out of me as I buried my face in her soft hair and sobbed incoherently for my beautiful bride. For my soul mate. For the one person who had loved me unconditionally. Who had taught me what love felt like. Who had warmed this heart of mine that had been cold for centuries. Whose soul had completed mine, making me whole for the first time ever.

"Alexis, my love, don't leave me." My words morphed into some kind of wail mixed with a howl. A sound of desperation that made me recoil, but I couldn't help it. I couldn't quell it. The pain, the anger, the overwhelming grief! Emotions that were too violent to be held inside. They erupted in shouts and screams and sobs. But still, the agony remained, ripping me apart from the inside.

When I could no longer muster the energy to yell, I silently rocked her in my arms as I recalled our lives together. The first time I'd seen her as an adult—young, barely eighteen and still very human, but nonetheless the most beautiful sight I'd known in my many years. I couldn't pinpoint exactly what it was about her, but she'd captured me and enraptured me from the moment I set eyes on her at this very monument.

Her laugh had been medicine for my damaged heart. Her love a salve for my wrecked soul.

And when I thought I couldn't possibly hold more love in my heart, I met our son for the first time. I'd never imagined I could produce such beauty, but of course, it had come from her. With the many hardships our poor child had suffered, he'd grown into a fine young man. But now . . . Although I'd been expecting this since the day I learned of his birth, a father could never be prepared to lose his son. I could only hope, for his soul's sake, he'd perished in the bombs before he ever reached the Daemoni.

They were both gone. I was left alone. With nothing left to live for.

I pressed my lips into Alexis's hair and murmured in her ear, praying she heard me. Or that *someone* heard me. "Lexi, *ma lykita*, I need you. Don't leave me here alone. Come back to me, my love. Please come back."

I closed my eyes against the brightening sky of morning and slumped backward against a large chunk of marble with my wife still in my arms, her head pressed against my chest as though she were only sleeping. I wanted to sleep with her. The night of fighting the dark magic of the sorcerers and Lucas, and then the Demons that had kept coming, combined with more grief than any one man should have to bear, drained me.

I'd lost my son. I'd lost my wife and our unborn child. The world seemed to have lost anything still good in it.

Take me, too.

"Is that what you really want? Would you come back home if that's where she is?" The deep, Otherworldly voice spoke the old language of the Daemoni Ancients as evil blanketed over me. I peeled one eye open. An orangish-yellow Demon balanced on the edge of a slab of marble a few feet away. I was too exhausted to fight. Too drained to give a shit anymore. "Shall I find her for you?"

My eyes fell closed again. I tightened my hold on Alexis's small body. The word came out as a whisper. "Yes."

The Demon's evil presence disappeared. As the sun rose higher, the odor of burning ozone filled the air. A distant part of my brain urged me to get up, to find shelter from the fallout that would likely blow this way from the mushroom clouds we'd seen near Baltimore and Richmond. Hell, Lucas probably planned a direct hit here in Washington, D.C., at any moment. If I knew him at all, which I did too well, he certainly had. But I couldn't bring myself to care. I slipped off into a doze.

"You will follow her where she goes?" The Demon's voice startled me partially awake.

I sighed. It didn't need me to answer. As a spirit, even an evil one, it already knew.

"Even into the dark?"

Again, it required no verbal reply. But I knew she wasn't there. Not my Alexis. She'd be in Heaven with the rest of the Amadis matriarchs.

"Come with me and make your choice."

I went with the Demon.

CHAPTER 1

$\mathcal{T}$he most important yet surreal question I'd ever asked hung in the air, suspended by the multitude of emotions surrounding it, the last word echoing around me: *Dead . . . dead . . . dead . . .* The only response came from my soul mate's wails, calling like a desperate love song, piercing the veil that separated the Earthly realm from the Otherworld.

That separated him from me.

My mind tried and failed to wrap itself around this fact, and my soul refused to believe it. I watched Tristan through the veil as his sobs and my question swirled together blocking out all else. The warmth of the tears on my cheeks wasn't enough to chase away the chill traveling down my spine.

He held my limp body in his lap, my face pressed into his chest. My hair flowed over his muscular arms that appeared unusually tan compared to the white of my skin. He rocked me back and forth, sobbing my name.

"Alexis, my love. *Please*, God, don't take her. Please make her okay."

I wanted so badly to answer him.

"I'm right here, Tristan," I called back to him, but, of course, he couldn't hear me.

I tried pushing my way to him, but the veil held me back, an invisible curtain that may as well have been a wall as thick as the universe. I could see and hear through it, as clearly as though I stood right before him, but in truth, my love, my soul mate, my other half was in an entirely different dimension.

How had this happened? How could I change it?

My hand pressed to the veil and tears streamed down my cheeks as I gazed out to a world that I was no longer a part of. I should have been relieved for my part to be over, especially with everything wrong in the picture before me.

Tristan sat among the boulder-sized chunks of white marble he'd thrown off of me, his legs spread out before him in a pool of blood. My blood, I assumed. Or, more accurately, the blood of our unborn child. The ruins of the Thomas Jefferson Memorial surrounded him, nothing more than a couple of broken pillars rising from a pile of rubble. We'd gone there to save our son and my uncle when Hell entered the Earthly realm in the form of Demons, nuclear bombs, and fire.

Across the Tidal Basin that looked like black ink, as if refusing to reflect the lightening sky, the Washington Monument resembled a broken toothpick. The once pyramid-shaped top had been cleaved off, leaving blackened, serrated edges reaching for the sky. Fire and ice shot through the air and blasted into the ground. Sparks trailed the fireballs and fell in an orange and yellow rain that ignited whatever they landed on. Fire blossomed everywhere and spread instantly, easily traveling through the trees and grass that had been dried out from the autumn weather, consuming everything in its path as it went. The ice balls shattered into shards on impact, and winged creatures exploded out of them.

The colors of the beings' mottled skin seemed to change as they moved, like a separate creature rippling over their somewhat human-like bodies. They had one head, though horns sprouted from it, some with two and some with many. Their thickly muscled torsos and powerful limbs—two arms and two legs—would make a body-builder weep. They had claws for hands and hooves for feet, a long tail with a barbed tip, and leathery, bat-like wings that spread out from their shoulder blades. They were the things of nightmares, but were part of reality on Earth now.

Demons.

Tristan had been fighting them when the memorial fell to pieces, crushing me. Now, all of the Demons flew toward the National Mall, where undead norms had been limping and shuffling around like zombies, which they'd essentially become. The Demons' shapes disintegrated into a black fog that enveloped the human bodies and then disappeared inside them, possessing them.

Lucas had brought Hell to Earth.

His words slithered through my mind: *The apocalypse is here, and you, darling Alexis, weren't able to stop it. And now you're out of time.*

He hadn't acted alone, though. With a little encouragement from him and the Daemoni, the norms had done their share. They'd gone to war against each other. Bombed each other's lands. Even allowed genocide. Some had committed these acts in the name of protecting their own, but others had been controlled by Lucas's hand of pure evil. And now the norms had done the ultimate act, resorting to nuclear bombs that had created a forest of mushroom clouds earlier in the night.

"There goes Richmond." Lucas's tone had been sharp, filled with a demented thrill. "And Baltimore. See what I mean about the Normans? So eager to destroy. Like I said, you can't stop this . . . It's just a matter of me opening the veil and letting Satan and his Demons in. I'm ready for him! And then . . . the spirits of my lord can come and save this world from itself. Humans are so eager to destroy their home and themselves. He will be a good king over

them. The true god who will empower them and give them everything their hearts desire. You can't stop this . . . you can't stop this."

That one phrase echoed, louder than anything else. Because he'd been right.

We hadn't been able to stop him. We'd been too slow, always five steps behind him. We'd been too naïve. Not even Tristan had anticipated Lucas would go this far, this fast. Because we'd been too *good* to fathom the depth of evil Lucas possessed. Too *honorable* to conceive such an outlandish idea as calling Satan to Earth so he could have the ultimate power over humanity. *Who does that?* My sperm donor. That's who. And I was supposed to lead the crusade to stop him.

But I'd failed.

As morning came, the sun rose on an unrecognizable world.

My vision through the veil panned out, and for as far as I could see, the land burned or was already blanketed in ash. The mushroom clouds had lost their shapes long ago, but their fallout drifted and settled. Homes and buildings were destroyed. And worst of all—thousands of blackened corpses lay in yards and on the sides of roads and highways. Tens of thousands sat in the shells of burned-out cars. They'd probably been trying to escape, but there'd been no place to go. How many more lay in their beds or in shelters not made for nuclear disaster? I didn't want to know.

But I already did.

All of them.

Nobody but Lucas and the Daemoni had been prepared for this final act. And now the only sign of life came from the Demons.

And my grieving husband.

I fell to my knees, clawing at my throat and chest as tears streaked down my cheeks. I'd failed everyone so miserably— the world and humanity, my people, my friends, my family, my son. I'd failed the man sitting before me who'd fought so hard against the evil that had created him, who'd fought so hard to learn goodness and love. Who'd loved me like no other being ever could. And I'd left him. Alone. Heartbroken. Weeping for me.

"How do I help him?" I asked, sensing the others behind me, although they'd never answered my first question and apparently weren't going to answer this one. "What will happen to him? What about Dorian?"

My poor son. *What had I done?* My eyes zoomed in on the broken wall behind Tristan, where written in dried, dark blood were Dorian's words.

"Is Dorian at least *alive?*" I demanded when no answers came. I could at least hope for that. Maybe Noah warned him. Maybe they found shelter somewhere. Maybe there was still hope for him. Or, with the state of the world as it was, perhaps even better would be that he was in Heaven. "Is his soul safe?"

Still no answers, and my stomach dropped. I didn't know what silence meant.

"Answer me!"

More dead air greeted me. Not even the whisper of movement. On this side of the veil, anyway. On the other side, Tristan's cries had deteriorated to moans as he scooted back to lean against a piece of marble with me still in his arms. I watched as his head dropped back, propped by the marble, and his eyes fell closed. The scene before me disappeared, erased, as if it no longer mattered. As if Tristan and I and the rest of the world no longer existed.

"Tristan," I whispered.

"Alexis." My mom's voice finally came quietly behind me, dismissing my string of questions.

"What's happening? Where is everyone?"

"Alexis." Rina's voice this time, and I didn't have to read minds to know from the tone of that single word that she wouldn't answer me.

Ignoring her just as they ignored me, I stared at the place where my husband sat on the other side of the veil, now obliterated by a thick mist. When he didn't return, I finally glanced around and found myself in a white, foggy space of nothingness seeming to stretch into infinity. I'd seen Stefan, Solomon, and Winston before, along with others, but nobody remained anymore, as though the fog had swallowed them up.

"Where am I?" I asked, because this vast emptiness couldn't possibly be Heaven. Where were the golden roads and the walls made of jewels? Where were the souls singing with joy? Where were my husband and son? My team? My people?

"We're in the Otherworld." Mom finally gave me a straight answer. Sort of. The Otherworld consisted of an entire dimension, vaster than Earth, perhaps larger than the universe. Full of many realms.

"But not in Heaven." I didn't state it as a question. I felt too much pain for this to be Heaven. Besides, I didn't belong there. "How do I physically *feel* when Tristan holds my body in the Earthly realm? How am I even here? *Why?*"

"No, not Heaven, but very near it," Rina said, evading my other questions.

The fog shifted in the distance, revealing a crowd of people. Stefan, Solomon, and Winston had returned, along with other Amadis whose funerals I'd attended. For as far as I could see behind them stood a sea of people.

"Everybody's dead," I whispered. Having seen the mushroom clouds on Earth and the lifeless world before it had disappeared, this truth couldn't have been more obvious. Confirmed by prolonged silence.

Tears slid down my cheeks as I stared at the endless crowd, looking for familiar faces. A large group of women with very similar looks—coppery hair, large, dark eyes, olive skin—stood up front, glaring at me. At once, they turned their backs on me, and then a thin cloud floated in, erasing everyone from sight once again. The previous Amadis matriarchs had made no effort to hide their disappointment in me.

They'd trusted me to defeat our enemy and win this war. I'd failed them, like I'd failed everyone else.

I swallowed hard. "So if not Heaven, where are we?"

"We are close," Rina assured. "At the gates."

I glanced around but saw nothing but whiteness. We couldn't be that close.

"We're as close as a twitch of the hand," Mom said. "As close as a final decision."

I understood her implication—I only needed to make the choice for my soul. "Are Tristan and Dorian already there?"

Mom's lips curved downward. "They do not belong there."

My stomach plummeted, and tears filled my eyes. I shook my head in denial. "No. This isn't right. If they don't, then neither do I."

"Darling . . ."

"*No.*" No part of me could accept this. Not this fate. Not this place. Not after what I'd done.

I rocked back onto my butt, crossed my ankles, and pulled my knees to my chest. The big, feathery wings that had burst out of my back in an explosion of pain only moments ago wrapped around me, closing me in, as though comforting and protecting me. I pressed my forehead to my knees and squeezed my eyes shut. I didn't deserve to be here. I didn't deserve comfort and protection.

I most certainly didn't deserve fucking wings.

Not these kind anyway. Not the huge, white, feathery kind that belonged to Angels. If I'd earned any wings at all, they should have been thin and leathery and accompanied by horns, a tail, and cloven hooves.

"Alexis, honey," Mom tried again, and the warm tone and term of endearment enraged me.

My wings flew back, and I jumped to my feet, spinning around to face Mom, Rina, and Cassandra, who'd suddenly appeared. They stood there with their white leathery dresses, swords strapped to their backs, and huge wings spread wide. Their wings weren't white, as I'd thought before, but a pearlescent color that gave off a pale lavender hue. All three women were inhumanly beautiful, even with the grim expressions on their faces. Expressions of displeasure with me. The feeling was mutual.

"How could you let this happen?" I demanded, waving my hand back toward where I'd seen Earth and Tristan holding my dead body. "How could you do this to me? To the Amadis, to humanity and the world?"

"Alexis, darling," Rina began once more.

I thought my soul would explode into pieces as anger and hurt, and every emotion that had been swirling together, built to a point where they could no longer be contained.

"YOU LEFT ME!" I bellowed at them, my hands balling into fists. "You said I was ready for this. You said I'd never be alone. No matter how many times I begged for help, no matter how many times I told you I couldn't do this, you insisted. But you never helped! You never gave me messages in my book. You left me to fight a war I could never win. You even took away my telepathy. My one advantage! You set me up for failure. And now look at what's left of the world. You kept saying we'd win, that I could beat Lucas and lead the Amadis to victory, but you *lied*. And now the entire world has paid for it."

Like a thick, hot waterfall, grief crashed over me and drenched me in misery. I fell to my knees again.

"Alexis, it is not over." Cassandra's voice remained calm in contrast to my rage. She'd moved to float right above me, and I lifted my head to glare at her.

"It is," I said through a tight jaw. "It's *all* over. Lucas and the Daemoni have won. I just want to be with my son and my husband and be done with it. I know I don't deserve any favors, but can you please bring them here? Or take me to them?"

"They cannot be here," Rina said. "They do not belong here."

My chest rumbled.

"I'm here, aren't I?" I snapped. "If that's possible, surely they can be here, too. They certainly don't deserve to be in that Hell down there."

"They still have a purpose to serve. As do you," Cassandra said.

I huffed out a breath. The phrase, the idea of it, the philosophy about serving one's purpose that had been driving me for so long sounded so contrite anymore. No, more like a joke. The insane urge to laugh bubbled up in my chest, but died instantly.

"I have no purpose now," I said flatly. "I'm dead."

"You do. It has not changed."

My gaze snapped up to her. "How can you say that? There are no souls to save. No humans to protect."

"No, Alexis. The war wages on." Cassandra swept her arm out, clearing away a thick fog behind them, and revealing a scene like none on Earth.

A fierce battle encircled the entire world, seemingly in a layer hidden between the troposphere and the ozone—between where I was now and the Earthly realm—and every one of the warriors were winged. Some had magnificent white, feathery wings that glowed, although there was really no light in this space. These were creatures of majestic beauty with powerful bodies that fought with finesse and skill. The others were no different than the Demons that had invaded Earth—horned, bat-winged, and terrifyingly ugly. The beauties and the beasts fought each other with a ferocity that could only exist between Angels and Demons.

Swords swished through the air, clanging against each other. Maces swung, and their spiked ends lodged into shields or flesh. Fangs were bared, and jaws snapped. Claws struck out. Silver and black blood splattered and mixed together. The hand-to-hand combat resembled bloody battles of the past, between Vikings or Romans and their enemies. I couldn't help but duck when a long blade swung toward my head, not knowing whether it could reach me here or not.

Cassandra's hand descended, as though closing a window shade to hide the scene once again. Our surroundings returned to the soft glow of white nothingness that was near the entrance to Heaven, like its foyer or ground floor. Since *I* was here, probably more like its sub-basement.

"The Angels and Demons have been at war in the Otherworld since the beginning of mankind," Cassandra said. "They fight for human souls. The Demons try to ensnare the souls before their time, and the Angels protect them until the humans decide their eternal fate. Never have they fought with such fierce passion and determination as now."

"Maybe someone should tell them it's over," I suggested.

"But it's not," Mom said.

My head flinched back. "But there are no humans left to fight for. There's *nothing* left to fight for."

"There is *everything* left." Cassandra's mahogany eyes sparked with the same resolve that filled her voice. "But the outcome has never been more at risk than now. The consequences have never been so dire. The future of the world, of humanity, is at stake."

Her tone had turned into one of urgency, borderline desperation. Her eyes and expression pleaded with me, as though I could do anything to solve the problem. My heart squeezed for her pain, but I lifted my hands in the air.

"I'm sorry that you put your bets on the wrong daughter. I really, truly am. But I warned you, and now I've destroyed whatever hopes you might have had, along with the entire world. What more can you possibly expect from me?"

"We expect you to keep fighting," Cassandra said simply, as though that were obvious.

My fingers pressed at my forehead as an ache set in, and I squinted at her. "Fight who? The Demons?"

Cassandra's head nodded once. "Yes, the Demons. And Lucas and the Daemoni."

My hand dropped to my side and hit my thigh with a soft thud as I stared at her. "But *how?* I'm dead. From what I can see, humanity is, too. Lucas and the Daemoni have already won."

"No, they have not. Not yet."

I stared at the very first matriarch, apparently sent to be the messenger on behalf of the Angels. Her words, their request didn't compute. Were they unable to see through the veil for some reason? Were they blind to the complete destruction Lucas had caused? Did they forget that I'm freaking *dead?*

"You must not give up," Mom said. She moved closer to me and took my hands into hers. "We still need you."

I closed my eyes and blew out a long breath as I slowly shook my head. "I think I've caused enough loss and devastation. I won't cause any more."

"The *Angels* need you, darling," Rina added.

Cassandra moved closer to me, and her voice softened. "There is still hope, Alexis. There is still love, which you know is worth fighting for. You only need to have faith, and we will be victorious."

My body, with these ridiculous wings, sagged, feeling so heavy that I was surprised I didn't fall through the floor. Faith? I had none left. Everything I'd believed in had died with my body . . . with the world.

"I can't fight for you," I said.

"You can," Mom insisted. "*You* are our hope, Alexis. The Angels depend on you to do your part. All of the souls of

Heaven and Earth need you. You are the *only* one who can finish this war."

I shook my head and let out a humorless chuckle. I couldn't even keep *myself* alive, let alone what remained of humanity. Either I'd missed the Angels' messages, or I never received any because I wasn't really one of them. Because I didn't really belong with the Amadis. Perhaps Lucas had been right—perhaps I had too much of him in me. He might have pulled the trigger or pressed the red buttons or whatever he'd done, but by failing to protect the world as I was supposed to have done, I was nearly as guilty for the destruction. The end of the world was just as much on me as it was on him.

"You're wrong," I said. "Everything I do benefits Lucas. I'm not one of you. How can I fight for the *Angels*? For *Heaven*?"

With a blast of air that lifted my hair and wings, our surroundings returned to the Otherworldly battle, only now we were smack dab in the middle of it. When a mace swung at my shoulder, it actually hit me, and the force knocked me back a few steps. I ducked as it came at me again.

"You *must* fight," Cassandra ordered as she drew her sword, twisted around, and stabbed a Demon in its chest. "We all must."

Confused and bewildered, I gestured behind me, to the limitless, empty space that was supposedly at Heaven's gates where we'd just been.

"But I don't even belong here!" I shouted.

An Angel, several times my size with blond hair and the face of Adonis, turned from the Demon he'd just decapitated and faced me. With a heated glare, he raised his powerful arms out to the side, a sword in each hand. I cowered backwards, stumbling over my feet as I stared up into his brutal but perfect face that looked familiar, like one of the angel statues that used to hang at the top of the meeting room in the Amadis Council Hall.

"Alexis Katerina," his voice boomed, "you are correct."

His hand came toward me, his sword barely missing my face as his fist shoved into my chest.

"You do *not* belong here!"

His voice echoed in my ears and brain as I began to fall.

Away from him. Away from my mom and Rina and Cassandra. Away from Heaven's gates.

"I know," I whispered, and the feeling of falling changed into the sensation of being swept away and pulled downward.

I didn't fight the tug. I didn't try to use these wings on my back that maybe could have provided a means of escape. I knew very well I didn't belong in Heaven or anywhere near it.

After passing through heavier white fog, the Earthly realm surrounded me with its dirty air and the pungent odor of life being torched. My wings broke and bent, extracting a scream as I fell into my body, but I didn't stop there. I was dragged through it, instead. I stared into Tristan's face, his eyes closed and his head lolled to the side as he still held me pressed against his body. I lifted my arms and tried to reach out for him, to touch him, to hold on to him or on to my corporeal self or on to *something* in the real world, but my hands only grasped at air as I passed through.

And I continued traveling down, down, down.

Heat blasted at me from below. Then fire surrounded me, hot and searing, singeing my broken wings. I screamed again as my skin blistered and bubbled, the sweltering air filling my lungs and suffocating me, the flames consuming me. But I didn't actually burn into ash. No, that would bring relief, and, it appeared, I would never have relief again. I'd live in the fire for eternity.

Except I didn't stop in the fire, either. Whatever dragged me maintained my downward descent, through the fire, and below it, into a cold so deep, my bones froze immediately, and ice crystals hung in the air as I continued exhaling the same breath I'd started with in Heaven.

And still, my fall through Hell continued, making me

wonder how many levels existed and just how far down I'd go. Apparently, to the bottom.

Perhaps, after all the deaths I'd caused, the lowest bowel of Hell was exactly where I belonged.

Just as I began to think that falling for eternity would *be* my Hell, I slammed into a hard floor, shattering my frozen bones. The cracks and snaps echoed in the air, and excruciating pain devoured me. Although I had no idea how I felt anything physical when my body remained in the Earthly realm, at least pain made sense here in the deepest, darkest pits of Hell.

Forever and a day seemed to pass as I simply lay there, on my side, my cheek pressed against a floor of solid obsidian ice that stretched out as far as I could see. I stared ahead into a darkness so black, I had no idea where it began or ended. The cold eventually went away, though the ice did not. My pain subsided as well, and I pushed myself halfway up, bracing myself on my hand.

Nothing surrounded me. Nothing to see. Nothing to smell. Nothing to feel, hear, or taste. Absolutely *nothing*.

And a very different nothing compared to the white, empty space of Heaven's lobby. There I could see those who presented themselves and the movement of the white fog. I could smell and taste the clean, crisp air, and feel tears on my skin. If anyone stood before me now, they could be a centimeter from my face, and I wouldn't know it. They could be breathing on me, and I couldn't feel it or smell their exhale.

This was a true void.

And apparently my Hell. This was how I'd spend my eternity—what the powers-that-be must have deemed as my punishment. I didn't find it surprising that my Hell would be one of nothingness. One that lacked any sense of touch, sight, smell, taste, and sound. After all, a warrior relies on all of her senses, as does an author. I'd used them to create beauty and to destroy it. Now I'd forget what it was ever like to watch a sunset on the beach while inhaling the sweet scent of my love or to feel the softness of my son's cheek. I'd never again hear either of them say "I love you," and even the echoes of previous times would fade.

"I hate you!" I yelled at said powers-that-be, my voice falling flat almost as soon as the words left my mouth. But I spewed more, hatred filling me. "You were as much at fault as I was. You were supposed to help me, but You abandoned me! And You allowed it all to happen! It was *Your* will! Now You've sent me *here*?"

My passion, my vehemence, my ability to care anymore slowly died away with everything else.

I do belong here.

Acceptance of this fate had come, and much easier than accepting any place in Heaven. I crossed my legs, pulled the remnants of my broken, charred wings around me, and sat on the hard, black ice. Immediately, the deafening silence filled my ears, the blankness in front of me pressed on my eyes, and the lack of feeling made my muscles twitch as though my body checked to make sure everything was still there. The pressure of the void compressed my head, and my brain felt as though it would be crushed like a watermelon in a vise. Yet, it never would give, but forever and always would linger right at the point just before implosion.

Without sensory input, I went mad.

And it didn't take long. Or maybe it had. Loss of all senses also meant loss of the concept of time. Although I'd arrived here with my memories and my imagination, they dissolved into the nothingness surrounding me, my mind becoming just as blank and dark.

I screamed only to hear the sound of my own voice, because at least it was *something*, but the sound was swallowed by the void. I dug my fingernails into the flesh of my arms to feel pain, because at least it was *something*, but it dulled quickly and my skin grew numb. My tears tasted like nothing, and then they stopped falling. My whole being seemed to teeter on the brink of nonexistence, but never fell over the edge.

And then the voices started. The screaming in my head. The images that came along, too. Apparently, I hadn't lost all memories. My soul hung on to the worst ones, the nightmares, the pain and grief others had suffered because of me. I relived every death I'd caused, from the werewolf I'd killed in Hades to those who'd died in the bombs on the fateful night that ended the world. If that wasn't enough, the voices of Hell's burning souls cried out for me, too. They filled every passing moment with grief and despair—thousands of needles tattooing their agony onto my heart and hot coals raking across my soul. I begged and pleaded for the nothingness to return.

"If you wanted mercy, you should have stayed in Heaven," a loud, gravelly voice thundered around me, and the sound made me jump at first, but then it sent chills over my skin and down my spine. The malevolent feeling went all the way to my soul, and I knew instantly this wasn't an everyday Demon with a sarcastic tongue.

Satan himself had spoken to me.

CHAPTER 2

"*P*lease. Call me Lucifer." The voice came as less of a boom this time. A flash of light and color—red or orange maybe, but too quick to be certain—flickered off to my right. My head automatically snapped that way, but it was gone before I could be sure I even saw it. "Satan, Abaddon, Apollyon, Beelzebub, Leviathan, Devil . . . The list of names I've been known by goes on, some more terrifying than others." Another flash, like an orange spark of fire, this time to my left, and my head whiplashed that way, but only pitch blackness remained. Like the sound of boulders falling but ending with a hiss, his words carried across it. "Lucifer, however, sounds the most civilized and refined, does it not? Less frightening? After all, it was the name my Father gave me."

The blackness separated for a longer moment now, exposing a massive, muscular shoulder, arm, and part of a torso with red and orange marbled skin. The body moved just enough for me to catch a glimpse of a head with horns that curved back and out to the sides and eyes that glowed a greenish-yellow. Then solid blackness fell once again.

"Don't get me wrong," he continued, his voice circling and

surrounding me at the same time, making it impossible to know where he was. "Terrorizing souls brings me a great thrill, and the names Satan and the Devil evoke so much fear. Ah, the smell of such dread! Like a ripe, wet pussy. It makes my cock so fucking hard."

Another glimpse—one that made me recoil. A clawed hand with the same dappled skin and curling black nails stroked an enormous red and black penis directly in front of me. I jerked back as bile launched into my throat, and instinctively shot a bolt of electricity at him. A shudder racked through him as he thrust hard into his palm before disappearing.

"Oh, yessss! You know how I like it," he said with an extra helping of joy, and laughter crackled around me.

I shivered with revulsion. It probably wasn't even real. He probably only wished he was that big—that he even had a penis. His laughter died down, followed by heavy breaths. Whether or not it was real, he was certainly getting off on himself as he mind-fucked me. Heh. *Disgusting.* But could I expect any better from Satan, the king of all things sinful, including lust and depravity?

"I apologize, Alexis. Sometimes I cannot help myself, especially with an Amadis daughter in my presence. Ahhh. I've been waiting for this day and began to wonder if any of them would have the intelligence to see that my way is best. I had nearly given up hope, but then you came along. Fiercely protective of all the wrong things—according to them, anyway. I, however, appreciate your selfishness—" he groaned and grunted "—your passion to protect your own interests—" a lustful sigh "—and your willingness to *kill* as long as it serves your needs." A sensual moan turned my stomach. "Yet you hold on to just enough of those repellent qualities of love, empathy, and generosity that the thought of *breaking* you makes me want to come. Almost there," he groaned. "Yessss. You're so sssssweet and tantalizing. Deliciousssss."

As though his tongue had actually slid up the side of my face, the serpentine hiss made me shudder, and the gurgling noise of release that followed made my stomach lurch. He fell quiet and dark for so long, I hoped he had left, but his presence was so heavy and commanding, I knew he was still somewhere nearby. Whether he expected me to say anything or not, I remained silent. Besides the fact that I had no desire to encourage him, I was afraid vomit would shoot out of my mouth if I so much as opened it. When he finally spoke again, his voice changed significantly.

"Oh, dear," he said, and now the longer he spoke, the less monstrous and more human he sounded. "I'm afraid I've gone and offended you. I am very sorry, Alexis. I'd so wanted to start off on the right foot." A hoof and a leg shaped like an ox's, but with the same skin tone as the rest of him, appeared briefly before hiding behind the blackness again. Deep laughter ensued. "Pardon my humor. Maybe this is better?"

Before me, a bright light shone, and I had to blink and squint against the sudden brilliance in the thorough blackness. As my eyes adjusted, the full body of a striking man with white-blond hair and cerulean blue eyes, broad shoulders, and wearing a black suit with a thin, red tie came into focus, looking as though a spotlight illuminated him, but from within. Although his coloring was like Lucas's, Victor's, and, I assumed, other descendants of Jordan, their attractiveness paled in comparison. He was breathtakingly beautiful.

But still a far cry from Tristan.

The sound of a deep growl rumbled around me.

"I *was* the most beautiful of them all," Satan said, his voice a mesmerizing song that I wanted to ignore, but could not possibly. "Still am, in any of my forms, if you ask me."

The beautiful man disappeared, replaced by the horned beast with red and orange skin, glowing eyes, a tail with a barbed end, and huge wings with claws on their tips. Like hot coals, his skin lit up, glowing in the colors of flames, and I lifted my arm to shield my eyes from the glare, so much more intense than before. Darkness instantly surrounded me, but when I lowered my arm, the attractive man stood before me.

"I will hold this form for you." He sounded as though he were doing me a great favor. "I don't particularly like it. It's quite uncomfortable, but my comfort matters not. I'm more concerned about yours."

I dropped my arm completely, my hand landing in my lap, and stared at him. My throat felt thick and dry, but I managed to form together a few words, because now he made no sense.

"You just said I'd receive no mercy here, but you're concerned about my comfort?"

"See there? It's easier to speak to me when I'm like this, isn't it? That is all I want. A conversation. And I am happy to make you comfortable enough for that."

I hesitated, knowing that by asking, I'd be entering into exactly what he wanted, and what Satan wanted was probably not a good thing for me to deliver. But bewildered and unable to help myself, I asked nonetheless. "A conversation? What on Earth about?"

"No, not on Earth. In Hell."

I blinked. Was that supposed to be a joke? He had the oddest sense of humor. "Okay. What in *Hell* do you want to talk to me about?"

"About this—your comforts, your needs and desires. I assume you don't like my home as it is, do you? The ice and the cold? I always laugh when humans talk about Hell freezing over. Guess what? It already has!" He let out a deep laugh that sounded more like his beastly self than this gentleman-like version, and then he quieted as he stroked his chin. "You do know I could provide you with every creature comfort of the world you used to know . . . and more. Right?"

A maroon, velvet-covered wingback chair suddenly appeared with him sitting in it, his legs crossed at the knee and a cigar between his perfectly shaped lips. The tip glowed as he puffed, and with long, elegant fingers, he flicked the ash into an ashtray that sat on a dark, polished wood table next to the chair. His hand twitched, and a whole sitting room appeared with me propped on a cushy settee, beautiful paintings hanging on the luxuriously covered walls, and a fire crackling in the oversized hearth. A grand piano sat in the corner.

"There's a suite upstairs with your name on it, Alexis," Satan said with the eyes of a lover. "A soft bed with the highest quality silk linens. A private bathroom with every essential you could need and more, including a hot, scented bubble bath. When was the last time you had a bath? Slept in a bed?"

He puffed on his cigar again, as though waiting for my answer. I remained silent, not wanting to reveal how enticing a bath and bed sounded. I didn't have to say anything, though. He already knew my selfish desires. A smile danced in his eyes as he exhaled smoke rings.

"And I have so much else to give you beyond a bed and a bath," he promised. "A castle, a claim on any part of that Earth that you want, or down here if you prefer, servants to grant your every wish. All the food you and twenty others could ever need. The freedom to do as you please, with no rules, standards, or expectations tying you down and limiting your potential." He leaned forward, resting his arms on his knee. "You see, I don't demand sacrifices or require that you deny yourself in any way. I want everyone to be happy, including you, Alexis. Especially you. I offer everything you could possibly want, as well as everything you don't even *know* you desire."

"In exchange for what?" I dared to ask, only out of curiosity. Because I knew there had to be something. This was Satan, after all.

He gave a sweltering grin that could easily seduce the panties off the most austere woman . . . or man. "Your soul, of course."

And there it was. At least he didn't beat around the bush. I rolled my eyes. I may have accepted my fate to be here, but I wouldn't simply hand my soul over to him. "I'd rather rot here in Hell."

The room disappeared, my butt hit the black ice, and I was surrounded once again by complete darkness. Utter nothingness. Except the screaming in my head. The images of those I'd killed played on a loop, their pain carving into my soul with the jagged edge of a dull blade. Then other faces, some I knew and most I didn't recognize. They were lives I didn't personally take, but my actions had led to their deaths, such as the children in the train car we'd abandoned in Moscow. Whether they actually died or not didn't matter. I still felt the guilt. I watched everyone suffer and fall, over and over and over again. My people. My team. Their screams and wails filled my head, pushing out everything else, and I clutched at my skull, screaming along with them as an eternity passed.

"Are you sure about that?" Satan asked, and the nightmarish images were gone, my head silent, the beautiful sitting room returned. "Your soul will become mine anyway, but in a way that is unnecessarily torturous for you."

"I deserve it," I muttered, lowering my hands into my lap, my heart still pounding from the onslaught of horrific memories. "Into eternity."

He studied me with a peculiar look in his blue eyes. "I don't think you realize just how long an eternity can be, child. You thought an eternity had just passed, but it had been mere minutes in your terms." He cocked his head to the side and steepled his long fingers together, tapping the tips against each other. "You have no idea the gift I am offering and how rarely it is given. You said you don't belong in Heaven, because deep down, you know you belong here with me. You can be *my* daughter. Be *my* princess. We can rule Hell and Earth, which is ready and waiting for me, together. You can be with your son."

My ears pricked. I narrowed my eyes.

He lifted his chin, acknowledging my reaction as minute as it was. "You know deep in your heart and soul that he belongs with me, too."

"He doesn't!"

"Of course he does. Why fight it any longer? You can be together now. He can rule, too. Your husband, as well, by your side as always."

"Leave him out of this," I seethed. Tristan's soul was not a bargaining chip. Neither was my son's, regardless of what he'd done. I would *never* stop fighting for him. "Leave them both out of this!"

"Well, maybe you should tell them that. Dorian's already made the first move, so it's only a matter of time before his soul becomes mine. Would you like to see?" He waved his hand, and the heavy draperies on the window parted, showing not a landscape outside, but the interior of a dark and dirty apartment. "Oh, yes, I can see into the Earthly realm, just like you can elsewhere in the Otherworld."

Crouched over a trash can, feeding balls of newspaper into a fire that blazed in the bin, was a man wearing black pants and a sweater. His long, brown hair was pulled into a low ponytail, and his chiseled face reflected the shadows and light of the flames. Thick, straight brows, one with a scar through it, pulled low over his dark eyes. Noah—Mom's twin, my uncle, and a Summoned son who was part of the Daemoni. With him, sitting on a stained, bare mattress on the floor with litter scattered around his feet, was a younger looking man, a teenager, with dark blond hair and hazel eyes full of determination. My son.

I gasped and sprang to my feet. "Oh my god! He's *alive*? On Earth?"

Satan hissed at my choice of words.

"For now," he answered, sounding annoyed. But . . . *he* answered. When Mom and Rina never would.

I ran to the window and pressed my hands and forehead against it as I stared at my son, new emotions welling within me. He still had on the same jeans and blue sweater he'd worn the last time I saw him. They appeared to have shrunk three sizes, though, showing how much he'd grown since the day I'd said "see you later" at the gates to the campus and he'd told me, "not if I see you first." I'd thought it a joke then. How had I not known?

"Dorian," I called out to him, but, being on the other side of the veil, he couldn't hear or see me.

When he spoke to Noah, though, his words came clearly across the veil. "Kali said I was the key to breaking the curse on you and the others."

My jaw slackened, and my fingers curled against the glass. "What?"

Satan snickered behind me.

Noah looked up from the fire that caused light and shadows to dance on his face. "I've heard that, too, and she would know."

"So she was telling the truth that if I offer myself to the Daemoni, my parents and baby sister will be okay?"

Those new feelings—a flicker of hope—turned upside down, and my heart sank. Was this the lie he'd been told? Was this why he'd left us? "No, Dorian. Don't you do it!"

"My understanding is that you must be offering yourself as a sacrifice." Noah dropped down to sit on the floor. He crossed his long legs at the ankles and rested his forearms on his bent knees. "The rest of us went willingly to the Daemoni. They offered us power, wealth, everything we could possibly want, everything the Amadis could not. Any power went to our sisters. We were *wanted* by the Daemoni. Not so much by the Amadis. The decision was simple. But that cannot be the decision for you, if you want to break the curse."

Dorian gnawed on his bottom lip. "My mother and father

love me. I love them. I don't *want* to do this, but I think I have to."

"No, you don't, Dorian!" I banged on the window, but in vain.

"A sacrifice might break the curse, but there's no guarantee it will save your family or anyone else."

"If I do break it and you're freed, though, you will fight for them?"

Noah nodded. "I will. But I might be the only one."

Dorian's eyes darkened. "Even after what Kali and my grandfather did to the others?"

Noah didn't reply at first, his own eyes storming, probably at the memory of what he'd been through when Lucas and the sorcerers controlled him. "I do not know. Some, such as Edmund, have already given their souls over, so it is too late for them."

"But the rest?"

"There's a possibility they will convert and fight for your mother."

Dorian leaned his elbow on his knee and dropped his chin into his hand as he gazed at the fire. The reflection of the flames danced in his eyes, looking so much like the eyes of his father at one time.

"Then I have to at least try," he said. "I don't want my baby sister to be a part of this war."

"NO! Dorian, no!" I screamed, banging harder on the window with both fists until the glass broke and cut through my palms and wrists.

I prepared to dive through, but the scene had disappeared, the window displaying a black wall beyond it. The draperies closed on their own, and I spun around, still shaking my fists. Blood droplets splattered on the thick carpet. How could I even bleed, or hurt in this place, for that matter?

"Oh, I ensure you feel physical pain, just as if your body were here," Satan replied to my silent question. "What fun would it be if you didn't? Emotional and mental pain is the best, but the physical just adds an extra dimension, so to speak." He held his hand out to the settee I'd been sitting on before he'd opened the view to the Earthly realm. "Sit down, won't you?"

I refused, standing there with my fists on my hips, blood still dripping on his luxury grade carpet. His finger jumped, the bleeding stopped, and the stains disappeared. I didn't acknowledge him.

"This is Dorian's purpose, don't you know?" Satan asked, and I only responded by glaring at him harder, my chest rising as I heaved for breath. "They would never tell you that, of course, but his purpose has always been to break the curse."

The breath flew out of me as though I'd been sucker punched. Why had nobody ever told me that? Mom, Rina, Cassandra . . . the blasted Angels? They'd kept this critical piece of information to themselves! He was *my* son, and they couldn't have told me this?

"Ah." Satan sighed. "I love the hatred and anger burning in you. Delightful."

I pulled back, quickly reigning in my emotions before he whipped his ugly dick out again.

He frowned, and then swished his wrist in the air. "Yes, that's what they want him to do. Something about helping you win the war and saving your daughter . . . blah blah blah. As if you could beat me."

"I lost the baby, though," I said, ignoring the taunts. "There is no sister to save. He's doing it for nothing."

"True. My girl Jeana took care of that little nuisance." Satan puffed on his cigar, his blue eyes seemingly thoughtful. "Too bad, isn't it? No daughters left on Earth means no reason for the Amadis to fight. Look how they've already given up."

He flicked his hand in the air again, and the draperies reopened, showing another scene. This one outside with a snowy landscape—the entrance to Hades. Lucas stood in front

34

of a large crowd, all of them on one knee with their heads bowed. I identified Chandra by her shiny black hair and spotted the eccentric hat and clothing Minh always wore. They'd sat on my council. On Rina's, too. And she'd tried to make me believe there was any hope left? I shook my head with incredulity as I recognized other faces in the crowd. In fact, I knew, all of them were Amadis. *Were* being the key word. They bowed before Lucas now. My heart shrunk to the size of a pea.

The draperies closed.

Satan tapped his fingers on the arm of his chair. "So I wonder, if there's nobody left to fight for or with, and there's no reason for Dorian to sacrifice himself, is he actually breaking the curse? Or is he simply coming to my side like every other brother—because it's the right side?"

I stared at the thick and heavy blue curtains as I pondered this question that sounded too much like a riddle. But the answer was not a joke or play on words. I dropped onto the settee, emotions coiling and slithering in my stomach like snakes. The draperies parted again, returning to the apartment with Noah and Dorian. My son stood at the door, wearing better fitting clothes now—how much time had passed?—and looking over his shoulder at Noah.

"I'll free you, Uncle Noah, and whoever else wants it. Just please, be there when my mom needs you." Dorian walked out the door, shutting it behind him, and a whimper sounded in my throat.

"Oh, look. I win!" Satan clapped his hands together and gave me an evil grin.

"No." I shook my head violently. "That hasn't happened yet, right?" The drapes closed again, and my gaze flew to the pretty face. "*Right?*"

Satan pondered me, taking his time, and I was about to lunge at him when he shrugged. "Does it matter? Accept it for what it is, Alexis. The end. Dorian hasn't given his soul over yet, but he will. So will you? Where are you going to put your faith? With the winners or the losers? Them, who have done nothing but lie and keep secrets from you, denying you your family? Or *me*, who offers you *everything*, including your son? And your husband, too."

My mind had been focused on the word *yet*—Dorian hadn't given his soul over *yet*—and wondering how I could stop him before he did. But the mention of Tristan snapped me out of it.

"I said to keep him out of this," I growled.

"He apparently doesn't want to be left out." Satan waved his cigar in my direction, but his gaze focused on some point beyond me. "Look who we have here. Welcome home, my son."

I sensed the new presence immediately, and when I looked over my shoulder, my heart rocketed into my throat. The most stunning face I'd ever known—far more attractive than Lucifer's, who had supposedly been the most beautiful Angel before he'd fallen—strode across the room, his legs clad in fighting leathers, but his shirt gone, leaving his muscular torso bare. His stomach muscles rippled as he moved toward me with a spark in his hazel eyes. Seated in the center of sin, I shouldn't have been so surprised at how quickly lust consumed me.

"Tristan!" I jumped to my feet and rushed to him, not believing he was really here, when I'd thought I'd never see him again. He wrapped me into his powerful arms. My body ached for his touch, but my brain quickly caught up and took over. "No. Oh, no. You can't be here. What are you *doing* here?"

"I follow you anywhere, even into the dark," he murmured against my ear. "I go where you go."

"No." I pushed him away. "You fought so hard *not* to be here."

"Maybe not hard enough?" Satan jeered from behind me.

I ignored him, knowing that wasn't true, and grabbed Tristan's face in my hands to look him in the eye.

"You *can't* be here. You don't deserve to be here. You don't belong here."

He pressed his lips to my forehead. Pleasure shot down between my legs, making me instantly ready for him. "Alexis, my love, I belong wherever you are."

My heart melted, and so did my knees while my breasts tightened with need. When his lips made it down to my mouth, my whole body tensed and throbbed.

"Why don't you two just fuck already?" Satan asked. "I'd be happy to watch."

Tristan and I both let out a low growl. I gave the lustful feelings a hard shove and returned to my senses.

"You do not belong *here*," I insisted. "Not in Hell."

"Neither do you, my love."

"Yes, I do. *I've* been sent here."

The sound of a clearing throat came from behind me.

"That's not . . . *entirely* true." Satan's words came out sounding like a mix between a guilty admission and pride for his deceit.

I peered over my shoulder at him with narrowed eyes. "What is that supposed to mean?"

He twirled his long fingers in a dismissive gesture. "It's called war, Alexis. You told the Angels you didn't belong in Heaven, and they agreed. You were probably supposed to go back to Earth, but since you seemed a little open to the idea that this was your fate, my Demon seized the opportunity and brought you to me. Technically, you *don't* belong here. But unlike them, I take any and all who want to join me. All you have to do is say the word. Give me your soul, and the world is your oyster. You can have *everything*. The offer stands to both of you."

I looked up at Tristan, anger and confusion churning

within me, and he gazed down with a determined love. "Like I said, I go where you go."

My jaw clenched, and my nostrils flared. "You will *not* rot in Hell because of me."

"I prefer that you don't, as well."

"Then let's get out of here."

Satan blew out a growly huff. "So be it."

And with a snap of his fingers, the luxurious room disappeared, immersing us in the cold black of Hell's deepest pit.

CHAPTER 3

"*I* was hoping we could reach an agreement and it wouldn't come to this." Satan sighed. "But you leave me no choice. Like I said, if you wanted mercy, you should have stayed in Heaven."

His debonair human form disappeared, and the repugnant beast returned. His red, horned head fell back, and he opened his mouth as if to scream, but fire blasted out, a river of flames shooting upward. As though that had been a summoning call, dozens of Demons appeared, similar in appearance to Satan, but smaller and with less vibrantly colored skin shining in the firestorm. And they were obviously the fighters, not the thinkers. Large swords and maces swung in the air before they even came close.

Satan's fountain of fire that he blew out of his mouth provided one benefit—we could see our surroundings. When I'd been in the void of blackness, I'd imagined an immeasurable cell that sometimes felt as small as a cardboard box and other times as boundless as the cosmos. Once Satan arrived, I'd imagined a movie studio and his beautiful parlor was a set with the false window that looked out at a brick wall, and when he'd made the room disappear, I was left on the empty, black sound stage. But as the flames from his mouth spread over a high ceiling as though it were covered in gasoline, I saw that the space was what I imagined the Devil's ballroom to look like.

The room was much longer than it was wide, with black marble covering every surface—the ceiling, pillars, walls, and floor. A long, rectangular pool, also made of black marble, stretched down one side of the room, and a black statue of a Demon stood in each end of the empty pool. Unlit chandeliers made of black crystals hung from the ceiling, and when the flames reached their chains, they traveled downward, lighting them up.

Satan turned his head and swung it around as he shot two additional balls of fire from his mouth. One sailed to the far end of the pool while the other hit and entered the Demon statue nearest us. Streams of fire shot out of the statues' mouths—a fountain of flames that flowed into the pool. And as though it had also been filled with gasoline, the pool lit up, too.

The real Demons carved their weapons through the fire, igniting them with flames that lapped and licked at the blades and spikes. Then they swarmed toward us.

Acting on instinct, I pushed my power at them to shove them away, but instead, I was the one who flew backwards and slammed into a marble pillar. Pain cracked through my head and spine, but I pushed past it to shoot a bolt of electricity at the closest Demon. The blue charge webbed over the creature's body, but my power did nothing to stop it or even slow it. In fact, the Demon's fat, leathery lips seemed to smile, reminding me of Satan's reaction when I'd tried to fry him. I attempted to shoot Amadis power at it, instead, thinking it wouldn't like that as much, but I had none. My time in Hell must have drained my power. As the Demons flew across the room toward us, my hand reached for my dagger, but I couldn't find it.

Satan chuckled. "Your physical weapons were left behind with your physical selves."

Panic threw my heart into overdrive. How could we fight them when we had nothing to fight with? How could we possibly survive this? Tristan dove for me and lifted me to my feet. Then he grabbed each side of my face, looking straight into my eyes.

"You must remember the pain isn't real," he said.

"But I *feel* it," I ground out against his tight hold on me.

"It's not real! Your body's not here. It's not in real danger. Just remember that. It's all in your head."

"And your soul," Satan offered.

My eyes drifted over to him, and Tristan gave my head a small shake. "Don't listen to him! Listen to me. Focus on what you want. You don't want to be here, right?"

"Not if it means you're here, too."

His eyes sparked for a moment—he didn't like that answer, but he ignored it. "We don't belong here. He admitted it. So it's up to you and me. He'll do everything to deceive us into staying, but in truth, it's our choice. Don't forget that, *ma lykita*. We *will* get out."

I nodded as best as I could against his grip. "How?"

"We run until we find our way." He slammed his mouth against mine, but only for a moment.

Then he dropped his hands from my face, grabbed my wrist, and ran. Unprepared, I stumbled after him at first, and he tugged me back to my feet. Once I gained my footing, we sprinted for a doorway at the far end of the room, the Demons chasing after us. Pain seared across my back as a sword found its target, but the burn felt like a freezer burn with thousands of icy needles piercing into my skin. My body arched against the pain as Tristan continued pulling me along. The doorway also filled with flames when we approached it, and without a glance behind us, we charged right through. More ice-cold pricked over my flesh and seeped into my bones creating the kind of ache that made me think I'd never be warm again.

"Hellfire," Tristan groaned as we entered a black corridor. The Hellfire provided barely enough light to see that the hall went to both our right and left, but darkness swallowed it up only a few feet away. "This way."

Tristan turned us right, although I had the feeling he didn't really know which way to go. The marble floor was slick, and when I crashed to my hands and knees, I realized it wasn't marble after all, but ice. Our feet slipped and slid as we tried to outrun the Demons, but they continued chasing after us, their fiery weapons providing enough light for us to see a few feet ahead at a time. My broken and straggly wings were completely useless, unable to lift me in flight, which could have come in handy against the Demons.

An onyx wall suddenly appeared in front of us, and Tristan made a sharp right, pulling me with him. We ran twenty or thirty steps before another wall appeared, and this time we turned left, trying to avoid circling back to where we'd started. But it quickly became apparent that we scrambled like rats through a maze, trapped in the lower levels of Hell. The Demons backed off, throwing us into darkness again.

Then the same images and screams that had filled my head before returned, bringing me to a screeching halt and down to my knees. Tristan gripped his head and fell into a crouch next to me as his own guilt-ridden memories from his Daemoni past overcame him. I knew because our minds and our souls were connected, and I experienced them along with my own. Tristan had already relived the horrors enough times, though, regurgitating them as a form of self-punishment. I'd brought him past that, and I couldn't bear for him to suffer through them again. Thrusting them away, I grabbed his hand and squeezed.

"We choose to leave, remember?" I pushed myself to my feet, pulling him up with me. Just in time, as Demons flocked at us.

We ran in the darkness again, although whether we actually made any progress was unknown to us, our only light still coming from the Demons' flaming weapons. They swooped down often, swinging their blades and bludgeons at us and trying to grab us with their claws. We ducked and turned, rolling when necessary to avoid the blazing swords and spiked balls swinging for our heads. One caught the edge of my wing, and my body lurched forward as I cried out in pain, at first from the cut and then from the sear as the remaining feathers went up in flames.

But the physical pain was nothing. It wasn't real.

The screaming in my head, however, was very real, and it lifted louder and beyond my skull into tortured wails coming from everywhere around us. Long, nerve-splitting, heart-wrenching howls, hundreds or thousands of them echoing each other. As we ran, gray-skinned, bloody-nailed fingers reached out of the darkness for us, but when I slowed and tried to grab a couple to help, they disappeared into smoke. Yet their agony remained, filling my nose and mouth with each inhale, slicing down to my lungs, shredding my heart and soul like sharp talons slicing up the fabric of life. When I didn't think I could take any more, the walls closed in around us, creating a black tunnel, and the icy floor began slanting upwards.

"Come on," Tristan said, pulling me along. "Up must be good."

The slope was steep and the floor slippery. We slid backwards several times, barely catching ourselves before we lost all footing. Although the tunnel was pitch black, I sensed something undulating in the walls even before the rumbling started, and then shapes in the walls pushed out at us, bumping into our arms and knocking us off balance. The ice of the walls seemed to form like a skin around some kind of Hellish beasts behind them—or *within* them—that tried to break free. They growled and snapped at us, their anger growing as we tried to pass by. I had no idea how close to the top we were when a head-shaped part of the wall pushed outward and swung toward me, slamming into my body and throwing me backwards. I rolled end over end all the way to the bottom. Tristan slid down to help me back up.

I felt as though we'd been running for hours, maybe days already, and the slope may as well have been Mt. Everest. And here we were, at the bottom of it again. Every part of my body ached, and I tried to tell myself it was all in my head, but everyone else's screams drowned out my own inner voice.

Tristan gripped my chin. "We can do this, *ma lykita*. No giving up."

But I was so close to wanting to give up. If Tristan's soul weren't on the line, perhaps I would have stopped trying. Curling up in a ball and losing myself to the madness might have been tempting. But his soul *was* on the line, so I would keep on.

I nodded. "I won't. I do it for you."

"And me for you."

He gripped my hand and began climbing again. We moved slower, avoiding the monsters in the walls as they pushed out at us, teeth clacking. As though they also feared the tunnel of beasts, the Demons didn't follow, except one. It flew behind us, quickly closing in, and a hoof rammed into my head, knocking me to the side. Large, bear-like paws stretched the membrane of the wall as they tried to grab at me. I sprang away and crashed into the solid body of Tristan, who had the Demon by its tail.

The creature's deafening screeches echoed down the tunnel as its wings flapped desperately. When it began to lift Tristan, I jumped up and latched onto its tail, too, and between the two of us, we were able to tug it back down. Then we whipped it to the side, slamming its body into the wall. The things inside the barrier roared and came for the Demon. It tried to fly out of our grip again, but when we let it go, it swung around with its blazing sword.

"AHH!" Tristan's shout of pain silenced the Demon's screeches.

It then began to laugh—if the sound of rocks sliding was a laugh—before diving down for Tristan. When I saw what it went for, I lunged for my husband and the fiery blade that had been lodged into his back. The Demon beat me to it, and Tristan yelled again when it jerked the sword free. But I was close enough to grab the end of the blade before it swung out of reach. Biting against the pain as the flames both seared and froze, I jerked it out of the Demon's hand. I flipped it in the air to catch the hilt and swung the blade out, decapitating the flying beast. Its head fell and rolled down the slope, and the body chased after it. Demons couldn't be killed, but they could certainly be inconvenienced.

As the walls of the tunnel disappeared, the tilt of the floor grew steeper, causing us to use our hands as well as our feet to climb, yet I still held onto the sword. The higher we clambered, though, the sharper the incline became until we were scaling the vertical face of a cliff. Darkness swallowed everything below, and although we'd been on the ground only minutes ago—I thought, anyway—we were in Hell. Everything could change at Satan's whim, and I had a feeling a fall now might never end. Too bad my stupid wings were useless.

Carrying the sword made it difficult to climb, but the flames lapping off the blade provided light to find hand and footholds. So I held onto the weapon as I followed Tristan upward, and when I felt the warmth, I thought at first the Hellfire from the sword put it off, but then realized the wall itself was warming. I craned my head back to see up ahead, and a wave of heat blew my hair and blasted my skin, feeling like a bad sunburn.

Then we suddenly hit the top and passed from hanging onto a frozen, icy wall to stumbling toward a low, swinging bridge of fire that crossed a flaming lake. And this fire was *hot*. I couldn't tell if we were in a high-ceilinged cave or not—the light of the fire surrounding us did nothing to illuminate the blackness above. To our right and left, fire and molten rock covered the banks that sloped down to the lake. We had no choice but to cross.

"Keep going," Tristan ordered, and still holding my hand, he sprinted across the bridge.

We ran as fast as our legs could push us, hurdling flames that leapt up in front of us and swinging at the Demons swooping down, knocking some into the flaming lake and others into the darkness beyond. The harder and faster we ran, though, the farther away the shore became. Hands reached up through the fiery surface of the lake, grabbing at the low bridge and our ankles. New cries and howls, moans and whimpers filled the air. Heat singed my nose and throat raw, along with the souls' agony I breathed in, tearing me apart further from the inside out. I stumbled several times, and so did Tristan, but we kept running. And the distant shore kept stretching farther and farther away.

A large group of Demons gathered at the far end and charged at us. We stopped, and I looked over my shoulder, really not wanting to return the way we'd come, and another group chased us from that direction. We had one flaming sword and powers that were useless against them. The cries of the tortured souls around us grew louder, and the number of hands reaching out of the lake at us multiplied, grasping with more desperation than ever. But we couldn't help ourselves, let alone anyone else. As my body began to sink from the weight of our seemingly hopeless situation, the flames licking at my legs forced me back up.

Tristan turned toward me, his face twisted with the same agony I felt, more on the inside than the physical outside.

"We need to get out of here," he yelled.

The Demons behind him closed in on us, and I felt the ones behind me quickly approaching, too. The lake of fire surrounded us. Up seemed to be the only way out—although I couldn't be certain if there was anything that way, either.

"How the hell do we get out of Hell?" I shouted above the wails filling my ears and mind.

I wondered if those souls in the lake, crying for help and reaching out for us, had been others who'd tried to escape. Had they been like us, souls that didn't belong in Hell, but couldn't find their way out? Had they eventually succumbed to the inevitable and let the fire consume them? Would that be us in the future? If so, it would be the very near future—the Demons swarmed in.

"I love you, Tristan," I said before I never had another chance to tell him, and I blocked my mind and soul to his to give me the element of surprise. I grabbed his waist, and his arms came up to wrap around me in an embrace. I ducked under his reach, and with all the strength I could muster, which was a hell of a lot for my size, I thrust my legs up and launched him into the air. "Go! Save yourself!"

His legs shot out into Aikido form as he soared over the Demons' heads, kicking several out of his way. He landed on the far side of the group, but instead of running toward the shore, as I meant for him to do, he charged back toward them and me.

His voice thundered angrily in my head. *"No way in hell am I leaving you . . . in Hell."*

Shit. I should have known. But I'd had to try.

The Demons' attention split between the two of us, their heads swerving side to side as though they tried to decide which one of us to attack first. Tristan glanced at the fiery blade in my hand and looked back to my eyes. I gave him a small nod. He distracted those closest to him by attacking with his fists and feet. While he fought them hand-to-hand, I sliced and stabbed the fiery blade at those in front of me, cutting my way toward him, severing a head here and an arm there. They returned my blows with their own weapons, but they must have been blind as bats, because their blades and spikes barely grazed me, if reaching me at all.

But that thought came too soon. The moment Tristan and I shoved the last Demon between us into the lake, a stabbing pain pierced throughout my lower back. I'd ignored the group coming from the other direction for too long, and one of the Demons had nailed me. I lurched forward and fell downward, my face only inches from the flames when Tristan's arms swept around me. He lifted me, but I could barely hold my weight, leaning on him as I tried to swing at the Demons.

They bared their yellow, craggy teeth in grins wide enough to expose their black gums. They knew they had us. I looked down at the lake of fire, wondering if it'd be better just to dive in rather than fight these beasts anymore. We'd die quick, at least . . . except, we wouldn't. We'd be like those other souls baying for our help. Dismissing that idea, I returned my focus to the Demons just as one's claws reached out for my throat. I batted at them with the sword and sliced them off. The Demon flew up and out of sight in the blackness. As my eyes followed it upwards, I automatically prayed for a miracle, although I knew prayers didn't work down here. They didn't work anywhere. And miracles would never come.

A bright light shot down toward us, followed by another, and I knew I'd been fooling myself that up was a way out. I envisioned dozens of Demons sitting on ledges on the sides of cliffs that reached high above us, reinforcements waiting impatiently to have their turn at attacking us. Then I realized how stupid that idea was. Why would they wait to take turns?

These had to have been some new kind of monstrosity sent to finish us off.

The Demons on the bridge screeched a horrible sound and lost interest in us. They sprang into the air, flying toward the white lights. Others came from seemingly nowhere, and they swarmed the white beings, swirling around them as though trying to snuff them out.

"*We have to go*," Tristan ordered in my head, not to hide his plans because our thoughts could not be hidden from those in this realm, but so he could be heard over the cacophony of shrieking Demons and howling souls.

He took my hand, and we ran again for the far side of the lake. Both of us constantly looked over our shoulders to ensure the Demons remained distracted by the lights twisting and swerving around them. When they came closer and began to take shape, I stumbled and stopped, pulling Tristan to a halt.

These were not Demons. They weren't Hellish at all. They put off a white light, a pure light, glowing from the inside out. Their wings were not black or brown and leathery, but white and feathery, pulled back behind them for the best aerodynamics as they shot like rockets in an extreme nosedive toward the lake of fire.

At the last second, they swooped over and hovered above us.

"You don't belong here," a male voice said, and the Angel who it belonged to grabbed my wrist and bulleted straight upward.

"Tristan!" I yelled, but the other Angel grabbed his upper arm and followed us.

A great rumbling sounded from below, and the fire lake churned like a sea, the flames growing and licking higher and higher. Some of the flames came together and took the shape of a hand the size of a bus. It reached for us, along with another hand, and then a horned head as big as a house. Lava poured off the colossal beast as its muscular torso rose from the lake.

49

Satan's voice boomed across the surface like thunder. "Bring them to me!"

The sound came from the behemoth, and I realized the monster was the true embodiment of Satan. But as hard as he tried to reach for us, he apparently couldn't break free of his own Hell. The rumbling turned into a furious roar that shook the very air and reverberated into my heart, making my breath catch.

Dozens of Demons screeched in response and chased after us. The Angels flew faster, but the Demons did, too. Talons groped for our arms and legs, trying to pull us back down. I kicked one off, and it tumbled in the air, only to latch on to Tristan. Another grabbed him, too, while two more attacked Tristan's ride. The fire below glinted off the Angel's sword as it lashed out, decapitating both Hellions with one powerful swing. But additional beasts swarmed onto Tristan, and the more he and the Angel fought back, the harder they twisted and pulled, until eventually they yanked him out of the Angel's grip.

"No!" I screamed as I hit at the forearm holding onto me, but my Angel ignored me, seemingly oblivious to what happened below us. My eyes blurred as tears filled them while I watched my husband fall away from me. "*Tristan!*"

His hands reached up for me and for his Angel, as the Demons pulled him down, down, down. His Angel flew after him. Tristan and the Demons crash-landed on some kind of land bridge that stretched across the abyss, far below me now. Hoping it would help, I threw the fiery sword to him.

"We have to go back," I yelled at the Angel carrying me away, but he ignored me and everything else, even his fellow Angel who'd gone back for Tristan.

We continued up, up, up. Up and away from Hell . . . away from my husband. Tears streamed down my cheeks as I kicked and twisted my body, trying to yank myself free, but the Angel's grip was too strong. I swiped the tears away with my free hand and watched in horror as my big, powerful warrior grew smaller and smaller below me, using the sword he'd caught to fight the Demons with the Angel by his side.

Don't give up, I silently called to him. *I'll come back for you.*

The promise echoed in my head as I watched helplessly while being pulled away from my love, my heart, my soul, leaving him in Hell.

CHAPTER 4

*T*he ascent lasted for eons, it seemed, even longer than it'd taken to fall. Which, I supposed, was true for anything in life. Tumbling down was easy. It was the getting back up and making the climb again that required effort. I yelled and thrashed the entire way, hoping to annoy the Angel until he turned around, but he acted as though he forgot I was even there. Except his grip—it remained tight as ever.

I expected to enter the Earthly realm at some point, but we only passed by it. The crash of metal on metal resounding in my ears meant we'd crossed out of Hell and into that space surrounding Earth where the battle between Angels and Demons carried on. The Angel dipped and lifted, twisted and swerved through it, narrowly avoiding Angels' swords and Demons' claws. My foot kicked a Demon's horn, and it chased after us, but at the moment its black nails scratched down my calf, two Angels ambushed it and carried it away. Finally, we passed through a blinding band of white light and then into the foggy area where I'd been before. The Angel deposited me at Mom's and Rina's feet, and I collapsed in a heap.

"Tristan!" I pawed at the beautiful creature's leg, trying to latch back on. "We have to go back for him."

The Angel shook me off and replied in a deep, smooth voice, "He has what he needs. Souls that do not belong there must make the choice themselves. He must decide where his faith lies."

My mouth fell open as I stared up at him in disbelief for as long as he allowed me to before he disappeared from sight. His words repeated what Tristan had told me in Hell, but if they were true, why hadn't he escaped? I spun on Mom and Rina.

"We have to save him," I deplored.

When they opened their mouths as if to respond, snakes tumbled out. Their eyes blackened, and horns grew from their heads. I screamed until darkness consumed me.

Monsters came at me with enormous snake-like arms that wrapped around me, constricting my lungs. I tried to fight them off, but the more I did, the more their squeeze on me tightened. When I finally broke free, their faces mutated to Mom's and Rina's, and I watched their bodies fall to the ground as bullets punched a million holes into them, spraying blood all over the grass . . . which began to undulate, each blade becoming a tentacle that tried to wrap itself around me.

"No!" I tried to scream as the visions cycled back to the start, but the noise that came out sounded like a toad's croak.

"Alexis, it's us." Mom's voice carried over a great distance, and I shook my head and squeezed my eyes closed because I couldn't stand to watch her die one more time. But even then, I saw it, the memory playing on the backs of my lids. I'd never escape the horrors of that night. "Alexis! Calm down!"

Something sharp hit my face. No, not sharp, but it left a sting. I lifted my hand to my cheek and peeled open my eyelids. Mom's and Rina's faces hovered in front of me, looking as beautiful as ever. And their wings . . .

Winged beasts . . .

Fiery monsters . . .

"Alexis!"

I blinked.

Right. Not in Hell anymore. Then I bolted upright from whatever I lay on. *I have to save Tristan. And Dorian! Is he still okay? Is he still with Noah? I have to stop him!* My mouth opened to say all of this, but my voice failed me. My tongue felt too large for my mouth, as though it had suddenly become a snake . . .

Mom placed a hand on my arm, but it wasn't a hand. A claw, with red and orange marbled skin and black, pointy tips. I jerked my arm away and stared at her without seeing her. Satan's face was before me instead. I recoiled and blinked. Mom's face returned. Her mouth moved as she spoke, but all I heard were the desperate wails and howls of the souls in Hell. They filled my ears, my mind, blocking everything else out, the weight of them pressing on my mind, my heart, my soul.

Vises tightened around my arms, my body shook, and my neck whiplashed. Hell disappeared again, and my gaze bounced around wildly finding nothing, although I sensed Mom's and Rina's presence. I couldn't face them, though. I couldn't watch their deaths for the millionth time. *No. Can't see them like that again.* I looked everywhere but at them.

"Honey . . ."

My head twitched at the patronizing voice that grated over my nerves. Something wasn't right. *I* wasn't right. I sprang off the bed and searched around for . . . I didn't know what. There was nothing here. Nothing but whiteness, a thick vapor surrounding us. My hands clasped over my head; my fingers dug into my hair. *Think, Alexis! Where are you? What are you doing?* Right. Okay. I was by Heaven's gates again. Right? And if so, beyond that fog was Heaven in one direction and the

Otherworld—the common part where Angels and Demons fought—in the other. And beyond that, Hell. I needed to go back there. I didn't want to go back there. *No, please, no. Don't make me.* I clutched at my head, trying to block the memories before they came.

But Tristan . . . he was still down there.

My head snapped up. My voice found itself.

"I need to go to Hell," I announced.

"Alexis, darling—" Rina began.

I held my hand up, refusing to look at her, afraid to see the memory of her death again. "I need to save Tristan."

"Honey, there's nothing we can do," Mom said.

"We can go after him!" I spun on them, momentarily forgetting the horror I would see. Blood poured out of a bullet wound in Mom's head. I didn't bother shutting my eyes this time. I'd still see it—Satan would mess with my mind forever. So I dropped my gaze, staring at the floor and the ends of her wings that lay on it. "Call for the Angel. He can go back and help Tristan."

"Tristan already has an Angel, yes?" Rina said.

"Only one. That's not enough. Not with the . . ." The horrors. Oh god, the *horrors.*

The screams, the shouts, the cries for help. I couldn't help them. I couldn't help the souls down there. Just like I couldn't help Solomon or Mom or Rina or those children in the train car.

Screaming filled my ears. My own. A hand pressed on my forehead, and darkness relieved me.

I opened my eyes and looked around. More white nothingness. The air tasted and smelled clean and fresh. The bedding under me was soft and silky to the touch. I wasn't in Hell, but I wasn't in Heaven, either.

And I wasn't alone.

Movement above me. Mom and Rina—the Angel versions, not the bloody ones—hovered, looking down on me.

"Did he bring Tristan back? Did you send the Angel?" I asked.

"I'm sorry, honey." The endearment set my teeth on edge. "There was an Angel with him. No one else can be spared from the war. We need all of the warriors we have to fight the Demons."

"Well, there are plenty of Demons down there to fight." Anger boiled up in me, and I swung my legs over the edge of the bed and jumped to my feet with restless energy.

"That is their home," Rina said. "And one Angel is enough if Tristan truly wants out. It is up to him."

"Like it was up to me to go down there? The *Angel* told me I didn't belong here. Pushed me down there."

"You *don't* belong here," Mom said.

Panic momentarily clawed at my insides with her words, and for a moment, I thought I'd be shoved away down to Hell again. But I forced myself to keep control, to not let the living nightmare overcome me. I needed to focus. On Tristan, who was still in Hell. On Dorian . . . Another thought occurred to me, wrapping me so tightly in terror, I thought my ribs would crack. *Dorian!*

If I didn't stop Dorian, Satan would eventually take my son's soul, too. My sweet, little boy, young and innocent, would be trapped in the fiery depths of Hell, hiding his fear behind a mask of courage in his hazel eyes. I could already hear him screaming for me in my mind. *Mom!* And I tried to yell back that I was coming, but I couldn't move. Couldn't breathe.

I suddenly lay flat on my back. My back with no wings. At least I didn't have to worry about those any longer. The Angels must have realized they'd made a mistake giving them to me.

"Focus on love." Mom's voice sounded normal, soft, not

grating, in my ear. Her hand stroked lightly up and down my arm. "You can make everything go away if you let love replace it. Let the light of love push the darkness away."

I closed my eyes and tried to picture my two boys and me with love surrounding us, not Hell. I saw us on the beach of Amadis Island the day Tristan and Dorian had first met, my towheaded little man running with abandon for his father's arms. I watched another moment on the beach as the three of us fell into the sand together, and Sasha bounced around us, barking and darting in for sniper-licks. I brought back other memories—Tristan and I making dinner while Dorian did schoolwork at the table, the three of us practicing Aikido, our family snuggled up and reading in bed. Back when the world had been normal. At least, closer to normal than it was now.

"Save them from Hell," I murmured sleepily. "Bring them here, too."

"This place is not for them."

"You said that about me, yet here I am."

"You are here so the Angels may give you what you need." Rina's voice floated from the end of the bed, by my feet.

I tried to comprehend her meaning, but my mind was slipping away. Warmth spread across my skin and into my flesh. Calming. Peaceful. My breathing came easier . . . slower . . . Until I drifted off.

I didn't know how long I dozed, but whatever the length, it must have been needed because I felt much better, much stronger, much *clearer* when I woke. I glanced around and found myself completely alone in the foggy space of Heaven's lobby. But not for long. Mom and Rina instantly appeared.

I scowled and pulled my arms tight to my chest with the way they looked at me. Pity? Or was that loathing? Maybe a mixture of both. I turned away, needing to keep my distance from them before they peered too closely. Before they saw the ugly, dark stains on my heart, on my soul—the blemishes left by Satan and Hell . . . shadows of the lives I'd taken.

"How do I get them?" I sat up, keeping my arms tight around myself, and looked at them expectantly. "If the Angels won't help, I'll get Tristan myself, and then together we can stop Dorian."

Rina's hand went to her throat. "You cannot return to Hell!"

"But it was okay to go the first time?"

She blinked. "No."

"But you sent me there anyway."

"That was not our intention."

I lifted a brow.

Mom hurriedly piped in. "When we said before that you don't belong here, we didn't mean you belong in Hell. The Angel didn't mean it, either."

"You do not belong in Heaven, nor in Hell," Rina added. "None of you do. You do not belong in the Otherworld at all. You belong on Earth."

"Then why do you leave Tristan in Hell?" I stood up to be at their height and pointed at my grandmother. "You, Rina, swore more than anyone that Tristan was one of us. You of all people know he doesn't belong there."

"It only matters what *he* believes, and if he believes that, he will return."

Unless he needs a little help from me, I thought but didn't say. How many times had the evil monster inside him tried to take over, and I'd helped him overcome it? Our love had beaten it. What if that was all he needed now? I grasped at the leather collar of the black fighting corset I wore, slipped my hand under it to press against the stone embedded over my heart, hoping he could feel me. It warmed at my touch, but that did nothing to calm me. The physical feeling wasn't even real in this place.

"You're saying I'm not supposed to do anything about him? About Dorian? What the hell *am* I supposed to do?"

"You can pray for them," Rina suggested.

"*Pray?* That's your answer? That's how I'm supposed to end this war?" If it were only so easy. But my prayers had been shut down long ago.

Cassandra suddenly appeared, as though she'd been listening all along. She floated above us, looking as much like a warrior Angel as any of the others, although she'd told me that she, Mom, and Rina were at the lowest level. The chestnut waves of her hair fluttered in a breeze, and her pearlescent wings opened wide to the side.

"There is a way, Alexis," she said, "a way to save Earth and the souls that remain."

"How? How do we stop everything? And please don't say I'll do it, because we know how well that worked out last time. I can't be the cause of any more deaths."

"But you *can* be the cause of many lives," she said. "You may not want to hear it, but it is the truth. We can still win this war, if you help us."

"What? From here?"

Cassandra shook her head. "On Earth."

I stared at her with disbelief. Did she forget that I was dead? I blew out a sigh, trying with difficulty to hold on to my temper as Lucas's words echoed in my mind, along with everything I knew about the Bible and the Book of Revelation.

"So let me get this straight." I thought out loud as I crossed my arms over my chest and popped my hip out. "God sent his four horsemen to Earth, brought on the apocalypse, took his own quarter of the population, allowed Lucas to rise as the Antichrist, and Satan to take over Earth, and *I'm* the one who's supposed to go down there and put a stop to it? Correct me if I'm wrong, but isn't that supposed to be Jesus's big gig? Or what? Are you going to resurrect me, too?"

"Alexis, that is not the apocalypse," Mom said.

I snorted. Hadn't she seen the loss of life that I had?

"This has not been God's doing," Rina clarified. "Nor the Angels."

"It is not time yet for the end of the world," Cassandra added. "There are many souls that can be saved."

I squinted my eyes, not understanding. "So you're trying to tell me I didn't personally witness and experience Conquest, War, Famine, and Death? That Lucas himself isn't the Antichrist trying to raise Satan from Hell? I *know* that isn't true. Lucas told me that was his plan. Satan himself told me he was coming soon."

Mom cringed at the mention of Satan talking to me. "*Lucas* has done all of this. He is arrogant and prideful. Power-hungry and aggressive. He brought on everything that you see as the four horsemen, turning Earth into a place that would welcome Satan. Maybe he does believe himself to be the Antichrist, and I'm so sorry for that, honey. I'm so sorry that you're in this position."

I could hear the sincerity in her voice, but part of me couldn't believe the apologies. They'd known this was coming and hadn't bothered to warn me. And maybe God or the Angels hadn't done this, but he'd allowed it to happen.

"He's always allowed humans free will," Cassandra said, apparently hearing my thoughts. "He's allowed the humans to choose their paths, and recently, the majority chose to walk away from what is right and what is good and followed their own desires. When dark times came, they chose to follow Lucas and evil. They did this to themselves and to Earth, and so yes, they must suffer the consequences of their choices."

"But it is Lucas who has taken it upon himself to start the apocalypse," Rina said. "He must be stopped before it is too late. You can make sure that happens."

I walked away from them, taking a moment to reign in my emotions. Still, the words came out through clenched teeth. "You still haven't explained how I'm supposed to do this. I'm dead, remember?"

"Not exactly," Mom said from behind me.

I spun on her and cocked my head. "What do you mean?"

"Your soul is here for a visit so we may give you the messages you seek so much, but your body remains alive."

"Which is why you cannot choose to go to Hell from here," Rina said. "If you do, you will be damning your soul there for an eternity."

My heart that wasn't really here stuttered. This news changed everything. "But what about Tristan?"

"His body is alive, too."

"But his soul is still in Hell," I surmised.

Mom tilted her head, looking off into the distance. "I cannot tell you that truth for certain."

"So it could be in his body? On Earth?" Hope finally rose within me. "What about Dorian?"

"Dorian is moving along the path he needs to take."

I couldn't help the quiet growl in my throat, my hope of just a moment ago quelled by what Satan had shown me. "Serving his purpose by giving himself to the Daemoni to break the curse. Satan told me when none of you would. How is it so easy for you to accept the sacrifice of one soul for many? Why can't they all be saved?"

"Dorian's purpose is much bigger than that," Cassandra said. "We do not know if he will break the curse."

"But you'll let him hand himself over to the Daemoni anyway and lose his soul," I accused.

"To serve his purpose, he must go to the Daemoni," Cassandra confirmed. "But Alexis, you must remember that his soul is like anybody else's—its fate is in *his* control. Only his. Just because he goes to the Daemoni does not mean he will lose his soul. He will face many challenges with that dark energy influencing him, yes, but in the end, the choice is up to him."

Another revelation that had my mind faltering, stumbling over itself. Why had I never considered this? All of those times everyone spoke of Dorian going to the Daemoni, I'd automatically feared not only for his life, but even more for his soul. I just knew that meant he'd lose it immediately, that he'd automatically belong to Satan and be damned for an eternity. Yet, I'd felt the hope in Noah when he'd been with us, and hadn't he made that same decision? If it hadn't been for the curse, I was sure he would have converted. Which meant that if Dorian made it to Lucas before Tristan and I could get to him, he wasn't completely lost to us.

Hope lifted again.

"Okay," I conceded. "What about the Amadis? Owen, Vanessa, Charlotte, Blossom, Jax, Sheree . . . ? Are they alive and well, too?"

The three of them looked at each other, and then their eyes glazed over again.

Cassandra finally answered me. "We can only tell you that there are many souls, many *lives*, still on Earth who need you and the Amadis."

"Fantastic," I muttered. They *couldn't* tell me more, or they wouldn't? Or was it something I didn't want to know anyway? Maybe this was their way of saying my friends were all dead. "I thought you were supposed to help me here."

"We've told you as much as we know," Mom said. "The Angels do not share everything with us. They have faith in you, though. That is all you need to know."

Heh. I wasn't quite sure I believed that. I wasn't quite sure what—or who—I believed anymore. And I certainly didn't return their faith, in me, or them, or anyone. It was broken, fractured into a million pieces, and I didn't know if it could ever be put back together.

But that didn't matter.

What did matter was that I wasn't dead. And neither were Tristan or Dorian. Perhaps some of those closest to me remained alive, too, although it was difficult to see how, knowing where they'd been when the bombs dropped—right in the heart of everything that was now dead and burning to ash. But if there was any possibility . . . if they were the only souls I could help, the only lives I could save, so be it.

I needed to return to Earth.

Tristan had taught me how to align my goals with Mom's and Rina's when they'd told me to build our army rather than search for Dorian. We'd figured out how to do both. So I'd tell them what they wanted to hear now, although I had no idea how I'd be able to actually follow through for them. I mean, if I found life and souls to defend, I definitely would. Of course I would! I just didn't expect to find them, and even if I did, if my soul was pure enough anymore to help. As for fighting the Daemoni and stopping Lucas . . . I didn't know how I'd do that, either. Hopefully, Tristan and anyone left of the Amadis could help me figure that out. It was a bridge we'd have to cross later. First, I needed to help Tristan and Dorian.

I had one question, though, before I agreed to their demands.

"If Lucas opened the veil for the Demons to enter Earth, why can't the Angels enter, too? Why rely on me when a few Angels could go in, stop Lucas, and finish this war for good?"

Cassandra came to stand in front of me, her eyes soft as they held mine. A small smile lifted her lips. "Because God's plan goes beyond simply stopping Lucas. We do not know it all—each part is revealed to us when appropriate—but we do know the Angels are preparing for so much more. And *you* are part of that plan. You were chosen to do this before I even started the Amadis, Alexis. It is not only this war, but what is to come after, that has always been your true purpose."

What is to come after . . . The words echoed in my head as I fixated on them. Certainly something would come after, but I didn't know if it would be good or bad. If the Angels would continue testing me by throwing me up against more evil, or if I could finally have relief.

"Focus on the good," Cassandra continued. "Find it in the world. It does still exist, but it's up to you to uncover it."

I blew out a breath. "Okay. Fine. If I don't belong here and I don't belong in Hell, then I must belong on Earth. I make no promises, but I'll do my best."

"Your best is exactly what we need," Rina said as her eyes lit up.

She held her arms open for an embrace, and Cassandra followed suit. I gave them each a hug, and then slumped into Mom's arms.

"You can do this, honey. Find the good. Start in here." She pulled back and tapped a finger to the left side of my chest, and I cringed away, hoping she didn't notice the dark blemish of Hell stamped on my heart, on my soul. "Love will get you through. Feel the love. Let it reign. And know that I always love you, no matter what."

I nodded, although my heart felt heavy, weighed down by the darkness inside. Before I could say anything more, the bottom dropped out from underneath me, and I fell.

CHAPTER 5

*W*hen I found her soul down here in Hell, I'd wanted to kill her. My own soul filled with joy to see her, of course, even if it was her essence in the Otherworld rather than her whole self in the Earthly realm. At least we were together. But finding her in Hell made me think she'd gone and done something stupid again, as she was known to do. It wasn't her fault—she hadn't had time to learn the rules like the rest of us had. We were born into a different world than her, even Rina and Sophia, who'd come from a different time. We often took for granted what we knew. With new challenges thrown at us nonstop, I'd been unable to give Alexis the lessons I'd gained in my hundreds of years. She'd had to learn as we went, trial by fire, so she was bound to make mistakes.

But to know that her soul's presence in Hell was not one of those mistakes, but Satan's doing, was quite the relief.

To see her leaving by the light of the Angel carrying her away made everything we'd been through down here worth it. As long as her soul was safe, I would be fine.

"*Don't give up.*" Her words carried down to me as I caught the flaming sword she'd tossed my way.

Never, I thought as I used the weapon to fight the Demons that had sabotaged my escape.

The lava-ensconced, monstrous body of Satan thrashed in the lake of fire, his molten fists pounding the air as Alexis flew away. He turned his attention on the Angel and me at the same time we dispatched the group of Demons that had brought us down. We stood on a bridge of black lava rock that stretched across the entire cavern, what appeared to be hundreds of feet above the lake's surface, although distance could not be easily judged or measured down here. Deceit was everywhere. Bound to the lake below, Satan couldn't quite reach us. With a roar, he sank into the flames. A moment later, a blazing serpent emerged and soared upward.

At the same time the snake rose, more Demons flew at the Angel and me. I swung the sword at the first one to reach me, and easily took it down, but the second one put up more of a fight. The ball of its mace slammed into my shoulder, the Hellfire on its spikes sending needles of ice into my flesh and bones. I spun away and arced my sword as I came back around. The mace's chain wrapped around my blade, and the Demon tried to yank the sword from my grip.

"No way in hell am I giving this up," I muttered as my hands tightened around the hilt. The Demon sword, along with the Angel's help, was my best bet of getting out of here. With a hard jerk, I pulled the blade free. It sliced through the chains, severing the ball from the handle. Weaponless, the Demon screeched a slew of obscenities in the old language. Flinging the profanity back at it, I charged, taking its head with one swoop. I spun to find not another Demon facing me, but the serpent.

Its enormous head had risen high enough from the lake to come eye to eye with me—its eye taller than my entire body. I glanced down to find its tail still immersed in the lake's depths far below. No telling how long it was. With an oval, yellow eye blazing through its red, magma skin, it peered at me for a long moment. It opened its mouth to reveal fangs dripping with red-hot venom. A tongue of fire flickered out, its prongs licking my uninjured shoulder, and this time, liquid heat rather than ice pierced into my skin. Then the snake twisted away before shooting higher into the air. One glance up and I knew why.

Alexis and her Angel were still in sight.

"I don't think so." I sprinted across the bridge until I came as close as I could get and then leapt into the air.

My sword pointed downward when I landed on the snake, and I plunged it in deep. Its body whipped to the side as its head looped around. I wrenched the blade free and swung at the tongue as it flicked out at me. I missed. As though deciding I wasn't enough of a threat, the head turned back up and aimed for Alexis. I ran up its back, trying to reach its head before it came within striking distance of my wife, but it was right on her heels. I thrust the sword again. The snake hissed and shrieked. It reared away from Alexis, whipping back and forth. I dropped to straddle the beast, hanging onto the sword's grip and gritting my teeth through the heat of the fire warming my leather pants.

Its head swung around to face me again. Its mouth opened, baring its fangs, then widened as though preparing to swallow me whole. With a violent yank, the blade came free, and I jumped to my feet, holding it in front of me. This time when the tongue darted out, I lobbed it off, but another one immediately replaced it. The mouth opened further, coming closer. The entire head lunged at me.

I jabbed at it, and the jaw snapped, nearly taking my head, but I ducked and rolled away. When I came back up, the Angel who had tried to rescue me stood in the snake's mouth, holding it open with his feet wedged into its bottom fangs and its sword piercing the top of the snake's mouth.

"No!" I yelled.

"I cannot die," he said. "But you can, and so can she. If your choice remains the same, I will be back for you."

Without hesitation, he dove into the snake's throat, his wings spread wide to scrape the sides all the way down. Flinging itself back and forth, the snake slithered into the lake, shrieking as it went. I missed the land bridge as we sank, but sprang off the snake's back as soon as I saw a ledge on the cliffside. Before the fiery serpent was even halfway down, it exploded. Balls of fire and massive drops of lava rained into the lake below. Whatever happened to the Angel, he was gone now.

I was left in Hell alone.

I glanced up to make sure Alexis was safe. Relief filled me when I could no longer see the light of her and the Angel who carried her. I could handle Hell for a while as long as she was okay.

"She may be gone, but you're mine again." Satan's voice rumbled all around me. "I knew you couldn't stay away forever."

"Don't think I'm here forever."

"We'll see about that . . ."

A Demon swooped down at me. I swung the sword at it, but it twisted away. Out of nowhere, something hard slammed into my head. I stumbled back, turned, reached for the wall, but it was too late. My feet landed on nothing. I began to fall backwards for the lake. Another Demon soared for me, as though to ensure I plunged deep into the fire. When it tried to shove me with its hooved feet, I grabbed onto its calves and clung. Its powerful legs swung back and forth as it tried to fling me off, but I held on until I saw black underneath me.

Nothing but black. No fire. No beasts, Satan or otherwise. Nothing at all could be seen below. The blackness could stretch forever, as far as I knew. Anything could be down there. But it wasn't the lake of fire or the serpent's mouth, which was good enough for me.

I let go with a prayer.

And crashed into a frozen floor. The Hellfire's ice in my shoulder shattered, jabbing pain through my entire right side. I rolled onto my knees and one hand and tried to look around. The darkness was thorough. A black as solid as wood.

But not silent.

The screams of earlier—the bays of souls—filled the air, my ears, my head. With no external visual stimulant, visions formed in my mind. Memories of things I never wanted to see again. The horrible acts I'd done on behalf of Lucas and the Ancients. The people I killed. The villages I burned using a flame from my very palm. The same palm I used to stroke my wife's skin, to cup her face for a kiss. I'd choked kind and generous men with these hands. Snapped necks of religious leaders. Seduced royals' women to start wars. I'd led ambushes, finished unfair battles, and caused the deaths of thousands. Hundreds of thousands.

The lamenting souls recalled each one. Reminded me that I belonged here in Hell. Pleaded with me to admit my guilt and accept my punishment.

I tried to stay steadfast in what I knew in my heart and soul. What had been promised to me. *I've been forgiven.*

"Have you?" Satan's voice asked, slithering around me. "Are you ssssure?"

"I'm certain."

"What about for thisss?"

A new vision showed—Alexis's distraught face as I walked out the door of the safe house in Virginia, leaving her with her mother and grandmother so I could meet Lucas. Abandoning her for seven years, seven months, seven days. Deserting her so she had to bring our son into the world without me . . . forcing her to suffer the circumstances of his birth alone.

"That is your fault, too," Satan taunted. "Dorian's arrival without a sister."

"I know," I admitted.

"I don't think you do. I don't think you fully understand. We needed *you* to mate with Alexis. We needed the child *you*, and nobody else, would produce. But we only needed one. Only the boy. He is important. So very important, with the blood of you *and* Alexis. The blood of Jordan *and* Cassandra. So powerful. And he isssss mine."

I growled and swung my fist, but it hit nothing but air. Satan laughed.

"It's too late for you to fight that inevitability. You know it as well as I do. And it's too late for you to change this next bit I'm going to share, but I'll tell you anyway, because it makes me happy. You see, two children from the two of you would not do. Not for our plans. Another Amadis daughter from anyone else would have been an inconvenience, but a daughter from you, born with this boy, would have ruined everything. And we actually had someone in place to ensure there wasn't a girl."

He paused, as though checking to make sure I was listening. I didn't want to, but it's not like I had a choice.

"Kali was such a good servant of mine," he finally continued. "Placed herself right where she was needed most— at the top levels of Amadis leadership. Dressed in Martin's body, everybody trusted her. Katerina, Sophia, their servants. If Martin sent supplies to the kitchen staff at the safe house where Alexis stayed during her pregnancy, nobody would question it. If those supplies were ingredients for her breakfast, in they would go without a second thought. If those ingredients were enchanted to attach to an extra X chromosome, and cursed to obliterate the fetus in utero, nobody would even know. Nobody did know. The circumstances of her labor—the unusual amount of blood loss that caused Alexis to lose consciousness—they blamed on natural causes. They were delusional in their security. Martin hadn't gone within a thousand-mile proximity to Alexis, yet Kali had succeeded in killing her child. *Your* child. For me.

Alexis would have been better off with children from anyone but you. Kali's son would have been a better choice for the Amadis. But you just couldn't help yourself, could you?"

Murderous red filled my vision. Every muscle pulled taut. When a Demon flew at me, I thrilled for the fight.

"It's your fault." Alexis's voice came from the Demon. Its form morphed into her shape. I hesitated. "*Your* fault that the Amadis didn't have another daughter. Why did you have to ruin my life, Tristan? Or should I call you *Seth*? You're selfish and evil! You don't deserve to be married to me. You don't deserve to father my children. Look at all of the horrors you've committed!"

Alexis's image disappeared. The Demon's mouth with her voice pouring out of it opened wide. It exhaled a colorful smoke that became another vision. No, not a vision. A window onto the Earthly realm. Showing Dorian and Noah. Dorian leaving Noah. Dorian saying goodbye as he headed out to find Lucas.

"LIES!" I bellowed.

Satan chuckled. "Oh, I'm afraid not."

"He's going because of you, Seth," Demon-Alexis said. "IT'S ALL. YOUR. FAULT!"

Her accusations grew, and she shouted an unending list of the many ways I'd hurt her and our son. How I'd caused the fall of the Amadis and the world. How I'd failed her and everyone else.

"*Have* you been forgiven for these trespasses against others?" Satan drawled. "For the sins you've committed against your own wife and children?"

"I died because of you. Our baby girl, too. You weren't there to save us!" Alexis's voice continued, and that was the one that broke me. The vision of holding her damaged, lifeless body as our baby bled out of her brought me to my knees.

Easily catching my reaction, Satan pounded me with that one. Never let me forget it. The vision blinded me as the

Demon's fists and club beat at me, its voice—Alexis's voice—driving home the pain I'd caused her and our children. Then they became a cry. Her sobs. Her keens of despair. And I wailed along with her.

At some point, another Demon arrived, carrying the voices of all the others I'd hurt and killed. The ones I thought I'd been forgiven for, but didn't know anymore. I could no longer believe in that possibility. How could one person cause so much agony to so many other people, including those he supposedly loved, and be forgiven? How could I be absolved for the many, *many* atrocious sins I'd committed?

"Impossible," I moaned along with the others.

There was no way. I didn't deserve to be pardoned. I didn't deserve to be anywhere but here. I only deserved to listen to these Demons with their howls and whimpers, their accusations, the guilt they hurled at me that stuck like black on tar. I deserved to suffer the pain, to relive the agony of my soul mate's death forever and ever.

Perhaps I belonged right here. In Hell. For eternity.

CHAPTER 6

I awoke with a start, my arms and legs spread out to catch myself and my heart pounding in my throat. The sensation of falling backwards for a great distance lingered from my dream. I blinked as I stared at the ceiling, taking in the familiar sight of gossamer fabric draped between the tops of four stone pillars at each corner of the bed. After a moment, my brain associated the view with our suite at the matriarch's mansion on Amadis Island, and my heart finally returned from my throat to its normal place and speed. I blew out a big breath of relief to know it really had been a dream. I couldn't remember the last time I'd been able to sleep so hard and long. My body must have needed the lengthy regeneration, because it'd never felt as strong and powerful as it did now.

Once my muscles uncoiled from the abrupt return to consciousness, I rolled over the thick mattress that lay atop the stone dais of our bed, and onto my side, facing my husband. He lay on his back, the silky sheet pulled up to just below his hip bones, his bare abs, chest, shoulders, and arms a sight to behold. I wanted to explore every mountain and valley of his body, preferably with my mouth, but his beautiful face was so peaceful, his long lashes resting against his cheekbones and his full lips slightly parted. I decided not to wake him. Yet. Just to be sure he was indeed asleep, I brushed my thumb over his scruffy jawline and then across his bottom lip. I lifted myself up on an elbow and leaned in to kiss him. His breath came soft on my lips, but he otherwise didn't so much as twitch. He'd been dealing with my nightmares for so long, he must have needed the deep rest as much as I had.

So I slipped out of the covers and treaded softly to the en suite bathroom, where I found my fighting leathers—a sleeveless top and pants—clean and folded on the stone counter, waiting for me. The pool-size tub always called to me, but I couldn't remember what we had planned for the day, so didn't know if I had time for the luxury of a bubble bath. So I took a quick shower and dressed.

When I came out and passed through the bedroom to the front room of our suite, the sheer curtain hanging in the doorway to the balcony caught my attention. Something about it wasn't quite right, but I couldn't pinpoint the problem. I shrugged and slipped through the door, closing it quietly behind me. Before leaving the suite, I reached out with my mind to identify who was in the mansion and where.

There was nobody.

No, I had to take that back. I couldn't tell if there was nobody because something felt odd in my mind as it tried to reach out. As though something blocked me. Had Tristan asked Owen to muffle our suite again so we could make love last night? *Had* we made love last night? I hadn't noticed any bruises on my skin when I showered. And surely I wouldn't forget that! But I honestly couldn't remember a thing about last night or yesterday or . . . My brow furrowed as I tried to recall my last memory, because my mind kept bringing forth events from my nightmare.

"I seriously need coffee," I muttered aloud as I left the suite.

I stopped at Dorian's room, but there were no signs of him

or Sasha, so I made my way downstairs. Ophelia, the mansion's head of staff and bringer of breakfast, was nowhere to be found, either. I sat in the fancy dining room where everyone staying in the mansion usually gathered for breakfast and dinner and waited until the sound of my own fingers drumming on the tablecloth drove me crazy. A mental search for Ophelia still found no one in the entire building. However, when I entered the gourmet kitchen, I discovered a hot pot of coffee waiting for me.

As I leaned against the granite counter and sipped my nectar of the gods, I stared hard at the rack of pots and pans hanging from the ceiling over the giant kitchen island. I could have sworn Ophelia used black-as-night, cast-iron pots, but these were the kind I preferred, covered in ceramic that was painted burgundy. Had she finally acquired new cookware? Seemed unlikely at her age, especially when hers had been so beautifully seasoned over the years. Then again, I couldn't recall at the moment if she'd actually been the one who did all of the cooking or if someone else did. Who had it been? Had they been replaced?

Why was my recent memory so freaking cloudy?

When I finished my coffee and still nobody had shown up, not a single mind signature coming into my range, worry needled its way under my skin. I searched the entire bottom floor for people. Owen, Vanessa, Charlotte, Sheree, staff, *someone*. But the mansion was like an empty museum, with sun streaming through the foyer and dust motes dancing in the rays.

"They must be in the village," I said, knowing full well I spoke to myself, but the silence was unnerving, and I'd needed to break it. "Are *we* supposed to be in the village?"

I tried to think if we had a council meeting or special event we should have been attending, but I couldn't remember anything at all. *Nothing.* My recent memory was more than cloudy; it was downright *gone.* I glanced up at the ceiling, as if

I could see two stories up to Tristan, but decided to let him sleep a bit longer and make the trip myself. Just a quick flash to the village to make sure everything was okay, and then I'd come back to wake him.

But when I tried to flash, I went nowhere.

I tried again and again, until I could only imagine how ridiculous my face must have looked with the concentration I put into the effort. *What the hell?* I strode over to the double doors at the front of the foyer and pulled on them. They refused to budge. I went to every door that led to the outside on the first floor, and none would open. And at that moment, I realized what had been off with the sheer curtain on our balcony: It had been hanging still and shadowed. It didn't billow inward as it usually did from the breeze off the Aegean Sea, and the light behind it hadn't been right. Neither was the light here in the foyer—there were no windows in the foyer for the sun to shine through. The only light usually came from the torches on the wall.

"What's going on?" I called out as the tiny seed of worry blossomed into a full bloom of concern. "Where is everyone?"

Nobody answered.

"HELLO?" My shout bounced off the stone walls, reverberating back to me. Concern exploded into panic. Something was wrong. I ran through the entire first floor of the mansion, throwing open doors to offices, bathrooms, staff rooms, parlors, the media room, closets . . . all except the doors to the Sacred Archives, which wouldn't open. "Dorian? Owen? Vanessa? Blossom?"

I yelled all of their names as I ran. I thought I caught a flash of pink and then a glimpse of white hair.

"Ophelia! Is that you? Are you here?"

Still no reply. I ran up to the second floor, throwing more doors open, and finding nobody. And then to the third story, even daring to enter Rina's wing for the first time since she'd died.

"Solomon?" I called. "Where are you?"

Not only was nobody around, but there were simply no signs of anyone being here. No coffee cup left on a side table. No hand towels in the bathrooms looking like they'd ever been touched. Not a single piece of trash in the bins—not a tissue or balled up sheet of paper to be found.

Adrenaline shot through my veins, and my heart sprang into a gallop. I ran back to our suite, throwing the doors open with a bang.

"Tristan, wake up! Something's wrong. Everybody's gone."

He didn't so much as stir, so I launched myself at the bed and gave him a shake.

"Wake up. Come on."

He continued to sleep, which wasn't like him. If anything, he should have shot upright, fists flying in natural reaction. But he did nothing except lay there.

"Tristan, please," I begged as anxiety turned to fear. I straddled him, grabbed his biceps, and gave him a violent shake. His head only lolled side to side. I peeled back an eyelid, and still no response. His pupil didn't even constrict. "What's wrong with you? Wake up, Tristan! *Please.*"

I yelled at him, jumped on him, hit him with a pillow. A shiny, royal blue stone that had been on the pillow under his neck slid to the side. Another one on my side of the bed caught my eye. I picked them up and studied them, but had no idea what they were. Faerie stones, maybe? Had a fae who favored the Daemoni done this to my husband?

I took off again, screaming for help. Still nobody came. I ran for the media room and picked up a phone, but dead air greeted my ear. No power in the media room at all.

"What's going on?" My frustrated screams echoed through the halls.

I blurred back to the Sacred Archives and tried the doors again. I yanked on them, punched at them, kicked at them, threw my shoulder into them, and then my whole body. I blasted a stream of electricity at them, and only then did they finally budge. With another shove, they flew open. Into a dark room no bigger than a coat closet.

Where were the shelves and shelves of books? Where was the sunshiny scent? Where was the Otherworldly glow that usually illuminated the room—which was supposed to be at least five times this size?

I slowly turned and left the room, then made my way down the corridor in a daze as I tried to solve the current puzzle of my life. My surroundings faded out as my mind strained to figure out what had happened to my husband. To my son. To everyone else. To my memories. Without realizing it, I meandered into the front sitting room, where the hearth was dark and cold for the first time I could ever remember. My head tilted as my gaze traveled across the small tapestries on the wall. They weren't quite right, either, like so many things in this house. I shuffled around to face the big one. The tapestry that stretched from ceiling to floor and wall to wall. The one that depicted the Ames Family Vine with the green silvery leaves for the women and the brown ones for the sons, each of those with their stems broken from the vine, showing how they'd defected to the Daemoni. All of the leaves for the sons were like that except Dorian's, whose had been brown, but had remained attached to the vine.

Until now.

"No!" I cried out when my eyes landed on his leaf at the top of the vine. It was no longer fully connected, only the tip of its stem still touching the branch. "Oh, Dorian. What did you do? What happened?"

I tried to focus on the last time I'd seen him, tried to figure out what events might have transpired to make his leaf pull away from the vine. The only answers came from my dream, a nightmare actually. One where Lucas had essentially brought Hell to Earth, where Dorian had freed Noah and taken off, where I'd died and gone to Heaven and then to Hell, where

Tristan had followed me, but when we'd tried to escape, only I had made it. I'd left him behind in Hell. But that had only been a dream. He was upstairs this very moment, still sleeping.

Right . . . ?

Reality slammed down on me, caged me like a monstrous Demon claw, capturing me within its talons of Hellfire that burned from both heat and cold at the same time.

"NOOOOO!" I screamed at the top of my lungs, the wail sounding like those from the suffering souls in Hell. I collapsed in a heap on the floor, and something in my corset poked me between the breasts. My fingers grasped the corners of thick paper stuffed into a hidden pocket inside, and I pulled it out, smoothed out the folded postcard, gazed at the picture of the Thomas Jefferson Memorial in springtime, cherry blossoms blooming all around the tidal basin. Tears filled my eyes and dropped onto the creased postcard. My head shook violently. "No, no, nooooo."

The visions of fire and black ice, of Satan in both his suave and beastly forms, of Demons swinging their weapons and monsters pushing through the walls, obliterated the scene around me. The howls and shrieks of burning souls filled my ears and mind. I sank into a crouch and fell backwards as my hands grabbed at my hair. This couldn't be happening. Everything from my dream—the war, the losses, the trips to Heaven and Hell—they *couldn't* have been real. The memory of Mom, Rina, and Cassandra with their Angel-like bodies in a white, foggy space flashed in my mind.

It was all real. So very damn real.

"How could you do this to me?" I screamed at them as I rocked up to my knees and lifted my face upward as tears streamed down. "How am I supposed to do anything here? I can't even leave!"

Exasperation brought another angry scream that started in my belly, tore through my throat, and launched itself out like a dragon finally set free. The power was so great, my back arched, cracking and popping, and I cried out again, this time with pain. It passed in a moment, and then a big shadow loomed over me.

I shrieked and jumped to my feet. Something very large and very dark was behind me. I spun, landing with my knees bent and my hands out, ready to fight. But it had moved with me. I twisted around again, and it followed. And when I knew this familiar game, I could no longer scream out my frustration. I could only double over with a fit of insane laughter.

"You've got to be fucking kidding me."

One side of the thing lifted and spread out as if to say, "Nope, not kidding at all." The tips hit the wall four feet away, and it wasn't even fully extended. My eyes cut sideways, looking at it out of curiosity, although most of me fumed over its very existence. Well. At least it was pretty. The other side spanned out as well, then they came together behind me, then back out, creating a breeze and a fluttering sound. The scents of baby powder and sunshine wafted in the air.

"Wings," I said out loud. "I have wings."

And here I'd thought I'd escaped the monstrosities.

I had to admit they were stunningly beautiful. Not white anymore or pearlescent like Mom's, Rina's, and Cassandra's. The feathers were purple, the deep, royal purple of the Amadis matriarch, gradually darkening toward the quill tips, which were a shiny black, as though they'd just been dipped in ink. Like no wings I'd ever seen, real or imaginary. My hand reached out and hung in the air, hesitating for a moment, before I caressed my fingers over the feathers. I gasped at how soft and silky they felt to my fingertips. A tingling, like my favorite sensation of someone brushing my hair, ran through the shafts and along the wings to my spine, causing me to shudder.

"Oh, those are nice," said a very female and very British voice behind me.

I spun around, my wings brushing the walls and knocking over a chair. The feathers had hardened with my surprised response, and the tingling sensation changed, becoming more like that of fingernails dragging across a hard surface. As more of a reaction than a thought, the wings closed in behind me, tight against my back.

A white-and-pink-haired woman with a voluptuous body clad in a fifties-style dress with cherries on it stood in front of me. She craned her neck, her big, blue eyes still trying to see my wings.

"Mine are pink, see?" A flash of gauzy, hot pink wings showed, shaped more like a butterfly's than a bird's, like mine. They disappeared before I could barely catch a glimpse of them. When my eyes flew to her face, it seemed to have momentarily changed, too—a more impish nose, eyes uplifted at the outside corners, and pointier ears—but when she frowned, everything looked normal again. "Been havin' problems."

My brows scrunched together, and I shook my head to clear it.

"What are you doing here?" I demanded, quickly realizing that she was a faerie. Had those been her stones in our bed? Was she holding us captive? She was certainly familiar. "I know you. You were in England. You're one of the faeries that sent us to the abbey in Whitby. Stacey . . . right?"

"That's right, chick," she said, friendly enough. "Debbie and me took care of you then, just like we took care of you now."

I crossed my arms over my chest. Faeries did not do so-called favors, like "taking care of you." Not without strings, anyway.

"How, exactly, did you take care of us?" I asked. "Did you poison us with your stones? What have you done to Tristan?"

Her eyes widened, sensing the accusations in my tone.

81

"We helped you! Tristan's missing his soul. That's what's wrong with 'im!"

I blinked. Missing his soul . . . because I'd left him in Hell. And he was apparently still there. My eyes burned, and I had to bite my lip to keep it from trembling, because I refused to cry in front of her. "Then *what* did you do?"

"We collected your bodies and hid them here. They healed themselves, but we protected you with the faerie stones so you'd be physically strong and good to go when your souls returned from the Otherworld."

I squinted at her. "What?"

"Your bodies were missing their souls, so even though they physically healed, they wouldn't last long without your essence. So we helped. Brought you here." She paused, and her baby blues misted over as her chin trembled. "I'm . . . I'm sorry about the baby. There was nothing . . . the blood . . ."

I blinked, caught off guard.

"Um . . . it's okay. I know. I'd already accepted it." Not that I didn't feel like a thick shard of glass had just been stabbed into my heart, but I knew she wasn't to blame for the miscarriage, nor was there anything she could have done.

"I'm so glad you're back," she went on, as though rushing to move beyond the awkward moment, "but shame 'bout Tristan. I know he'll come, though. 'Course, I can't hardly stand to be here myself with what the norms did to the planet, thanks to Lucas." Her voice had become watery with emotion, and she cleared it with a cough. "The fae folk are creatures of nature, Earthly nature or otherwise. We can't survive on a near dead world like this one. Didn't know if you two would make it, either, so we got you as far away from the nastiness as we could." She tilted her head and crossed her arms over her ample chest, mirroring my position as she studied me. "Seems like you're okay. Better'n okay by the looks of ya."

I uncrossed my arms and placed my hands on my hips instead. "Hold on. Just so I understand. You're saying that you moved our bodies to the Amadis mansion to protect us from the nuclear fallout? And your faerie stones have kept our bodies alive, waiting for our souls?"

"Yeah, that's right—nuclear and other fallout. Except we're not at the Amadis mansion. I just gave you that illusion so you'd feel at home when you came back. I've never been there, so I did me best copying your memories."

My mouth dropped open, although I shouldn't have been surprised. I'd noticed the inconsistencies in the mansion. The weirdness. Her explanation was weird in itself, but at least it *was* an explanation.

"Then where are we? Where is everyone else? Do you know if they survived? My people?"

The corners of her mouth quivered as though she fought a frown. "You're in a safe place for now. I don't know about anyone else, or the rest of the world. All I know is the Daemoni seem able to roam anywhere they please, so maybe it's safe for you and the rest of the Amadis, too?"

"You haven't seen anyone through the veil when you're in the Otherworld?"

She shook her head, making my stomach drop, and her hands wrung together. "There is so much going on in the Otherworld . . . too much to focus on this one when we are there."

She meant the fighting between the Angels and Demons. The faeries probably watched it for entertainment, passing buckets of faerie popcorn between them.

"Why?" I asked.

She blinked at me, reflecting my bewilderment.

"Why would you faeries go through all of this trouble for us?" I clarified. "You don't take sides in the war."

Her eyes brightened. "Oh but we have, haven' we? Some of us have, helpin' one side or the other out since the very beginning. And the Amadis need you. This world needs you. So Debbie—remember her in York with me when you were looking for your lad?—she and I did what we could to help."

"You saved us for the Amadis and the Angels?" I asked skeptically. "For the norms? You don't even like norms."

"Sure we do," she said unconvincingly. "Except when they destroy the natural energy that gives us life." She looked away and sucked her cheeks in, pursing her lips together as though for a kiss.

"There's something else," I guessed.

A grimace flashed across her face for the briefest moment, and then she looked back at me with a bright smile. "Well, there is one tiny thing."

And here it comes. The payback they'd require for saving Tristan's life and mine. Of course, I couldn't argue that I owed them, although I'd much prefer Tristan's soul be in his body. That wasn't their fault, however. I mentally cringed from the horrible visions threatening to fill my mind and gave them a hard shove out. I couldn't break down now, as much as I wanted to at the thought of Tristan still in Hell.

I inhaled a deep breath and blew it out. "What can I do for you?"

"It's not really anything specific. We just need you to win. You have to beat Lucas and make sure arsehole Satan stays where he belongs. And, well . . . maybe save our folk while you're at it."

I cocked my head. "What do you mean, save your folk?"

Her gaze slid away as she averted her eyes. My question hung between us for a moment.

"Would you like a cuppa tea?" She suddenly produced a tray in her hands with a teapot and two cup-and-saucer settings. "Let's sit."

Her head gave a small jerk, and the chair I'd knocked over with my wing righted itself. She sat down in it, placing the tea service on the coffee table in front of her. I moved over to the leather couch and began to sit down, but my wings got in the way. I tried sweeping them to the side, but they were too huge and unmanageable. So I straightened up.

"I'll stand," I said.

"Can't you make them hide?" she asked as she poured a cup of tea.

"Hide?"

"Unless you plan on rompin' all over the place with those whoppin' things on your back?"

I frowned. Could I hide my wings like Sasha could hide hers? With a simple thought of "hide," they disappeared. My excitement over this revelation was instantly extinguished, though, with the thought of the lykora. Another family member whose whereabouts were unknown. I hadn't seen her since she'd chased off a Demon at the Jefferson Memorial, right before I'd died . . . or whatever I'd done before waking up here. I sat down with a heavy heart.

Stacey handed me a cup and saucer, and although I took it, I didn't plan to drink the contents. No telling what was in faerie tea.

"I'm not goin' to poison you," she said. "I need you. All the fae folk do."

I pretended to take a sip and then set the cup on the coffee table. "Explain."

Her white brows scrunched together with concern. "Some of us are missin'. Lots of us, really, 'specially anyone who helped the Amadis. They've just been disappearin'. Like Debbie."

I recalled the faerie who'd been with her that night in York, when we'd followed Kali, Owen, Noah, and Dorian through a portal to England. She'd looked similar to Stacey, but with purple in her hair rather than pink. "Debbie's gone?"

Stacey nodded. "She was here with us, making sure you and Tristan were okay, and then she went outside and poof! Gone."

"Maybe she's in the Otherworld?"

"Oh, I know she is. I know they all are. Just not in a place I can go. Unless I'm taken there." Her voice filled with fear with that last statement. "Those of us who are left believe Satan's got them. Punishing them for helping his enemy."

"You think Satan's locked up the fae?"

"Not just fae. Several others, too. He's had entire races locked up for eons. Anyone who doesn't support him. He'd gone after them before, and now he's goin' after the fae."

"And you think I can help how?"

"Satan's only as powerful as the souls in the physical realm allow him to be. *They* give him the power. If you take out the Daemoni, you knock his power down several notches. My people can free themselves then."

Okay. No pressure there. She made it sound so simple, but what she asked was no different than what the Angels asked of me. I didn't even know if she told me the truth or had some ulterior motive.

I leaned back against the couch and studied her face, since I couldn't read her mind. Fae minds came as blank slates to me. She seemed sincere with genuine concern, but she was a faerie, known for their trickery. Would she tell me such dire stories in a time like this just for the fun of it? I didn't know. I didn't know her well enough, and I really didn't trust the faerie. Even if she had helped us before. Actually, *because* she had helped us before, which gave her all the more reason to jack with me. Regardless of what she said about some fae leaning one way or the other between good and evil, they didn't do anything for free.

"I'm not askin' you anything you won't do anyway," she said. "You wanted to know why we helped you, so I told you. That's all." She stood up. "I better go now."

I jumped to my feet. "No! You can't leave us here. I don't even know where we are!"

She lifted a brow, and I immediately regretted the outburst. If she stayed, she could demand anything of me.

"I'm sorry, but I can't stay in this world for long bouts anymore," she said as she headed for the door, "but I'll be back."

I followed the faerie out of the sitting room and into the foyer. "What's it like out there?"

"In the Otherworld? Didn't you see it?"

"Yes. I mean on Earth."

She turned to look at me and frowned, a deep sadness filling her eyes. "It's dire. If you feel up to it when I return, you can go out and see for yourself."

"Can you tell me where Dorian is?" I asked. That was a favor I didn't hesitate to request.

"I'll take a mooch in the Otherworld and let you know what I find out that will help you." Well, that was better than what anyone else had done. She tugged at the double wood doors that hadn't budged for me, but she had no problem opening them. "But I can make no other promises."

Panic rose as the reality of her leaving us here alone hit me. "What do I do about Tristan? How do I help him?"

"I don't know," she shouted over the howl of a wind outside. "Stay here until . . . bring . . . back . . ."

The wind drowned out her last words, and the doors slammed shut behind her, leaving me staring at them in bewilderment. The *hell* I was just going to sit around here, waiting. I needed to figure out how to get my husband back.

Except I couldn't leave. I fought the doors myself, used my powers and superhuman strength, but they failed to open for me. We were trapped.

At first, I told myself she'd come back, as promised, because that only made sense. How did she expect me to do anything when I was held captive here? But after a while, doubt crept in until it became a full-blown monster. And that monster morphed into the beasts of Hell, taking over my mind while the screams clawed and scratched at my soul. I tried to fight the nightmare, coming in and out of consciousness, begging Stacey or someone, anyone, to return.

After what could have been a day or a month—just like in the Otherworld, I had no concept of time—the illusion of the Amadis mansion around me disappeared, leaving Tristan and me in a cold, dark room with a rounded, dirt ceiling and rocky walls. He lay perfectly still in his black leathers on a stone slab while I sat in a ball on a dirt floor.

And I knew then that Stacey wouldn't be returning.

CHAPTER 7

The realization that we were completely alone and on our own snapped me out of my personal darkness. If we wanted out of here, it was all up to me now. The sense of purpose gave me a rush of adrenaline.

After I pushed myself to my feet and stumbled around for a moment, I gained my bearings and an idea of our surroundings. Based on the dirt floor and rocky walls and ceiling, I assumed that Debbie and Stacey had hidden us in some kind of cave. Feeling my way around the room, I found my little leather backpack and a small pile of packaged food, but no exits, no openings except a tiny, irregularly shaped fissure several feet above my head, where the wall curved into the ceiling. Low gray light seeped through it. Was that outside? Based on the wind howling through the cracks in the dirt and stone walls, I assumed it was. What sounded like great forces of water splashing against a hard surface also came from the other side of the rocks, although I couldn't be sure if waves caused it or rain from a storm. Wedging my fingers and toes into crevices and pushing away the image of scaling the wall in Hell, I climbed up to peek out and saw that I could fit my body through the hole.

I wiggled my way out and found myself on the top of a mound of huge, gray boulders that made up an island as tiny as our suite back at the mansion. An infinite, dark sea heaved and rolled all around the island, with massive waves crashing onto the rocks and spraying foam high into the air. The droplets fell back down, peppering my face. Dark clouds hovered low enough to kiss the sea, and wind gusts nearly knocked me off my feet. My hair slapped and stung my eyes, and ice crystals blew in my face. A small cloud poofed out of my mouth with each exhale into the below-freezing air, and snow quickly piled up on the boulders. Standing at the top of the mound, I turned in a complete circle. No land could be seen on any of the horizons.

Nothing at all to tell me where we were except in the middle of a cold, raging ocean.

My mood as dark and tumultuous as the sea, I squeezed myself back through the hole and dropped to the floor below. Darkness had fallen outside and swallowed me in here, where Tristan still lay completely unaware on the stone slab. The cold didn't usually bother me, but this was like the cold of Hell, seeping deep into my bones, making my body tremble and my teeth chatter. I almost wished for Hell's fire. Almost. If only I could shoot a flame out of my palm like my husband and son could, because sparking a web of electricity around me did nothing to warm my body. So I climbed up on the stone slab, lay down on top of Tristan, let my wings come out, and enclosed us within them to hold the heat in.

And my mind churned over ideas of how the heck we were going to get out of here.

Flashing was probably too high-risk. The norms' traps would likely be defunct now from the war, and even if a trap caught us, there were no norms out because of the radioactive fallout. But according to Stacey, the Daemoni could roam freely and would likely be the ones to catch us. And me against all of them, while trying to protect Tristan's body, didn't make for good odds. Besides, flashing required a destination, and since I had no idea where we were, I had no idea what was in flashing range.

Tristan was the mastermind with this kind of stuff. He'd seen all parts of the world so many times, he could probably pinpoint exactly where we were and also be able to determine the best place to flash from here. But nobody was home in Tristan's body, and there was no way I could save him while stranded on this island. I had to figure out a way to go back to Hell to help his soul and bring him back. Rina had said I couldn't choose to go to Hell while my soul was in the Otherworld, which made me think that I *could* choose to go from here.

"Mom! Rina!" I called desperately. "I need you. I need to go to Hell!"

My pleas echoed noisily around the cave with no response. Or, more likely, the lack of reply *was* my response. I really was on my own. What were the faeries thinking, stranding us here? Or had that been their plan all along? If so, that meant Stacey had been lying to me about needing my help, which didn't feel right. But I couldn't care about her or the rest of the fae. Get off the island. Go to Hell for Tristan. Save our son. Maybe, along the way, find the good people. If there were any left. Those were my objectives.

And Hell would probably be the hardest part. I doubted I could walk up to a Demon-possessed zombie at a bus station and request a ticket downward when I had no intent to stay there. On the other hand, the Demons didn't seem too bright, so maybe I could convince one to take me. But since I hadn't noticed any flying around the island in their native form, I was back to my other problem of getting us off this mound of rocks.

Flying around the island . . .

Oh! My breath caught. I'd provided my own answer . . . assuming these wings could fly.

"I'm going to get us out of here, Tristan," I whispered against his chest. "I'm going to take care of you like you always take care of me. I'll make you proud, baby. Just stay strong, okay? Promise me you won't give up, and I won't, either."

I lifted my head and rested my chin on his chest, staring at his face. How I missed his sparkling hazel eyes and the way I'd get stupid when he winked at me. His glorious grin that still made my knees weak after all this time. His way with words, always knowing what to say to calm me, or excite me, or make me feel better about all the hell we'd been through and still had to face. He wasn't my Tristan like this. Just a shell with a heartbeat.

"Please come back to me." Thinking that maybe he needed to feel my love like he'd had in the past, I pressed my fingers to the stone in my chest while kissing his soft, cool lips. I tried to push love and Amadis power into his body at the same time. He didn't wake up. "Guess you aren't Sleeping Beauty, are you?"

I prayed for his soul next, that it would stay strong enough to escape from Hell, but then I chastised myself for thinking prayer would help. Nobody was listening. So I returned to my plans for learning what these wings could do until I fell asleep laying on my husband.

After what felt like several hours of sleep and regeneration, I stared upward at the fissure between the rocks, waiting impatiently for the morning light. It seemed to take forever, making me wonder if the sun would ever rise. Had I not slept as long as I thought I had? Were my hours turned around? Finally, dark gray light came through the hole. I'd barely scaled the wall, squeezed through the opening, and explored the little island when it began to fade again. That and the blizzard that still blew full force clued me in that we were near the North Pole in winter. Or were we? Without knowing how much time had passed while I'd been in the Otherworld, I didn't know the month, or even the year, here on Earth. So for all I knew, we could have been off the coast of Antarctica, near the South Pole, in June or July.

Only one way to find out.

"Here goes nothing," I muttered as I brought my wings out of hiding.

Although they were enormous and covered in feathers, I could barely feel their weight. I even looked over my shoulder to make sure they were actually there. They kind of cupped against my back in a vertical position, the tops of the arches about an inch over my head and the bottom tips by my feet laying on the cold, wet rocks under me. As they spread out seemingly on their own—it took me a moment to realize I'd commanded them to do so in order to see them better—the shock slammed into me like a freight train.

I had wings! Freakin' *wings*!

How was this even possible? I knew I was far from being an Angel, but these weren't Demon wings either. They were thick and feathery, and I was unable to help myself from admiring their purple and black beauty, even when their presence shocked and confounded me. What did their shape and colors—their very *existence*—mean about who and what I was? I considered this question only fleetingly before telling myself not to go there. I probably didn't want to know the answer.

"Wings," I said aloud, although my voice was lost on the wind. I just needed to speak the word because some weird part of me thought doing so would somehow make this moment less surreal. It didn't. "Well, let's see what you can do."

I thought of my wings opening up further and spreading out to my sides, and they responded like any other part of my body would. The tips lifted from the ground, stretching out and away, each feather reacting and moving appropriately. I hadn't even fully extended them yet, and they each reached over a foot beyond my fingertips, making my wingspan at least seven feet across.

"These are kind of awesome," I had to admit.

I'd been assuming I could fly with them, but it occurred to me now that maybe I couldn't. Maybe they didn't work like that. But what other good would they be? What other purpose would they serve? Perhaps none except to be an annoyance, but that made little sense. I'd received them in the Otherworld, so surely they'd been given to me for a reason. Cassandra had said I was there to be prepared, so the wings must have been what she meant. Whether I believed in the Angels' purpose for me or not, I knew firsthand that their gifts didn't come lightly. So unless this was a punishment, which it very well could have been, I'd go with my first assumption that they were useful. This had to mean they'd allow me to fly.

I just wasn't sure how. Did I jump in the air and flap them like a bird? Did they somehow lift me off the ground on their own? Testing my control, I wiggled my back and shoulder muscles, pulling them in and pushing them out, and then I stretched them further outwards, imagining how birds spread theirs wide when they took off for flight. I made them as big as possible.

Then the wind gusted up, caught my wings like sails, and launched me off the boulder.

"Ack!" I yelped as my feet caught against the rocks, and then in the crevices between.

I stumbled backward, stepping on my wings several times, unable to figure out how to catch myself because the wings kept getting in the way. I tripped and rolled all the way down the mound of rocks, the momentum and the wind working together to push me along, with no chance of grabbing onto something. My breath flew out of me as I stopped right before plunging into the angry sea. I lay facedown with a jagged rock jutting into my stomach, salty spray hitting my face, and a string of profanity spewing out of my mouth back at the water.

"Son of a mother-effin' witch," I swore as I pushed myself up with my hands.

I couldn't help the glance around to make sure no one had seen that. And then I wished someone had, because I desperately missed all of the people who would have been laughing at me. Tristan, Owen, Vanessa, Dorian . . . Where were they all now? Would I ever see them again?

Rather than letting it bring me down, the feeling of loneliness gave me a surge of determination.

"Nobody can save Tristan but me, and I have to do that before I can worry about anything else."

I stomped up the pile of rocks again, stood at the top, and turned my back to the wind this time before spreading the weird, feathery appendages emerging from my shoulder blades. This time when the wind gusted up, I sprang up and out, away from the rocks. I thrust my shoulders back and forth, and then undulated my whole upper body in an attempt to flap my wings. They didn't respond, and I could only imagine how ridiculous I looked. If not for the howling wind, I'd probably hear the shouts of hilarity from the Angels watching me through the veil.

"Look at the noob!" they were probably yelling through their laughs as they imitated my moves—thrusting their chests in and out, doing the worm in midair. A worm having some kind of a grand mal seizure.

My body had moved, though—about five feet from where I'd been, but only because gravity brought me down lower on the mound of boulders.

Why couldn't I just lift off like a rocket and soar upwards? Wasn't that how the Angels did it?

And with that thought, my body jetted into the air.

Ice and snow pelted into my face as I shot twenty-five feet above the top of the rock island before I even realized it. With another thought, I spread my wings to slow my ascent and gain some control. Thinking of Dorian and birds in flight, I leaned my body forward. And I soared.

"I'm freakin' flying!" I shouted, fist-pumping the air as I sped over the violent sea below. I'd figured it out. I'd done it. I would get Tristan and myself off this island in the middle of frozen nowhere.

But then the wind died down, and the dark sea rapidly came closer, the foam on the white caps growing as I plummeted toward them.

"Shit!" I screamed. I hadn't been flying after all. I'd only been catching and drifting on the wind like a kite or a discarded plastic bag.

Before I crashed into the freezing water, I pulled myself more upright, tried to bank left and then right, and those motions worked, but now I headed face-first for the pile of snow-dusted boulders. With another twist of my body to the right, I swerved around the island, the tips of my wings scraping against the rough edges of the rocks. As I tried to turn back around to attempt a landing, another wind gust caught me, and sent me tumbling ass-over-end in the air, rolling like a tumbleweed until I smashed into the rocks. Any birds in the sky had certainly joined the Angels in their resounding guffaws. The earlier list of profanity was nothing compared to what came out now.

"Why do I have these stupid, useless, piece-of-shit things anyway?" I muttered as I climbed to the top of the mound, hid the worthless things, and slid through the opening to drop to the floor inside. My bloody lip and scraped up palms and knees were already healing, but my ego wasn't. I was done for the day. Maybe forever. Since amputating the things sounded quite painful, I wondered what would happen if I just kept them hidden forever. Nobody would need to know they even existed. Assuming I ever saw anyone again.

"Guess what, Tristan?" I snapped as I walked over to his

unconscious body on the stone slab. "Chalk up one more slash under the Failure column for me. Not surprising, is it?"

I stopped by his side and sighed as I picked up his hand. My anger immediately deflated, pooling into sorrow from seeing him like this. My imagination didn't have to work too hard to picture him in Hell, battling the Demons and probably Satan, too. At least, I hoped he was still fighting. I just wished he would hurry up and win and return to where he belonged—with me.

"Please come back to me, baby," I whispered against the lump in my throat.

I stared at him for a long moment, but of course, he remained motionless. My stomach growled and ached with hunger, but I had to force down one of the wrapped little cakes Stacey had left, my throat too tight to swallow. Then I climbed up on the slab, sat next to Tristan, pulled my knees up under my chin, and stared into the darkness, feeling sorry for myself. It didn't take long for tears to moisten my cheeks as I replayed all of my failures, questioning what I could have done differently. My heart felt small and heavy as I thought about Dorian and how I hadn't done enough to keep him with the Amadis, and then it broke when my mind moved on to Tristan fighting the Demons in Hell and how I'd left him there. I was officially the world's shittiest mom and wife. Nobody could argue that. Because really, who else would let their family end up in Hell? *I* was the one who belonged there. Not them. My self-pity quickly spiraled into a dark depression.

After an unknown amount of time passed, I lay down and curled up next to Tristan, wishing I could pull on his strength and the calming effect he always had on me. But this body was soulless. He wasn't really here with me. Even his unique scent was fading. I grasped his hand again to bring it to my lips and frowned. It felt cooler than it had before. Pushing myself up, I studied his face in the darkness. He looked the same, although his skin seemed paler than it had been.

By the time the dark gray light shone through the opening above many hours later, the corners of his lips were blue.

"Oh, no!"

I grabbed his wrist between my finger and thumb while holding my other hand over his mouth. My own heart and lungs stopped as I focused on feeling for signs of life. His pulse and breaths still came steadily, although disturbingly slow.

"They said the supernaturals weren't affected by the radiation," I told him as my hand slipped under his neck, feeling the smooth rocks pressing into his nape. "The faerie stones are still here, so they should be—" My heart stuttered as something occurred to me. "Are they not working anymore because the faeries are . . . gone? Is that what's wrong with you?"

My stomach tilted at this possibility. I couldn't lose him! I slid my hand under my corset and fingered the stone embedded in my chest, which was like a piece of his heart, connecting us. It warmed slightly, as did his skin under my other palm. But not as much as usual.

"Stay with me, Tristan. Don't give up." I pushed the thought, the *feeling* to him, hoping he felt me. Hoping it would make a difference.

As soon as my hand pulled away from the stone, his skin cooled again. Was he not able to regulate his temperature without his soul? Did his body retain *any* of its supernatural powers? The thought scared me, and then another took my breath. *What if his body is just a normal body without his soul in it?* Taking him out into the world with all of the poison from the bombs could kill him. But as his face grew paler while the short span of daylight passed, I knew that staying here would definitely kill him.

Lying on top of him, trying to warm him with my own body heat, I pressed my forehead to his. "I need to save your soul, and that's not happening as long as we're here."

With renewed commitment, I climbed outside, brought

my wings out of hiding, and tried flying again, not caring that it was dark or that snow and ice battered my skin. I wasn't going to give up. I *was* going to save my husband and then my son, no matter what it took. Hours passed. Cuts and bruises covered my body from all of the crash landings I made into the rocks. But finally, after a couple hundred attempts, I flew. And then I landed. Neither was graceful, and I honestly wasn't sure I could do a repeat performance, but I'd achieved the basics.

With a small sense of accomplishment, I dropped down to check on Tristan before practicing some more, my feet crunching on the wrappers of the cakes that were long gone now. He looked worse than he had before. Faint purple half-moons showed under his eyes. His normally luscious lips were chapped and turning bluer. His hands were cool, and his fingertips downright cold. I didn't know how much longer he could last. At least if I could get him somewhere warm, his body might have a better chance of surviving until I could bring his soul back.

We needed to go now.

I picked up the two blue faerie stones and tucked them into my backpack. Standing next to the slab, I slid my arms under Tristan, knowing I could easily lift his weight, even as big and muscular as he was. But being able to lift the weight and actually being able to hold him were two different stories. He was so much bigger than my little body, and while his weight wasn't an issue in itself, all of the other physics were. The only way I could manage to hold him tight enough to fly with him was to loop my arms around him from behind and lock my fingers together over his chest, but then his legs dragged on the ground. Not a problem once we were in flight, but landing would be an issue.

And then I looked up toward the opening and realized I had another problem. While I could squeak out of it, I couldn't possibly get Tristan through.

"Damn it!" I shouted.

After carefully laying him back down, I aimed my hand at the opening and blasted electricity at the rocks around it. A few pieces crumbled away, but mostly only dust rained down. I clambered up the wall and while hanging onto the opening with one hand, I pushed and pulled at a rock with the other, using all of my strength. It moved about two inches outward, then stopped. I tried to use my power, but it still wouldn't budge. I poked my head through the hole and saw why. One of the larger boulders blocked it. So I climbed out and tried to move it, but other boulders, some the size of small cars, kept it in place. As I studied what I'd called a mound of rocks before, I saw that they were actually very carefully arranged and packed together to create the cavern without collapsing in on it. And I had a feeling norms had nothing to do with the structure. Something supernatural probably bound the rocks together.

Awesome.

I had no choice but to flash us. I just didn't know where to go.

"I'll be back in a bit, Tristan," I called down through the hole, as if he could hear me. And then, because I apparently had a morbid sense of humor, I added, "Don't go anywhere, okay?"

Using newly found takeoff skills, I launched into the air and flew. I imagined myself looking like a graceful Angel from a beautiful painting, but in reality I knew I looked more like a poorly made paper airplane wobbling through the air. Every shift in wind current sent me sideways for a moment before I could compensate for it. One big gust threw me into a tailspin that I barely recovered from before crashing into the sea. But eventually, I became accustomed to these strange things on my back and improved my control. I was still no beautiful bird, but I managed to do well enough where I could concentrate less on keeping myself from falling into the water and more on evaluating my surroundings.

The wind remained unforgiving and the air cold. Snow and ice blew sideways at times. The cloud cover never dissipated, blocking out any moonlight. The ocean below was black and heaving, throwing itself on a few other rock islands that were much smaller than ours. I flew for a good twenty or thirty minutes until finally I saw land. A sheer-faced cliff covered in snow faced the ocean, and as far as I could see, snowy land stretched beyond it. I still had no idea where we were, but it was a starting point. From there, I flew my attempt at a circle, as rough as it was, around our tiny spot in the sea, but found no other place to go.

"Well, at least we have something."

When I returned to the cave, Tristan's body was ice cold.

CHAPTER 8

"Oh, no," I gasped as I pressed my hands against Tristan's frozen face. "What—?"

Oh, crap. I pulled the faerie stones out of my backpack and stared at them before closing my eyes and cussing myself out. What had I done? In my rush to leave, I'd forgotten to leave them behind to keep Tristan's body protected. Hot tears burned my cheeks as I pressed the stones against his chest.

"Stay with me, Tristan. Please, baby. Stay with me."

I lay on top of him, trying to share my warmth and energy, and it was like lying on a popsicle. After creating a bubble of Amadis power within me, I pushed it out of my body to engulf him in the warm goodness. I lifted my head to watch him as moments that felt like lifetimes passed, and panic began to set in. Finally, a little color returned to his skin. I blew out a breath I'd been holding forever and collapsed on top of him, wrapping my arms around his shoulders as best as I could.

"I'm so sorry. I promised to take care of you, and I will. But I have to try something. I have to try to flash us out of here."

Time had run out, and I had no other choice. After

putting the faerie stones in the inside pocket of his leather jacket, I moved to sit behind his head, spread my legs around him, and slid my arms under his and around his chest. I heaved him upward, into my lap. Then I held on as tight as I could, hoped we wouldn't be snagged in a trap, and flashed.

We appeared on top of the snowy cliff, and a breath of relief rushed out of me.

Based on where we'd been before Debbie and Stacey rescued us—Washington, D.C.—and where their cottage was —York, England—I took a guess that we were somewhere in the North Atlantic Ocean. Maybe Iceland? Greenland? I groaned with frustration, debating whether flashing here had been a big mistake, because I didn't have a destination for where to go next. My relief had been short-lived.

When I pressed my cheek against Tristan's cold one, though, I knew I'd had no choice. And I had to keep going.

With my arms tight around his chest, I lifted into the air to gain a bird's eye view of our surroundings. For as far as I could see with my keen eyes, I saw no towns or cities or even military installations. My telepathy found no mind signatures anywhere around, even as I began to fly over the top of the cliff and inland. Gray lines appeared in the snow, confusing me at first, but as I came closer, I realized they were evergreen trees. Except there was no green to them anymore. Nor brown, for that matter. Only gray, bare trunks rising from the ground with spindly branches naked of any needles.

And good thing for that because my eyes landed on an aged wood cabin nestled in the woods that I wouldn't have seen through the cover of leaves.

Our landing was clumsy as we plowed into a bank of snow, but then I could use my power to lift Tristan up the wooden stairs and across the porch to the front door. With another shove of power, I slammed the door open, then guided Tristan inside the cold, one-room cabin.

When I glanced around, my eyes instinctively went up to

look for a hole in the roof because a blanket of white covered the entire interior. There was no hole, though, and when the back of my hand dragged across the top of the couch as I directed Tristan to the hearth, the white stuff didn't feel cold. It plumed into a cloud when I lay him on the floor. I rubbed my fingers together. It was thicker than normal dust, more like ash. Was this fallout? I had no idea, but that was my best guess.

There was no wood in the cabin, so I had to go back outside and hunt some down. Once I had a few logs stacked in the fireplace, I had to hunt some more for matches or a lighter, and blankets and food would have been nice. I didn't find any blankets at all, but I found a matchbook with a single match and one can of sausages. Miraculously, I managed to light the fire with the one match, and then I cut open the can with my dagger. The sausages smelled like farts and tasted like ass, but I couldn't remember the last time I'd eaten. So I shoved them in my mouth and forced them down as tears spilled over my cheeks at the memory of my son, my husband, and my team choking down sausages just like these on the train in Russia.

The fire barely warmed me and did nothing for Tristan. When the few logs I'd found crumpled into coals, I went outside to find more wood. A new blizzard howled through the woods, blanketing any fallen logs. I found one piece that lasted another hour or so, but it quickly became apparent that we couldn't stay here.

So where to next? And how?

Since I'd been successful in taking off and landing to bring Tristan from the cliff's edge to the cabin, I considered flying us out of here, but decided to give something else a stab first, because flashing was so much faster and more efficient. So I focused on my destination of "one hundred miles south of here" and hoped that didn't send us farther away from civilization. Well, not that there was any civilization left on this world, but I needed to go closer to the equator. *Oh.*

Maybe that was how I needed to think it. I clarified my destination, one hundred miles closer to the equator, and flashed.

We appeared on the edge of a dark, lifeless village. No mind signatures around. The place was eerily still, but I couldn't stop and contemplate. Tristan could be dying. I had to keep us moving. I tried flashing again. This time, I sensed the minds—all Daemoni—close by the moment we arrived in another village, but before I could concentrate on a new flash, a red light streaked toward us and blasted into my wing.

The shock of impact rattled throughout my body, making me yelp. After a moment, though, I realized that I otherwise felt no effects from the mage's spell. The feathers of my wings had hardened and taken on a steely edge along with a silvery glow. Another light shot at us. I immediately folded myself over Tristan and pulled my wings around us, enclosing us within their protection. More spells pinged against them. I peeked out through a crack between feathers. Several Daemoni witches had emerged from the town's buildings, standing on the roofs around us, firing their spells as we sat in the middle of the road. But none did any damage. My opinion of these wings improved drastically.

Knowing the witches couldn't hurt us but sensing the mind signature of a more powerful mage nearby, I focused on another hundred miles closer to the equator and flashed us out of there.

We slammed into what felt like a brick wall.

The Daemoni had trapped us, blocking the flash. We still sat in the middle of the same road. My mind and body picked up on the more powerful mind and magic of a warlock, and a moment later, a spell blasted at us, feeling like a sonic boom that crashed into us. The pressure hit my ears, and my heart stopped for a long moment. I couldn't pull in a good enough breath. The mages circled us, following the warlock's lead. More spells soared at us. I covered us with my wings, wiggled my legs out from under Tristan's body and still hanging on to him, crouched upward as best as I could without removing the protection of my wings from his legs.

"Don't worry, Tristan. I'll get us out of here." My promise was made more to boost my own confidence than anything.

I lifted my palm up just enough from his chest and parted my wings. An electric bolt shot out of my hand at the same time that I launched us upward.

More spells streaked up at us as we climbed to a few hundred feet above land. I swerved and twisted, dodging them and throwing my own powers back downward while somehow managing to keep a hold of Tristan, too. Then I turned us to head toward what I felt in my gut was south. As we flew farther away from the mages, I thought we might have made it. But apparently the warlock had flashed ahead, because a powerful spell surged at us again. The movement in the air sent me flying backwards, and then tumbling uncontrollably. My hands' grip on each other loosened . . . then broke. I lost my hold on Tristan.

He plummeted for the ground.

"Tristan!" I screamed as I nosedived after him.

Another spell hit me, sending me off course and farther way from him. I arced around to fly for him again while zapping electricity toward the warlock, having no idea if I actually hit him and not caring. Tristan's limp body plunged toward the ground entirely too fast. I focused on zooming toward him, hoping that even if I caught him, I didn't slam us into the unforgiving ground. A spell flashed by me. I twisted and swerved. Shot Amadis power blindly behind me.

Almost there, baby. Almost there.

Another sonic boom carried through the air. And I immediately knew I wasn't going to reach Tristan before it hit him. I reached my arms out, trying to grasp his ankles, but he was still too far away.

"Tristan," I tried to call again, but the wind carried his name away as my chest tightened and my throat closed.

A gold streak flashed before the boom hit us. Something wrapped around my wrist. I yelled one more time for Tristan when everything around me disappeared.

The air changed—the smell of it, the very feel of it. The sounds of growls and grunts and metal clashing against metal reverberated all around me. When my eyes adjusted to the new scene, my mouth fell open. Angels and Demons surrounded me, swords and other weapons flying, lodging into shields and flesh. Silver and black blood flowed like water.

I blinked, but the scene remained. I stood in the Otherworld, facing a golden-haired fae who held Tristan in her arms.

"Bree!" I squealed, but when I was about to lunge at Tristan's fae mother, she shook her head.

"I need to get him out of here before he suffers the consequences. Where are the faerie stones?"

"In his pocket."

She nodded. "Good. I'll be right back. You stay here."

Her head flicked to the side, and the veil to Earth parted.

"Wait! Where are you taking him?"

"Where he'll be safe until you can get back to him." She disappeared, taking my husband with her.

My heart didn't even beat once before she returned without him.

I glared at her with my hands on my hips. "It's a good thing I trust you!"

"Duck!" She grabbed my shoulders and pushed me down right before a Demon's mace swung my way. The air swished over my head, blowing through my hair. "Come on."

She became a gold blur darting through the battle, pulling me along with her. I had to tighten my wings close to my back before an errant sword sliced through them. I didn't know if they'd stand up to the weapons of the Otherworld as well as they did those of Earth.

"Where are we going?" I asked.

"I'm taking you to Hell so you can save my son. We have to hurry before it's too late for him."

"*What?*" I came to a screeching halt as my heart leapt into my throat. "What do you mean, too late?"

She jerked me back into motion. We left the fighting behind and became swallowed up in a sea of gray. The light blinded me, and I could no longer see Bree, but could only hear her. I followed her voice.

"His past is bogging him down, Alexis. He's letting the pain of other souls—pain he caused—to get to him. His soul will succumb soon. Only *you* can reach him. Only you can save him."

We emerged from the gray fog into a dim light where I could see again. We stood on the pointed edge of a blackened cliff. Far below us, at least hundreds of feet, raged a river of lava, parts of it glowing orange and yellow. The smell of death and sulfur made me gag, and I had to swallow down burning bile.

Bree turned to look at me with piercing golden eyes. "You'll save my son, Alexis?"

My eyes widened, and I pulled back with surprise. Her golden locks flashed in the darkness.

"Of course!" As if she had to ask.

"You're going back to Hell."

As though hearing the words from her rather than myself made the prospect more real, fear suddenly grabbed hold of my soul and twisted it up. What was I thinking, wanting to go back to Hell? Hadn't I already lived through enough of it? The memories nearly suffocated me. But my poor husband was still suffering through it. And if what Bree said was true, I was about to lose him forever to it. I *had* to go to Hell.

"I know." I nodded while expelling a long breath. "I was planning on it."

"You have your physical body with you this time," she said. "Any injuries you sustain are permanent. You may not heal completely, if you even survive. And if you die here, nobody can save you."

I pressed my lips together as I let this warning set in. But what good was my body if my soul was damaged beyond repair? "I don't care. He's the other half of my soul. And he doesn't belong here."

"No, he doesn't."

"Then I'll save him."

She nodded. "Okay, then. I'll take you down as far as I can go."

"What's the plan?"

She shrugged. "You'll have to find him, convince him to come with you, and fight your way out."

My eyes bugged. "That's it?"

My life and soul—and Tristan's—were in mortal danger, and that was her plan? She didn't answer me. Golden wings sprang from her back, and her hand encircled my wrist as it had before when she'd rescued us from the warlock. Without any warning, she launched us off the edge of the cliff. My wings covered hers as we soared downward, colliding into the heat that waved off the lava.

"Use your wings to protect you," Bree yelled at me, letting go of my wrist as we headed straight for the burning river. "It's an entrance to Hell, so we're going to dive through it."

"Oh, crap," I muttered as I pulled my wings around me to enclose my entire body. They hardened right before I plunged into the lava. The warmth surrounded my wings, but didn't penetrate them, and they didn't burst into flames. The thickness of the lava slowed my descent down, and I began to wonder at Bree's so-called plan. What if I didn't make it through? Surely she wouldn't have set me up for failure when her son's soul was at risk. Would she? Was she any better than the Angels?

Cooler air surrounded me. Far from cold, but not as hot as the lava.

"Okay, you're through," Bree said, and I opened my wings.

Darkness surrounded us, but the familiar odors of Hellfire and Demons greeted me, sending my emotions spiraling as panic tried to take over. A fear-filled voice in the back of my mind screamed at me to turn around, to save myself before it was too late. But saving myself was impossible if it meant abandoning Tristan. Again. I shut that voice off as we continued our descent downward until we came to a land bridge that I thought might have been the same one I'd left Tristan on. But he was nowhere to be seen.

We landed on the edge of the lava rock, overlooking the fiery lake below. The distant light shone on Bree's face, revealing features that were close to what you'd think a fae should look like—large, upward tilted eyes, a pointier nose and chin, and elongated and pointy ears protruding through her golden hair.

"He's fallen farther down," she said. "But my part ends here. You need to get through to him, Alexis. If anyone can, it's you."

My heart stammered with fear, but I nodded. "I'll save him, Bree. Or die trying."

"Focus on your love and your—" Her body suddenly jerked into the air, and she was sucked away into the blackness beyond the bridge, screaming what sounded like "fae."

"Bree!" I yelled, springing after her, but unable to catch her hands that reached out for me.

Her golden hair and eyes disappeared, swallowed by the blackness.

CHAPTER 9

"BREE!" I screamed again as I flew after her, but she was gone.

My heart hammered against my ribs as my stomach sank away. I landed back on the land bridge, trying to catch a breath but unable to. What had I done? She shouldn't have been here! I should have remembered Stacey's story about the fae disappearing. Did Satan have her now? *Crap!* I should have known better than to let her come this far with me. What was going to happen to her? Tears stung my eyes at the possible answers, all of them horrifying. She was in Hell. And it was all my fault. She had probably known better herself and had come anyway, but I could have stopped her. Maybe. I could have at least tried, if I'd only been thinking. Instead, war had probably claimed another casualty, continuing to take people I loved.

I wouldn't let her efforts be in vain. I wouldn't let it take Tristan, too.

I dove off the land bridge, farther down into Hell, the burning lake coming closer by the half-second. At the last moment, I veered up and soared across it, searching for my Tristan. I felt out for him with my mind at first, but my telepathy only worked down here when Satan wanted it to, so I pressed my fingers to the faerie stone in my chest and reached out with my soul instead, hoping it would find its mate.

I so did not want to have to face Satan, but when the wails and howls of souls filled my ears again, I wasn't sure which was worse. Horrific images began to flash in and out of my vision. The deep agony of all of the souls in the lake were like three-ton blocks of cement, weighing me down.

"Did you missss me that much?" a slithery voice hissed in my head.

I ignored him, focusing my search on my husband. *There.* My soul caught it—our connection—and pulled me to the right and down. I followed the sensation, skimming over the lake barely out of reach of the hands that extended from the burning lava, like some kind of morbid forest of arms. When I thought I was about to careen into a stone wall, I saw the opening. I flew through the pitch-black tunnel that came to a dead end where a flaming monster had cornered my husband.

At least, my soul recognized my husband, but my eyes did not. His large self was crouched into a ball, as though he tried to make himself as small as possible. His arms were folded over his head, and his eyes squeezed tightly closed. The blazing sword I'd thrown at him lay discarded to the side. The sight of my powerful warrior cowering from this beast broke my heart and infuriated me at the same time.

"Tristan!" I yelled, and his eyes popped open. He looked at me, showing recognition and love at first, but then his face filled with the most tortured look I'd ever seen.

"No." His voice was hoarse, sounding like he'd been shouting for weeks. "Alexis, not you, too. Get out of here. Go!"

His words came weakly, lacking any energy or power.

"No. Not without you." I lunged for him at the same time the fiery beast did.

Tristan's eyes widened, and he shook his head vehemently.

"Go, Alexis," he yelled as he sprang to his feet with sudden energy. If the fear of something happening to me sparked fight back into him, I was okay with that. "Get out before he gets you, too!"

I landed in front of him. "Not without you."

"I can't! Their pain is too much. I need to be here to take it from them."

"What—?"

The beast behind me sucked in a deep breath, and I spun as it blew it out. I expected fire to rage, but instead, only sound did. The sound of thousands of people screaming for mercy, for help, for their lives.

"I caused that," Tristan said through a clenched jaw. "It's mine to bear. I have to take their pain."

Full understanding nearly brought me to my knees with sadness. His guilt over his past life as a Daemoni warrior anchored him to this spot here in Hell, and he didn't even want to fight it. He wanted to take on the agony from the souls here, as though doing so would lessen theirs.

I couldn't remember how many times I'd told him that he needed to forgive himself, and I thought at one point he actually had. Apparently, though, he'd only been hiding the guilt from me, and doing everything he could to be good and right and overcome the horrors he'd committed.

"Tristan, this—" I flicked my hand at the monster "—it's not real. Those aren't the people you hurt or killed. Their pain has been relieved. You *can't* take this on."

"I must."

"But you can't."

"I deserve it."

"No! You don't."

His tortured expression deepened, breaking my heart. "I see them and feel them all around me, Alexis. Their cries for mercy. I only want to give that to them. Mercy and peace."

"But you can't! Not the souls here, Tristan. They chose their damnation here. The damned are the ones you hear, not the ones you think. Look, it's not even real." I kicked the fiery sword I'd given to him off the ground, and it flew into my hand. I swung at the beast in front of me, severing its head. The cries surrounding us ceased. Only those in the distance remained. "See? It's not real. *They're* not real. You're letting the guilt bog you down. Letting *Satan* get to you."

He stared at the flaming monster as it collected its head and disappeared.

"Come on. Let's get you out of here." I grabbed Tristan's hand as I prepared to lift off.

But he wouldn't budge. "I can't. This is where I be—"

I spun on him, my eyes wide, and slapped him before he could finish the declaration.

"Don't you say it!" I stepped right up against him, feeling the coldness his soul had become. My hands clamped onto the sides of his face. "You listen to me. You are stronger than this. You are better than this. You overcame all of this, and you've been forgiven. *Everybody* has forgiven you, Tristan. Everyone but yourself. And I need you to do that right now." I pulled his face down to me and pressed my lips to his. "You are a man of love and kindness and righteousness. You are my rock, my everything, and I need you. Dorian needs you. I need you to believe in us, in our love."

He stared into my eyes, his full of bewilderment and more pain. He shook his head slowly. "He says I belong here."

"Who? *Satan?*" I shook my head. "Are you going to believe him, or are you going to believe me? Your wife, your love, your *soul mate?* You're always telling me to have faith, Tristan. So tell me, where does *yours* lie?"

His brows pushed together. A spark lit up his eyes. After blinking a few times, his eyes, his mind, his whole self seemed to clear. He straightened up, breaking the hold I had on his gaze, and rose to his full height, pulling his shoulders back and nodding. Now *this* was my man.

"Ready to fight our way out of here?" I asked as two Demons came soaring at us.

"Damn straight."

I swung the sword at the first Demon, expecting to decapitate it immediately. This time, however, the blade went through the Demon, but had no effect, as though it only sliced through air. I tried again, and the same thing.

"Throw it here," Tristan said, holding one hand out as his other fist slammed into the second Demon's temple, making it recoil.

They both attacked him, ignoring me. I tried to use my powers, but they were ineffective on the Demons, so I punched and kicked. My fists and feet went right through them. Meanwhile, Tristan landed blow after blow, while they did the same to him. At the same time, screams and wails ripped out of their throats, full of despair and guilt. One's voice sounded like mine, and I realized: These were his Demons to slay. Nobody else could do it for him.

So I flew out of the way, silently cheering him on while I could only watch the battle in the glow of the fiery weapons. I didn't even realize as the darkness started to fall over me, until it was nearly blinding. Cries for help sounded distant at first, but then everywhere around me, on top of me, within me. My head filled with the sobs, my vision with nightmarish images, and my soul with a heavy grief that weighed me down. To the floor, into the ground. At the last moment, when I thought I was going to fall through, my eyes locked with Tristan's, and I knew I had to fight this. He'd come here for me, and he'd stay for me if I didn't battle my way out of here.

I heaved myself up to my hands and knees and struggled against the invisible weight as I rose to my feet. Tristan had defeated one of his Demons, but still fought fiercely with the other one. When we'd locked gazes, though, the Demon had noticed. Its black, inky eyes had flown to me, before returning to Tristan. Now, as I barely regained my balance, still struggling to breathe, it swung around with its fiery sword arcing around and down. And I remembered what Tristan had said so many years ago: *You are my weakness.*

I also recalled Bree's words: *If you die here, nobody can save you.*

My hand flew to my chest. The pain as the blade cut from my right shoulder to barely missing my heart seared at first and then blossomed into a full-on burn that seemed to explode like the bombs on Earth. My lungs expelled the air they held and refused to pull any more in. I wanted to scream with the agony whipping through my chest, but my throat was too tight to let any sound pass. Gray crept in on the edges of my vision, and I stumbled forward. My hand dropped down to catch me, landing on a rock. No, not a rock. A head. The Demon's head.

"Let's get out of here," Tristan said, wrapping his arm around my waist.

I tried to answer, but only gasps came out. *I . . . can't.* I didn't know if he could hear my mind-talk.

"Where's your faith, Lex?"

Unlike the other times I'd been asked, his question didn't leave me grasping for unknown answers. Because at this moment, I knew exactly where my faith lay. In us. In our love. Together we could conquer anything, and today, that would be Hell.

Although I could barely breathe, I bit back the pain and wrapped my arms around Tristan's neck. Then my wings lifted us into the air, and we flew through the tunnel, out to the fiery lake. A whole swarm of Demons greeted us with an enormous, lava-dripping snake behind them. I beat against the air harder, pushing us upward. Every move of my wings pulled at the wound in my chest, tearing it open further, but I pressed on.

The Demons attacked, and Tristan fought them one-armed with the sword blazing in Hellfire while I struggled to lift us higher. The snake rose in front of me and released a breath of fire. I dipped us down, barely missing the flames, and then swerved us around its head before it tried again. Tristan must have severed a Demon arm because a sword came flying at me. I caught it, just in time as the snake's head lifted to meet my gaze. I swung out, slicing through its liquid eye as I gave my wings a hard push against the air.

A piercing screech followed us up. Heat engulfed us as the snake exhaled another breath. I beat my hardened wings frantically while swinging the sword at the Demons who came near. One caught my blade with its mace and jerked it out of my hand. At the same time, another knocked Tristan's sword free, too. Without weapons, we could no longer fight. We had to rely on flight. By the time we reached the bridge where I'd lost Tristan last time, though, I could barely force myself to go on. The wound, the flying, and the fighting had drained my energy. The slash in my chest not only burned from heat, but sharp icicles filled my lungs and heart. The souls of Hell were like anchors chained to my chest and pulling me down.

"Tristan," I croaked.

"You can do this, *ma lykita*."

I gave him a weak nod. "For us."

But the harder I tried to lift us up into the blackness that led to the Otherworld, the more Hell dragged me down. The hotter and colder the wound in my chest burned. As much as my wings fought to fly us upward, we went nowhere. With a deep, feral growl, I gave my wings every bit of energy I had to push us up and away. But we only hung in the air, like a kite losing its uplift and about to dive for the ground. I looked Tristan in his eyes, the gold around the pupil reflecting the flames below us and the outside of the irises a deep emerald green shining in the glow. They were void of any fire within them, though. Instead, they were filled with complete trust and confidence in me.

And once again, I was about to let him down.

"I'm . . . sorry," I said as we began to fall.

The defeat, the loss, the acceptance of yet another failure of mine was so much worse than the pain. I closed my eyes, unable to look him in the face a second longer. I'd tried so hard to save him, to save us both, but as usual, I wasn't enough.

"*Believe in love.*"

The whisper was so quiet in my mind, I almost missed it. But it was enough to give me one last surge of strength. With only sheer will and perseverance—and the love of my soul in my arms—to power me, we shot upwards, into the blackness, toward the Otherworld.

CHAPTER 10

A thousand-pound weight sat on my chest. At least, that's what it felt like, especially when I tried to breathe. I rolled to the side on the hard ground, hoping that would help. The smell of leather with the mouthwatering scent of mangos, papayas, lime, sage, and a hint of man filled my nose. I tried to inhale my favorite scent in the world, but air wheezed through my throat, making me cough, which made my chest feel worse. Was I sick? Why wasn't I healing? My eyelids felt glued shut, and I had to force them to separate. They felt like sandpaper over my eyeballs as they slowly peeled apart.

All pain was forgotten when I saw the sight in front of me.

"Tristan!" I tried to say with excitement, but it came out as an underwhelming grunt.

He sat next to me, lighting some twigs on fire from a flame cupped in his palm. He twisted toward me and smiled. I wanted to jump up and into his arms, but my body failed to cooperate, remaining anchored to the stone floor with my head pillowed by his coat.

"Shh." He brushed his fingers across my cheek. He leaned down and kissed my forehead. I wanted more than that, damn it. "You're hurt, and you're healing very slowly. I did what I could to help, but—"

"Bree said it would be lasting," I muttered as I gingerly felt my chest with my fingertips.

My bustier had been cut open, and a long line of scar tissue stretched from my right shoulder to the valley between my breasts. I didn't dare look at it—the feeling alone told me it was raw and ugly. I did my best to close the leather over it.

"At least you *are* healing," Tristan said. "Not as fast as I'd like, but you're making progress. Here. Drink."

He held a water bottle to my lips, and I drank the cool liquid greedily, reveling in the feeling as it slid down my throat and pooled in my stomach. I couldn't remember the last time I'd had any water. I'd been parched on the rock island, and the heat of Hell had dehydrated me further. I drained half the bottle before Tristan pulled it away, my mouth following after it.

"I don't want you to get sick. Let that settle for a moment. I have food, too."

My stomach growled in response.

"Where are we?" I asked as I glanced around. The dim, square room, lit only by Tristan's fire, seemed vaguely familiar with its aged stone walls, and its musky odor. "Amadis Island? Why aren't we in the mansion then?"

His face darkened, and he looked away from me, towards the fire. I supposed that meant I didn't want to know about the mansion . . . which only made me want to know more.

"What's wrong?"

His jaw muscle twitched, then he finally replied, "We're safe and hidden here in the dungeons."

The dungeons—what I'd called the prison cells under the council hall where they'd kept Tristan when he'd been on trial, and where we'd taken refuge during the bombings when the world began falling apart.

"But the council hall was destroyed," I said.

"Up top, yes. We're completely buried here and can only flash in and out."

"How did we get here? Did you—"

"I woke up here, too."

"Ah," I said after a moment of thought. "Bree. She must have brought your body here before she took me to Hell. Oh, no! Tristan—"

My jaw snapped shut. Tears burned my eyes. I couldn't bear to tell him . . . but I had to.

"I think Satan has Bree," I said, and I told him the full story.

Well, sort of. I didn't tell him about the mishaps with flying. He'd seen the wings in Hell, but they were hidden now, and I didn't want to bring them up. I'd have to deal with his reaction eventually, of course, but I didn't have the energy to right now. He handled weird much better than I did—he'd grown up and lived hundreds of years with weird—but I still didn't know what the wings meant about me. They were feathery, but also dark. I could only assume I wasn't good enough for the Angels' colors of light and purity, but what else it all meant, I didn't know.

And they didn't matter at the moment. Bree and the rest of the fae folk did.

He rubbed his hand over his face when I finished telling him what Stacey had said and what happened with Bree. "We'll find a way to save her. Them. Everyone. But right now, you need to build your strength back."

He finally gave me the rest of the water, and then carefully lifted me and leaned me against the wall before feeding me soup from a can.

"Where'd you get the food and water?"

"There's plenty of it scattered across the island."

"And none of it's contaminated?"

One corner of his mouth lifted in a half-smile. "The Amadis know how to safeguard their goods. You wouldn't believe what some of the mages had hidden—most of it useless or magically protected, and the majority of it . . . bizarre. Even for us."

I chuckled before he fed me another spoonful. I peered at him closely.

"How are you so okay?" I'd been a mess when I escaped Hell, unable to tell the difference between now and then half the time. I thought my little bit of time at Heaven's gates before returning to Earth had helped—that the Angels had taken me back there for that very reason—but Tristan hadn't been granted that relief.

His eyes cut sideways at me, the light of the flames flickering in them. "My physical body was here. I felt the pain down there, but it didn't actually injure me."

"No. I mean, *you*. Your soul. How are you doing so well after so much time down there?"

He set the can down, dropped the spoon in it, and lifted a hand to my cheek, his eyes soft and appraising. He brushed away the hair that was matted to my skin, and then grasped my chin between his thumb and forefinger.

"Because of you, *ma lykita*. You're here, alive, talking to me. That alone makes me okay. Makes everything right in my world."

I gave him a brief smile, but then let out a harrumph. "Everything in the world is far from right."

Although I wasn't intentionally listening to his mind, I sensed what he was about to say—that I would make it all right—but then he changed his mind in mid-thought.

He said instead, "I saw Dorian through the veil, when I dove down after you."

I opened my mouth to yell at him for that, but he held a finger to my lips.

"I follow you, my love. Don't argue with me about that. Just don't plan on any more trips to Hell, and we'll both be okay."

"Never again," I promised.

He took my hand in between his and folded his fingers over. His words came quietly. "So I saw what Dorian's doing."

"We can't trust what we saw in Hell, but if it's true, we need to stop him."

He frowned, and I hated seeing him so sad. "But if it *is* true, it might be too late."

I clapped my free hand over my mouth and shook my head slowly. "No. It can't be. We can still save him."

He placed his palm over my heart, settling its chaotic rhythm. "We will. We'll do whatever we possibly can. But we do nothing until you're strong enough."

With no light in the dungeons, I didn't know how much time passed while I concentrated on resting and regenerating my body—a few hours, maybe a day. My growing restlessness was a good sign I was ready, and the dark cell was making me stir crazy. In fact, it reminded me too much of Hell and the horrible days on the rock island. I was so tired of being underground. Finally, Tristan let me flash outside, and I went straight to the mansion on the other end of the island.

The light blinded me for a moment, and then the scene that greeted me made my stomach fall, my heart tumbling after it.

"Oh, no."

The grand marble mansion of the matriarchs, which had been protected by the Angels and hadn't been so much as scratched by the Norman bombs before, was flattened. Decimated. A pile of stone, wood, and broken furnishings among the surrounding sticks of dead cypress trees. Everything was coated in the same thick, gray dust as the cabin in the woods, and all color was gone, as though the bombs had bleached the world, washing out all the hues from the grass, the trees, the ruined items under the marble rubble.

"H-how?" My voice shook. "I thought . . . Ophelia said . . ."

I couldn't form coherent sentences, my mind too shocked as I tried to take it all in.

"Apparently, it wasn't entirely indestructible."

I climbed up on a boulder-sized chunk of stone and surveyed the debris, my eyes burning with tears. So much history. Over two millennia of matriarchs had lived in this mansion and led the Amadis from here. The items inside were not only antiques amassed over recent centuries, but some of the furniture, the tapestries, and other items—the very walls—came from *ancient* times. A collection more valuable than those in many museums. And now it was all nothing but rock and shards.

Jumping from stone to stone, I tried to search for anything that might be at least somewhat salvageable. After poking around for a while, I found the family vine tapestry covered in dust, but still intact. It took some pushing around of stones and debris to free it completely, and after unsuccessfully trying to shake off the thick coating, I folded the fabric, although I didn't really know what I would do with it. The lineage of the Ames matriarchs no longer mattered. There was a very real possibility that there was nobody left to care except us, but maybe I could hang it up wherever we settled after retrieving Dorian. A reminder of what once was.

I found another tapestry, and for some reason, I folded it, too, although I couldn't even tell through the dust which one it was. I placed it with the big one. All of the beautiful knickknacks Rina had left behind in her office were destroyed, as were Solomon's collection of souvenirs from his past. Just like their owners. Besides the tapestries, the only other item I found in one piece was one of my fighting tops, enchanted with protection spells. At least I could wear one now that hid the ugly scar on my chest. With my back turned to Tristan, I slid off the ruined one, unable to repair itself because the damage had been inflicted in Hell, and pulled on the vest.

"That wasn't very nice," Tristan said from behind me as I zipped up the front. "You couldn't let me watch?"

I ignored him, pretending like something had caught my attention, because the embarrassment over the scar felt petty, but I felt it nonetheless. When I hopped over to where I figured the Sacred Archives would be, though, I found nothing. What had happened to them? Had the Angels saved all of those books that had lined the shelves? Or were they gone forever like apparently everything else? Did those in Heaven even care about any of this? I began to wonder if they cared at all, based on the sight in front of me, angering me and breaking my heart at the same time. They hadn't protected the mansion because it was no longer needed. Like the rest of the island.

That must have meant there was no Amadis to occupy the village, no society in need of a matriarch. With no matriarch, there was no need for the mansion or the goods inside. And apparently, no need to safeguard our history, because there was no future to appreciate or learn from it. They'd told me to look for the good, but the most good of all had been right here, and it was destroyed.

"I'm sorry, my love," Tristan said as he reached a hand up toward me once I'd gone back to where he stood.

I didn't need it, but I took it anyway before hopping down. I forced a smile.

"It's just stuff, right? Nothing compared to everyone who's been lost. I just can't believe they tried to make me believe there's anything left here to fight for." The little bit of hope I'd gained in Heaven dissipated into the tainted air.

Tristan kissed the top of my hand. "There's still us to fight for. And our son."

"Yes, and we will. But I don't think there's anything else." My chin trembled with despair, and my eyes stung. I blinked against the tears and bit my lip hard enough to draw blood, the physical pain distracting me from the emotional pain of my heart breaking. Again. Once I thought I had control of the emotions building within, I inhaled a ragged breath. "Let's get out of here."

When Tristan bent over behind me to pick up the tapestries, a ripping sound tore through the dead silence. I spun around and stared at him with my mouth open, thinking it was his pants, but when he growled loudly, I stifled the laugh. Something was wrong. The tone of that growl didn't indicate anger, but pain.

"What's—" I began to ask when Tristan fell to his hands and knees, and his back arched upward and then down, like a cat stretching. The frrrrp sound came again, and he snarled. "Tristan! What do I do?"

His muscles tensed and coiled, and his jaw clenched. The only time I'd seen so much pain etched into his features was when I'd hurt him. But that had been emotional pain he'd suffered then. This was the first time I could remember seeing him in real, physical agony.

"I . . . I don't know," he said through his teeth before he let out another growl. "I don't know what's wrong. It's . . . my back."

He'd no more than finished the sentence when his shirt and skin tore open further, and two big, dark shapes sprang out of his shoulder blades.

"Oh my god!" I squeaked as I jumped backwards and out of the way.

He remained on all fours as they uncurled from his back, growing and stretching up toward the sky until they reached their full height at least five feet above him, casting a shadow on my face as I stared in awe. Dark, silvery gray feathers that became a shiny black at the shafts glinted in the sunlight as the wings came back down and closed in around his torso.

He jumped to his feet, grabbed the pieces of his ruined shirt, and tore it off completely, and then he craned his head to stare over his shoulder.

"What. The. Fuck. Are. THOSE?" he bellowed.

Then he turned in circles, like a puppy chasing its tail. The shock worn off, I doubled over, cackling with laughter.

Not very nice of me, I knew. I'd felt exactly as he had when my wings first appeared and surely looked just as comical, if not worse. But something about seeing my Tristan, whose heart and soul were stronger and more righteous than almost anyone I'd ever met, with wings as dark as mine felt like a huge weight had been lifted. I still didn't know what they meant about us and who or what we were, but at least we were alike.

He stopped turning and glared at me. His wings opened wide, spreading out to the sides, monstrous yet more stunningly beautiful than I'd seen on any Angel in the Otherworld. Although, I liked mine a tad more with their purple coloring, especially now. But even so, I couldn't possibly have looked as breathtaking as he did, standing there with no shirt, his muscles taut, like a powerful, avenging Angel.

My laughter died with the sight, and I rose to my feet and un-hid my own wings.

"I don't know if they're from the Angels, Hell, or something in between, but yeah, I have them, too."

His face softened, and his wings retracted closer to his body as he walked around to investigate mine.

"I thought I saw them in Hell," he said, his voice filled with awe. "I swore we flew over the lake of fire. But when I woke up and you didn't have them, I figured they'd been a figment of my imagination while down there. Wishful thinking."

"You can hide them, just like Sasha can." I made mine disappear and reappear. He did the same.

Then a huge, lovely grin lit up his face, and he bent his knees and jumped upward.

"Wait!" I called. "It's not that easy . . ."

KRISTIE COOK

My voice trailed off as I watched him soar over the island, bank his turns, swoop down and back up again, even make loops in the beautiful blue sky as puffy white clouds skimmed high above him. I crossed my arms over my chest and scowled. Well, didn't that figure. It took me hundreds of attempts, crashes, scratches, and bruises, and he just did it naturally. What a jerk. I no longer felt guilty about laughing at him.

He made a perfect landing in front of me, the gold in his eyes sparkling beautifully as that sublime smile still covered his entire face. "This is . . . incredible."

"I hate you," I muttered, staring at the lines and curves of his bare chest and abs, the beauty of which eradicated any meaning I might have had in the three words. "Do you know how many times I crashed into that stupid pile of rocks?"

"Hmm . . . Well, you said we were in the North Pole with wind, snow, and ice, right?" he offered. "That couldn't have been easy to stand in, let alone learn to fly."

I narrowed my eyes, wanting to be mad at him for patronizing me, but I couldn't hold it. He looked sincere. God, I loved this man so much.

"Yeah, that's it," I agreed, although I was sure I would have crash-landed even on a day as beautiful as this one.

He took my hand. "Come on."

He launched himself in the air, pulling me with him. He had to release my hand when our wings spread out, but we flew side-by-side over the ugly remains and lovely beaches of Amadis Island. Almost the whole island was a grayish-tan color, like the sand, and the few parts that weren't had been blackened from fire. No green grass or leaves. No more eclectically colored homes the mages had built. Everything just a dull, dead gray.

My heart hurt at the view, but flying with Tristan by my side made it all a little more bearable.

After surveying the island, we neared the council hall, and

he pulled himself more upright, and I came up, too. I turned to face him as we hovered in the air.

"How do you feel?" he asked, a sparkle of mischief in his eyes.

My wings beat against the air to keep me upright while my stomach quivered. "Physically? Good, for the most part." I gave him a flirtatious little smile. "There might be a few places that could use a kiss to make them better, though."

His hands lashed out, grabbed my wrists, and yanked me into him so that only a breath of space remained between us. His eyes smoldered as his palms braced my face, and then he leaned in and captured my mouth with his full, delicious lips. Electricity jolted through me with the light but passionate kiss, and I melded against him as we floated thirty feet in the air. I parted my lips, and when his tongue slipped in, I met it with my own. He tasted better than ever, which I hadn't thought possible, and I deepened the kiss, wanting to devour him. Our wings dropped, nearly vertical, and closed around us, my tips brushing against his feathers and sending a brand new sensation through me that tingled all the way to my core. He must have felt it, too, because the bulge in his leathers instantly grew, pressing against my belly.

His hands slid back, into my hair, gripping and massaging as he pulled me even closer. My whole body pressed against his, and I ground against his erection as the kiss sent torturous levels of desire through me. Slowly, we lowered to the ground, landing on a big slab of marble, his mouth never leaving mine. With the same thought on our minds, our wings disappeared. His hands glided down my back, his fingers curling into the tips of my hair and pulling, tilting my head back. My lips were suddenly cold, abandoned by his as they traveled over my chin and jaw. His mouth lingered over my throat as his tongue swirled arousal into me, drawing a sigh from me as my hands gripped his thick shoulders.

A warm electrical web spread over my skin as his hands

slipped between my top and the waistband of my pants. His fingertips slowly caressed the bottoms of my ribs as they moved around to come between us. His mouth had reached my collarbone when his fingers went to the top of my vest, and my breasts tightened with anticipation as he pulled the zipper down, separating the two sides. When they fell apart, his head pulled back, and he frowned. The expression of disdain and repulsion sent a dagger through my heart. I stepped back and yanked the two pieces together.

"I know," I said, tears stinging my eyes. He'd never, *ever* looked at me that way before. "It's ugly."

CHAPTER 11

My muscles tensed when I saw the look on her face, heard the hurt in her words.

I covered her small hands with my large ones and shook my head at her misunderstanding. "It's beautiful. It's part of you. Of all the battles we've been in, you have this one scar that serves as a reminder of what you did for me. Because you love me. You should be proud of it."

Her bottom lip trembled. "It's ugly, Tristan. I saw it on your face."

My eyes snapped up to hers, and the pain in them nearly killed me. How could I make her understand that she was still the most beautiful creature on Earth? In any realm? That it wasn't the scar that sickened me, but the fact that I'd essentially been the one to put it there?

I was glad to have awoken before her, because the fit of rage I'd felt when I saw the injury would have sent her back to the Otherworld if she'd seen it. The guilt had nearly sent *me* back to Hell. I'd barely been able to control myself—not all of the destruction in the village had been from Norman bombs and the Daemoni, some had been caused by my own hands—

but I forced myself. She had that scar *because* of my guilt. When I told her last night how I'd asked the Demon to take me to her in the Otherworld, she'd thrown a fit, but I knew without a doubt she'd do the same. She already had—she'd followed me into the darkness when I couldn't break myself free. I wasn't about to risk her life and soul again because of my weakness.

"What I don't like about it," I tried to explain while keeping my voice steady, "is that you wouldn't have it at all if I'd been strong enough."

Her eyebrows pinched together. "But you *were*, in the end. We made it. Together." She glanced down at the scar, and then lifted her warm, brown eyes back to mine. "If this is a badge of honor, then it's for both of us—showing what we do for each other."

I stared at her for a moment, always amazed at the love she had for me, and then I nodded before lowering myself to my knees. "Like I said. It's beautiful."

My hands pushed hers apart to let the vest fall open, and I pulled the sides over her shoulders. She let it slide down her arms and drop to the ground. Then I leaned in and pressed my lips to the tip of the puckered skin at her shoulder. She smelled like her usual dark chocolate and raspberries and tasted the same, too. I thanked the Angels for that, because I'd been afraid of what might linger under the skin. When I first saw the wound gaping open after I'd regained consciousness, I'd tried to heal it, but my best efforts left her like this. I wished I could kiss away the blemish completely as she'd done for me, but the dark magic that had been left behind by the Daemoni didn't compare at all to the Hellfire that had done this to her.

Because of me.

I continued kissing down the scar, hoping to show her that it was no different to me than any other part of her glorious body. And speaking of glorious—I found myself in the valley between her breasts. My gaze rolled up to look at her. She stared back at me with half-lidded, smoldering eyes, and her lips parted slightly. When I skimmed my mouth to the side, along the softness of her breast, her skin pulled taut and her dark pink nipple hardened. She moaned as my tongue tasted her, and I ached to hear her do it again. My mouth clamped over her breast, sucked it in, and I couldn't get enough of her. When she whimpered, I nearly came undone. She caused a short circuit in my brain, as she always did, and my body acted on its own. Without thought, my hands, mouth, and tongue roamed over her soft skin, tasting every inch of it. Never getting enough.

Her fingers skimmed over my shoulders and upper back, and then her nails dug into my flesh. As I took her other breast into my mouth, her entire body quivered under my touch. I pulled back and blew on her nipple. Her knees gave out from underneath her. I easily caught her in my arms and laid her down on the smooth, marble slab. I lay next to her on my side, propping myself on my forearm, admiring the alluring creature in front of me. I cupped her cheek with my free hand and gazed into her eyes, full of desire, and then her perfect lips. Her tongue darted out, and I couldn't control myself. My mouth crashed down on hers.

Her lips parted. Her tongue delved into my mouth. My hands explored again as hers reached around my neck and pulled me closer, deepening the kiss. She twisted up so her breasts pressed against my chest, and she hitched her leg over my hip. Her pelvis ground against my erection. I grabbed her ass, pulling her tighter as we moaned into each other's mouths.

"I need you, Tristan." Her voice came thick and husky with desire.

Her hands slid over my chest and abs to the button of my pants. She had it undone in a second, and while I kicked off my boots, she slipped her hands under the waistband, pushing my clothes off and freeing me. I about lost it with the look she gave me. I'd had to move and shift to remove my pants, so now I rose up and straddled over her. Her eyes widened at the view in front of her before making their way up my body to my face while her hands encircled me. My eyelids dropped closed as I tried to think of something horrible before I lost myself completely.

"You're so beautiful," she said as she stroked, and my eyes popped open.

"I think that's my line," I murmured as my hands grasped hers to pull them away, and my gaze roamed over her half-naked body. "But you're entirely too clothed."

I reached behind me and removed her boots while she unbuttoned her leather pants. Before she could slide them off, I grabbed the waistband and yanked them down. She lifted her butt to pull them off, her hips raising to nearly my eye level. My throat went dry. Her pelvis dropped, but then her legs fell open. My mind blanked out. After shoving her pants out of the way, the only thought that remained was how much I needed to taste her. My tongue slid over my bottom lip in anticipation.

"Make love to me, Tristan," she whispered. After a heartbeat or five, my eyes reluctantly flicked up to hers, but then back down. I couldn't help it. I had to touch. To taste. My mouth already watered for her. My hands slipped between her thighs and pressed them further outward. I lowered my head. "No, make love to me. I need *you*."

Not happening. I glanced up at her, wanting to beg but forcing my voice to take command. "Just a taste. I need to taste you."

Before she could argue, I dipped my head down and swiped my tongue over her. I knew full well that would shut her up, and she'd let me have my way. As expected, her pelvis thrust against me, and she let out a cry. Her reaction sent a thrill of excitement through me, and I had no choice but to give her more. I licked and lingered, my tongue pressing and twisting, lapping and tasting her in every way possible. And she tasted so damn good. Dark chocolate and raspberries sprinkled with honey.

I glanced up at her, watched as her chest heaved and the perfect globes of her breasts bounced while my mouth continued to ravage her. My beautiful, brave, warrior wife mewled like a kitten as she bucked against my face. Her hands clasped onto my head, her fingers curled into my hair, and her nails scraped my scalp as she pulled me closer. My need for her skyrocketed, but first I'd make her scream, and then make her beg. My thumbs rubbed circles into her upper thighs and the soft flesh between them as I devoured her until she shouted my name with breathless cries. I loved seeing her lose herself like this, knowing that I brought her to these heights of ecstasy. It made me so rock-hard, I was about to explode.

My mouth moved upward, over her pelvis and trembling stomach, kissing my way back up to her breasts. Our eyes locked as my tongue swirled around her lengthened nipple, then I pulled up to appraise her entirely. This girl. This *woman*. Her soft curves, her luscious skin, the mischievous spark in her eyes as she panted for me . . . perfection in one tiny package. Every time I looked at her like this, I felt like I'd been punched in the stomach, but in a good way. The kind of breathtaking blow I'd crave the rest of my days.

"Please," she panted.

Shit. That one little word nearly ended me. But slowly, trying to maintain control, I rose and settled between her legs. I gave her a smirk, even while I ached and throbbed against her.

"Now I'll make love to you." My hands circled her legs behind her knees and spread them as I lifted her hips off the slab. My entire body tensed up with anticipation as I slowly slid just an inch inside her. "Unless you want more."

My gaze held hers, and her brown eyes widened. She nodded. I pulled out, and this time, I thrust hard and deep into her, all the way in, sending a ripple up through my body. I couldn't stifle the groan.

"Yes," she said. "*More.*"

I could deny neither of us any longer. I pumped into her, again and again, my eyes focused on her swollen, red lips as my mind gave over to the physical sensations. She felt so good. So tight. So perfect. My hand left her thigh for her swaying breast, and I kneaded and pinched it as I stroked in and out, harder and faster, her hips bucking up to meet me every time.

"Yes, Tristan," she begged. "Harder."

My eyes fell closed, and I groaned as I gathered her into my arms, plunging deep and relentlessly. Her mind opened and sucked mine in as she shared the intensity of her pleasure with me and I shared mine with her. It was an experience like none other, something only the two of us could ever share. Indescribable. Not *needing* to be described. Pure, unadulterated ecstasy as our hearts, souls, and bodies unified. I pounded until we exploded into oblivion together. Soared into another time and space. Shouted each other's names and gasped for air in our aching lungs.

Floated weightlessly on a shared high before slowly drifting back down.

"I love you, my beautiful, Sexy Lexi." I heard myself speaking before my brain could even function, my mouth spewing words that came from somewhere deep—from my soul. She sighed as I dropped kisses all over her face as I laid her down on the slab. I lay next to her, the smooth marble cool against my flaming skin.

Our rest didn't last long because my fingers couldn't stop touching her, wouldn't stop trailing up and down her bare back, and her lips wouldn't stay off my face. A thought occurred to me, and I revealed my wings, brushing the tips over her legs. She gasped, and her eyes lit up, but what she felt couldn't compare to what I felt on this end. The tips of the feathers that could become as solid and unbreakable as a titanium shield, according to her, had the most sensitive nerve endings at the moment that ran all the way to my center. My eyes widened, and her brows lifted at my reaction, then her wings came out, too. With a smile, I wrapped my arms around her and lifted us in the air. She cupped my face while devouring me in a kiss. Our legs entangled as we hovered twenty feet above the ground, and then her wings disappeared so mine could wrap around us, enclosing us in our own world.

We may have looked like Angels at first glance, but the way we made love next was borderline sinful.

Later, we lay side-by-side on the marble slab with exhausted bodies and pounding hearts. I turned my head to look at her.

"Merry Christmas," I said. "I gave you some of me. That fits the rules, right?"

She laughed, but then her head rolled toward me, her brows scrunched. "Wait. Christmas?"

I looked back up at the dark blue of the sky as the sun hung over our toes, about to set over the water. "Based on how the sun crossed the sky and where it's setting now, I'd say it's late fall or early winter. Around Christmas, maybe Thanksgiving, but definitely not New Year's."

She didn't reply at first, seeming to take this in. "You can determine that so easily?"

"Mmm . . . I've spent enough time on this island—on this world—to make an educated guess."

"Wow," she said after another moment, and I smiled at her ceaseless wonder. "So we lost over a month, maybe two in the Otherworld?"

My smile faded. "I'm afraid so."

"Huh." She huffed out a breath. "I honestly thought it was longer. It sure felt like an eternity."

I took her hand and gave it a squeeze. "Yes, it did, my love. I'd rather not do it again."

We lay in comfortable silence as the air began to chill our naked bodies with the setting sun. With a moan, I pushed myself to sit up.

"Up until a few hours ago, I thought my strength had fully returned, and we could go," she said as she still lay on her back. "I'm not so sure now."

I chuckled. "You've sapped my strength, too. Another day of rest, and then we take back the world."

She didn't respond. My girl, who had always had trust issues but had still managed to hold on to a childlike wonder as well as her spiritual beliefs, had become a jaded cynic. She'd lost her belief in pretty much everything. She still believed in love, though, and that was important. Otherwise, she would have never done for me what she had. I had to figure out how to bring the rest of her back before I lost her forever.

As we pulled our clothes on, she leaned over and studied the edge of the marble slab and started laughing. I cocked a brow.

"We made love on the council table!" She continued chortling, and I couldn't help but laugh with her. "I wonder what those uppity council members who tried to oust us would think of that."

"Maybe what he does." I nodded toward a mound of broken marble where the stairs to the council hall had once been.

One of the statues of the warrior angels that had hung in the main room lay there—part of its wing and head, anyway. But rather than the fierce expression they always held, this one, with chunks of its jaw and forehead missing, seemed to be staring at us with a lifted brow and a small, knowing smile on its face.

Alexis returned its expression with a frown. Then she threw a bolt of electricity at it, effectively shattering the marble into small pieces.

Nice, I thought with a silent sigh. With an attitude like that, we were in more trouble than I realized. But I vowed to restore her heart and soul—and her broken faith—no matter what it took.

CHAPTER 12

$\mathcal{I}$ sat upright in the dark, a gasp in my throat. "Dorian."

I'd been dreaming about him, but only bits and pieces came to me now. Dorian as a baby, always grabbing at my necklace. Then Dorian flying away from the Thomas Jefferson Memorial. And then Dorian in Hell, Lucas by his side, in the luxurious parlor with the dark blue curtains and thick carpet. Satan's beastly form sat in the chair by the fire, his animal-like legs crossed and his black-nailed fingers lifting a cigar to his mouth, only it wasn't a cigar but a baby's arm. Dorian took a knee in front of him and bowed.

Although I knew now that such a scene would only happen if Dorian chose it—and my sweet boy would never do such a thing—I couldn't shake the terror blanketing me.

"It's time to go," I told Tristan, who'd sat up next to me.

"You're ready." It wasn't a question.

Good thing, because whether he agreed or not that I'd regained my strength and health, I *was* leaving today. Using one of the bottles of water and a blanket we'd found in the village that we'd no longer need, we did our best to clean up and then dress in our fighting leathers.

"Where do we start?" I asked as I laced up my boots.

"See if we can find Noah."

"He's the last we know who's seen him," I agreed. "But how? Where? If you're right that it's December, he could be anywhere by now, with or without Dorian."

He pulled on a t-shirt he'd found yesterday after our . . . escapades. "One guess would be Noah would go to his homeland of Italy."

"Okay then. I guess we head there." Then I added halfheartedly, doubt bringing me down, "Maybe we'll find Amadis on the way."

Tristan nodded. "Keep your mind open."

After stuffing my little backpack with as many bottles of water it could hold, we stood outside the demolished Amadis council hall one last time before launching into the crisp air. Flying several hundred feet over Earth alongside my man and a deep blue sky above us, should have been an incredible experience. Although the wind blew through my hair and against my cheeks in the same way, riding a motorcycle didn't come close to comparing to this feeling of freedom and thrilling release. But the beauty of the day was ruined by the way the sun's yellow rays shone brightly down only to fall flat on an iron-black sea and a gray Earth below. The peace was suffocating, because the feeling of being the only two people on Earth was more than an illusion. I was beginning to truly believe that it was our reality.

I watched the ground with eagle eyes, searching for any sign of life, Norman or Amadis, but I saw none. Not even fish in the sea. No birds in the sky with us. No fishing boats out for the restaurants' catch of the day. Once we flew over land, no restaurants open or people to go to them for a night out. Not even a green leaf on a tree or a blade of grass. Granted, if Tristan was right, winter might have set in, but Greece had a mild climate. It shouldn't look like a thin layer of dirty snow had stained everything an ugly gray.

The smaller villages we flew over showed wear and tear, but most buildings remained standing. Still, though, no people. Not a single mind signature to be found or heartbeat to be heard. No cars or buses traveling on the roads or trains chugging through the countryside. Trucks didn't carry goods from source to consumer. As the villages became suburbs and the suburbs the city of Athens, my breath caught at the sight. Half of the city was blackened from fire, and the rest destroyed. The ancient structures had been demolished. A greenish haze hovered over the city with an acrid smell that burnt my nose and eyes.

My heart sank at the sight of such overwhelming loss. Millions of people should have been living their lives, going to work or coming home, shopping for food, picking up children from school, walking dogs, visiting the Parthenon . . . going about their normal days or enjoying their long awaited and much deserved vacations.

So much beauty and history . . . so many people . . . gone, I thought to Tristan.

He didn't answer, but swooped closer to me, slid his wing over mine so he could reach my outstretched hand, and gave it a squeeze. Then he pulled me along, farther west.

You're sure about Italy? I asked him as Athens disappeared behind us. *What if Satan lied to us? What if Mom and Rina were wrong? What if both Noah and Dorian died in the bombs with the rest of the world?*

"*Did you see Dorian in Heaven?*"

I frowned. *They told me he didn't belong there.*

"*And he doesn't belong in Hell, so he can only be here, somewhere on Earth.*"

That was pretty much what I'd concluded before, too, but I wasn't sure I trusted Mom, Rina, and Cassandra anymore. Or anyone else, really. Especially when it came to Dorian.

"*Italy is the closest option of where Noah could be,*" Tristan continued, "*so we may as well check there first. Keep your mind open.*"

Without the millions of Norman signatures filling my head, my mind could reach much farther than usual, allowing us to do a quick sweep over southern Italy. Every now and then, I picked up on some mind signatures, especially as we approached Rome. All Daemoni, but none Noah. No Amadis or norms, either.

We headed north from there, flying nonstop until we hit a snowstorm over the Alps. We tried to press on, but the wind gusts kept flipping me over, and I'd careen into Tristan. Even he had a hard time fighting the wind, and when we flew over a castle still standing on a mountainside, we dipped down to check it out. No mind signatures were around for as far as my sense could reach.

The castle apparently had been a hotel most recently, and no guests or caretakers had stuck around, although it was far from any city that had been bombed. We gained entry through a side door into the modern, industrialized kitchen, and found a couple of bottles of soda water and wine, some jars of olives, anchovies, and artichoke hearts, and a box of crackers—the only non-perishables in a place that had probably served gourmet meals made with the freshest of ingredients. The rest of the food left behind stunk up the place, and we hurried beyond, through a fancy dining room and into a beautiful sitting room. Well, it was probably beautiful at one time. Now, it was as gray and ashy as the rest of the world.

"I can't believe this place is so untouched," I mused as I brushed my hand over an antique coffee table, flinging a plume of dust into the air, before I set down the ingredients for our dinner. "This would have been a good place to flee from the Daemoni, so they must have left to take shelter from the fallout."

"Actually, there's a ski resort not too far from here, and you know how the Daemoni like to prey on vacationers." Tristan picked up an antique goblet and rubbed a coating of gray ash off with his thumb, exposing a smudge of gold underneath.

"So not a good place for refuge?"

He studied the cup for a moment and put it down. "No, not good for norms. Or if any had come here, it'd be the first place the Daemoni would hunt and harvest for their human farms."

"I wonder where they are." I meandered around the room for a quick inspection, trailing my fingers through the dust on the spines of books that sat on a bookshelf spanning an entire wall. "Surely the Daemoni did something with the norms to protect their food source from the nuclear fallout."

"I'm sure those camps were strategically placed near bunkers," Tristan said. "But I don't think those were nuclear bombs. Not all of them."

I looked over my shoulder at him. "We saw the mushroom clouds when Lucas was boasting about what he'd done."

"Any large impact can create a mushroom cloud. The damage we've seen doesn't make sense." He picked up a piece of cut wood from the stack next to the fireplace and blew across it. A cloud of gray dust rose and scattered. "Here, for example. There weren't enough nuclear bombs in the world to hit every town or even small city. Targets would have been chosen strategically. There's no reason there would be fallout way out here in the mountains, in the middle of nowhere."

"Couldn't the wind have carried it?"

He shook his head as he placed the wood in the hearth and reached for another piece. "Normal nuclear fallout wouldn't be like this. Not covering everything so completely and evenly. The thoroughness is unnatural."

I brushed a layer of thick dust off the camelback sofa, sat down, and leaned my elbows on my knees. "You think it's supernatural?"

"I think Lucas and his sorcerers, maybe even the Ancients themselves, did something, yes. It looks like they tried to scrub out every bit of life-form on Earth. Except, of course, for the ones they specifically chose to save for their own purposes."

I dropped my chin in my hand and sighed. "Not *try*. They *did*."

Tristan lit the pile of wood with his hand, and the fire caught quickly. The flames cast their orange light on half of his face while the other half remained in shadow as he looked at me.

"I don't think so. I think humans are more resourceful and more resilient than the Daemoni know. And so is this world. Life will come back from this, if we can give it the chance it needs."

I pursed my lips together as I began opening jars for our supper, staying silent on the matter. Nothing we'd seen so far had given me any hope. In fact, the desolate landscape that had passed below us today had sucked out nearly every iota of belief I had that anything good remained in this world. The lack of mind signatures confirmed what I'd believed in the beginning—humanity was gone.

The blanket of nickel-gray snow we woke up to the next morning did nothing to change my mind.

We flew over all of Austria and then to Prague, which looked even worse than it had when we'd been there before. We continued on to Berlin and farther north, until we came to the sea. We stopped at all of the bomb shelters Tristan knew about, hoping to find people hiding in them, but we only found charred skeletons. I picked up pockets of Daemoni mind signatures, but no Norman life.

Are you sure Noah wouldn't have gone to Hades? I asked Tristan, not for the first time.

"*Positive. He had no interest in Hades, like most of the Summoned once they realized Lucas had no intention of giving them any real power. Some went rogue, like Edmund, and the rest*

145

scattered, doing their own thing. They created their own little empires, taking over small towns or leading gangs and mafias. But Noah just disappeared. We crossed paths a few times before I left, and there are a couple of places we can still check. I think we should go west and south before we head east toward Hades." He banked to the left as he finished.

But as we made the turn, something caught my mind just ahead in a large German town that wasn't quite a city.

No, not something. Some*one*.

Tristan, there's a norm down there!

We dropped to the ground a mile outside of the town and hid our wings before running the rest of the way. As we approached, she didn't move at first. The girl, in her early twenties, sat on the curb with her jeans-clad legs stretched out into the street, her feet rocking side to side on the heels of her Converse All-Stars. One gloved hand held her blue, puffy winter coat together while the other lifted a cigarette to her lips. Curly locks of black hair stuck out of her knit hat. We were almost close enough to touch her when she finally looked in our direction.

Her cheeks were sunken in, and her skin, which had probably once been a pretty coffee tone, was a sickly pallor. Her light brown eyes, ringed in purple, opened wide when she saw us, her pupils dilated unnaturally large for being out in the sun. She jumped to her feet and ran.

"Wait!" I called after her, but she sprinted down the street and around the corner. "Let's go. There's probably more."

My hope began to lift again. If this human could be out here in the air without succumbing to the fallout, then others could, too. Maybe Tristan had been right last night. Maybe there *was* a chance for this world.

We jogged after the girl, and up ahead, I sensed the many mind signatures. A mixture of them—Norman and Daemoni.

I think it's a camp, I said to Tristan as we rounded the corner. The block was short, ending at a large building that looked like a mall. The girl disappeared inside. We stopped jogging, but continued heading down the street.

"*I sense a couple dozen Daemoni inside,*" he said. "*Any others around?*"

I reached out with my mind and then shook my head. *We can take these.*

But I'd no sooner spoken the words when several more minds popped into the area, surrounding us. Except, not all were Daemoni. Not enough mind signatures accounted for the physical bodies on the roofs above and the sidewalks to our sides. The extras looked Norman, but they had no thoughts for me to grasp. And on closer look, they all had the same, inhuman eyes—no irises, no pupils, not even whites. Their eyes were black with flames dancing in them, like Tristan's used to be when the monster inside him had tried to take over his soul. These were Demons, wearing human bodies.

The door to the mall ahead of us swung open, and the Norman girl in the blue coat came running out, tugging at the hand of a dark-haired vampire. She spoke in German.

"She says we tried to kill her," Tristan said quietly. The vampire leaned down and pressed his mouth close to her ear. "He's promising to take care of her."

The girl looked up at him and smiled as his tongue traced the line of her jaw. Her coat had fallen open, exposing bite marks all over her throat and chest. Other norms came out of the building, also sporting scars and also hanging on to more vampires. Tristan and I exchanged a sideways glance. Our one communication before I shot Amadis power at the Demons, and he paralyzed the vamps in mid-motion as they'd made their move to attack. The Demons poofed away, and I turned my palm toward a female bloodsucker.

A norm stopped me, his voice pleading as he spoke in German. I looked at him with disbelief, noticing the fresh wounds on his throat.

"Ich liebe sie," he said, and I didn't know much German, but I knew that meant he loved her.

"They're blood slaves," Tristan murmured, before speaking to them in their language. The man answered him, shaking his head. "He says that's his wife. She was before she was turned, and she still is. This is her nest. They're all claiming to be family."

"They're not Amadis," I said.

Tristan shook his head. "Not at all."

"So they're using these norms."

"Retters!" a woman said, and her thought translated to "saviors." My head snapped toward her with another spark of hope, thinking she meant Tristan and me, but she jabbed at the vampires to each side of her. "Safe."

And my heart sank. This was exactly what Lucas had wanted—the norms to believe the Daemoni would save them and take care of them.

Some can be saved, even some of the vampires. Some of them still love, so there's hope.

Tristan said more in German, a vampire hissed, and the Norman man responded, eliciting a harsh breath out of my husband. "They don't believe we can help them. They don't want us to help them. They said the nest saved them right before the bombs and has kept them safe all this time. They *want* to give them their blood. They claim it's no different than cooking dinner for their families."

I opened my mouth to ask him what we should do when gunfire ratted through the street, coming from the doors to the mall. Several norms dropped to the ground, pulling their vampires down with them. More Daemoni and Demons appeared around us.

After scanning the minds of several people, I came to the depressing conclusion that there was nothing we could do. These norms wanted to serve the Daemoni. They truly believed what they were doing was right. And since none of them stopped the shooters, they obviously didn't want us there. They had masters and caretakers and were perfectly fine with that.

Tristan gave me a nod, and we rocketed into the air, exposing our wings to wrap around our bodies, blocking the bullets still spraying toward us. Once we were high enough, we spread our wings and soared toward the southwest, flying for hours. No matter how far we flew, though, I couldn't get away from the images of the norms and their perforated throats. Those were the people I'd failed when Lucas had claimed his victory. Those were the people who needed my help, but I had no idea how to give it. Especially when they didn't want it.

We spent the night on the sacred grounds of a cathedral outside of Paris after sensing only Daemoni in the city. My hope that had dared to spark earlier was once again snuffed out, and I didn't know how much more of this roller coaster ride I could take. My heart felt so heavy in my chest, I was surprised I could even lift it off the ground to fly.

Where are we headed now? I asked Tristan the next morning as he steered us in a southwesterly direction.

"*Noah once had a hideout in Morocco,*" he said, the only explanation he gave.

We flew for hours over gray land, then over charcoal-gray sea that swallowed the sunlight rather than reflected it, and then over more gray land that should have been the color of sand. Even the deserts of Africa had been scorched of any beauty. And there were no signs of life anywhere, not even Daemoni. Not until I could see the ocean far ahead did I sense a lone mind signature.

The singularity of it made my heart sink.

He's here, I told Tristan. *Noah. But not Dorian.*

I led him as I followed the mind signature to where the edge of land met the ocean. Cliffs overlooked the beach, some jutting out into the water in unique arched formations that had probably been breathtaking before, but the monotone colors and strange shapes made me feel as though we were on an alien planet. We landed on the gray sand and hid our wings.

Up there. I focused on a point about halfway up the cliff where there was an opening in the stone. Tristan nodded, and we both sprang up there together, landing at the entrance to a cave deep enough that I couldn't see the back walls.

"Noah," Tristan called.

No reply came, but we sensed him nearby.

"We're not here to hurt you," I said, although I felt no fear from him. More like misery. We stepped farther inside so our eyes could adjust better to the shadowy darkness.

"I know why you're here. I'm not ignorant." Noah's deep, throaty voice came from our right, at about the two o'clock position, and we both turned in that direction. A large figure moved in the shadows. "But you're too late. Dorian's long gone."

My throat went dry, although logically, I'd already known Dorian wasn't here. The finality of Noah's voice felt as though he carved the words into my heart.

"Where then?" I asked, sure I didn't really want to know, although deep down, I already did.

"He should be to Hades by now."

My eyes fell closed, and my jaw snapped shut as the lump in my throat muted me.

"When?" Tristan demanded, his voice steel-hard.

"We parted ways in Prague a while ago. That's as far as I would go. I don't know exactly how long it's been—a few weeks, maybe a month or two. I came here to get away from the others."

"What others?" Tristan asked, his thoughts lined with hope that Noah meant Amadis.

"The Daemoni and the Demons, of course," Noah snarled.

"And you just let him *go*?" I asked, my voice found again. "You let a little boy travel to Hades by himself?"

Noah scoffed. "He's not exactly a little boy. And I'm sure he wasn't alone. This was all his doing, but many have been waiting for him. He probably had a royal escort."

"I was trying to save you!" My voice rose until I yelled at him. "I helped you! And this is what you do in return?"

Noah stepped out of the shadows completely, revealing himself, wearing only leather pants and combat boots, his broad chest bare and his long, wavy brown hair reaching his shoulders. His lip curled up in a sneer as he looked down his nose at me with hazel eyes, the scar in one eyebrow looking extra severe. "How many times do I have to tell you? *You* can't save me. But Dorian could have had a chance."

My ears pricked at the use of the past tense. "What do you mean *had*?"

With four long strides, he crossed the cavern and stood at the entrance, making us turn to see him, a silhouette against the light outside. "He should have been there by now. So either he never made it, or he didn't break the curse."

"What do you mean? How do you know?"

He turned and glared at me with narrowed, red eyes, his nostrils flaring and his hands fisting. "Because everything inside me is fighting to kill you."

The look in his eyes was far more frightening than Tristan's had ever been. Tristan had been resisting the monster inside him for years before he came near me, and he'd already been converted. Noah had nothing but whatever self-control he might have possessed. Which probably wasn't much.

Tristan stepped in front of me, his arm out protectively. "What makes you think he could break the curse?"

"What difference does it make? I was obviously wrong. Kali lied."

"Of course she did," I muttered. "And now because of you, my son is in Hades."

"We need to know what she told him," Tristan persisted.

Noah growled. "She told him about how Eris cursed all of Cassandra's male descendants, so that they would all bow down to Jordan's direct line. Since Dorian descends from them both, Kali surmised that the curse can stop with him, but only if he gives himself willingly. At least, that's what she told Dorian and he told me. It must have been her lure to reel him in to the Daemoni."

Now I understood why Dorian had been so broody during his last months with us. He'd carried the weight of the world on his young shoulders. My battered heart broke into smaller pieces with what he must have felt every time we were attacked, every time we saw a norm die, every time one of our own was injured or killed. He'd been led to believe he could stop it all, and the sense of responsibility must have crushed him. He had to have been working up the courage to make his move from the moment he watched Lucas kill his Mimi, but his love for his father and me had held him back. His worry for us and the sister I'd been pregnant with had been the catalyst for him to make his move. And all that time I hadn't known. I hadn't been able to help him. I could have stopped him if I'd had any idea.

My blood boiled at the turmoil he'd been suffering. At what he was going through now. He was so young. *Too* young! How dare that fucking bitch plant lies in his head! I almost wished she'd come back to life so I could kill her again.

Especially because Dorian's sacrifice would all be for nothing.

He hadn't broken the curse. The Summoned wouldn't help us win any war. There was no sister of his to do this for.

"It's time for you to leave," Noah said. "I can't—"

His words were lost as two Demons swooped into the cave's entrance, grabbed him in their claws, and carried him away. Tristan and I ran to the edge of the opening.

"Noah!" I yelled, opening my wings to take off after them.

"You can't follow them."

The female voice came from below us, where a dark-haired woman dressed in a bikini with a sarong wrapped around her waist stood on the beach. She disappeared and reappeared on the ledge right before us, only her toes hanging on. Tristan and I both stepped backward, and I had to control the urge to wrinkle my nose at the sight of her. Her skin was a sickly pale gray with blisters and boils oozing yellow pus on her arms and chest. Her face might have been pretty with better coloring, except for the irregularly shaped, yellowish-orange irises of her eyes. She made the disgusted face I'd been holding back from making myself.

"I know. I'm atrocious," she admitted. "But if you think this is bad, you should have seen what I looked like when I first took this body. I'll get her back to normal soon enough."

For the briefest moment while she spoke, I caught a glimpse of her true self—with oily, mottled skin, horns, and a tail. Her eyes changed, too, from the weird, spiky irises to none at all. No whites or pupils, only fire. Another zombie possessed by a Demon.

"Where are they taking Noah?" Tristan demanded.

The whites of the Demon-woman's eyes bled back in, and the fires returned to the freaky irises. "To Hell, where he belongs. And you've overstayed your welcome down there . . . for now."

I shook my head. "No."

I didn't believe Noah belonged there. I still held hope for his soul. He'd promised Dorian he'd fight for us, which meant he wanted to convert.

"Or maybe they took him to Lucas. I don't know, and I don't care," she said. "I'm just glad it's all almost over. My lord and master will be here soon, and you will die. The boy is all Lucas needs."

"*What?*" I gasped.

Tristan's huge wings came out as he advanced on her.

"What does that mean?" he growled.

Her ugly eyes filled with fear as his wings curved in toward her, but her full mouth curved into a smirk. "That boy is all Lucas needs to drop the veil and open the gates to Hell. Everything else is done and ready for my lord Satan."

CHAPTER 13

Tristan shoved the Demon-woman against the cave wall, and his wing curved around, the feathers pressed against her throat. But the feathers weren't soft and light, giving at the pressure. Their edges had become hard and razor-sharp, drawing a thin line of black blood.

"Where's our son?" he demanded, his voice frightening even me.

"Almost home," she sneered.

"Is he with Lucas?"

She didn't answer. Tristan pressed his feathers harder into her skin. The line of blood grew thicker, dripping downward like a line of oily paint on a canvas.

"Where. *Are.* They?" he roared.

"I don't know. On their way to Hades? Maybe in Hell by now, talking to our lord. Making preparations." She gurgled out a laugh. "It doesn't matter. You can't stop it. But it's not too late to change your minds about who the true god is."

Tristan's wing swished outward, slicing across the Demon's neck. The body slumped against the wall and slid down to the floor, while a black smoke emerged from it. The Demon

155

gathered into its natural shape and flew out of the cave, then disappeared.

I ran outside and leapt to the beach below, where I spewed out a string of profanities while pacing back and forth. Tristan landed on the beach, too, but he stood perfectly still, his wings out wide, his arms crossed over his chest, and his eyes staring out at the water as black waves crashed onto the gray sand. The peculiarly shaped cliffs cast dark shadows over us.

"We have to go to Hades," I declared. He didn't respond. "We have to go to Hades, get our son back, and . . . and . . ."

I floundered for our next step, not knowing what to do after that. There wasn't much left to life on this Earth, but it didn't matter. As long as we had Dorian back and the three of us were together, we'd figure out the rest. Right now, all we had to focus on was getting to Dorian.

"It might be too late," Tristan finally said through a clenched jaw.

I stopped pacing in front of him and stared at him with lowered brows. "No, it's not! Don't say that! As long as the veil hasn't been ripped down, we have time. We're going to go to Hades and get him back before it *is* too late."

"We'll be severely outnumbered. It's just the two of us."

"And from what we've seen, it will always be just the two of us." My voice fell, my heavy heart weighing it down as what I'd been thinking was finally voiced. "The Amadis are . . . gone. The Angels were wrong. We're all we have now. You and me. And Dorian. He's our son, Tristan."

He finally looked over at me, the gold in his eyes glinting. "I know. I'm ready. I just want to be sure you are."

I spread my arms out wide and turned side to side. "Look at our lives. At the world. We have nothing more to lose, do we?"

"We could lose each other."

My arms dropped to my sides, and my teeth gnashed at

the thought of losing Tristan again. I forced my tight throat to swallow.

"We just can't let that happen," I said firmly.

He gave me a sharp nod. "Then Hades it is."

We were about to launch when three winged women suddenly appeared in front of us.

"You cannot go to Hades," Cassandra declared.

The impersonal greeting immediately set me on edge.

"We have to stop Dorian." I placed my fists on my hips. "Make him see the mistake he's making."

They disappeared.

"He is not making a mistake." Rina's voice came from behind me, and I spun around. She sat up on the ledge of what had been Noah's cavern. Her voice came softly, but easily heard. "Dorian is doing what he needs to do."

"He's doing what he *thinks* he needs to do because of Kali. But she lied to him. This is not what he needs to do."

"But it is, honey." Mom stood on the edge of one of the stone cliffs that jutted out into the water. The sun behind her created a glow around her body and wings.

"Why? To break the curse?" I threw my hands in the air. "Except, he won't be. He won't be saving the brothers. He won't be doing anything except giving himself to Lucas, who will then drop the veil and open the gates to Hell. Is that what you guys really want? I thought you wanted me to stop him!"

Cassandra appeared to my right, hovering inches above the water as the waves slid in under her feet. Their movement was giving me whiplash. "You cannot prevent Dorian from doing what he needs to do. You must allow him to go. But you will stop Lucas."

I turned and squinted at her, confused. To stop Lucas, we had to stop Dorian.

"What do you mean?" Tristan asked, his voice steady but with that steely undertone that meant his patience ran thin.

"You must trust us," Cassandra said, turning her full gaze on him. "You must believe in us, in the Angels, in your God. You must have faith that they have a plan and make God's will your way. Dorian is following his purpose. You must not stop him."

"So letting Lucas rip down the veil is also God's will?" I scoffed. "You said this whole apocalypse wasn't God's doing, but now it *is* his will? He wants Satan's chains to break so he can come to Earth? Because that's what Lucas is going to do."

"You will not let it come to that," Rina said, now on the beach, standing behind Tristan.

"Exactly," I said, "which is why we need to go to Hades. Now."

"Not now," Cassandra said. "Not yet. You need your army."

I fisted my hands in my hair and dropped my head back to stare at the sky as a frustrated chuckle escaped me. After exhaling a sharp breath, I lifted my head to look at her.

"There is no army," I said, and my voice deflated with the dark reality of my words. "They're gone. You told me to search out the good, and I tried. You gave me hope there was something worth fighting for. That I'd find Amadis and norms, and we looked. But the only souls we've found so far are part of the Daemoni. Anyone still alive have given themselves over. We don't have an army anymore, Cassandra. This is it." I waved my hands between Tristan and me. "This is our army now. And the little bit of good left is the love of our family, including Dorian. And that can be enough for us, if we can stop him and Lucas."

"Do you give up on your people so easily?" Mom asked, still perched on the cliff above us. "On Owen and Charlotte? Vanessa and Sheree? Blossom and Jax?"

My stomach clenched as though she'd just punched me, and I blinked against the tears forming at the mention of their names. I'd been trying so hard to block them out, to not think about them, to not wonder what happened to them. I didn't want the visuals that came to mind, the ones I'd watched on repeat while in Hell—their horrific deaths while they'd been trying to help the norms. And now the loss and despair all flooded over me, and I gasped at the pain in my heart.

"They're . . . gone," I whispered.

"Don't give up on them." Mom's voice was distant, muffled by the pounding in my ears. "They're still out there."

I shook my head and scrubbed at the tears on my cheeks. "I watched them die a thousand times."

"Then you witnessed lies," Cassandra said, still hovering above the water. "They are out there. Other Amadis are, too. They need you, Alexis. As does humanity. They will fight for you, with you. Find them. Build your army. Then you will go to Hades."

I wanted to believe her. I truly did. I wanted nothing more than for the world to be saved and restored. My heart, my whole chest, ached with such longing.

"There's nobody to find," I choked out against the thick lump in my throat. "Looking for what isn't there is a waste of time."

Mom suddenly appeared right in front of me, her eyes narrowed.

"Alexis Katerina." Her voice took on her mom tone. "You were angry at us for not providing direction before, and here we are, providing direction. Giving you the answers you claimed to want. Telling you what to do. Now listen to us rather than fighting us. Why do you treat us like the enemy?"

I blinked, then huffed out a breath. "Because I never know if you're telling me the truth or not. Or setting me up for failure again."

"We've never lied to you."

"But have you ever given me the full truth?"

She didn't answer, but averted her eyes.

"That's what I thought. And because you hadn't told me everything I needed to know before, the world is left like this." I waved my hand in the air.

Rina dropped down to stand by Mom. "We only interfere when we need to."

"And you didn't think you should have interfered *before* all this happened?"

She shook her head. "No, darling. You did as you needed to."

My jaw dropped open, but I was speechless.

"But we are here now," Rina said. "What does that tell you?"

"We are here to help you, Alexis," Cassandra said, closing in on me, too, "but it is up to you to accept it."

I frowned and looked sideways at Tristan. He held up his hands and gave me that man look—that I'm-not-getting-in-the-middle-of-a-bunch-of-women expression. My frown deepened. Some help he was.

I looked back at the women before me. "So tell me where to find my people, if you really think they're still alive, so we can gather our army."

None of them said anything at first.

"You will need to search them out," Mom finally replied.

Unbelievable.

"We don't have time for that. There's a ticking clock! In fact, Dorian's probably already at Hades, and it's only a matter of time before Lucas drops the veil. Just tell me where to go."

"Dorian is not with Lucas yet," Cassandra said, and for the first time in I didn't know how long, she actually said something I wanted to hear. Something that gave me true hope. "He is with a neutral party, receiving objective counsel. He has many difficult decisions ahead of him. Before you ask, no, we do not know where. Just know that he is safe. When he does go to Lucas, there will be signs. Watch for them. The veil will not fall and the gates will not open the moment Dorian meets Lucas. There will be time. You will still be able to stop Lucas from proceeding. First, you need your army."

And my hopes fell with the word *when*, rather than *if*.

"But you won't tell me where to find said army." I looked at each of them in turn and realization came over me. "Because you don't know."

"We are not told everything, no."

"We've spent the last several weeks scouring Europe," Tristan said, finally speaking up. "Everywhere we've seen is the same—gray and lifeless. The only human life we've found is possessed by Demons or serving the Daemoni."

"You must look closer," Rina said. "We might not be able to tell you where they are, but we do know you are not alone."

"They're hidden deeply," Mom added. "They don't know that it's safe to come to the surface, and it's not in many places. You will have to search for them, but they are there."

"I can't even find their mind signatures, though," I said. "There's *nobody* but Daemoni."

"Then you're not looking in the right places or hard enough."

My mouth fell agape again. Tristan and I had flown over pretty much all of western Europe and a good portion of northern Africa. We'd checked the shelters where they could have hidden. At least, the ones Tristan knew about. If we hadn't found signs of life in any of those places, where else were we supposed to look?

"Search for the good, and you will find it," Cassandra said. "As long as you expect to find evil, though, you will, just like my brother. That is all that you will find. But if you open your heart and soul to the good, Alexis, you *will* find that. And you will win this war with it. It is not over."

With that, the three of them disappeared.

My hands balled into fists, I stomped my foot, and a scream of overwhelming frustration rose from deep within and erupted like a volcano out of my mouth. Then I glanced over at Tristan. He stared at me with his arms over his broad chest and a brow lifted.

"They infuriate me," I muttered in explanation.

He unfolded his arms and held his hands up.

"No judging here. I understand." One side of his mouth lifted in a crooked smile. "But your tantrums are . . . endearing."

I narrowed my eyes at him, half-tempted to shoot a bolt of lightning at him, but that would be *endearing*.

He shrugged. "What can I say? I've always had a thing for your hotheadedness."

He walked closer to me, hiding his wings as he did. I made mine disappear right before he snaked his arms around me and pulled me close against him.

"What are you thinking?" he asked.

"I don't know." I banged my forehead against his hard chest. "I don't know what to do. Part of me says run for Dorian before it's too late, but . . ."

"But part of you knows they're probably right. They do have a broader perspective than we do."

"One they won't share with us."

"But that doesn't mean they're not right."

I growled. "I hate it when they're right."

Using two fingers, he lifted my chin to look me in the eye. "Even if it means that there's still hope for this world?"

I didn't answer him. I could only wish. But the chances for rebuilding this world were about the same as the odds of me spitting out a bunch of babies: pretty much nil. As long as I had the family I knew was still alive, though, I was okay with that.

"Do you really think there's any chance Owen and Vanessa and everyone are still . . . around?" I asked.

"I don't know why Rina and your mom would lie to us about it."

"Doesn't mean I completely trust them." I gnawed on my bottom lip. "And Satan showed me their bodies. Made sure I knew I was to blame for their deaths."

"And *he* would have every reason to lie."

"Would he? What ulterior motive would that serve?"

He lifted a brow as he looked down at me. "Are you really asking me if I know all of Satan's ulterior motives?"

"He was the only one who told me the straight-up truth about Dorian's purpose. Maybe he's the only one who's been honest about everything."

"Or maybe he was trying to make your Demons as big and powerful as possible so you'd believe you couldn't slay them." His hazel eyes pierced into me, driving his point home. "Who do you think you should believe, Lex? Your mother? Or the Devil?"

I dropped my gaze and pressed my lips together, hoping he didn't see in me what I truly felt. Because although the answer should have been clear and easy, it wasn't. I loved my mom and grandmother, and I knew they loved me, but I also knew they'd do almost anything for the cause, including lifting my hopes so I'd obey their commands. After all, they were at war, too, and war required deceit.

Ultimately, I could only trust myself, and Tristan, and the strength of our love.

"The only way to know for sure is to search for them ourselves," I said. "So where do we start?"

"Since we're this far, we may as well check on Jelani's village, but I'd say we need to make our way back to D.C., since that's the last place we saw our group."

Jelani had been one of my council members I'd inherited from Rina. The last we'd known, he'd been in Kenya, so we took off and flew southeast. What passed on the ground below us sickened me. Besides the gray dunes of the desert, dried up lakes and rivers, dead trees and grasslands, indigenous tribes who'd had no part in any of the world's politics had been obliterated. Their corpses and skeletons were scattered around the remains of their villages. And the animals. The poor animals. Lions, tigers, hippos, hyenas, birds of all kinds . . . and the extraordinary elephants and giraffes. So beautiful at one time, but now barely recognizable as rotting remains. What had Lucas done? Why the animals? Why wipe out every centimeter of Earth and the life on it?

To make Satan feel at home.

The thought made sense . . . sort of. Except, if Satan and his Demons liked Hell so much, why bother taking over Earth? If he had all the human souls anyway, why was he so anxious to come topside if it was just like Hell itself? Was it the destruction that he loved so much? If so, wouldn't he have wanted to be a part of that himself? Or did Lucas need to prove his worthiness or something?

Why am I spending so much time contemplating Satan, Hell, and Lucas's motives?

I tried to clear my mind of such darkness, but that was difficult to do when I saw nothing else before me.

We found no evidence of Jelani's survival or the Amadis village where he lived. No mind signatures, no animals, no life at all. Everything grayed out and dead. Not even Daemoni were-animals roamed the land—because there was nothing there for them to hunt.

My heart felt like a two-ton anvil by the time we stopped for the night.

"Maybe we'll find things better in the States," Tristan suggested as he curled his body around mine on the gray sand beach we lay on.

"Yeah, maybe," I said while suppressing a snort. If no part of Africa, with its sparse population, had escaped unscathed, I hardly expected America to be any better.

"Do you think we can fly across the ocean?" I asked as I stared out at the waves crashing onto the beach, the moon's reflection off the crests making the water sparkle. It was the first thing of real beauty I'd seen on this Earth since my trip to the Otherworld. Besides my husband's face, of course.

"I don't know. We've been flying pretty far stretches, but we're over land. The winds over the ocean will be tougher to navigate, and if we get tired, there aren't too many places to rest if we go straight across."

I rolled onto my back to look up into his face. "I know you have a plan."

His full lips curled into a half-smile, and the gold in his eyes sparkled confidently, confirming my guess. "We'll go back north, all the way up to Iceland. Check out the parts of Europe we haven't hit yet on our way, and then turn to the west. We'll hug Greenland and then Canada, so if we get tired, we'll always have land nearby for a stop."

"Sounds like a plan."

Although we were too close to the equator for it to be cold, I snuggled closer to him as I gazed up at the sky. With no light pollution to obliterate their glow, the stars shone like billions of little pinpricks in the fabric of the sky. This world was but a dust mote in the universe, and the stars made me feel so tiny and insignificant. And so lonely.

Tristan and I could be the only ones left to gaze at their beauty.

And maybe Dorian? Tears pricked my eyes as my mind wandered back to him—where he was, who he was with, what he was doing. I'd gone through all of this before for half a year and had only had him back for a couple months before he left. And here I was again, a mother whose son had disappeared. But this time felt different. More final. There was no one to be angry at but myself. I couldn't even blame him. He thought he was doing the right thing. He was no longer my little boy, but a young man on a mission. Tears burned my eyes at the thought of his bravery.

I blinked them away and focused on the sky, pretending that my son lay on the ground somewhere in this world, gazing at the same stars and wondering if his parents saw them, too.

CHAPTER 14

Alexis

e took a few weeks to search for life in Africa and Europe before we followed Tristan's flight plan north, scouting the ground below as we flew several hundred feet over the ground. The scenery should have changed with different vegetation and architecture as the miles passed under us, but the trees were nothing but bare sticks pointing like accusing fingers at the sky, and any buildings were in ruins. I supposed there was some variation to the view, but the grayness of it all camouflaged the differences. We didn't know exactly where we were until we landed for the night, taking refuge in the remains of hotels or people's homes.

We'd check for bomb shelters each morning, but any humanity that survived remained elusive. For the most part, the only mind signatures I found or creatures we saw were Daemoni or Demons. The few pockets of norms were like the ones we'd found in Germany—servants to the Daemoni. We hadn't even found any Norman farms, and I began to wonder if those people who'd been in the camps had voluntarily turned to the Daemoni when they realized there was nothing else left in this world. Hadn't that been Lucas's plan, to become the norms' saving grace?

"There must be somebody left in their right mind," Tristan said when I'd told him this theory while he made us a fire.

We'd found an ice cave in Greenland to spend the night. I hated it here. Winter this close to the North Pole sucked. There were no nearby towns to scavenge for food, and we hadn't eaten since leaving Iceland this morning. My stomach growled, but it was drowned out by the wind howling outside that sounded like an eerie whistle. And I'd had enough of the freezing cold that reminded me of Hell—the real thing and the time on the rock island when Tristan was only a shell and my mind floundered in my own private hell. The ice on the air and in my veins brought back the memories and the visions and made the scar across my chest ache.

"T-t-tell m-me how," I replied through chattering teeth as a tear froze to my cheek. "B-b-because I have n-no hope."

He sat down behind me with his legs around me and wiggled us closer to the fire. Then he draped his arms over my shoulders, curved his body around mine, pressing his chest against my back. His breath came warm near my ear.

"Do you love me?" he asked.

"Of c-course," I answered automatically.

"Do you love Dorian?"

"T-tristan . . ."

"Where there's love, there's hope, *ma lykita*. And we have enough of that between the two of us to blanket the world with hope."

"B-b-but if there's n-no one else to f-feel it . . ."

He tightened his arms around me. "There is, though. There must be. Why else would they insist we look for life? Since you're so skeptical about their motives, think about it this way, Lex. If the war is that heated in the Otherworld, why would they send us here if there's no benefit? Why wouldn't they have kept us there to fight? You said they told you the Angels needed all the help they could get. So if they were only worried about their own souls and not about Earth's, why would they leave us here? Why give us wings and more powers, only to send us back here for no reason?"

I frowned. "Because we don't belong in Heaven *or* Hell."

"We belong here. For a reason."

"Yeah, because there's no other place for us to go."

"Or maybe because this world is not as hopeless as you think."

I stared at the fire for a long moment. "I don't understand how you have so much hope, after all you've been through. You were in Hell longer than I was."

"How many times do I have to tell you? I have you. I've been fighting my demons my entire life, but only because of you have I finally slayed them. I have faith, Alexis. Faith in us, in humanity, in the Angels . . . most of all, in God's plan. We're right where they want us to be. We only have to believe that they know best."

"Hmph. If that's the case, then they must think the best thing for Earth and humanity is to let Satan have it, because that's where we're headed. But I honestly have a hard time believing God or the Angels care one iota about us anymore."

Tristan sighed, his breath heating my cheek. "As long as you believe that, you will always live in the dark, *ma lykita*."

The defeat and despair in his voice made my heart hurt. But after all we'd been through and all we'd seen of the world so far, I couldn't help my feelings. If God hadn't abandoned us, then where was he? Why had he let the world come to such destruction? I used to believe in him. I used to think that in the end, good would win, just like Owen always said. I doubted even Owen would believe that now, if he were still alive.

My chest tightened at this thought. If God or the Angels really cared, how could they take souls like Owen's, Sheree's, and Char's out of this world? And Blossom and Jax, and even Vanessa, who'd never lost her hope for a better life. Why take them and their faith, while leaving me and all of my failures?

Because they wanted them in their realm. Where they belonged. And probably the only reason Tristan was here with me was because he followed me here, just like he'd followed me to Hell. For that reason alone, I should have tried to believe, for his sake. But as much as I wanted to, as much as I searched myself for it, I came up empty.

As we lay on the hard ground by the fire to go to sleep, Tristan prayed out loud for me to see the light. My soul cracked. I'd failed everyone else, including my son, and now I was failing Tristan, too.

Two days later, we flew over New York City. What remained of New York City, anyway. Many of the skyscrapers had been mowed down with their rubble in mountains on the streets. No bright signs flashed on Times Square, and the thought that the ball would never again drop on New Year's Eve felt like a sinking weight. We swooped over 34th Street, where a banner advertising the upcoming Christmas season half-clung to the Macy's building as it flapped in the wind. Christmas had long passed, but there had been no holiday season. My throat tightened as I recalled all of the Thanksgiving Day parades I'd watched on TV, knowing there would never be another. The crowds would never fill these streets again.

Except for Daemoni. Vampire nests, mage covens, and shifter dens and packs roamed freely as though they owned the city. I supposed they did now. Their human pets gazed at them adoringly, practically bowing down and kissing their feet. When the mages shot spells at us as we flew by, the norms laughed. We didn't bother fighting back, but flew off, headed farther south.

As we approached Washington, D.C., my breath became trapped in my lungs. Even from a distance, I could see that little remained. At some point after the faeries had rescued our bodies and Lucas must have evacuated his followers, someone had bombed the hell out of the city. Or maybe other sorcerers, besides Jeana and Merrick, had been nearby, waiting on Lucas's orders to destroy the capitol and everything around it.

Not until we approached the university campus where we'd left Carlie, A.K.'s Angels, and the hunters did I realize I'd been holding on to a thin thread of hope. Because at the sight of its decimation, that final trickle drained away. Charlotte, Blossom, Jax, and Sheree had been here, too, and Owen and Vanessa were headed here when Lucas brought Hell to Earth. Or, at least, the first wave of Demons.

I thought I'd already accepted the loss of my friends, my extended family, but I'd never been so wrong.

Anger exploded in my chest as I circled the remains of the campus, knowing there was no way anybody survived what happened here. All emotions burst out in a guttural scream. My breaths came shallow as grief threatened to shut me down.

"Why?" I shouted at the world, at the Angels, at God as my circles became tighter and faster. "*Why?*"

Sobs tried to push up from my gut, but I shoved them away while grasping on to the anger. I flew off, soaring south, far away from this place of death and destruction.

"*Alexis,*" Tristan mentally called out as he flew to catch up with me.

I . . . I can't, Tristan. I can't take any more.

I pushed myself as hard as I could, soaring south fast enough for the land to become a blur under me because I couldn't stand the thought of seeing any more. The movies and TV shows about zombie apocalypses, nuclear wars, and alien invasions hadn't come close to depicting what it was truly like to see the world void of life. Nobody could ever be prepared for the deafening silence left behind, the eerie stillness of the land, the overwhelming loss of billions of men, women, and children. No animals, no plant life, not even a spark of color except the blue of the sky. My eyes watered from the wind in

KRISTIE COOK

them—or so I told myself, not wanting to admit to the tears streaming over my cheeks and flying off behind me.

"Damn it!" I screamed as loud as I could, my fists balled at my sides.

Something crashed into me, and I careened in the air. I thought it was Tristan at first, trying to stop me, and I was ready for the fight. I came to a halt and spun on him, my fists flying. They didn't meet Tristan's body, though. They thudded into the side of a Demon. It pounded a fist into my back, and I whirled and kicked, my foot slamming into its head with a satisfying thunk. As I spun and ducked under a swing at me, I caught a glimpse of Tristan fighting another Demon several yards away. I didn't know why the Demons had left us alone until now. Perhaps these guys had simply been bored when they sighted us. But they'd attacked at the wrong time. I took pleasure in beating my fists and feet into the Demon's thick flesh, even though I caused no damage, and I welcomed the physical pain it dished out on me because it smothered the emotional agony in my heart and soul.

"Fuck you. Fuck you. Fuck. YOU!" I shouted with each blow that landed.

Its razor sharp claws scraped over my side, digging through my leather vest and into my skin. I palmed my dagger at my hip and brought it out, swiping it across the Demon's barrel of a chest. It soared away from me, and a putrid stink poured out of the gash along with an inky ooze. The Demon let out a long howl before flying headfirst at me. I swung the silver blade out and carved a new orifice into its face, and then I spun in the air, away from its outstretched claws, and arced my dagger around. The entire length of the blade sliced into the Demon's neck, all the way through, until my blade broke free at the other side. Its horned head rolled backwards and hung from the thick hide at the back of its neck before falling completely away. The Demon's wings formed a V behind it as the body shot down after its head.

Tristan had already decommissioned the Demon he'd been fighting, and I'd felt the weight of his gaze on me. I barely glanced at him before flying off, back on course going south. I didn't think I knew where I headed until the Gulf of Mexico came into view, and I was nearly at my destination. For some reason, my subconscious must have thought going to the Captiva safe house would have made me feel better. Or perhaps returning to our house a few miles away on Sanibel Island. But both were destroyed. Nothing remained of the structures, the Amadis colony, or anything else on the islands. They were no different than the rest of the world.

The adrenaline from the fight leaked away, and emotional and physical exhaustion began to set in. But I pushed on, afraid that if I stopped flying, the gravity of reality would pull me completely under. I flew until I ran out of land at the tip of Florida. And finally I landed.

In front of the house Tristan had built for me in the Keys.

I stared at the structure with a mixture of awe and confusion. Beams from the setting sun bounced off the gray, metal roof of the three-bedroom beach house that held so many memories for me. For us. The second-story screened-in porch remained intact across this side of the house that faced the water, and hurricane shutters covered the windows, seemingly unharmed.

"It's still standing," I mused aloud when Tristan dropped to the ground beside me.

The house still stood, indeed, but the paint had faded to a dull gray and it curled away from the walls in many places as though it had blistered up and popped. The yard was overgrown so there was no longer delineation between it and the brush that used to only line the edges of the property. All of it was dead now. Dead and gray, like the rest of the world.

I flashed inside to the island kitchen with the granite countertop that was no longer cracked, fixed by Owen before we'd left the house for the last time after my *Ang'dora*. With a mere swish of my hand, I opened the hurricane shutters over the sliding glass doors to allow some light in, and then I opened the doors themselves for much needed fresh air. The inside of the house was dank, having been closed up with no power to run the air conditioning for months. Although the shutters had enclosed the interior, the same ashy-dust coated everything, sapping away from the décor what had been pretty colors of the ocean and the beach.

After one of the longest and more miserable days of my life, I strode into the Caribbean room that should have been renamed the Room of Blech because all of the pretty jewel tones on the curtains and accessories were washed out to grays and whites. I collapsed onto the dusty bed, wishing I could fall into unconsciousness. But my stupid brain wouldn't allow me, forcing me to relive all of the atrocities of my life since the first time I'd walked into this house on my honeymoon. Losing Stefan, Tristan's disappearance, living without him for seven long years, my first real fight with Vanessa, the *Ang'dora*, battling the monster inside Tristan . . . the trial, Lilith, Martin and Kali, Owen's abandonment, Rina's months-long coma . . . skirmishes with the Daemoni, the trunks with Vanessa's chopped-up body, going to Hades, escaping Hades, finding Dorian missing and our mages slaughtered . . . hunting Dorian, Rina's and Mom's deaths . . . and the war that started right after. When I tried to revert my train of thought and focus on all of the good parts of life, I only felt worse. Except for Tristan, none of those people I shared the good times with lived anymore.

Well, hopefully Dorian did, but he was almost as lost to me as the dead.

Silent tears fell over my nose and down to the comforter, soaking it under my face. The other side of the bed creaked and sagged as Tristan settled in next to me. I was thankful when he curled around me but remained silent. There was nothing I wanted to talk about. There was nothing more to say. I'd been right about the world, after all, but I didn't feel good about it. Quite the opposite. My despair hit rock bottom.

Eventually, I fell into a deep sleep full of nightmares.

When I awoke, the sun shone brightly from the other side of the house, meaning it was still morning. That had been the longest night of sleep I'd had in months, and although nightmares haunted me throughout the night, I hadn't felt so rested in a long time. After finding a can of tuna in the cupboard, I flashed outside to the tiny sliver of beach, sat down in the sand, peeled the lid off, and ate with my fingers while staring at the murky water. It reflected the darkness of my mind, my heart, my soul.

We'd gone snorkeling several times on our honeymoon, and then later, Tristan, Owen, and I had swum the depths of these waters when I was learning my new abilities from the *Ang'dora*. Although there had been more fish out by the reef, the water here had supported a decent amount of life at the time. Now there was none. Too bad, because half a can of tuna wasn't enough to satisfy my hunger. If I didn't love Tristan as much as I did, I probably would have devoured it all. Then again, my stomach felt like a rock, so I didn't know how much it could actually hold.

"Thank you for saving me some," he said, as though he was the mind reader in this relationship. He sat beside me and lifted the can. "But you can have it. I can wait until we find something else."

I shook my head without removing my gaze from the water. "Don't be ridiculous. Eat."

I didn't tell him that I suddenly felt ill anyway. It wasn't quite a sick feeling, and I didn't think the tuna itself had caused it. Just food in general. The thought of putting anything more in my mouth nearly made me gag. Where had that come from? I hadn't been sick since before the *Ang'dora*. Was it because it had been so long since I'd really eaten much?

175

Either that or the depression was taking hold, because even if I'd somehow contracted something, my body should have regenerated after yesterday's taxing flight.

"Do you think the water's safe to go in?" I asked, really wishing I could wash myself off. It wouldn't be the same as a hot bath, it wouldn't soothe the soul, but at least I'd be somewhat cleaner.

"I don't know. Whatever black magic was in those bombs that killed all life forms on land probably killed everything in the sea, too, including any bacteria. It's probably safe . . ." He leaned forward onto his knees and reached his fingers out for a wave that slid onto the sand. My breath caught, and I cringed at the sizzle as the water washed over his skin. He jerked his hand back and held up his raw fingers. "Or maybe not."

The skin on his fingertips immediately healed, but I couldn't imagine what it would feel like to immerse my whole body in that acidic water, if only for a moment, even if it did heal.

"There should be fresh water in the water heater," he said. "We should conserve it, so no bath or shower, but at least we can drink it."

And for some reason, the inability to wash myself set me off once again.

I snapped.

Total desolation overcame me. I leaned forward on my knees, curled my body over them, and let the sobs ransack me until I couldn't breathe. Then yesterday's anger returned, fueled by exhaustion and guilt. Although I'd been saying it all along, yesterday's flyovers had brought home the truth, and the stupid water reinforced it.

"I was right. The world is *gone*. Our friends and family are gone. We can't even take a fucking bath in the ocean!"

I slammed my fists into the sand. Something sharp, a broken shell or piece of glass, I didn't know, sliced into the side of my hand. I jumped to my feet, swearing up a storm as I turned toward the house.

"Damn it!" I screamed as I shook my hand.

The pain immediately vanished, and the skin was already closing up, but the blood that had trickled out sprayed in splatters that landed on the dead brush of the yard. Bright red dots contrasting against the endless gray. Splashes of color in a monotone world, like those artistic black-and-white photographs with a single hue that caught the eye. Photographs that didn't exist anymore, that would never again be taken.

Tristan wrapped his arms around me from behind, trying to settle me down, and something about the gesture drained me of all energy worse than a sorcerer could do.

"I'm so done," I said quietly as I sagged against him and closed my eyes. Tears seeped between my lashes. "Everybody we love is gone. Why can't we be, too?"

"It's not our time," he murmured against my ear. Not what I wanted to hear, but at least he didn't argue with me about the hopelessness of the world. Maybe he'd hoped to find something different back in D.C., but he'd finally accepted what I'd been saying all along. At least, I thought he had, until he spoke again a few moments later, and the tone of defeat in his voice had disappeared. "Alexis, open your eyes."

I didn't reply, and I didn't immediately open my eyes. The scene was clear on the backs of my lids, and if he was trying to be cute by filling my vision with his face, I wasn't in the mood. Yes, I actually thought that for probably the first time ever—I wasn't in the mood to see my love's beautiful face. Even when it was the only thing of beauty and life left in this world. That's how done I was.

"Lexi, my love, open your eyes," he insisted, his voice even lighter now. Almost excited.

I reluctantly obeyed. And gasped before falling to my knees.

"What the hell?" I breathed as my finger traced over one of the branches of the brush in the yard. A branch that had been dead and gray only moments ago, but now began to turn green, starting at a little dot in the center of the stem and growing outward. My eyes lifted as more little specks of green caught my attention. "I don't understand."

"I think it's everywhere your blood drops landed," Tristan said as he kneeled down behind me.

"My blood will bring back life?" I started laughing hysterically, but not the kind of joyous laughter that was appropriate. This was a maniacal howl that made me sound like a lunatic. "Classic. Just fucking classic. What am I supposed to do? Spread my blood all over the damn world to save it? Is that their oh-so-wonderful plan?"

I leaned back against Tristan and stared up at the sky, wondering what the Angels were doing on the other side of the veil. Probably cackling their heads off.

Tristan snaked his arm over my hips. "I don't know, Lex, but it shows that there's hope."

I looked back down at the brush. Only a few branches had shown signs of life, and it wasn't spreading very quickly. I'd bleed out before we could revive this yard. How the heck would this do any good for the world? My eyes fell on a new color that wasn't gray or green. Something tiny and purple in the dirt. As I watched, it pushed its way up, becoming a purple bud that blossomed before our very eyes. I clamped my hand over my mouth, and new tears welled.

I reached for the flower, and at the same time, my stomach jumped.

For a brief moment, I thought my tuna was trying to come back up, but the nauseated feeling had passed.

Then my belly fluttered again.

"What was that?" Tristan asked as his hand pressed against my lower abdomen.

"You felt that?" As soon as I spoke the words, my body did it again. "Oh my god."

"Alexis . . ."

Another flutter made him trail off.

My heart leapt and swelled. I clutched the flower I'd accidentally picked to my chest and turned around to face him. The biggest and most sublime smile beamed from his face.

"You believed in hope, and you were right," I breathed.

I threw my arms around him, and he lifted us both from the ground before swinging me around.

"Faith, my love. The tiniest bit goes a long way."

He spun us around again, and I felt like the heavy weight of despair peeled away and flung off of me in chunks with the centrifugal force. For some reason, realizing I was pregnant now felt different than last time. The world was in a lot worse condition than it had been then, but something told me that this—the baby's kicks and the flower—were the signs of hope I was supposed to discover.

"We're going to have a baby," I shrieked as I held onto Tristan's neck.

"Wicked awesome!" The familiar male voice came from near the house, and Tristan suddenly stopped his spinning.

"I told you we'd find them here," his female companion claimed, and I ran for her.

$\mathcal{T}$he brush slowed me down, so I leapt up and sprinted across the tops of it toward the couple standing by the corner of the house. I launched myself at them in a tackle hug, taking them both down.

"You're alive!" I squealed as I sprang to my feet and grabbed their hands to help them up.

"The last person who came at me like that got their head bit off," Vanessa said, brushing herself off and flicking her long, white-blond hair over her shoulder as she leveled me with ice-blue eyes. "Literally."

"I can't . . . I just can't believe it!" Ignoring her threat, I threw myself at her again, tears streaming down my face. And then I turned to Owen with a huge smile and hugged him again. "I thought you were dead! I thought everyone—"

I cut myself off, not wanting to ruin the moment by mentioning everyone else we'd lost.

"We didn't know what happened to you two, either," Owen said as he held me tightly before letting me go to give Tristan a man-hug. His straw-colored hair was longer than his usual style, and worry lines spread out from his sapphire-blue eyes. I wondered what kind of hell they'd been through since the last time we saw them.

"We thought we'd lost you," Vanessa said, and although she tried to hide it, I could hear the fear in her voice. "We've been looking ever since we figured out we could come to the surface without dying from radiation."

"We only got here yesterday," I said.

Owen shook his head, his eyes full of wonder as his gaze swung back and forth between Tristan and me. "I still can't believe it. Why Vanessa thought you might come here is beyond me, but cheers to her for insisting we come all the way down here."

Vanessa rolled her eyes. "It's a girl thing. And believe it or not, I *am* a girl."

I nodded. Owen should have known this place was important to me, but guys just didn't think the same way.

"What happened to you? Where did you go? Where have you been?" My questions gushed out like a geyser.

"We have the same inquisition for you," Owen said, "but first, did I hear something about drinking water?"

I narrowed my eyes at him. "How long have you been here, Mr. Eavesdropper?"

"We popped in under a cloak," Vanessa admitted. "Looked like you two were having a moment, so we didn't want to interrupt."

In other words, they saw my stupid tantrum. Now, at least, I could blame it on hormones. *Baby.* Oh my god, we were going to have a baby! *That's what you thought last time.* I mentally frowned as my hand automatically covered my abdomen, as if to protect it, and then I pushed the negative thought out of my head. I didn't want to worry right now. I wanted to bask in the little glint of hope today had brought. I knew it would be brief, so I'd enjoy this little escape from the shitty truth of reality while I could.

"The hot water heater's inside," Tristan said without

missing a beat. He headed for the stairs to the screened-in porch. "Let's see what's in there."

Vanessa and I followed the guys up, but we stayed out on the lanai when they went inside.

"So the baby's going to make it?" she asked. "I thought you'd be showing by now."

Both hands went to my stomach this time, and I tried to smile though more tears filled my eyes. Yep, my escape had been brief. "I lost the other one when I, uh, died and took a trip to the Otherworld."

She stopped in front of the patio chair and stared at me with brows raised. I shrugged.

"Just a brief visit with Mom and Rina . . . and others. They sent me back." I sat down in my old favorite chair, trying to blow off the whole thing. Wishing we could forget everything that had happened and celebrate the good, like the baby and finding each other again. But we all had too many questions.

Tristan and Owen came outside holding coffee mugs full of stale tasting water with a metallic aftertaste to it. At least it was something drinkable, though. I drained the entire cup, and Tristan handed me another.

"Hold on," Owen said as he took a seat next to Vanessa. "Start at the beginning."

Tristan and I exchanged a look, and then he began telling our story, leaving out the parts of our lengthy stays in Hell. Although we'd never actually discussed what we'd say if we ever found people, we were apparently on the same page that we didn't want to share the nitty-gritty with anyone. If we mentioned it at all, you could bet they'd want to know everything about our times in Hell, and those details were too personal, too shameful for comfort. They questioned us plenty about the Otherworld as it was.

"I didn't see anything really," I said, and I quickly moved on to the rest of the story. "We left Amadis Island and flew over Europe—"

"Whoa, whoa, wait a minute. You *flew?*" Vanessa asked.

"But we heard Dorian . . ." Owen's voice trailed off, and he looked away from me. So they knew Dorian had left for the Daemoni.

"We need to save him," I said, and we told them what the Demon said about Dorian being what Lucas needed to drop the veil and open the gates to Hell.

"So we need to find Dorian," Owen agreed.

"Wait. Go back," Vanessa said. "How did you fly over Europe and Africa if not with Dorian?"

Tristan and I exchanged another glance.

"They're going to find out sooner or later," he said, and I nodded.

Then we both pushed our chairs away from the table and stood up. We exposed our wings.

"Holy shit!" Vanessa spat. "I guess that explains the holes in the back of your vest."

"Sweet," Owen said with awe. They both stood up to inspect our wings, which we had to hold tightly against our bodies because of the confines of the space. "You can *fly?* What do they mean? And why are they dark? I thought Angel wings would be white."

"Obviously, we aren't Angels," I snapped. Owen frowned, and I immediately felt bad. It wasn't his fault the Angels were a pain in my ass. I hid my wings and sat back down with a frown. "We don't know what they mean. Nobody's explained. We had them when we came back from the Otherworld, though. I guess the Angels thought they'd be useful."

"And they are," Tristan said as his wings disappeared, and he also returned to his seat. He gave Owen one of those boyish can't-wait-to-show-you-my-new-toy grins. I rolled my eyes. "They're pretty badass. Wait until you see."

"Wow." Owen dropped into his chair, his eyes bouncing between the two of us. Everything I'd ever accomplished suddenly disappeared, and I once again returned to my teen years, when everyone stared at me for being a freak. "Wicked awesome!"

That seemed to be Owen's new phrase. Outdated a bit, but then again, the whole world seemed to have gone back in time.

"So what's the rest of the world like?" Vanessa asked. "We've seen some, but not as much as you."

"Dead," I said. "We found no one but Demons, Daemoni, and a few norms who think the Daemoni are gods. No plant life. No animals, except shifters. Nothing."

"Until just now." Tristan lifted his chin in the direction of the brush by the beach. We all turned to look. Tiny blotches of green stood out against all of the monotone gray.

Vanessa shook her head. "I knew your blood was good, but not that good."

"Yeah, well, it's not like I can revive the world," I said miserably. "So what good is it really?"

"It'll bring hope," Owen said. "We need that. So will that baby. In fact, just seeing you and Tristan alive will make a huge difference."

I frowned. "A difference with who?"

A corner of his mouth lifted in a crooked smile. "Everybody. You'll see."

Tristan leaned forward over the table. "There are others alive?"

Owen laughed. "Well, yeah, dude. What? Did you think you two were the last ones on Earth?"

His tone made the theory sound ridiculous.

"Pretty much, yeah," I admitted.

He shook his head. "Not even close. I mean, we don't have millions in our group or anything, but we're growing all the time as we find more survivors."

"*Seriously?*" My jaw dropped open. "But we've seen nothing . . . nobody . . ."

"You've been looking in the wrong places. We can show you whenever you're ready."

I sprang to my feet, knocking my chair over from the force and speed. "I'm ready!"

We didn't leave immediately. We rummaged through the beach house first, collecting towels, blankets, pillows, soaps and shampoos, and everything in the kitchen, packing it all into boxes Owen magically created from supplies around the house. He and Tristan drained the rest of the potable water from the hot water heater into smaller containers. Then we scavenged the other four abandoned houses on our little key. Hardly anyone knew these homes even existed, hidden from the highway and view of the general public, so nobody had come and looted them. Until now.

"Biggest jackpot yet. We're gonna be heroes," Owen said as he appraised the pile of goods we'd collected, including mattresses and other furniture. He rubbed his hands together, and then pulled them apart, opening a portal. "Oh, they'll be glad to see you, too, Alexis."

Vanessa lifted a stack of boxes into her arms and walked through the portal. Tristan, Owen, and I used our powers to raise the rest of the pile from the ground.

"Ladies first," Owen said when I didn't immediately move forward.

I hesitated, suddenly scared for who I'd find there—or wouldn't find. I needed to be prepared.

"Owen . . . your mom?"

He didn't answer me. My bottom lip trembled as I sucked in a jagged breath. "Blossom? Jax? Sheree? Heather and Sonya? Carlie?"

"Just go," he said. "You'll see."

I inhaled another cleansing breath to gather myself, and then pushed my pile through the portal before I followed it in. On the other side, I arrived at what appeared to be a garage door set into a hillside, once covered by trees and undergrowth that were now nothing but gray, scraggly branches wearing a dirty blanket of crusted snow. Vanessa stood next to the door, holding the boxes and tapping a foot. Not until I moved up closer to her did I notice the tiny wings and A.K. initials carved into the metal jamb, with a line of strange, but vaguely familiar symbols underneath. Owen ran over to us and tapped the symbols in a specific sequence, and I remembered where I'd seen them before—on the trunks Vanessa's body had once been delivered in.

"Hold on, before you go in," he said, turning toward us as the garage door began to open from the ground up. "Gotta decon us."

"What?" I asked.

"There's lots of nasty stuff out in the world," Owen said as he rubbed his palms together then held them out toward me. A wave of energy washed over me. "Don't want to bring it in to the more sensitive among us."

I opened my mouth with more questions as he did the same to Tristan, but snapped it closed when I looked behind Owen.

Behind him, just beyond the mouth of the doorway, a group of eight figures dressed in white haz-mat suits greeted us with the barrels of automatic weapons pointed at our heads, a long tunnel stretching out behind them. Tristan immediately threw his hands up, but not in surrender—in fighting stance —but as soon as the others saw Owen and Vanessa, their guns dropped. And when they saw Tristan and me, a few of them gasped. My eyes landed on these faces and recognized them immediately as a murmur spread over the group. Those three had been part of the group of hunters that had been on the university campus back in Georgetown. The rest of the faces behind the shields of their hoods were unfamiliar, though.

"Welcome to The Loft," Owen said, ushering us and the supplies inside. Once we were in, he waved his hand at the door, closing it behind us. Darkness swallowed us for a moment, and then the comparatively dim light of a single fluorescent bulb overcame the gloom.

Tristan looked up at the light. "Electrical power? I figured EMPs fried everything."

"They did," Owen said. "Everything above ground or unprotected, but not down here. I have to do my magic on everything we bring in to get it to work." He wiggled his fingers at us before gesturing at the group of people. "We've found more hunters, as you can see."

"You got that a little backwards there. We found you," a tall, middle-aged man with dark hair and a graying goatee corrected Owen.

"Yeah, yeah, and I'm lucky you didn't blow my head off when we suddenly appeared by your camp. As if you could." Owen clapped a hand on the man's broad shoulder. "Alexis, Tristan, this is Shawn. One of the original hunters, so the story goes. You can learn it later. I think there are others you might want to see first."

With a flick of his hand, he lifted the piles of supplies we'd brought and directed them in front of him.

"Hold up there just a minute," Shawn said as he and three others moved toward the four of us, each of them holding some kind of device with an antenna in their hands.

"I already—" Owen began, but he shut up as they moved closer and the small, rectangular boxes started chirping with a kind of clicking noise. At least, the ones closest to Tristan and me did.

"Radiation detectors," Tristan murmured in explanation.

"Not a good enough job!" Shawn barked at Owen. "You trying to kill us?"

Owen set the supplies down and turned toward Tristan and me. He did his decontamination spell again, on both of us and then on Vanessa and himself. The hunters swept the detectors over us again, and the little boxes remained quiet.

"Where you two been?" Shawn inquired as his dark gaze

studied us.

"Everywhere," I said. "Feels like it anyway."

"New York? Washington, D.C.?" he asked.

"And several other cities," Tristan said.

The man nodded. "Makes sense then. We've figured that only a few cities got the real nukes. The rest of us just got the dirty stuff."

Tristan lifted a brow as he stared at the man.

"I'll tell you everything later, bro," Owen said. "Come on."

Using magic, he lifted the supplies again. We left the hunters by the door, presumably to guard it, and followed Owen and Vanessa down the tunnel that had been carved into the rocky hill, big enough for a truck to drive through. The floor had the slightest bit of downward grade, and about every twenty feet, another fluorescent light flickered from above, the lamps joined together by a cord that snaked along the ceiling.

"Are you going to tell us where we are?" Tristan asked as we curved around a bend in the tunnel.

I wondered the same thing. Owen and Vanessa had made it sound like they had quite the encampment here, but the only mind signatures I sensed belonged to the hunters up by the door. I couldn't get a feel for anything ahead of us. The air had a cool, crisp feel to it against my cheeks and smelled like it filtered through something synthetic with only the faintest threads of damp earth and stone.

"It's an old limestone mine," Vanessa said.

"Actually, it's several mines joined together," Owen corrected.

"With an air filtration system and electricity," Tristan noted. "So mines that have been reclaimed and developed."

"Pretty much," Vanessa said.

"By who?" Tristan asked, skepticism and a bit of annoyance lacing his tone. I didn't blame him. I was growing impatient for answers, too.

"Almost there," Owen said, ignoring the question. "We have the place double-shielded to keep the Daemoni from finding us. An exterior shield and an interior one, like they do in Hades."

"That explains the lack of mind signatures," I muttered. "Who's 'we'?"

We rounded another bend, and on the other side, the tunnel widened to the left into a space big enough for three or four semi-trucks to park. Owen moved ahead of us, magically directing the pile of supplies into the open space. On the far side of the area was a wall with a door, a sign hanging over it that said *Intake*. Vanessa headed for the wooden door, and when Tristan and I passed into the space to follow, the air gave the slightest bit of waver around us. We'd passed through the barrier of the interior shield.

And hundreds of mind signatures popped into my brain.

I drew in a sharp breath when I picked up the one on the opposite side of the door. My legs sprang forward, and my feet moved with no command of my own. I practically bowled Vanessa over to get through that door.

"Hey," she snapped.

"Hey what?" another female asked. The blonde had been facing a whiteboard with colorful markings all over it and turned around to look at the doorway, apparently thinking Vanessa had snipped at her. Her jaw dropped open.

"Charlotte!" I squealed as I ran for her.

Her arms sprang around me at the same time I collided into her, holding onto her thin body as though it had given me life. She could never replace my mom, but she was the closest I had here in the Earthly realm, and seeing her alive definitely built on the hope for the possibility of a new life. A hope that had only sparked barely more than an hour ago.

"I thought you disowned me," Char said over my shoulder.

"What? Never! Why?" I squeezed her even tighter.

"I couldn't stop him. Dorian. I tried, but he's so powerful, Alexis . . ."

Her voice trailed off, and I closed my eyes. I'd never even thought to blame Charlotte, Blossom, or any of the others whom I'd asked to watch my son that fateful night. I knew they would have done anything and everything they could, so Dorian's escape would have been no fault of their own.

"I don't blame you," I said quietly. "Dorian . . . when he's determined to do something . . ."

"He's like his mother and Mimi," Charlotte finished.

I let out a small chuckle. "Yeah, exactly."

She grasped my upper arms and pulled away enough to give me a good once-over. When her gaze fell on my belly, she frowned.

"You lost her, too?" she asked.

I blinked back tears as I nodded, but at that exact time, the new life inside me fluttered.

"I'm pregnant again, though." I tried to sound chipper to lift the mood as I placed her hand over my stomach. The baby kicked again, but Charlotte didn't react, except to look at me with her brows raised expectantly. "I guess you can't feel it yet. I'm surprised I even can."

Tristan had felt the movement the first time, too, but maybe our heightened senses explained it. I could only be about two months along anyway, at the most.

"Well, that's good news," Charlotte said, pulling me into a hug again before we finally let go. She leaned against a table that was one of four set up in a U-shape, facing a wall of whiteboards. The room could have easily been a basic conference room or classroom, but the charts marking the whiteboards made it feel like a command post. "So what happened to you? Where have you been?"

"To Hell and back," I blurted, and Tristan gave me a sideways look. I flipped my hand in the air. "You know, that hell up there on the surface."

"How many times do you want to tell your story?" Vanessa asked, her arms crossed over her ample chest and her light-blond hair hanging over her shoulder as she cocked her head.

"Oh, of course," Charlotte said. "Let's get you processed so you can see everyone."

She went over to a row of long, low cardboard boxes full of four-by-six-inch index cards. She stopped at the first box in the row and fished out two cards from its front.

"I've been optimistic," she said, waving them in the air. My eye caught Tristan's name on one and mine on the other. "This is how we keep track of everybody and know who's here, when they go out and come back. Everyone gets their own card when they first arrive, but I made yours in the beginning. Normally, we ask new arrivals if they have any family or friends they've been searching for so we can see if maybe they're here, but I already know who you'd like to see."

While she used a pencil to jot down something on the cards and put them back, I reached my mind out across the sea of others putting off a signature in my range. A few hundred of them were scattered for what felt like a mile or two away, all underground. My heart did a little flip each time my mind landed on a familiar signature.

CHAPTER 16

"New arrivals?" asked a deep, male voice. I'd sensed the vampire's approach, and now he strode into the room—tall, barrel-chested and thick-armed, a ramrod spine, and his strawberry-blond hair cut short, screaming ex-military. He handed a folder to Char, his eyes barely flitting to Tristan and me at first. But then he did a double take, dropped to a knee, and bowed his head. His voice came out softly, embarrassed. "I'm sorry, ma'am, sir. I'm new to this."

"Please, don't worry," I said as I looked over at Char. A small smile played on her lips as she eyed the man. "You don't need to bow."

He stood up and then at attention, his hands clasped behind his back and his eyes staring at a point straightforward on the wall. "Sorry, ma'am."

"Relax, Brogan," Charlotte said, amusement still alit in her eyes. "I told you. She's not like that."

Brogan's green eyes cut over to Char and then down to me. I nodded and gave him a small, but encouraging smile. His body relaxed. If you called a slight drop in the shoulders relaxed.

"Alexis, Tristan, this is Brogan," Char introduced. "He used to own this place."

"*Used* to own it?" Tristan asked.

"I've given it over to the Amadis," Brogan said without the tiniest hint of remorse. "I'm not a good leader since being turned, and Charlotte . . . the Amadis can do more with it than I could on my own."

"What *is* this place?" I asked once again.

"We'll tell you on the way to get the others," Owen said as he moved for the door.

Char held up a walkie-talkie. "I could just call them."

"I thought we'd surprise them and give Alexis and Tristan a tour at the same time," Owen said. "They're probably starving, too."

"Definitely." Tristan rubbed his stomach with one hand while he slid his other arm over my shoulder. "We *all* need to eat."

I nodded. "Drink, eat . . . a bath and bed would be amazing."

"We can take care of the first two," Owen said from the doorway. "The other two . . . well, we have them, but they'll have to wait."

Char eyed us. "That's right. You two owe us a story before you get the good stuff. And it better be impressive, considering everything we've been through, looking for the both of you. I'll be here when you get back."

We followed Owen and Vanessa out the door and to the left, farther down the tunnel. About ten yards down, it opened up into another, much larger space. Owen pointed at the wall at the corner of the junction where a gridded, upside-down egg shape had been etched into the limestone.

"This place is huge and can be a maze if you don't know where you're going," he said. "So I put maps up. You can see how the entire space is divided into sections, each about the size of half a football field. We use the section numbers as part of addresses, so to speak."

He indicated the orange signs hanging from the ceiling next to the lights, each numbered and spaced about fifty yards apart. The map engraved into the limestone wall reflected the section "addresses" that appeared to be numbered like a hotel's rooms—the bottom row where we were was in the 100s and each row up the grid incremented by a hundred. The Intake area and the room where Charlotte was, at the bottom center of the egg, were Sections 104 and 105. *What happened to 101-103?* I was already confused.

"We pretty much have everything we need here," Owen continued as we walked past the section marked 106. This section and the next consisted of row after row of floor-to-ceiling metal shelves holding boxes and large plastic buckets and containers.

"Not everything," Vanessa muttered.

"No, I guess not everything," Owen admitted. "But enough to keep us surviving, as long as we're careful and keep working."

"All of this was already developed?" Tristan asked as he craned his neck to look around. "Before you found it?"

"How *did* you find it?" I asked. "And so quickly?"

"You're going to love this," Vanessa said, rolling her eyes. "Your friend James was holding out on us."

"He wasn't my friend," I snapped, my jaw tightening at the mention of the hunter's name. Tristan had tensed next to me, as well. "More like my punching bag."

Tristan relaxed and even smiled. Neither of us had fond feelings for James. He'd been one of the last people I'd trusted and been betrayed by as a teen, leading me to punching him in the nose when he called my mom a whore. Of all the people who could have shown up, he'd been with Carlie's group in D.C., one of the supernatural hunters.

"Well, he certainly won't be your friend now." Owen

turned to face us, walking backwards. "He'd known about this place all along. Shelter, food, a water supply, weapons . . ."

"*What?*" I demanded. "*How?* And he never mentioned it to Carlie?"

"Claims he thought it was too far away for the group to reach safely," Vanessa said. "Which, you have to admit, it probably was for the norms. We're in Kansas, of all places. James didn't know about Owen's portals, and probably wouldn't have used one anyway because of his whole issue with the supernatural." She snorted. "So it would have taken weeks for them to get here from D.C. They would have never made it with the gangs and Daemoni out there."

"When he had no choice, James finally spilled, though. He knew about the place because Brogan's his uncle," Owen said. "Although Brogan won't have much to do with him anymore. He agrees with the rest of us that James is an ass."

"So who is Brogan exactly, and what is this place?" I asked one more time.

Owen stopped walking, and so did the rest of us. We stood among shelves stacked with fifty-gallon plastic boxes marked "FLOUR" and "RICE."

"Brogan was a general in the Army, and when he retired, he started The Prepper's Stash House," Owen started.

"*The* Prepper's Stash House?" Tristan interrupted as though he knew what that was.

"The world's biggest supplier of survival gear and know-how," Vanessa confirmed, sounding as though she quoted a motto. It sounded vaguely familiar to me.

"Supplier of the goods *and* the knowledge," Owen added. "Said he saw the writing on the wall when he was in the military and knew something was coming down, so he wanted to help people learn how to survive the end of the world as we'd known it. He had no idea supernatural creatures would bring it on, though, so he'd never expected to be turned."

"James thought Brogan was dead, so he took off and left

him." Disgust colored Vanessa's tone. I thought she might despise James more than I did. "Brogan got attacked by a Kansas City nest and woke up as a baby vamp with nobody around to help. James brought us here at the last minute when he saw the mushroom clouds, and we had to subdue Brogan right away. He missed out on the first week of the apocalypse while being converted."

And now I fully understood Vanessa's contempt for James. His betrayal of my trust when we were teenagers was nothing compared to what he'd done when shit hit the fan. What a coward.

"So Brogan's one of those doomsday prepper guys?" I asked. "Like the ones everyone used to make fun of?"

"The king of them," Owen said. "Started his business from scratch and made himself millions, all of which he used to develop this place."

"And what, exactly, is this place?" I asked once again. "His bugout bunker?"

"Oh, it's much more than a bunker," Vanessa said. "I hate to admit it, but even I was impressed when I first saw it."

"Because this *is* The Prepper's Stash House. And more." Owen lifted his hand to indicate the rows of shelves we'd stopped next to. "Food, first aid, equipment, filled water tanks . . . His company's whole inventory was stored down here, enough to keep him and several hundred people going for many months—years if we can keep supplementing it."

"But that's not all," Vanessa said as she began walking again. I started to feel like we were in a late-night TV infomercial. The kind that didn't exist anymore. "This was also his training facility, where people would come on their vacations to learn all kinds of survival and preparations for the worst. So he had a lot of the facilities and space already here for that."

"People spent their vacations *here*? Underground?" I shuddered at the thought. At least this place was large and somewhat illuminated, rather than small like the rock island or pitch-black with screaming souls, like Hell. But still—not exactly my first choice of a vacation destination.

"Crazy prepper people, huh?" Owen asked, sarcasm lacing his tone.

"I'd say pretty smart, considering," Tristan said. He took my hand and gave it a squeeze. "Means there are a lot of people out there who were prepared for the worst."

I didn't reply. How many of them really expected how bad the worst would be? Had they truly been prepared? Considering the fall of religion and the declining number of people who believed in God before everything went to Hell, I highly doubted they had been. But maybe, just maybe, there were some who'd managed to survive anyway.

We followed Vanessa and Owen around the corner of Section 107 with its rows of shelves, and fifty yards farther, we came to a junction in the road that made me mutter "whoa." Tristan let out a low whistle.

"It's *huuuuge*," Owen said, drawing out the word. With the amount of pride in his voice, you'd think he'd built the place himself. "Over three million square feet, with air filtration, electricity, and some of it even has basic plumbing. Dude, we couldn't have *wished* for a better place. It's a gift from the Angels."

The lane we stood on stretched out in front of us for at least a quarter-mile, the end disappearing into the edges of darkness. The crossroad, for lack of another word, intersected ours right in front of us, going a few hundred yards to my left and a couple to my right. The ceiling stood at least twenty-five, maybe thirty feet high, lined with neat rows of pipes, cords, and fluorescent lights. Only every third light worked, however, the others empty of bulbs, presumably for conservation. After all, who knew when light bulbs would be manufactured again?

Owen pointed to our left, where faint gunshots sounded

like pops. "There's a huge area here for various kinds of training. A gun range, an archery range, a gym with machines and weight room, classrooms, etcetera, etcetera. But this way —" he turned to our right "—we have the Armory, Medical, Engineering, and a Conversion Center."

I tilted my head to look down the hallway. "Conversion Center?"

"Exactly the kind you're thinking," Owen said. "I promised you food, though, so we'll come back if you want to check it out."

He led us down the road between limestone pillars that were at least ten feet wide and thirty feet long. Between each support, cinder blocks had been stacked to create walls to block off the different sections. The smell of freshly baked bread and some kind of meat wafted down the hallway, making my mouth water. But that wasn't what had me nearly running in its direction. I could barely contain myself when I found the two mind signatures.

I jogged through a huge, open section, winding around mismatched tables and pushing chairs out of my way, past another pillar, and through a swinging door in a cinderblock wall. A dozen or more people hustled and bustled around the kitchen, preparing large vats of food. I continued to the back, where three industrial ovens lined the wall and found a slight woman with big boobs and a bun of blond hair piled on her head pulling out a tray of bread loaves. She almost dropped them when she saw me.

"Alexis!" She squealed, practically throwing the tray and the oven mitts at the counter and running to me. She wiped her hands on her short, black cotton dress before throwing her arms around my neck. "Oh my god! You're alive! Are you okay? Where have you been? Everybody's been worried sick, looking for you guys. I'm so glad you're here! And I'm so sorry about Dorian. One second he was with us, and the next he was gone. We thought he just went to the bathroom, but . . .

I'm so sorry, Alexis, I really am. I was so devastated, and I know you'll never be able to forgive me—"

"It wasn't your fault, Blossom," I said without letting her go. "He was apparently hell-bent on leaving. He's on a mission . . ." I couldn't get into it now. "Just know that there's nothing to forgive you for. You did nothing wrong."

"I don't deserve it, but thank you." Her whole body relaxed in my arms, and the tone of her voice lifted. "This place is amazing, and we keep doing more with it. Did Owen and Vanessa tell you? I guess you saw Charlotte already. Hey, what about the baby? Is she okay? You don't look big . . ."

She finally trailed off when she pulled away from me and looked me over. Her babbling didn't bother me, though. I'd missed it so much. Even before the worst happened, she hadn't been her normal ninety-miles-a-minute talkative self. I could already tell that being here, especially in the kitchen, was what she needed.

"Hey, hands off! That's *my*—Princess?" a deep voice with an Australian accent asked from behind us as Tristan and Blossom hugged.

I spun around to find a stout, bald man with a large box of flour on his shoulder. "Jax!"

Other people around the kitchen gave us a quizzical look. A few recognized Tristan and me, and I knew their faces from Carlie's group, but others must have been newcomers who'd joined them.

"Are you hungry?" Blossom asked, and she must have seen the answer written all over my face. "Of course you are. Go find a seat out there so we can let these guys work, and I'll get you some food and bring it out. Oh my gosh, I can't believe you're really here!"

She gave me one more hug before shooing us out the swinging door and into the dining room. Right by the door to the kitchen, flanked by another door on the far side, was a serving bar. As we weaved our way through the path of picnic tables, plastic patio tables, round wooden tables, and cafeteria folding tables, I could see around the corner of the kitchen, where there was another set of doors with a serving bar between them, allowing two food stations for a large crowd. Mismatched plates were stacked at the end of both bars, but the centers, where trays of food should sit, were empty. I had no idea the time of day, but it must not have been a normal mealtime. Except for a few people sitting at small, round tables on the outer fringe of the dining area, we had the place to ourselves. Owen led us to one of the larger, cafeteria-style tables.

"How many people are here, Scarecrow?" Tristan asked as he lifted his long legs over the bench seat. I joined him as Owen and Vanessa sat across from us.

"Mom said 438 as of yesterday . . . 440 now. And a half." He gave us a grin. "And we still have tons of space. We could easily take double or even triple that as long as we can keep the food and water supplies going."

"One nice thing about being a vamp," Vanessa said. "We're not high maintenance."

Owen cocked his head and lifted a brow.

"What?" she asked. "Blood is a renewable and sustainable resource . . . as long as we don't kill the supplier."

Owen snorted. "Anyway, as I was saying . . . we use magic to keep some things operating, but there's not a lot we can do about food and water. Not when it's as bad as everything is up top. There's a huge garden area where Brogan had already started growing vegetables and grains, but that won't be sustainable for a while."

"I sense a lot of Amadis among the norms," I said. "At least a quarter of the people here?"

Owen grinned. "They'll want to know you're here, if they don't already. Thought we'd keep it on the down low until you're fed and cleaned up."

"As if we can't smell you," a familiar female voice said from behind me, and I thought my face would crack when I spun around on the bench.

I'd sensed her mind signature before from the area Owen had called Medical, and I'd been too afraid to explore it further. I was sure she was still laid up in bed, barely holding on to life, as she had been the last time I'd seen her. I'd wanted to eat, rest, and mentally prepare myself for seeing her again. But here Sheree was, up on her two feet, her tall, thin body hobbling between the tables, using a crutch under her right arm for support. Tears filled my eyes as I stood to greet her. I wanted to give her a bear hug, but was afraid I'd hurt her.

"I'm okay," she said with her signature warm smile that exposed almost all of her teeth and lit up her brown eyes. "My leg doesn't work quite the same as it used to, when I'm human anyway. It's annoying, but that's all. Fit as a tiger, otherwise."

We embraced in a tight hug before she joined us at the table. Blossom and Jax brought out soup and bread, and Tristan and I had barely taken our first bite when the questions started flying again.

"I think Char plans on all of us meeting at that Intake room," I said around a mouthful of delicious, warm bread. "There's lots to talk about. Tristan and I aren't done fighting. We have to stop Lucas . . . and Dorian."

"Of course we aren't done fighting," Owen said. "As long as the Daemoni walk freely, we're still at war."

I paused with the spoon midway to my mouth and looked around. Everyone nodded in agreement with Owen's declaration. I hadn't expected this after seeing them so happy with being here in The Loft. Why would they want to leave the security of this place to fight an unwinnable war? Tristan and I had Dorian to worry about, otherwise, I couldn't say I'd be so willing to go to battle again. Not when there were no other souls left worth saving.

"We haven't stopped fighting," Sheree said. "Which means,

I better get back to work. I just wanted to come say 'hi' for a minute, but we can catch up later."

"Where's work?" I asked as she pushed herself up to her feet.

Before she could answer me, a loud alarm buzzed throughout the cavern. Sheree's head snapped up.

"Yep, definitely got to go," she said.

I jumped to my feet and followed after her. "Where? What's going on?"

The walkie-talkie hanging on her jeans-clad hip came to life with Charlotte's voice. "Sheree, the group's returned, bringing two in for you. Do you need help? Over."

She slowed her fast-paced hobble, unclipped the device, and held it to her mouth. "Ten-four. We should be fine, thanks. Over."

"Two what?" I asked as we hurried down the passageway. We passed the Medical sections, and then hung a left. At that moment, Charlotte turned into the corridor, using her magic to guide two unconscious people—a red-headed man and an Asian woman—down the way, toward a door in the far corner of the entire space. Silver blades protruded from their chests, at their hearts. Vampires.

"Conversions, of course," Sheree answered as we followed Char through the door marked, well, Conversion Center. "That's my work."

My mouth fell slightly open as I looked around the space that took up a whole section, some areas blocked off with shower curtains and sheets turned into curtains. Three beds in one corner were occupied with what I sensed as an Amadis shifter and two vampires. The energy coming off of them told me they were newly converted. Two Amadis vampires sat with them, their discussion topic one that was always covered during faith healing. My heart and soul dared to lift just a little bit with more hope.

"Do you get a lot?" I asked.

Sheree shrugged as she picked up a clipboard and handed it to me. "A few a week."

"Really?"

"There were a lot of people turned against their will, Alexis. Sonya and Alys go out with the hunters, and they're finding them, slowly but surely."

She hurried off to help Charlotte get the two newcomers situated. Blossom jogged into the room, followed by another Amadis mage.

"Kitchen's good," Blossom said as she rushed over to Sheree's side. "I can help."

I glanced down at the clipboard that contained a chart of names listed with their species, intake dates, location found, and release dates. I flipped through three pages of them, totaling ninety-five newly converted Amadis. That was nearly as many Amadis as I'd sensed in the entire compound, which meant we hadn't found many of our own, but those here were successfully helping others. Increasing our numbers.

Building our army.

Huh. Leaving that thought for later contemplation, I set the clipboard onto the makeshift desk—a piece of plywood sitting across two stacks of buckets—from where Sheree had grabbed it. Charlotte and Blossom had already secured the vamps to two beds with silver handcuffs, ankle chains, and magic, and they were about to remove the blades from the vampires' hearts, so I sauntered a few steps closer. I wasn't sure I had enough power in me to help. When they slid the blades out of the hearts, the vamps awakened, and both of them jerked against the magical constraints, lifting their heads and shoulders off the beds. Their glowing red eyes immediately landed on me. Evil energy surged into the air.

The room fell dark.

"She's ours," they both hissed, only their voices didn't sound right. "*OURS.*"

No, they sounded like Satan. Satan's voice yelling at me,

calling for me, sending his Demons after me, and I was suddenly back in the blackness of Hell. The hospital-like area of the Conversion Center had disappeared, and I stood by the lake of fire, hands grabbing at my ankles, my calves, my thighs . . . pulling me down.

"*Alexis.*" The voice came from far away.

CHAPTER 17

A jolt in my stomach made me gasp, and for a moment, I thought the burning souls had me. But another twinge brought me back to the Conversion Center, my heart racing and my palms sweating. I blinked. Everybody was focused on the two vampires. Nobody seemed to have noticed my momentary freak-out that I could only blame on the demonic energy in the room. The little being inside me was going berserk, making my stomach clench and turn.

"Alexis," Vanessa said again. She'd been the one calling me a moment ago.

"Bathroom?" I choked.

"This way." She waved me through the door.

I followed her out and down a corridor that passed on the other side of the Medical sections from the main road. As we came closer to the kitchen again, approaching it from a different angle than before, my stomach actually settled rather than worsened from the smells. I still hurried through the Women's door, just in case, past a bank of six sinks with mirrors over them, and down a short passage with a line of six showers on one side and six doors to toilets on the other. By the time I reached one safely, the urge to puke had subsided, although the smell in the room didn't help.

As I leaned against the bathroom wall to slow my breaths and heart rate, I considered how it actually hadn't been an urge to vomit that had overcome me. Baby Girl—she *had* to be a girl—inside me had reacted to the Daemoni's evil energy just like I had. What had me worried was that I didn't know if she responded to it in the same way I had, with fear and repulsion, or if it had beckoned to her.

"Are you okay?" Vanessa asked from the sink area.

"Um . . . yeah, fine." I exhaled a long breath as I stepped out of the bathroom stall. I gave her the best smile I could manage. "False alarm."

She eyed me with her icy blues. "Good thing. You can't afford to lose the food you just ate."

I nodded as I walked up to a sink and turned the water on. Or tried to—nothing came out.

"This one." Vanessa tapped the porcelain edge of the one closest to her. "There are all kinds of limits on water here. You get two showers a week on your designated days. All of the sinks' taps are only open in the morning for quick hand, face, and teeth washings. The rest of the time, water's only supplied to this one, and the faucets only let so much out before they shut off for five minutes."

The last point proved itself when the faucet I'd been washing my hands under suddenly went dry. I rubbed the water on my hands over my face before making sure the handle was turned to the off position.

"And one of their number one rules for more reasons than one: If it's yellow, let it mellow. If it's brown, flush it down." She wrinkled her nose. "Disgusting."

My nose lifted to match her expression. "That explains the smell."

"It's awful. So glad I don't have to worry about that."

"So how do you and the others get blood?" I asked as we

left the bathroom, and she led me back toward the dining area where Tristan and Owen still sat at the large table in the middle of the vast space. I'd probably help Sheree later, but at the moment, I didn't think my body or soul could handle it. Especially my soul. An ironic thought of how I myself needed faith healing tried to niggle its way in, but I pushed it out as I listened to Vanessa.

"I've been out a lot with Owen, so he's been my supplier." She gave me a little grin. "My favorite, of course. Well, besides you or Tristan. But we do have a blood bank here, over there with suppliers of other goods." She nodded her head sideways, toward our right.

"Like a marketplace? With money?"

"No money. Everything's based on need and barter right now. All on the honor system. If we grow much bigger, though, we'll need to figure out something better."

"*We?*" I asked.

"Charlotte pretty much runs the place, but we all help her with big decisions like that. Your council at work."

Huh. I would have never thought . . .

"Show me everything," I commanded.

Vanessa and Owen started us back in the kitchen, this time introducing Tristan and me to the people they knew, who in turn introduced us to the others. Most were norms, besides Blossom and two other witches who directed the rest of the staff. Jax was nowhere to be seen.

"Jax oversees deliveries," Owen explained when I asked about him after we left the kitchen through a door that faced the same bathroom I'd been in minutes ago. "We've decided to save as much power as possible, so we don't use the golf carts and forklifts Brogan has stored up front unless necessary. Don't need them as long as we have mages, vamps, and shifters to do the heavy lifting."

Next to the bathroom was the marketplace Vanessa had just been telling me about, looking like a makeshift flea market. The section blocked off for it was quite large, although most of it remained empty. A few stands were clustered together alongside the dining area, made up of plastic tables and cardboard boxes with sheets and blankets hanging between them to separate the "shops." The blood bank was here, along with a kiosk with dried herbs and other reagents for the mages. A witch and several older, Norman women sat in a larger booth, busy at work mending clothing and blankets or knitting and hand-sewing new pieces.

"As long as we can find them material, they'll work all kinds of magic," Owen said as he pulled out a couple balls of yarn from the inside of his jacket and tossed it into the basket next to one of the women. She gave him a wrinkled smile, adoration filling her gray eyes.

"Explains why you raided the yarn basket at the house next to ours," Tristan said. I hadn't even noticed Owen had done that when we'd been back at the Keys, looting the homes. "I thought you'd taken up a new hobby."

"Har-har," Owen retorted.

"This young man here saved my granddaughters' lives," the woman said to Tristan and me. "I'll make him anything he ever wants."

"How old are they?" I asked her.

"One's six and one's eight. They're the sweetest things. Their mama and daddy had gone out for food when the big bombs dropped. We ran for the old fallout shelter my husband, God rest his soul, had put in our backyard back in the day. My son and his wife never came home. We'd eaten our last bite of food two days before this young man came along."

"Oh, wow." I sighed, my heart hurting for what they'd had to go through.

"They're doing as good as can be expected," the grandma said. "They're over at the school with the other kids, many of them in the same situation—one or both parents gone. But at least the young'uns made it. Gives us hope for a future." She shifted one of her knitting needles into the other hand and reached out to lay her palm on my belly. "You're bringing us more hope, child."

My brows furrowed. How did she know?

She grinned. "Word travels fast around here."

She reached for my hand now and gave it a squeeze. I noticed she had an A.K.'s Angels tattoo on her inner wrist. Her smile widened, showing a capped tooth toward the back.

"I'm a new fan. Once I learnt how so many of these folk found each other, I was curious. Especially when they said they learnt how to survive because of your books. You bet I'll be making my girls read them as soon as they're old enough."

I didn't know what to say except thank you. The shocks to my system were never-ending today.

We let her return to her work, and Owen and Vanessa stopped us by the Medical section, where Carlie and another woman doctor ran the hospital that had a surprisingly decent setup, if not all of the equipment they needed.

"This was the residential area where Brogan had originally bunked his guests," Carlie explained after we greeted each other with excited hugs and exchanged the two-minute versions of our stories. "The larger rooms he used to reserve for families are what we use for surgery and admin. The single rooms allow the patients privacy."

"I guess you get a lot?" I asked.

She nodded. "Enough. We require all of the humans to spend a few days in quarantine when they first arrive to make sure they don't bring in anything contagious. The last thing we need is a virus. And we constantly have hunters in here." She made a face. "I had to stitch up James' ass once after he'd sliced it open on a broken window. It was gross."

"Ugh." I suppressed a shudder. "I'm so sorry."

She shrugged. "Having no anesthetic at the time made it better."

I shook my head and laughed. "You're a little evil, aren't you?"

"Only to assholes."

Once we left the Medical area, we walked around the dining space and entered the School Zone. Like the marketplace, the section was divided with cardboard and sheet walls, each with kids surrounding plastic tables and boxes. In the room with the children about Dorian's age and a little younger, a familiar face greeted us.

"Alexis! Tristan!" Heather jumped up from her four charges and rushed over to hug us. She looked around, as though searching for someone else, and frowned. Her voice came out in a whisper. "I'd hoped the rumor wasn't true about Dorian. I'm so sorry."

"We'll get him back," I said firmly while the backs of my eyeballs pricked.

"I'm glad you're both okay." She looked over her shoulder at the two girls and two boys at her table. "I better get back to work."

"Teacher, huh?" I asked, forcing a smile. "It seems fitting."

She let out a small chuckle. "I guess. I do my best. It's three parts teaching and one part grief counseling, though. These poor kids . . . but at least they're still alive. We have hope."

I bit my tongue, holding back a sigh while we checked out the rest of the school. We found Teah and Teal, the cousins who'd been with Heather and Sonya in Cape Heron, teaching other classes. I counted forty-two children between the ages of three and fifteen. Vanessa said anyone over fifteen was put to work, and there were a handful of toddlers and infants who stayed with their parents. Sure, seeing that children had survived gave me the tiniest bit of hope, but compared to how many had died . . . I couldn't accept the optimism everyone here seemed to embrace. The events of the day had improved my outlook, certainly, but there was a reason I'd woken this morning with a heavy heart.

"This is the part you'll both love," Owen said as he led us to the area marked Training. At least three-quarters of the mind signatures in the entire place were here. "What Brogan had built before."

"Except this part. This is the boring stuff," Vanessa whispered as we passed by the sections closest to the rest of the compound. Shelves of books and photo albums lined the cinderblock wall that separated the Training section from the dining area. "Horticulture and plant identification, which I guess is necessary for the norms so they don't eat poisonous plants, although nothing grows anyway, so I don't know if it really matters."

"Also so they can learn how to grow food," Owen added, apparently hearing her, and Vanessa shrugged. "Brogan collected a huge library of information for everything from first aid—" he pointed to a space where a dummy lay on a card table surrounded by gauze, dental floss, and other items "—to shoemaking to making your own batteries to welding. There are classrooms over there to our right for when something special comes up. Some of the best stuff is how to recycle the junk we scavenge and create or repurpose useful items. Without magic!"

"Yeah, who knew," Vanessa muttered teasingly.

We paused by the gym area, where several people worked out on treadmills, stair-climbers, and stationary bikes or lifted weights, before heading toward the back. The first insanely huge room we entered, the size of four footballs fields and walled off on all sides, was the archery range. People of all ages, from sixteen up to sixty, men and women both, target practiced with compound bows and crossbows. An instructor walked behind them, adjusting stances and holds for better aiming. After that, we peeked into the shooting range, which was even bigger than the archery range and where the walls were padded to absorb a lot of the sound, but it was still necessary to wear earmuffs.

"I keep a muffle spell on that place," Owen said once we left. "Otherwise, we'd all be suffering migraines."

"Do they have silver bullets?" Tristan asked.

"Not for practice, but in the armory. That's why we scavenge anything silver. In the back is a machine shop with a forge." He stopped in front of a large, open section covered in mats. "I expect you'll be spending some time here."

Dozens of paired-off people practiced martial arts, kickboxing, wrestling, and boxing. Brogan walked among them, stopping now and then to correct someone's form.

"He has a strict training regimen," Owen said. "He's pretty good, and Mum helped for a while, but she's been too busy with managing everything and conversions. I think you, Tristan, can do even better."

Tristan crossed his arms over his chest as he watched and nodded. "They're not doing badly, but they can do better with a little help. Do they all train in weapons, too?"

"Of course," Vanessa said before she strode off to show a woman how to angle her hand to hit her partner's weak spot dead-on.

"Who do they plan on fighting?" I asked. "They can't even go above ground, can they?"

"The air's clean in some places," Owen said. "We'll explain when we can all sit down together. There's a lot to figure out."

"I know there's a lot we need to discuss," I agreed, and I lifted my arms to indicate the norms surrounding us. "But these people aren't a part of it. They need to stay down here, where it's safe. Because they really may be the only hope for the future."

"They want to fight, Alexis," Owen said. "Look at them. Look at the determination on their faces."

"They can't fight our war," I protested.

"It's not just your war," Brogan said, suddenly by my side.

"These people have lost everything. Their homes. Their businesses. Their ways of life . . . Their loved ones. They—all of us—have just as much vested in the war against those Daemoni sons-of-bitches as you do, if not more. You won't be able to stop us from fighting with you."

I tried to push my hand through my hair, but it got caught up in the ratty tangles. "Those people *can't* fight. They're human. There's no way they can defeat the Daemoni."

"You know that's not true," Tristan said. "If we can train them properly, they'll be prepared."

I stared at him for a long moment before shaking my head. "No way. We've already lost enough humans *and* Amadis. What are we going to do? Take the few hundred here to face the hundreds of thousands of Daemoni and their Demons? I don't think so. You and I have one more battle to fight for our son, Tristan, but we're *not* leading these people into another war that can't be won."

"Ye of little faith," Owen said as he clipped his walkie-talkie to his belt. I'd only noticed him talking into it out of the corner of my eye. "It's not just us here. There are people and Amadis around the world."

I rolled my eyes and snorted. "Bullshit. Tristan and I have been around this world. You're the first and only souls we've found that don't belong to the Daemoni and their *volunteer* servants."

"You're wrong, Alexis. Let's go see Mum, and you'll see proof. A messenger has just arrived."

As we headed back to the front of The Loft, I reached my mind out to find the new arrival's signature in the same room we'd been in earlier at the Intake section, and I frowned. Robin, the were-falcon whom I'd kicked off my council, was with Char.

"Ms. Alexis?" Robin's greeting was a mix between a chirp and a squawk when I walked through the doorway, and she immediately dropped to a knee with her head bowed.

I entered the command post farther and tilted my head as I studied her. Was she kissing up to me now? She'd been one of Rina's council members to put Tristan on trial, and then when I took reign, she hadn't exactly been supportive. She'd questioned my methods and abilities too much for me to feel comfortable with keeping her on my council, so I'd dismissed her, along with a handful of others. And now here she was, bowing to me. I wasn't sure what to make of it. Her thoughts matched her actions, but she'd expect me to check them and would prepare for it, so that didn't mean much.

"Please, get up." I circled around her to Charlotte's side.

Robin rose to her feet, but rather than look down her long nose at me with her round, beady eyes as she usually did, she gazed at the floor.

"I'm very happy you're safe and sound," she said quietly. She paused, and then, as if she'd been waiting to say her next words for a long time, they came bursting out of her. "And I apologize greatly for my actions before. I should have believed in you."

I let out a harrumph. "But you were right. I failed."

Her head snapped up, and she looked at me with widened eyes. "You saved the Norman soldiers. You did exactly what you said you'd do. What needed to be done to protect the Normans."

"Protect them? They were far from protected. And I haven't stopped Lucas and the Daemoni. Human lives have been lost. Amadis, too. The world is only worse."

"Well, the war continues, but that's how war is. It must get worse before it can get better. You told us that. And you will have victory in the end."

I narrowed my eyes and gnawed on my bottom lip. *Who was this woman, and what happened to the real Robin?* I would have asked if I hadn't been able to feel her very authentic mind signature. She was definitely Robin the were-falcon who'd once served on the Amadis Council.

"So you have news for us?" Owen asked as he turned one of the plastic chairs around and sat on it backwards, propping his elbows on the table in front of him.

"Wait another minute before you start," Char said to Robin. "We're not all here. I've sent relief for Blossom and Sheree so they can join us."

A few minutes later, my team had assembled around the U-shape of conference tables in the command post. *My Team.* Just thinking the two words lifted my heart after so many weeks of thinking I'd never see them again. Of thinking they were dead. This room, with its cheap, plastic furniture and whiteboard-covered walls, was a far cry from the grand room of the Amadis Council Hall, but we were all here. Well, except Solomon and Bree. But the rest of us were alive, and that's all that mattered now. Tristan and I stood with Charlotte and Robin at the front of the room, and I looked at each of their faces—Blossom and Jax, Vanessa and Owen, Sheree—and smiled, fighting tears of happiness to have us reunited.

"Stupid hormones," I muttered as everyone watched me wipe my eyes, earning a chuckle.

"So have you found anything since the last time you were here?" Charlotte asked Robin, whose gaze had jumped to my midsection. Tristan and I quickly moved over to lean against the front of the closest table so she could face us all at once, and I self-consciously wrapped my arms over my belly.

"I've found several groups of Normans and Amadis spread throughout the United States," she announced, and I gasped.

"Alive and . . . normal?" Tristan asked. "Not possessed or serving the Daemoni?"

"Not including them, yes," Robin answered. "There are many of those, but there are also pockets of people in hiding, just like those here. Many are in underground, sealed-off compounds like this. In some areas, they've been able to go to the surface for short amounts of time, so I was able to find them. A lot have Amadis mages keeping them cloaked and protected."

"Wow," I breathed, but then the air caught in my lungs. "Dorian?"

The word came out as a demand, and Robin bit her thin lip. I wanted to shake her.

"Have you seen Dorian anywhere?" Tristan asked.

She shook her head. "I thought he . . ." She looked at Char, Owen, and Vanessa before her gaze came back to us. "He left . . . right?"

"We don't know where he is," I said. "There's no evidence he's crossed over to them yet, but we found no trace of him, either."

"I did overhear a couple of Daemoni say he was with a fae. I don't know where, though. They also said Lucas is waiting on Dorian, because he can't force his decision. So there's nothing for the Daemoni to do right now, but enjoy their victory. And that's exactly what they seem to be doing."

A fae? Was that what the matriarchs had meant by a neutral party? Wasn't that just dandy. We could only hope the fae was actually unbiased and didn't have Daemoni leanings. Maybe Dorian would even fall for the faerie magic and never want to leave. If only that were a real possibility, but I highly doubted it. Too much was at stake. He was probably with a male fae for that very reason, but at least he wasn't with Lucas. Yet. At least he was alive. As far as we knew.

I sighed, fighting back more tears. Damn hormones. "How many people? Norman and Amadis?"

Robin lifted her broad shoulder in a shrug. "It's hard to say. I've found a few larger groups like this one that are a mix of Norman and Amadis. And a lot more smaller ones that are one or the other. The ones with Amadis who can spend longer times on the surface say their groups grow every day as they find new survivors or Daemoni who want to convert."

I straightened up at this. "Where are they? Nearby?"

"A couple smaller ones are, but the big ones are off in the mountains. In what was Colorado and Arizona. The Arizona group has a whole network of connected caves. They're pretty established and constantly growing."

"Really?" *Huh.*

She shifted her weight on her bird-thin, jeans-clad legs, and nodded. "I'm sure there are many, many more. It's difficult to scope areas out very well when you're a target as the only bird in the sky, so I know I've missed some. And I've flown as far south as Mexico, where another Amadis were-falcon has been searching. There are more survivors in Central and South America, which means there must be groups all over the world."

Now I shook my head, and my shoulders dropped as I slumped against the table again. "Tristan and I have been all over Europe and Africa. There was nobody except Daemoni."

"Are you sure?" Robin asked. "They're hiding very well, for good reason. Deep underground."

I tapped my finger against my temple. "We searched with more than our eyes and ears. I found nobody's thoughts. Until Owen and Vanessa found us, I truly thought Tristan and I were the only ones left on Earth."

"But if they're shielded and cloaked, you can't hear their minds, right?" Owen asked. "Did you detect the hundreds of people here?"

"Well . . . no," I admitted as I rubbed my chin. "But you and Charlotte put up the strongest cloaks. And not all of the groups have Amadis at all, right, Robin?"

"A few don't. The really tiny clusters of Normans. But the Amadis are out looking for them and bringing them to the larger groups that *are* cloaked."

"So how many are we talking about? What are the estimates for survivors?" Tristan asked.

Robin squinted her little eyes as she appeared to be doing

math in her head. "At least a couple million Normans in the Americas. So probably a hundred million worldwide?"

I gasped audibly. "You really think so?"

I wasn't sure how I felt about this news. That was a hundred million more than I'd thought had survived, even when Mom, Rina, and Cassandra had tried to convince me otherwise, but that meant over six billion lives had been lost. All in a matter of weeks.

"Considering what I've found so far, and what others have found, yes, I do," Robin answered me.

"Does that include the Daemoni's slaves and the norms they'd put in the farms?" Vanessa asked.

"Farms?" Robin asked. "You mean the concentration camps?"

Vanessa nodded. "They're using those people for food. Harvesting them."

Robin scowled and shook her head. "No, it doesn't. But I think tens of thousands of those Normans are alive, too."

"And if the Daemoni were truly farming them, there might be many pregnant women under their control," Blossom said.

"*Seriously?*" I asked. *Wow. Just wow.* Where was everyone, though?

Tristan rubbed his hand over the back of his head. "It makes sense. There are dozens of government compounds around the world that are nuclear safe. They each hold thousands of people."

"We checked those, though," I reminded him.

"We checked the ones I knew about in Europe," he corrected me. "I'm sure there are more there, as well as around the world. Now granted, most are probably occupied by the Daemoni since Lucas's fingers were in all of the governments, but then think about the many private shelters like this one."

"Brogan said he had over one-and-a-half million

customers," Char said. "Those are people who were prepared for catastrophes."

Could this really be true? Were there still people whose souls were worth fighting for? And babies' souls, too?

Of course, I'd known about the Norman farms, so I knew the Daemoni had kept some norms somewhere. Victor had told us they were nice and safe—from the bombs, anyway. I'd figured they were the ones serving the Daemoni voluntarily now, but I hadn't considered the possibility of babies. Of another generation who'd either be controlled by the Daemoni . . . or could rebuild this world.

Their future was possibly up to us. This news changed everything.

CHAPTER 18

"What about Amadis? How many survived?" Tristan asked, and my eyes flew to Robin.

She didn't hesitate to count this time. "A few thousand. Maybe ten or twelve?"

"And Daemoni?" Sheree asked.

"All of them," Vanessa muttered. "They knew it was coming."

Robin nodded. "They were prepared. Their numbers are about the same as they were."

"Over half a million then," Tristan said, and my heart sank. "And they have the Demons now, too."

"More Demons than Daemoni," Robin reported. "Most of them are hiding in Norman skins."

Now my heart fell through the floor. All hope that had been building in the last several hours had been dashed to nothing in mere seconds.

"There's no way," I murmured.

"No way for what?" Blossom asked.

"No way to beat them. Ten thousand Amadis versus over a million of them?" I shook my head.

"There are the norms—" Vanessa started.

I looked at her with disbelief. "We're talking the Daemoni and the Demons. I'm not putting the norms against them. That would be asking them to commit suicide."

"Many of them are trained," Owen said. "The hunters, to start with. They do well against the Daemoni."

"What?" I turned on him. "When they're five or ten on one?"

Owen shrugged. "We could hit those numbers."

My brow shot up. "There are that many hunters?"

"No, but we can train other norms," he insisted. "Look at all of the people in the training rooms here."

"We're not doing that. This is *our* war. We're not putting them in that situation."

"It's their world, too, *ma lykita*," Tristan said. "Maybe they should at least get a say in it."

"There are a lot of military and ex-military who probably want nothing more," Char added.

I paced a few times across the room and back, pushing my hands through my hair that still needed a good washing. I finally turned toward Tristan.

"So what are we going to do? Do you have a plan?" I asked. "How would we even pull all of these people together?"

He held up a hand. "Slow down. The Daemoni aren't making any immediate moves, are they? Anything we know about?"

"Nothing Vanessa and I have seen," Owen said.

"I've noticed nothing," Robin said.

"Alexis and I didn't see anything, either," Tristan said. "They're just lazing about, complacent in their victory. They have no reason to be planning anything if they think they've won."

"Except Lucas—" I started, but Tristan looked at me and gave a small shake of his head.

"*We'll talk about his plans with your council,*" he silently said to me as his eyes drifted to Robin.

But if she's a messenger and can tell others . . .

He gave me a slight nod this time.

"The Daemoni aren't going anywhere, so we have time to create a strategy," he said aloud. "Alexis and I have just learned a few short hours ago that we're not the only ones left to fight them. So we'll discuss and come up with a plan. Robin, are you making rounds to all of these groups you've found?"

She nodded. "This is the second time I've been here. I can come back when I have more news."

"We should probably get regular check-ins." Tristan glanced at me.

"Right," I said, reassuming my leadership role. "I'd like you to come back every week."

"Actually, every two or three weeks would be better," she said. "That gives me time for longer trips. I'd really like to find out more about Asia and Europe."

I pressed my lips together, wondering if she was really trying to challenge me again. If she'd been faking her whole apology.

"There are ways for you to communicate with the other groups, though," she said quickly, before I could open my mouth. "The big ones like yours have amateur radio, like you do here."

I looked over to Charlotte, and she nodded her confirmation. "Ham radio."

"This is actually why I stopped by this time." Robin dug her hand into her back jeans pocket and pulled out a small piece of folded paper. "Here's the code for the frequencies. They change them every four hours in this order—" she tapped the paper in one place and then in another "—and then when they get through those, they'll go in this order. See the pattern?"

Tristan glanced over at the paper. "I see it."

Robin turned back to me. "So, Ms. Alexis, you can receive news that way if there's anything to report before I can return."

"Okay," I said with a nod. "Every three weeks, I'd like to see you here with a full report of what you've found and who else you've reported our news to."

"Anything to tell the others this time?" she asked, glancing at my belly. "Or did I imagine the comment about hormones?"

"You imagined it." Tristan answered before I could open my mouth. Robin looked at him with a sharply arched brow. "We don't want the Daemoni to know, so it's better to keep it under wraps for now. Can we trust you with that?"

She peered at him with her birdy eyes for a moment longer. "Of course," she finally said. "But the news would really help with morale."

Her tone and her history with us made me suspicious, but today she showed a different side to herself, so I tried to do the same and be nice. "Robin, I was pregnant before, and I lost the baby. Since my mom's the only Amadis daughter to have a child after the *Ang'dora*, we have no guarantees. There's a good possibility I could lose this one, too. I don't want to get everybody's hopes up and then have them decimated. Let's wait, okay?"

"Of course, Ms. Alexis." She bowed her head for a moment.

"For now, we want norms trained as much as possible," Tristan said. "Spread the word that they need to at least be able to defend themselves against the Daemoni and Demons."

"Does anybody know how to fight the Demons?" Sheree asked.

"From what we've seen, they seem very interested in finding fresher bodies than the ones Lucas provided," Vanessa said. "And the ones who don't have human bodies would like to have them. I have no idea why, but that's what we've noticed."

"If you cut off their heads, they disappear," I offered. "That's about all we know for now. Some seem to have a lot of power, though—more magic than a sorcerer—but most are all about brute force."

"I don't think norms will be able to get close enough to defeat them," Tristan said. "They just need to make sure they don't allow the Demons to enter their bodies. They react to silver, so using it might be enough for the humans to get away."

"The hunters are researching other ways," Owen said. "Legends and myths. Holy water burns them, but not severely enough to make a lasting difference. Plus it makes them angry as heck, so better to conserve the water."

Robin dipped her head. "The hunters in Oklahoma said the Demons react to verses from the Bible, or anything about Jesus. It makes them angry, like the holy water does, but it also wears on them, draining them of energy. Simply repeating the Lord's Prayer can give norms time to escape."

"Of course, we need to keep the norms away from the Daemoni and the Demons so they don't *have* to fight them," I said. "We want them trained and prepared, but not actually fighting."

"The Amadis, however, need to be prepared," Tristan said. "When the time comes, we'll need everyone who's physically able to fight."

"I'll spread the word," Robin promised.

"Do me a favor," I said. "Keep your eyes open for Dorian. Whoever you talk to—make sure everyone's looking for him. I've received a message from the Angels—" I stopped, unable to flat-out lie that they'd told us to stop Dorian, and glanced at Tristan. "We just need to know where he is. Let us know immediately."

She nodded again. "I'll keep an eye out for him."

"You know where the dining room is," Charlotte said to her. "Get yourself some food, and you can use the same room you slept in last time to grab some shut-eye before dark. I'll have numbers for you to share before you leave."

Robin strode for the door.

"Thank you," I said, stopping her as her hand grasped the knob. "And if I don't see you—be careful out there."

Her auburn brows knitted together, but then she gave me a small smile. "The Angels are with me. I have faith in their plan, whatever it is. That's all we need, right?"

She left and shut the door behind her. As soon as she did, Char muffled the room, and my team immediately began lobbing the questions at Tristan and me. We told them everything we'd already told Owen and Vanessa, once again keeping out the part about going to Hell. But we did tell them what the Demon in Africa had confided about Lucas and Dorian, and that Mom, Rina, and Cassandra had confirmed it. Although, I called them the Angels to simplify the explanation. They might have thought us crazy for talking to the dead.

"So we need to stop Dorian," Owen said.

I also might have failed to mention that we were told to let him go. But I couldn't bring myself to correct Owen. Apparently, neither could Tristan, because he didn't say anything, either.

"But you don't know where the lad is," Jax said, "which creates a gnarly problem."

"Except *you* can look for him," Vanessa said, leaning back in her chair and crossing her long, leather-clad legs at the ankles.

"Yeah, you forgot to mention something." Owen lifted his arms out to his side and gave them a quick flap.

I threw an annoyed look at him before Tristan and I

stepped to the front of the room and revealed our wings. They received the reaction I'd expected—gasps and *whoas* and a *holy shit* from Charlotte. My team sprang from their seats, even Sheree, to inspect them more closely.

"They don't mean we can easily search and rescue Dorian, though," I said as they stood around us, poked, and prodded, jumping back when we automatically reacted with a twitch of a feather. "We've already scoured half of the world, and I never found his mind signature. He's likely heavily shielded and cloaked. If Robin or her people saw him, it would be by accident. The were-birds may be the only animals in the sky, but they're a lot less conspicuous than we are."

I didn't know if my team heard me at all through their infatuation with our wings. I hid mine to remove the distraction, and Tristan did, too.

"And you can make them disappear," Blossom noted. "Too cool."

"The Angels gave you those?" Sheree asked after hobbling back to her seat.

"I guess," I said. "I don't really know. We were, uh, knocked out at the Jefferson Memorial in D.C., and we woke up with the wings . . ."

I trailed off. We were about to be caught in one of the many holes in our story because we'd woken up in different places, at different times. And the only reason we'd even survived was because of the faeries. Although I had no idea how we'd be able to save the fae, I wanted to tell my team about them, including what happened to Bree. And that meant telling my team about going to Hell and Tristan getting stuck there.

"Why are your wings dark if they're from the Angels?" Blossom asked.

"How did you get out of D.C. before it was destroyed?" Vanessa added.

"And what were you doing for the first couple of months before you started searching for life?" Charlotte wondered.

Tristan and I exchanged a look.

They're my team, I told him. *We should probably tell them everything.*

He pressed his lips together, but gave me the tiniest nod. *"They need the full story to do their jobs of advising and supporting."*

So after blowing out a full breath, I said, "Hold on. There's more to what happened to us."

And we divulged the rest. All of it, from my death, or whatever it was, that sent my soul to Heaven, how I ended up in Hell, and how Tristan let the Demon take his soul there because that's where I was, to my waking up in the faeries' cave in the middle of the North Atlantic, Bree's help in taking me back to Hell to rescue Tristan, and what happened to the faeries.

"And Heaven wasn't the last we've seen of Mom, Rina, and Cassandra," I finished, deciding that since we'd come this far, we needed to tell them everything. I couldn't ask them to act against the Angels' wishes when they'd been led to believe they were doing the opposite. Otherwise, how could I blame Rina and Mom for their half-truths and omissions if I did the same? "They came to us in Morocco and said we aren't supposed to stop Dorian, but I do need to stop Lucas."

Several silent seconds ticked by as my team absorbed all of this.

"Well, that makes more sense," Char finally said. "Rina knew Dorian had a purpose."

"To open the gates of Hell?" I snapped, and then I immediately felt guilty.

She shook her blond head. "There must be more to it, Alexis. If that's what they want, there's a reason for it."

"How do we stop Lucas without stopping Dorian?" Blossom asked, which was exactly my question. The question

I'd been asking myself and Tristan since the day Mom, Rina, and Cassandra had told us this in Africa.

"We don't," I said, which had been my answer to myself every time. "I've let my son down too many times. His heart and soul are still good. If he knew what's going to happen when he goes to Lucas, he wouldn't be doing this, and I won't let him have to live with the consequences for the rest of his life. I *have* to stop him. And that will stop Lucas."

Thankfully, nobody argued with me. Perhaps because all of them except Sheree felt guilty that Dorian wasn't with us this very minute.

"But we have to find him first," Tristan said, breaking the silence.

"Have you been to Hades?" Vanessa asked.

I pressed my palms to my eyes. This day felt never-ending, and the more we talked and shared, the more I realized we were still in the same place as we were yesterday or several weeks ago when we'd been standing on the beach in Morocco. "We were told not to. Not yet. The Angels want me to build my army first."

Charlotte lifted her hands in the air. "Then that's what we do."

And I supposed we *were* in a different place than we were yesterday or two months ago. Not just physically, but in regards to our situation. Before, I'd thought there was no hope for an army. That Tristan and I would have to stop Dorian—and Lucas—by ourselves. At least now we'd have some help with saving our son. And possibly the world.

Then I recalled the numbers we'd discussed only a short time ago. I wanted to protect the millions of Norman and Amadis souls we'd learned were still alive, but drawing them into a war would be the opposite of protecting them. Yet . . . there was no doubt that bringing Dorian back to our side would ignite a battle until the end.

I'd said many times before that nobody's soul was more

valuable than anybody else's, but how many was I willing to risk to save Dorian?

After discussing our options, I reluctantly agreed that we'd wait for news from Robin before Tristan and I defied the Angels' wishes and went to Hades to find our son. After all, as soon as Dorian made the move to officially join Lucas and the Daemoni, we'd surely find out. As the matriarchs had suggested, Lucas would make a point of us knowing, wanting us to watch as he made a big ordeal out of Dorian handing himself over, and we could act then. In the meantime, as long as everything was quiet, Dorian must have been hiding out somewhere, probably under somebody's protection. Every time I thought of him as my little boy out in the world by himself, tucked away somewhere and scared to death, I had to remind myself that he was none of that. He'd known what he was doing when he left.

And he was probably more powerful than any of us.

Blossom and Sheree returned to the Conversion Center, and Vanessa and Owen showed us to our sleeping quarters. Several sections made up the residential area, each section divided into fourteen individual rooms that could sleep up to four people each, according to Owen. They gave us a room in the back, away from everyone else, and our mattress we'd brought from our beach house had been placed in it, along with some linens.

Although it wasn't technically our evening to shower according to our last name, they allowed us an exception. Probably for everyone else's benefit as much as our own. We were pretty rank. Timers regulated the water, so there was no standing under the warm stream for relaxation, nor was there much privacy in the communal bathrooms. I fleetingly wondered if Tristan and I would ever be able to enjoy a shower together again, but at the moment, I was just glad to be clean. Blossom used the spell to clean and refresh our fighting leathers, but we'd been provided a few sets of Norman clothes, too. Although my leathers fit like a second skin, it was still nice to hang out in yoga pants and a hoodie for a change.

As I lay on the same mattress I'd woken up on in a very different place this morning, I thought about how much everything had changed in the last sixteen hours. Well, actually, nothing had changed except Tristan's and my perspectives, and I had a feeling mine more than his. He'd remained much more optimistic than I had, believing that we'd eventually find what had found us—other souls that weren't swimming in evil.

For months, I'd been focused on saving Tristan and Dorian with a private hope that I could convince the Angels to allow all three of us into Heaven, because there was nothing left in this world worth staying for. In a matter of hours, I'd learned that not only were my closest friends—aka my extended family—still alive, but so were thousands of my people and millions of humans. And to top it off, a new life grew inside of me. Not only me, either, but perhaps thousands of Norman women harbored a new generation in their wombs. Would the Angels be so cruel to give us such promise for a future when they knew it would all be destroyed in the end? I certainly hoped not. All of these new developments made this world worth more than just staying for—it made this world worth fighting for.

If only we could figure out how.

We spent the next few days settling into a routine with the rest of The Loft's residents and finding our places in the workload. Tristan, of course, belonged in the Training section, teaching various classes from Aikido to weapons to everything about the Daemoni, including each creature's weaknesses. I, on the other hand, floated all over the place. As official leader, I worked with Charlotte in running the place, although she really did most of the work. I helped Tristan, Brogan, and the others with some training classes, too, and when the hunters and Amadis brought Daemoni in, I'd help Sheree with conversions. A few times, when being underground twenty-four/seven began grating on the nerves, Tristan and I would go out with Alys, Sonya, and hunters to find more Daemoni to convert. But I was needed for the conversions that followed, so escaping the compound was a luxury.

Weeks passed, Robin returned with news of more groups found throughout the world, and my army was growing in both number and strength. The most significant improvements were in the norms, who trained diligently, but I still didn't want to involve them in any war waged on Lucas, the Daemoni, and the Demons, if at all possible. Every plan Tristan devised included the norms, though, and I'd make him go back to the drawing board.

"They want to fight," he'd told me repeatedly. "They tell me this every day in training. It's *why* they come to training and work their asses off. This is their world, too, *ma lykita*."

"And if we let them go against the Daemoni and the Demons, there won't be any of them left by the time it's all over."

"You underestimate the norms."

"*You* underestimate Lucas and those vile creatures. And you, of all people, should know better. How can you be so willing to risk their lives?"

After enough of these arguments, he stopped answering this question because I always ignored how he explained his optimism.

"We need more Amadis," I said. "More converts."

I ordered all Amadis who Robin and her fellow messengers could reach to become more aggressive in finding Daemoni who wanted to convert, and we did build our numbers that way. According to Robin's reports and what we learned through the ham radio, we'd add a few dozen new Amadis each week. But that was hardly anything compared to the Daemoni's numbers.

And there was still no word about Dorian.

This was both good and bad. Good because it meant he hadn't joined the Daemoni yet, and as each week passed, that meant more converts for us and more training for the norms before Lucas made his next move. But bad because it was another week that I'd heard nothing about my son. Another week of wondering and worrying about him. Another week of not being able to show him where he truly belonged—with us.

"I just can't imagine where he could be," I said to Sheree one afternoon after we'd completed a new conversion. We sat in the dining area, drinking tea while I waited for Tristan. We were going to see Carlie for a minute, and then he'd give me what I really needed after a conversion—the kind of true, deep love only a soul mate could provide.

"Do you think he could have gone back to Noah?" she asked as she ran her long, thin finger over the rim of her ceramic cup.

"I doubt it. When we saw Noah, Dorian had already been gone for weeks."

"If Noah was telling you the truth."

I rested my chin on my hand. "He seemed to be."

"But he's Daemoni and therefore a liar."

I started to nod, but then frowned. "I don't know that he's ever lied to me, though. At least, when he wasn't under Kali or Jeana's control. Besides, the last time we saw him, Demons had taken him away. For all we know, he could be trapped in Hell."

She opened her mouth to say something, but the overhead buzzers rang out an alarm. Our walkie-talkies lit up with Charlotte's voice.

"New converts you're going to love," she said. "Tristan and Owen, I need you here stat. We'll need all the help we can get. Over."

Although we'd just completed a conversion, Sheree and I had no choice but to jump up and respond. We rushed to the Conversion Center in time to meet Tristan, Char, and Owen struggling with three conscious Daemoni—one woman and two men.

"*Warlocks?*" I asked in surprise as the three new mages whipped their bodies against the bindings holding them, murmuring spells under their breaths.

Tristan's chest rumbled. "This will be . . . interesting."

CHAPTER 19

"*Y*ou don't need to tie us up like this," the black woman seethed as she arched her back against Owen's hold on her. "We came because we wanted to."

"We're not taking any chances," Tristan replied calmly as his power moved the black male warlock to a bed.

"You really want to convert?" I blurted, although they wouldn't be here if they didn't. I just couldn't believe this.

"I don't know. Are we coming to the stupid side?" the white man with black, curly hair snapped. His arm suddenly jerked free of Charlotte's hold, and a spell shot wildly across the room. A glass bottle on a shelf exploded.

"If you don't want to be here, we'll take you out," Owen growled, and the way he said *take you out*, you couldn't be sure if he meant out of The Loft or out of the world.

The woman's eyes bulged and glowed red as she looked at me. "No. Please, no. You don't know what they're doing . . . what they're planning. *Please help us.*"

Her plea hit me right in the soul, and I rushed to her side. My heart swelled with love and concern as I placed my hand on her arm. She jerked and cussed when the Amadis power hit her, and a spell surged out of her palm. A ceramic coffee cup on the makeshift desk melted into a puddle of goo. These were going to be some of our hardest—and most interesting—conversions ever.

Vampires were easy to subdue—stab them in the heart with a silver knife or stake and don't remove it until they were tightly bound with silver cuffs and chains. Shifters were a little more difficult during full moons, but in general, they could also be contained with silver. Warlocks, on the other hand, could be tied up with silver rope from neck to toe, but as long as their mouths could move, they could shoot off a spell. Many could do so without their mouths. And during conversion, there was no telling what they'd do when the evil fought back.

Mages who wanted to convert were a rare score, though. Vampires who came to us had usually been turned against their will, or in a few instances when they'd wanted to be turned, they'd regretted their decision soon enough to save their souls. Most of the were-creatures who came to us had been bitten and infected, and like the vamps, usually against their wills. Some shifters, and all mages, however, were born, so Daemoni or Amadis from birth. All the Daemoni mages had ever known was evil and darkness. They learned dark and black magic from an early age, and delighted in the powers they could use for personal gain. Rarely would they give that up to come to the other side. And that natural Daemoni blood made their conversions all the more difficult.

"What's your name?" I asked the female warlock.

"Call me Molita."

"Okay, Molita, we'll help you," I promised, and the look she gave me—full of fear and determination—reminded me of when Sheree had been so desperate to convert.

As expected, the conversions pushed us to our limits, and I'd already been so drained of power. Every Amadis with any amount of power had to come help at some point or another, just to give us a chance at beating the evil drenching their souls and coursing through their blood. The baby inside me must have grown accustomed to the dark energy several conversions ago, because she no longer reacted like she had the first time, and now she seemed to have retreated completely, becoming quiet. Probably sleeping like I wanted to after days of staying with the mages.

When I could finally leave, knowing they were going to be okay, the woman's dark hand wrapped around my arm, stopping me. Her black, bloodshot eyes, ringed in red, rolled up to me.

"Thank . . . you," she whispered hoarsely. She closed her eyes and swallowed, and I thought she was done, but when I started to pull away, her grip tightened, and her eyes opened. "There are more of us. More Daemoni who want to convert. Lucas . . . has gone too far. Others know . . . too. They just don't know . . . how . . . to leave."

My heart felt like it shrunk with the desperation in her voice, but at once, exploded with the news. I placed my hand over hers and gave her a squeeze. "We'll help them. I promise."

But as soon as I uttered the words, inexplicable fear sent me into a sudden panic. *How* could we help them? How could we help anyone? Any hope drained out of me. *You can't. You will fail again!* Satan's voice rasped in my head. My heart raced way too fast. My breaths came quick and shallow. Sweat beaded on my forehead, and my knees knocked together from the tremble in my weak legs. Gray splotches crept in on the edges of my vision, and then blue and black dots wavered and grew until I could see no more.

Strong arms caught me as I went down.

"You need a break," Tristan murmured as he carried me out of the Conversion Center. "Too much dark energy."

"I just need you." I leaned my head against his shoulder and pulled on his love as his concern poured out of him and into me. I could already feel a difference. "I need you to hold me, to strengthen me."

His jaw clenched as he looked down at me. "I want Carlie to examine you."

"I'll be fine," I argued. "It's just been a long, exhausting week. You know how I get with these conversions."

His steps paused, and I realized we were already at the Medical station. He looked down at me, worry written all over his face.

"Just let me regenerate with you tonight. I promise to see her tomorrow. I'm just too tired to deal with prodding right now."

His lips flattened out for a moment, then he finally nodded. He didn't put me down, though, but carried me to our room.

"You know how worried I've been," he said after he laid me down on the mattress. He pushed the hair away from my cheek and leaned down to press his lips to my forehead.

I sighed with the relief that small kiss brought. "I just need more of that."

He took off my boots and leathers, and he gave me exactly what I needed—love and comfort. After a night with him and regenerating in his arms, I felt fine the next day. But as I'd promised, we went to see Carlie. He and Charlotte had been concerned for a while, anyway, and, honestly, I couldn't argue. I had to admit something had changed in the last week or so.

"She feels more active to me, but Tristan can't feel her anymore," I explained to Carlie as she had me lay on the exam table.

"I still can't believe either of you felt her as early as you did," she said.

"She's our power baby." Tristan gloated from my side as he held my hand like any good expecting father would do.

"She has to be to come into this world," I mumbled.

"I'm worried about her heart, though," Tristan said. "None

237

of us can hear it anymore. If Alexis didn't still feel her moving around . . ."

He trailed off, unable or unwilling to voice the worst-case scenario of another pending miscarriage. Carlie frowned as she pushed around on the barely noticeable baby bump.

"Unless I just have bad gas, trust me, she's still alive and kicking. Literally."

Without a reply, Carlie donned a stethoscope and placed the cold disc against my skin. She moved it around several times, the crease between her brows deepening with each move.

"That's odd," she murmured. "I can pick up the heartbeat, but it's really faint. And there's something . . . Tristan, there's another scope in that box. Come listen."

Tristan shouldn't have needed a stethoscope, but he found the one Carlie indicated in a box on the counter, and then both of them hovered over my belly, sliding their discs around.

"Huh." Tristan looked up at me with interest in his eyes. "I can hear it now."

"It's so faint," Carlie said. "And now come over here."

She moved his end an inch or so over. After a moment of listening, his eyes darkened, and his mouth pressed into a scowl.

"I don't like that look," I said. "What's wrong?"

"You hear it, too?" Carlie asked Tristan, and he nodded. "Well, lucky for us, Owen was finally able to fix the ultrasound machine the scouting group brought back weeks ago. Let's take a peek."

A few minutes later, after Carlie turned off every light and electrical device in the medical unit so she could power the ultrasound machine, I again lay on my back with cold jelly being smeared on my abdomen.

"I've had a little training on reading these things, but it wasn't exactly my forte," she warned as she pressed the wand against my skin. "Do you know how, Tristan?"

"Not so much, but between the two of us, we should surely be able to figure it out."

They took turns moving the wand around while strange noises sounded in their throats.

"I didn't think it would be this hard," Tristan said.

"The placenta seems unusually thick, I think." Carlie's brows pinched together. "Would that be possible with you guys?"

Tristan's forehead wrinkled as he looked at me, one corner of his mouth lifting. "Maybe she has a little more supernatural protection after what happened last time."

The Angels? I wondered. "Well, that would be nice. Good news for once. So why the frowns earlier?"

A moment later, when Tristan moved the device lower, Carlie answered with a little squeal as she clapped her hands together, her eyes transfixed to the screen. "There it is!"

I studied the monotone image, trying to figure out what she saw in the gray blobs surrounded by a black area at the bottom of what looked like a tunnel of more gray. "What?"

She placed her hand over Tristan's on the wand and moved it to highlight one of the gray, peanut-shaped blobs. Something small flashed in it. "One," she said, and then she moved to the other peanut with another pulsing smudge. "Two."

My breath caught as I realized what she meant, and my eyes remained locked on the screen. My own heart forgot to beat for several of those blips on the monitor.

"No," I said, shaking my head, refusing to believe it. "This can't be."

"You're having twins, Alexis!" Carlie said excitedly.

I shook my head harder, tears springing to my eyes. My voice came out in a hoarse whisper. "That's not good. I can't do this again."

"Carlie, can give you us a moment?" Tristan asked as he passed her the wand, and then picked up my hand between his and brought it to his lips, his darkened eyes never leaving mine.

"Of course. Just let me take a quick look." She moved the wand around for what felt like an eternity but was probably only a minute or so. My lungs refused to function, and my hand tightened around Tristan's with every second that passed while I tried to suppress the tears. "From what I can tell, everything seems to be okay. I can't see gender on the one, though. He or she's behind the—" She paused and looked at us. "Do you want to know?"

"We already know," Tristan said quietly.

"Oh. Um, okay." She handed me a tissue to clean off my belly. "I know twins are a lot of work, but if anyone can handle it, you two can."

She squeezed my shoulder before leaving us.

Tristan sat on the exam table and gathered me into his arms. We held on to each other tightly, as though if we let go, we might fall to pieces.

"At least we're certain there are two babies," he said after a while, his voice thick with the same emotions roiling through me. "No tricks this time."

"If we're lucky, which we never are."

"They're protected."

I sniffled and wiped my eyes against his shirt. "But even if we keep them, we *have* to break the curse. I . . . *we* can't lose our sons."

He pressed his lips to my forehead before tucking my head under his chin. "Do you remember on our honeymoon when you talked about the children you wanted?"

I closed my eyes, recalling the beautiful memory. One of the last clear memories I had up until the *Ang'dora*, when I'd aged backwards to that exact time. The seven-and-a-half years between had been virtually wiped out, except for a handful of moments with Dorian that were embedded so deeply on my soul, I could never forget them. On that day, Tristan and I had lay in bed in the Caribbean room at the beach house, discussing our future. That was back before I knew hardly anything about our world.

"I'd wanted a boy so badly, one just like you, and I have him. Or, I did. You said then that a son was a bad idea, and I get it now. God, do I ever get it." I opened my eyes and tilted my head to see his face. "Not that I regret having Dorian at all, but it just goes to show we should be careful what we wish for."

He pulled his head back enough to look down at me. "You'd said you wanted three or four children."

"And you said that was impossible."

"Right. And now look."

I'd have my three, four if we counted the one I lost—actually five, if Satan's story to Tristan had been true about Dorian's twin—but we'd be lucky if we could keep one. I sighed. "Again—be careful what you wish for."

He brushed his lips over my cheekbone. "I prefer the cliché of anything is possible."

After a moment of pondering his unending optimism, I nodded and said with determination, "Including breaking the curse."

News about the twins traveled quickly, and while the norms found the prospect exciting, the Amadis among us knew what this meant. My team, especially, loved Dorian and understood the heartbreak I already suffered . . . and the intensifying need to stop Dorian while figuring out the real way to break the curse.

A few days later, Char came rushing into the training room where Tristan and I had been leading an Aikido class. "We have news on the radio. Hurry."

While Tristan dismissed class, I mentally called out to the rest of the council in The Loft, and we met them in the radio room at the command post up front.

"This news is for anyone listening, hopefully including the

mother ship one," the man on the radio said, referring to The Loft here, since I was the mother. "Movement has been seen toward the land of the great white. Almost seems to be a migration. Take note." He paused, then started the message again.

"Daemoni are moving toward Hades," Tristan translated.

I nodded. "The great white of Siberia."

"Why?" Blossom asked. "What do you think's going on?"

Dread sent a shiver up my spine when the answer hit me. "This must be one of the signs the matriarchs told me about. Lucas must be getting ready to act. Which means Dorian—"

"Let's not jump to conclusions," Charlotte interrupted. "Daemoni heading to Hades may not mean anything. There could be many reasons for them to go to their biggest city."

"He said a migration," I pointed out.

"Which is different than a swarm or a rush," Char said. "They're moving slowly. Right now, it doesn't sound urgent."

"Agreed," Tristan said. "It's just information at this time. But that could change."

"We should check it out," I said to him. "See for ourselves what's going on."

He nodded. "Maybe find out Lucas's plans."

Charlotte pointed at me. "*You're* not going anywhere."

"Don't be like the others," I said harshly. "You know damn well that I am. Tristan and I are the only ones who *can* go."

"Hey," Owen protested. "Vanessa and I did fine before we found you."

I turned to look at him while crossing my arms over my chest. "So you're going to open a portal to Hades and let a sorcerer or Lucas trap you?"

"Fuck no," Vanessa replied before Owen could open his mouth.

"We'll have to eventually," he said. "If we're going to battle at some point. Why not beat them there now?"

"Because we're not talking about going to battle," Vanessa

said. "You're talking about the two of us going there alone to scope things out. On land. *Alone*. At *Hades*."

Tristan rubbed his chin. "She's right. We need more intelligence before you take the risk of a portal and getting stuck there like we did last time. We won't take the chance until we're ready for that point of no return."

"Tristan and I can do a flyover, maybe pick a few brains, and get back," I said.

"You hope," Charlotte corrected.

I swept my hand in front of me. "We have a better chance than anyone else here."

"We're stronger than ever, Char," Tristan said, clapping his hand on his own shoulder, gesturing to his wings. "Alexis is right. We can be there and back. Trust me—nothing will happen to her and our children."

With only a scowl as a reply, she turned her back on us and strode out of the room.

"I'm with Char on this," Sheree said, her eyes sad as she looked at me before hobbling through the door.

Blossom stood up. "Sorry, Alexis, but I am, too. Maybe you should let someone else do the dirty work for a change."

"My life is no more valuable than anyone else's."

She glanced down at my belly. "Considering there are *three* lives in that package, yes, your body *is* more valuable."

She left, too, and I stood there in shock for several long moments while those who remained in the room stayed silent. With a split vote, Tristan would be the tiebreaker, although the final decision always belonged to me. But I didn't think this was really a split vote. Owen, Vanessa, and Jax showed their support of whatever I decided by staying here, but that didn't mean they liked it. I could sense their conflict in their brainwaves.

Tristan broke the silence. "Since we agree it's not urgent yet, why don't we wait a few days or so before we go? Let Robin and the other were-birds continue watching."

"You were just all for us going," I argued. "You know we can do this."

"Yes, we can. And eventually, probably soon, we'll *have* to. But for now, you should listen to your council's advice." He lifted his brow as I stared at him, and I opened my mind to his. "*You need them one-hundred-percent behind you when the time comes. Show that you can listen.*"

I blew out a harsh breath.

"Okay, fine," I acquiesced. "Have Robin and the others gather intelligence for now. But if something changes, we're out of here."

Giving in to their wishes went a long way with my team, which was good because less than a week later, something did change. Daemoni moved more rapidly and in larger numbers toward Siberia and Hades, according to the reports coming in on the radio. And then Robin showed up.

"I wanted to come tell you myself," she said as soon as she saw me with Tristan on my heels as we entered the command post room. "Lucas has been sighted."

My stomach tumbled with fear. "Is Dorian . . . with him?

"Not that anybody saw. We found it bizarre, though, that Lucas was moving to the east, away from Hades."

"While everyone else is headed toward there," Tristan said, as though finishing her thought.

"Exactly."

I clutched Tristan's arm. "He might be going after Dorian, tired of waiting on him."

"That would be stupid of him," Tristan said. "He knows Dorian must come to him. To the Ancients, more precisely."

"Unless he doesn't care about winning Dorian over and only wants him to open the gates to Hell."

Robin made a noise that sounded like a freaked-out chirp. "*What?*"

Tristan eyed me. I threw up my hands. "The time has

come for our people to know. From the sounds of things, we won't be able to keep it from them much longer."

So we told Robin about Lucas's need for Dorian to open the gates to Hell and bring Satan to Earth, knowing she'd spread the word to the groups hiding around the world.

"Keep this among the Amadis only," I ordered her. "The norms will panic."

"Everybody will want to fight," she said.

"Not yet," I said firmly. "Tristan and I will go first and find out what Lucas is doing. Nobody moves until you hear from us. Got it?"

She gave a sharp nod. I turned to face my council who stood behind me.

"Any objections this time?" I asked. "Or do we agree the time has come to move?"

"I still don't like it," Char said as she stepped up to me and put her hands on my shoulders. "You're like a daughter to me, Alexis. Those babies are family, too."

"And if we want them to have any hope for a future," I started, and she nodded, not needing me to finish.

"You two find out what you can," she said. "We'll worry about preparing the Amadis."

"Nobody does anything until we say," I repeated. "If we get lucky, maybe Tristan and I can take Lucas down, and we can avoid going to Hades to fight the rest of the Daemoni."

"Wishful thinking," Vanessa muttered under her breath. Probably, but I ignored her.

Robin took off to begin alerting the rest of the Amadis, while Tristan and I hurried to our room to change into our fighting gear. Then we headed to the Armory where Char and Brogan met us. I had my trusty dagger on my hip and my knife in my boot, but I didn't hesitate to grab a silver-bladed sword and two handguns. Brogan fitted straps over my chest and back to hold the sword, gun holsters, and ammo clips, ensuring they wouldn't get in the way of my wings. Tristan also strapped on a sword and a couple of guns, although he contained the deadliest power in his hand. We loaded up on as much silver-coated ammo as we could hold.

"Weren't you the one who taught me guns were pretty useless in our world?" I asked Char as she made sure my leather straps were tightened.

"They are if you don't want to kill, which has always been our way," she answered as she pulled the guns out of the holsters and inspected them. "But weren't you the one who started this war saying we'll do whatever it takes, even if it means slaying Daemoni?"

I'd said it, but that was before I'd actually done it. I still had nightmares about giving the Daemoni vampires in London their final deaths, as well as Kali, Jeana, and Merrick, even when I knew their souls were damned.

The image of Molita's dark eyes pleading with me about the others sent a stab in my heart.

"I'm hoping it won't come to that," I muttered.

"Me, too, Alexis, me, too." She shoved the guns back in their holsters, and then grabbed my face between her hands and tilted my head to look up at her. "But if it's your life or theirs, don't you hesitate. Do you understand me?"

"Don't worry. I don't enjoy it as much as some people think I would, but that doesn't mean I won't kill if necessary."

"That's my girl."

My entire council walked Tristan and me to the front door of The Loft, where a group of hunters guarded. They let us out into the night, but closed the door behind us to seal out any radiation and residual black magic in the air. Although norms were probably safe in our area with brief exposure, as many of the hunters experienced when they went on search and recovery trips, we weren't taking the chances of letting the contamination inside.

"Two days to Hades, one day scoping, and two days back?" Owen clarified.

"It shouldn't take us longer than that," Tristan confirmed. "Maybe less time, depending on how far this way Lucas has already moved and where we intercept him."

"Don't do anything stupid," Charlotte said, eyeing me specifically. "You wait for the rest of us if you see him. Recon only."

"And if you're not back in five days, we're coming," Owen said.

Vanessa nodded. "And ready to fight, because that's the only way in Hell you'll get me back to Hades."

"Don't worry, sister, I have a feeling you'll have that chance soon enough."

Tristan and I jogged down the gravel driveway, revealed our wings, and spread them out wide before launching into the evening sky. Although the Daemoni had supernatural hearing and sight, we hoped our black clothes and dark wings would make us little more than shadows against the night as we followed the sliver of moon over the land. We flew northwest, hoping to be far enough north into Alaska before morning, because up there, sunrise would come late in the day this time of year.

We'd barely passed Seattle and crossed into Canada when my mind, always open as I searched for mind signatures, stumbled across one that felt very familiar, but also different from what I remembered. I mentally yelled at Tristan.

Dorian!

CHAPTER 20

Up ahead, about seven miles, I told Tristan as I took
the lead.

We circled the area where I found Dorian's mind signature
in a small cabin hidden deep in the woods. I sensed no other
minds nearby, but worried there might have been Daemoni
hiding under a cloak. If that were the case, then Dorian served
as bait to bring us into their trap.

Dorian, I called out to him.

"*Mom?*" His mental voice sounded deeper than it had
before, just as his mind signature no longer felt childlike.

Are you alone?

"*For now. Where are you?*"

I gave Tristan the signal, and we dropped to the snow-
covered ground in front of the cabin. The front door opened,
and a man came running out. I gasped, and my hand flew to
my mouth. At first, my mind saw Tristan come to a halt at the
top of the steps to the front porch, but my husband stood next
to me. With the same hair and the same beautiful facial
features, this man was still a little shorter than Tristan and not
quite as broad. Yet. It was only a matter of time, and by the
looks of it, not much time at all.

"You shouldn't have come," Dorian greeted from the porch.

"We're your parents," I said simply. "We love you, until the end of forever, remember? And we've been looking everywhere for you."

"I told you not to. I told you to leave me alone."

"Dorian, you need to know—" I began, but he cut me off.

"I know everything I need to know. I know what I'm doing, Mom. You need to leave me alone and just let me do it."

"Dorian, please." I wasn't beyond begging. "You're making a big mistake."

He suddenly stood right in front of us, a growl rumbling in his throat.

"Dorian," Tristan said in warning.

Dorian's hazel eyes flew to his father's face and then back to mine. "I said to leave me alone!"

"Problems, Dorian?" The icy cold voice pricked our ears before its owner showed himself. Lucas appeared out of nowhere right behind Dorian.

Tristan and I both shot power at him.

"No," Dorian said curtly as Lucas's hand lifted, and our powers ricocheted into the woods, never hitting him. Dorian's eyes narrowed at us, and his chin lifted. "They were just leaving."

Dorian, please, I pleaded again, silently to Lucas's ears. *You don't need to do this. He's only going to use you to open the gates of Hell.*

"I said I know what I'm doing. Now go!"

"Dorian, you belong with us, not with them," Tristan said.

"I said to GO!" Dorian bellowed, and his hand suddenly shot up, his palm facing us. A strong gust of wind whooshed out of it, blowing Tristan and me backwards several yards. We landed in the snow and sprang to our feet. We tried to shoot at Lucas again, but Dorian deflected our power just as

249

easily as Lucs had. He *protected* him. "I'm ready, Grandfather."

"No!" I blurred toward them and latched on to Dorian. "Don't do this. It's a mistake. You've been told lies, Dorian. All lies."

He tossed me away with one easy shake of his arm. I turned on Lucas.

"Take me," I said. "Spare him, and take me instead. Use *me*."

"Alexis, no!" Tristan barked from behind me.

A wicked grin spread over Lucas's face. "Are you begging?"

Ignoring Tristan, I nodded vehemently. Even dropped to my knees at his feet. I couldn't let my son have to live with what he was about to do. I'd take the hit to my soul. "Please, *please* take me instead. I know what you're doing. Use me."

My neck craned backwards to look up at him, and like Hellfire, his ice-blue gaze sent prickles of cold into my skin as he seemed to appraise me. Maybe even considered the trade.

A bar of an arm enclosed around my waist and jerked me backward, up to my feet. Tristan held me against his body as Lucas watched on. Now he seemed to be appraising both of us. His nose and one side of his upper lip curled upwards when his gaze landed on our wings.

"I have no use for you anymore," he snarled. "Let us go, Dorian."

"NO!" I screamed as I pulled my dagger free while lunging for them, but I landed face down in the snow. They were already gone. "No, no, no!"

I pounded the snowy ground as tears streamed down my cheeks, and a scream ripped out of my throat. Out of my soul.

"Follow their trail!" Tristan grabbed my hand and flashed before Lucas's trail disappeared.

We appeared in another snow-covered area, but no trees surrounded us here. No flash trail lingered, either. We'd taken too long to follow the first one. Or, Lucas had wizened up and ensured he didn't leave a second one.

"We have to go to Hades," I said.

"Shh," Tristan replied. "Listen."

Voices tumbled over the air, and I opened my mind to find the owners. Lucas and Dorian were nowhere in my reach, but many, *many* Daemoni were. Hundreds of them. They didn't bother to cloak themselves as they traveled, all of them nearby headed in the same direction—west and slightly north.

Where are we? I asked Tristan.

"Middle of Siberia. Between Alaska and Hades."

We flashed that far? Our normal range had been about a hundred miles, give or take, but that had been before we'd been given the wings and who knew what other powers.

"Or Lucas did, and we were simply able to follow."

Of course, we weren't the only ones who'd gained in power. Lucas had, exponentially.

We need to find him. We have to figure out how to stop him.

"Come on."

He shot into the air, and I followed before anybody saw us. We trailed the Daemoni, and I'd been wrong about the number of them. *Thousands* of them headed in the general direction of Hades like a march of ants. Except . . . they didn't go as far as Hades. As we flew over a snow-covered mountain range still to the southeast of the Taymyr Peninsula, we had to turn back, because they were gathering in a wide valley, still hundreds of miles from the Daemoni's main underground city. Camps were spread across the expanse surrounded by mountains, with fires dotting the landscape. The deep thump of Shaman drums echoed across the valley. For as far as we could see, Daemoni came from all directions as though following the sound—thousands upon thousands of them. Mages flashed, vampires blurred over the mountains, and shifters sprinted through the forests of pine trees that looked like looming monsters, their branches naked of needles but dripping with icicles and covered in snow.

Holy shit. I knew the Daemoni severely outnumbered us, but seeing this many in one place provided an entirely new perspective—a reality check that felt like a slap in the face.

"*We need to get out of here,*" Tristan said as a horde of Demons flew through the sky straight for us.

Of course. We couldn't forget the Demons. They'd apparently been hiding in the cover of the night sky as we had been. And thankfully, they ignored us, too focused on their destination, I supposed, because they flew on past us.

What are they doing? I asked as we sped away. *Do you think it's a celebration or something else? The Daemoni minds are just gross bubbles of excitement and anticipation.*

"*Dorian's made his move. Lucas has what he needs to drop the veil.*"

Dread quivered through my chest and into my stomach. We hadn't been able to stop Lucas when he was alone. How could we possibly do so now, with a whole sea of his people surrounding him? Even if we had our army, trained and here with us, I didn't think we had a chance.

We're going to fail again.

Something unseen, warm and too strong for me to fight, suddenly gripped my wrist and stopped me in midair. Tristan jolted to a halt, too. The warm goodness flowing into my arm subdued any desire to try to escape as we flew toward the face of a mountain at the south edge of the valley. The force pulled me downward to the top of one of the pine trees that looked like an alien creature covered in a foot of snow with multiple thick, white arms dangling with icy tentacles. My feet landed on a branch, and a cascade of snow dropped through the limbs below. Tristan settled next to me, and when I reached up to grab an overhead branch to balance myself, I found Mom and Rina sitting above us.

"You *must* stop Lucas," they said at once.

"It's good to see you, too," I mumbled.

"Alexis, you are out of time," Mom said.

"You must gather your army. The final battle is coming," Rina added. I'd never heard her sound so urgent.

Balancing on the branch, I turned to face the valley below. From here, the campfires looked like fireflies flickering in the darkness. The rhythmic beat of the Shaman drums sounded as though they were right below us rather than a few miles in the distance as the snow and mountain faces threw all sounds into sharp relief. My heart pounded along with them. The air should have smelled crisp and clean, but instead left an acrid aftertaste in my nose and throat that must have come from the concentration of evil.

"There's so many of them," I said to Mom and Rina. "And so many more coming. Tens of thousands of them. Maybe *hundreds* of thousands, not including the Demons. There's no way we can stand up to them."

"Gather your Amadis. Your Norman armies, too," Rina said.

"*What?* You can't expect me to bring the norms into this. That's a death sentence for them." For all of us, really.

"The Norman militaries *want* to fight," Mom replied, "and they deserve the opportunity to go to war as they're trained to do. They've watched the Daemoni slaughter their loved ones, their friends, and neighbors. They've lost their communities. The very people they've sworn to protect. As a warrior, you know what that means."

"But *we're* supposed to protect *them*."

"You are to protect their souls, darling," Rina clarified.

"So sending them to their graves is okay as long as their souls are safeguarded from evil?" The question was rhetorical. I already knew their answer—they'd told me before that was exactly how it was. "It's not their war, though!"

"You're wrong, honey. It's always been their war."

Rina nodded. "More than their lives are at stake if Lucas brings Satan to the surface—their very souls are."

"They're right." Tristan shrugged when I looked at him. "The Daemoni were always after the Normans' souls, long before the Amadis even existed."

"Yes," Rina said. "The Angels only interfere in the Norman world when necessary. They started the Amadis because they needed an army on Earth to assist and protect the Normans."

"But that's all we've ever been," Mom concluded. "The Amadis may be the Angels' army, but we are the Normans' soldiers, fighting in their war on Earth while the Angels fight for their souls in the Otherworld. Things have changed and will continue to change until this battle is over. But what hasn't changed is that this *is* the Normans' war just as much as —or more than—it is ours."

Holding on to the branch above me, I leaned back and stared at the thick, dark clouds growing in the night sky as I contemplated their point. What they said made sense, and the truth rang through me, but . . .

"You're asking me to bring them to their deaths. I—" I tried to swallow, my throat dry and tight. "I don't think I can do that. I can't in good conscience lead them into this battle. I don't even want to bring the Amadis into it."

"You can, and you will," Rina said. "How do you say? The wheels are already moving?"

Tristan straightened up. "What do you mean?"

"It is time," Rina replied. "Time for good to face evil, for love to face hatred. Those souls down there—" She swept her arm out toward the sea of darkness below, the lights of fires like pinpricks in the evil haze settling in the valley. "They are the product of evil and hatred that filled this world and led to this. Many of them were once humans who became more focused on themselves than on others and the world."

Mom nodded. "Rather than follow the example of our Lord, they put words in His mouth and twisted them around for their benefit, to serve their own selfish agendas. We were asked to do one thing—love our neighbors. And some of those lost souls did, as long as their neighbors were like them. But we were not given conditions to that rule. And so the opposite of love came to be. They forgot what true love for God and for good really looked like. Contempt led to hatred and hatred to evil and evil to what we see here."

"The souls lost their faith," Rina said as she looked at me, her eyes showing the agony she felt on behalf of everyone down there. "Do not be like them, darling. Be the good that brings this world back."

I blinked and nodded, although my heart tremored. Like the fog of dark magic below, fear had drifted in and curled its way into me.

"Just tell me what to do," I said, trying to sound braver than I felt. "Tell me how to defeat Lucas, how to lead my people in this war."

Mom pointed to a snow-covered meadow at the backside of the mountain perpendicular to us. A clearing the Daemoni wouldn't be able to see from the valley—but Demons and were-birds could see fine from the sky. "The Amadis and the Norman armies are already coming together under your leadership. You will gather them right there."

I waited for her to continue, but she didn't. "And then what?"

"You will know," Rina said.

I turned back toward them and stared with my mouth half-open. Their dark eyes were full of an unfathomable depth of wisdom, shining on me with assurance.

"Hold on. You want me to bring my little army of ten thousand Amadis, join them with maybe fifty thousand norms, if there are even that many, and what? Hang out until the Daemoni attack? Or wait. You probably want us to march into the valley first and then just stand there, facing *that*?" I flicked my hand toward the Daemoni camps in the distance.

Rina bowed her head. "This is what you must do."

"But . . . that's absurd!"

"Trust us, Alexis," Mom said. "Follow our instructions, obey the Angels, and you *will* defeat Lucas."

I grabbed the back of my neck. "This is ludicrous. Give me *something* other than this . . . insanity. Something for me and my troops to believe in."

"You know what to believe in," Rina replied flatly.

"That is the plan, honey. That is all we know. Follow it, and you will be victorious."

"And what about Dorian?"

Something flickered in her eyes, and the corners of her lips twitched, but she censored any true emotion. "Let him serve his purpose, what he's been prepared for. Remember, we are given our children on a temporary basis, to raise, to teach, to provide as much wisdom and guidance as we can so they can become the best person they can be. But they are not our possessions. They belong to themselves and to the world. Their impact goes far beyond their childhood home and family. That's why they say it takes a village to raise a child, because one or two people alone cannot provide the foundation a child needs to become a contributing member of society. In various ways, we've all been preparing Dorian for his purpose. You, Tristan, and all of us have given him much love, and that will carry him through. Never forget, in the end, *he* decides the fate of his soul. Nobody else."

I understood what she meant, but that didn't make me feel any better about what was about to go down. Nor about what they'd requested us to do, and what that would mean to so many lives, so many souls.

"It is time." Rina tilted her head in another bow. "Remember, Alexis. Believe in what you cannot see with your eyes, what you do not know in your mind, but nonetheless feel in your heart and soul. And be the good."

And with that, they disappeared.

I turned toward Tristan who leaned against the trunk with a confident glint in his eyes.

"Do you have any idea what the hell that was supposed to mean?" I demanded.

One side of his mouth quirked up. "Somebody has a plan, but hasn't revealed it yet."

"Well, that's freakin' helpful." I hopped up to the next branch to try to gain a better view of the surrounding area. The pace of the Daemoni coming this way seemed to have increased—both in their speed and their numbers. "So what's *your* plan? Because theirs sucks."

"My plan is to follow theirs."

"You can't be serious." I looked over my shoulder and down at him. He appeared to be completely serious.

"First of all, they're our commanders. You may be the leader of the army here on Earth, but we serve the Angels. We obey their orders."

"Orders that will get us all slaughtered."

He straightened up and stepped away from the trunk. He leaned over and rested his arms on another branch in front of him, putting his head nearly level with mine. "I'm sorry, *ma lykita*, but I have no other plan. You're right. We'll be severely outnumbered and out-powered. I see no other solutions except retreating, which is not an option if we want to stop Lucas and save Dorian, as well as the rest of the world. We'll *have* to trust that there's more to their plan. You heard them—it's the only way we'll win."

"There must be something else." I scowled as I wedged myself between branches and watched the Daemoni and Demons below, trying to figure out why they came here to this particular place. What were they doing? Were they also preparing for war? But why would they be? As far as they were concerned, they had their victory. I reached out for a couple of minds in range and recoiled at the evil thoughts filling them. Thankfully, they weren't completely clear, fuzzed over by inebriation. They matched the sounds that traveled up the mountain to our ears—songs and cheers, noises of celebration. This was all a big party to them.

"I'm not learning anything here," I finally told Tristan after we watched for a while. "I don't really want to, but we'll have to move closer to get any good intelligence to take back."

"Our best intelligence came from Rina and Sophia," he replied. "They told us everything we need to know."

I heaved out a sharp breath. "Everything they said is ridiculous. If I can even bring myself to obey their orders, I won't be the blind leading the blind into this."

I ran along the branch until I could launch myself into the air without catching my wings on spindly branches and icicles. I shot straight up, higher than the Demons flew, although their attention remained focused downward. Tristan followed me as I moved closer to the center of the valley, while remaining high and on the western fringe. As though they'd purposefully built their camps this way, a wide circle in the heart of the valley remained clear of everything but snow. The main thought I could grasp among them echoed Rina's words. "*It's time*" rippled over the Daemoni below as they began to crowd toward the expanse in the middle.

Tristan and I hovered about halfway up the mountain above them, watching as the crowd began to part directly across the clearing from us. The mind signature approaching the center elicited an involuntary growl from my throat, but when I couldn't find the mind that I thought would be with him, foreboding and hope battled within me. Where was Dorian? Had he changed his mind and escaped? Or was he being held captive somewhere, such as with the Ancients? Was he nearby and cloaked, or was he soaring away to safety, perhaps even looking for Tristan and me?

We should look for Dorian, I told Tristan at the same time Lucas produced a ball of orange fire between his palms. Curiosity froze me in place. He spread his hands wide, growing the flames until they surrounded him, and then he rose a few feet above the ground, floating like he had when he'd cornered us at the Capitol building.

"What the hell?" I breathed.

Lucas's voice boomed over the valley. "Indeed. It is time, my faithful children."

He glided over the snow to the center of the clearing, and with a flourish, lifted his arms upward. Underneath him, the snow and ground began falling inward, at first in a tight circle, as though a drain had opened in a tub. The spiral grew quickly, though, sucking away the earth and snow, and within minutes, a sinkhole at least fifty feet in diameter yawned open like a gaping mouth. Lucas, still wrapped in a fireball, swooshed around the sinkhole, corkscrewing down into its pit, and then zoomed upward. The entire space filled with fire.

The Daemoni cheered before their voices fell into a low chant, and they stomped their feet in rhythm. Shaman continued beating their drums, and caught up in the excitement, shifters began transforming, the wolves howling a background chorus.

"The Ancients are coming," Lucas said, his voice reverberating across the valley floor and up the mountains. "Soon, our lord will be here. For now, let us welcome the rest of our brethren who have been trapped in the wrong realm for millennia too long."

The orchestra of voices, stomps, drums, and howls grew louder as Lucas lifted his arms again, like a conductor signaling the crescendo. The wind suddenly picked up, whooshing against my ears and knocking me off-balance as it blew in every direction, but mostly upward. Lightning cracked across the sky, illuminating low, dark gray clouds. Snowflakes the size of saucers began to fall over the valley, sizzling in the pit of fire, where the flames grew larger and jumped higher. An orange glow lit up the area nearly bright as day, reflecting off the thousands of faces and the sides of the snow-covered mountains.

A large and dark object shot out of the pit, high into the air before soaring across the valley and slamming into a mountainside. The chunk of black ice shattered, the sound resonating across the land, and a Demon burst out of it. Many more followed at quick and regular intervals, as though shot out of a cannon from the bottom of the pit, like the fireworks that blast several balls into the air, one right after the other. They all careened into the surrounding mountains and exploded, freeing the Demons inside.

Dozens of them.

Hundreds of them.

Thousands.

"The veil has dropped," Lucas yelled over the ruckus. "Soon, we open the gates to Hell."

CHAPTER 21

*M*y heart thundered against my ribs. "Oh my god."

I turned in midair to face Tristan, but a large body soared toward us in my peripheral vision. Tristan grabbed my hand and took off. Like rockets shooting through the air, we flew toward the south end of the valley, back to where we'd been before when Mom and Rina spoke with us. I'd called their instructions absurd then. I'd had no idea just how ludicrous and dangerous they really were.

Whether it grew bored or had been called back, the Demon that had been chasing us turned away and returned toward the fire pit that resembled the lake of fire in Hell. No other Demons chased after us. Not even Lucas paid us any attention, though surely he was aware of our presence. He obviously didn't care about us anymore. He didn't need to.

Tristan and I flew wide circles around the area, searching for Dorian, but when I couldn't find his signature, we assumed he was cloaked. So we returned to the same tree we'd been in before and watched the ceremony or celebration or whatever you'd call the horror playing out below in the valley. The hours stretched into the next day, I thought, although it was hard to tell because the sun never rose.

"It's too late in the year for constant darkness," Tristan murmured at one point. "There should be several hours of daylight by now."

"So they're doing this?" I glanced up at the starless sky where huge, low clouds hung.

He did, too. "The pending storm wouldn't make it this dark."

"There's hardly any smoke rising from the fire pit," I noted.

He looked down at me with dark eyes. "It's the evil energy rising from Hell, blocking out the light."

I recalled the thick black of nothingness in Hell, and a shudder racked through me.

Demons continued shooting out of the pit, the number countless, and those in the Earthly realm kept on with their party. Lucas disappeared, although I sensed him nearby in a large tent. Unfortunately—or maybe fortunately—Dorian was not in there with him, as far as I could determine. We kept waiting for something new to happen, to see if we could figure out what came next, but nothing ever did. Lucas kept his thoughts guarded, signaling that he knew I was close, so I didn't know what "soon" meant to him when he'd made his statement about opening the gates of Hell.

"This is pointless," I said to Tristan after a few more hours. We'd discussed ways to sneak into Lucas's tent and kill him, but we weren't cloaked, which wouldn't have mattered anyway. The magic of the numerous warlocks and sorcerers surrounding him would break through any kind of cloak and shield our mages could produce, if they were even here. "We should be looking for Dorian more instead of wasting our time here. I'm not learning anything from their minds that are drunk on evil except that Satan is coming. Maybe we can stop—"

"*Alexis.*" The familiar male voice sounded in my head, and it didn't belong to Tristan.

"Owen?" I gasped. Tristan lifted a brow, and both of us spun on our respective branches, searching.

"*Over here.*" Owen showed himself standing on the very space on the side of the other mountain where Mom had said to gather my people. Tristan spotted him first and gestured at him. Then Owen disappeared.

We flew off the tree and swooped that way. We passed through the shield to find Owen standing in the clearing and others appearing out of nowhere, coming through his portal.

Apparently, I didn't have to gather my army. They were coming all on their own.

Charlotte, Blossom, Vanessa, a tiger I knew as Sheree, Jax in human form, Sonya, Alys, and Brogan . . . and more people pouring through the opening. Dozens at first, but the crowd quickly grew into hundreds of Amadis. Then Owen disappeared for a moment before coming through a new opening, bringing more bodies, and then he disappeared once again.

Tristan and I landed on the ridge above them so we could see both them and the Daemoni. When they saw our wings spread out, people below gasped, and murmurs floated over the crowd, which continued to grow. And not only with Amadis. My heart sank when I spotted Heather, Teah, Teal, and other norms at the front. Then Kristen, Olivia, and more from the London cell of A.K.'s Angels came through a new portal, followed by Ammi and Terrence, two vampires who could still be considered newborns.

Our people talked excitedly among themselves as they gathered into groups, climbed trees, and perched on boulders. Adrenaline pumped through their veins, fueled by a healthy dose of fear, but a disconcerting amount of eagerness, too.

"Guess we know what Rina meant when she said the

wheels were in motion," Tristan said. "Apparently, your army was already on its way."

"Yeah, they're definitely gathering. So now what?" My hope that the fiery pit would swallow up Lucas and the Daemoni before it sealed itself shut again didn't appear to be coming true. God and the Angels weren't coming through for us. "What do we do?"

"I'd say we're going to battle." Although Tristan didn't yell the words, he didn't quite whisper them, either.

A cheer rose up among the crowd—those with inhuman senses apparently having heard Tristan's declaration and passing it along. Their enthusiasm was more than disconcerting; it was insane. A mixture of anger at the Angels for putting us in this place and fear for my people grew within me bigger and louder than the crowd, filling my ears with the flow of my own hot blood. I launched myself into the air. Which only made them cheer louder. I flew a circle around them—a tight circle because, although more came through the portals, my army was not very large. Not large at all.

As my circle brought me to face Lucas's Demons across the valley, a boulder of emotions slammed into my chest, taking my breath. The extreme difference in sizes between the two armies was terrifying. I swooped back to face my people, and rather than a growing crowd, I found only dead bodies littered over the clearing, crimson staining the snow. *NO!* I mentally screamed to myself as I squeezed my eyes shut. When I opened them again, the crowd below me had returned to normal, psyching themselves up for battle. But every time I looked at the Daemoni and back at my people, mine were all dead.

Visions from Hell. *Lies*, I told myself, but I wasn't so sure. They could have just as easily been premonitions.

Rather than growing confident with each person that came through the portals, my fear grew. The pour of people diminished into a trickle, and then the flow stopped. My heart shrunk.

I flew toward Owen. *This is it?*

"*This is enough.*"

Are you serious? This is a small handful compared to the legion of Daemoni and Demons! And the norms, Owen? What were you thinking, bringing them here?

"*Following orders.*"

Not mine.

"*No. Theirs.*"

Whose? I dropped down next to him, my fists on my hips and my eyes hard as I glared at him. "I give the orders, Owen. You're sworn to obey me, and this is not what I wanted."

He leaned his head back and stared at the sky. "But they do. And I'm sworn to them over you."

Although I knew nothing was there, my gaze swept upward anyway. "The clouds, Owen? The stars behind them? What the hell is wrong with you?"

"Funny. What the hell is wrong you? The Angels, Alexis. The Heavenly Host. Whatever you want to call them. You know, those people we work for?"

I ignored his sarcasm. "The Angels told you to bring these people to their deaths? Or do you mean Rina and Mom? Either way, they're wrong."

He looked over at me with hands rested low on his hips. "Actually, when the Demons started coming, we figured we'd better make our move since we hadn't heard from you yet. That was a pretty obvious sign that the veil was falling. Everyone went on high alert, all of us feeling in our gut that this was it."

"So you brought all these people here? All of these untrained norms?"

"They're not untrained."

"They're not ready to fight that!" I gestured toward the Daemoni side of the mountain. "Send the norms back!"

"No. They wanted to be here for you. For us. For the world. We're *all* here to fight and to win."

I shook my head emphatically and returned to mind-speak. *They're going to die. We all will. Not even your shields can protect us against the black magic over there. We will lose.*

His lips curled up in a confident, almost cocky grin. "*Don't you know? Good always wins.*"

And he gave me a wink. A wink!

I returned it with a blank stare, feeling the same as I had one of the very first times he'd stated that to me—standing on the porch of the beach house in the Keys when I'd learned exactly what the Daemoni were and that they'd declared Provocation against my people. The words had felt like a slap in the face then, when I'd believed the Daemoni had already won because they had Tristan. The sting felt just as real now.

You've lost your fucking mind, Owen. We've lost before we've begun.

He turned to face me more directly, his sapphire eyes alit with anticipation. He spoke aloud. "Alexis, they *have* to fight. The Demons aren't just here. Not all of the Daemoni have come. They're *everywhere*. And the norms and the Amadis are prepared for whatever comes. If they're not here, they're fighting anyway. You can't stop this. You can't stop them. These people here? They're here for *you*, for this battle specifically—to stop Lucas and to save Dorian. Let them help you."

My heart hammered. What had the Angels gotten us into? Why were they doing this to us?

Gasps and murmurs broke out over the crowd, more excitement filling their voices and their minds. Fingers pointed in various directions as whispers were exchanged. What was wrong with them? They acted like they were at a party! Even my team chatted giddily. They'd all drunk the Kool-Aid.

Owen glanced around at the mountainsides, and then his neck craned as though he tried to peek at the Daemoni's

266

camps in the valley, but there was no way he could see them from here. Then he gave me a casual shrug. "Stop worrying so much. We'll be fine, Alexis."

Tristan dropped down beside me then, and they fist bumped. Fist bumped! What was wrong with them? A deadly battle loomed over us, and they acted like we'd already won. As though blood wouldn't be shed and lives lost. Their confidence was borderline arrogance. Anger, frustration, and most of all fear for these people rushed through my veins. My head snapped backward when a Demon soared over us.

"We need to get out of here. Lucas's minion just spotted us."

"We're cloaked," Owen reminded me, but I wasn't so sure the Demon couldn't see through it. I wasn't sure of anything at the moment except for my hatred for Lucas. And a very strong dislike for the Angels.

"We need to wait for our orders," Tristan said.

I spun to face him. "I just gave orders."

"But *you* aren't following *our* orders."

My rage teetered on the edge of an explosion as my team gathered closer. I glared at each of their faces in turn, and they all stared back.

"We can do this, Princess," Jax said as he rubbed his hand over his bald head.

"It's *what* we do," Owen agreed.

"Win or lose, we have to try," Blossom said from Jax's side before giving me an encouraging smile.

Owen chuckled. "Oh, we'll win."

"Damn straight," Vanessa said.

Charlotte placed a hand on my shoulder, the weight noticeable, discomforting. "The only true failure, Alexis, is not trying at all."

While everyone else had sounded like a cheerleading squad, the truth of her words knifed into me, digging into the dark spots on my heart and soul. The blemishes of my previous failures, of my time in Hell.

My body jerked. Charlotte shook me back to the present. "Remember, Alexis, this life is only temporary, even for the supernaturals. None of us are getting out of here alive."

"Exactly," I muttered.

"I mean out of this world. As soon as we were born, we were dying. But it's the soul that matters. You know that. So help these people defend their good, loving souls against that evil."

She released her grip on me and stared at me expectantly. Without a word, I sprang into the air, flying up and away from them before I lost it. As I soared away, I heard Sheree's voice in my head, although she was in her tiger form, thinking something about a mustard seed.

I shot into the sky, my wings tight against my body, making me into a missile. I didn't have to read minds to see and feel the hope and excitement gurgling within everyone below me, and I couldn't believe how thrilled they seemed to be about the massacre they apparently wanted so badly. Their own massacre.

Tristan followed me, mentally yelling at me to stop, but I ignored him. I flew a larger circle around the valley, and again I saw my people dead on the battlefield, but only for a moment. My mind showing me what was about to come. A future I couldn't prevent if I wanted to stop Lucas.

"Ma lykita, *you're letting your emotions rule.*"

I halted, bringing myself vertical as I hovered over my people hundreds of feet below. Tristan hung in the air in front of me, his wings spread wide, and light dancing in his eyes. Not sparks or flames, like they used to hold, but the light of hope.

"No," I refuted through gritted teeth. "I'm trying very hard *not* to let them rule, because if they did, everyone would be headed home. But then, we wouldn't be able to stop Lucas or save Dorian, so either way, I lose."

"Alexis."

"What, Tristan? What am I supposed to do? Watch them die on the battlefield? Or wait for Satan to have his way? We're not ready for this! Especially not the norms!"

His mouth turned down into a frown, and he let out a breath that sounded so sad, my heart faltered. The hope that had been all over his face a moment ago had disappeared. "My love, I wish you would only believe."

"Believe in what?" I flicked my hand toward the Daemoni and Demons who were already celebrating. "I believe what I see, and I see our imminent annihilation."

"And that's your problem. You believe only with your eyes anymore."

I opened my mouth, about to argue, but movement beyond him stopped me. Coming over the mountain behind our people, a sizeable beast with wings flew close to the ground with figures much larger than the average Norman man marching behind. The crunches of their boots on snow carried over to us, and white plumes billowed up behind their feet as they continued pouring over the top of the ridge, hundreds, then thousands of them. The ground trembled, shaking the tops of the trees and sending small piles of snow sliding down the mountainside.

My chest tightened even more. "They're going to cause an avalanche."

"Our people are fine," Tristan said confidently.

I shook my head slowly, not believing what I saw with my eyes or felt with my own mind. All of those oversized men, marching in military form, were norms. Norman super-soldiers.

I peered at the figure flying in front of them that I thought at first had been a new-to-me kind of Demon. "*Sasha?*"

A wolf the size of an elephant, her fur white as snow with

269

stark black stripes like a tiger's, flew toward us with wings several times the size of mine. She circled around us, giving a dip of her head before dropping back down to the men she'd brought. *Her* men, loyal to her above anyone else, much to Lucas's chagrin. She'd led the Norman super-soldiers here, to fight for us now that they were no longer controlled by Lucas or the Summoned sons.

The last time I'd seen the *lykora*, she'd been chasing a Demon away from the Jefferson Memorial the night Hell arrived on Earth. I'd tried hard to believe she'd made it, but since we'd never found her, I had only assumed the worst and mourned her like I had the rest of my team. But she'd survived.

Just like everyone else.

"Is this supposed to convince me?" I asked nobody in particular as I turned in the air. "Because it doesn't. Just thousands more who have marched to their deaths."

"Alexis." Tristan flew right up to me and braced his hands against my face. "You're outnumbered."

"Don't I know it."

"I mean by your own people. They want to fight. They know they can win. They know we have the Angels on our side. But you're not helping."

"Do we, Tristan? Do we have them on our side? Because I don't see the evidence." Tears pricked my eyes. "But it doesn't matter, does it? We're going to have to do this, aren't we? And I don't know what to do. I can't help the fear I feel knowing that either way, these lives are at risk. All those people . . . so many, but not enough . . ."

"No, not enough people." His eyes, full of love but hard with certainty, bored into mine. "But enough Angels to win. If you could only see them."

I blinked back the sting in my eyes. "All I see is death below me. All I feel is the truth of our defeat. I'm going to fail them again, Tristan. The Angels entrusted me to lead us to victory, but there's no way. I can't do this. *We* can't do this."

"But *they* can. Please, *ma lykita*, I beg you to feel the truth. In here." He pressed a hand to my chest. "Where is your faith?"

I closed my hands over his, folding my fingers to hold him tightly. "In us," I whispered. "My faith has always been in us. In you and me. In our love."

His brows scrunched together. Sadness filled his eyes. "That's it? Only in us?"

I flinched. "*Only?* That's always been enough. We've survived everything we've been faced with—your years away with the Daemoni, the trial against you and us as a couple, what Kali did to you, Dorian's kidnapping—we've survived it all because of our love. We escaped *Hell* because of our love, Tristan. Because of you and me. Our love has always been enough. Until now . . ."

"But it still is. Because it's more than just you and me, Lex. It always has been."

Tears pooled, threatening to spill over the rims as I shook my head. "No. In the end, it's only been us. Nobody else cares. Not the Angels. Not God."

"The Angels brought us out of Hell, Alexis. We didn't do that."

"Not the second time. They wanted me to leave you there! *I* went back for you, Tristan. Bree and me. *I* got us out of there." I swallowed the lump that had formed in my throat as I still fought back the tears. The next words came out as a whisper. "I could only save us, though. Not Bree or the rest of the fae. And now, not the Amadis or the norms. Maybe not even our son."

His eyes held mine as they pierced even further into my heart, into my soul, as though searching for some underlying belief I wasn't voicing. But I'd put it all out there. Exactly how I felt. Exactly what I *knew*. Ugly dark stains and all.

With a sad sigh, he pulled me closer to him and pressed his lips against my forehead for a long moment. Then he backed away, holding me at arm's reach. When he spoke, his voice held more torment than it had when he'd found my body buried in the marble remnants of the Jefferson Memorial.

"Alexis, my love, as long as you believe everything we've accomplished has been on our own, without any help, you're just as arrogant as Lucas. You'll never be better than him or the Ancients or Lucifer himself."

CHAPTER 22

*J*blinked, speechless.

"I love you more than life," he continued as he took several steps backward, away from me, "but I can't stand by your side on this."

My mouth fell open. I snapped it shut, but my jaw went slack again as I stared at him, opening and closing my mouth like a fish as no words came. My heart felt as though he'd physically shoved his hand into my chest cavity, grasped it in his fist, and wrenched it around. The dam broke, and the tears that had been threatening finally spilled.

"What do you want me to do?" I cried. "I can't change any of this!"

"That's what I'm trying to tell you, Lex. You don't have to change any of this. It's not up to you. All you have to do is find your courage and believe. Put your faith in the right place. If you could see what we see . . ." His gaze lifted, sweeping over the mountaintops around us. "You would know. You only have to change your own heart."

"Let go and let God?" I asked skeptically. "That's what you're telling me will win this war?"

"That's exactly what I mean."

I blinked against the tears. *Easier said than done.* I could so easily say it if the words alone would bring us victory. But it's one thing to say everything had been handed over to God, or anyone else, and an entirely different thing to live that way. Nearly impossible. Decisions still had to be made. We still had to take action and move forward. We had responsibilities and people depending on us. The world in fact! Wouldn't it be nice to simply let go?

But I *wanted* to. I wanted to trust God and the Angels and hand everything over to them so badly that I physically hurt inside, as though my heart and soul were twisting up and shriveling in on each other. A debilitating tightness in my chest squeezed each breath I tried to take. My stomach clenched and cramped. The weight of responsibility pulled me down, too heavy to lift and hand over, crushing me instead. I could almost feel it physically trying to anchor me into the ground, into that pit of despair, paralyzing me with hopelessness.

"If only I could," I whispered. "But I'm so scared."

"Ah, *ma lykita.*" He stepped back over to me and held my face in his hands, rubbing my tears away with his thumbs. "Remember the definition of courage. Find yours, and you'll find your faith." He pressed his fingers to the rise of my breast, over my heart, over the stone that connected us. "*Feel* for it, Lex. I know it's in there. I've seen the glimmers of hope in you. The flickers of faith. All is not lost. You just need to stop focusing on the evil, on the negative, on everything that could go wrong, and focus on the good instead."

He leaned in and brushed his lips across my forehead before swooping down to join Owen, Char, and the others below. The plans they made—following what Mom and Rina had instructed—drifted up to my ears as I floated in the sky, still reeling from his words. I thought I'd felt alone before, when Mom and Rina had died and left me to lead the Amadis, but I hadn't known true loneliness then. I'd had Tristan. And

Dorian. Owen, my sister, my best friend, and the rest of my team.

Now I had no one. Because nobody else truly understood the weight I carried.

Whatever they saw, whatever they thought they knew was lost on me. Because still, all I could see before us was defeat and death. The true end of the world. How much longer before Lucas opened the gates? Before Satan joined the Earthly realm? Not much, I knew, because there was no way we could stop him. Not when that army of a million, maybe even more, surrounded him, while only thousands had gathered under me. Not when he had dozens of sorcerers and countless Demons with their blackest magic, while we had Owen, Charlotte, and a few dozen warlocks with a fraction of their power and the inability to use any kind of dark powers.

Tristan led those below into formation, and they began their march around the mountain to the valley. My team followed behind him, then the Amadis, then Sasha's super-soldiers with the rest of the norms after them. Tristan motioned a hand signal, and a third of the army branched off to march to the mountain to the east of the valley, another third—which included Tristan and the rest of my team—headed for the west side, and the last third stayed on this mountain to the south. What was he thinking?

The definition of courage was to do what needed to be done despite your fears. But there was a fine line between being brave and being stupid. How could they not see they were about to cross it?

I soared down to Tristan's side.

"What are you doing?" I demanded as I fell into pace next to him.

"You know," he said without pause.

I did know. I just couldn't believe it.

"Tristan! How can you do this?" I swept my arms around at the landscape surrounding us. "You of all people know what a stupid maneuver this is. Our tiny army is split up. We don't have enough troops or firepower to be surrounding the enemy like this. We'll have mountains at our backs, and nowhere to fall back for retreat. You know more than anybody what a bad plan this is. You taught me!"

He stared straight forward, not looking at me. "And you of all people know these are the orders we've been given."

I blew out a breath of exasperation and threw my hands into the air.

"So you're just going to follow them in blind faith?"

His eyes cut sideways at me. "As a matter of fact, that's exactly what we're doing."

A multitude of emotions slammed into me. Most of all, that deep-seated, debilitating fear.

Tristan spoke into my mind, his voice softer. "*We're all afraid to some extent, ma lykita. But we know in our hearts that we're doing exactly what we're supposed to do. Please believe that, too, because they're following me for the moment, but you'll have to give the final order.*"

I turned around, walking backwards, as my eyes traveled over our measly army spreading itself thin across the mountainsides. Stupid. So incredibly stupid.

But we had no choice.

The wheels were already in motion, as Rina had said. In fact, they'd started long, long ago, and now everyone's moves had been made. Including ours. And Tristan was right. My people were looking to me to lead them into this final battle, regardless of how much I didn't want to. As Vanessa had told me before, I needed to pull up my big girl panties. I needed to face this head-on, despite my fear.

Charlotte was right, too. If I accomplished nothing else in this world, I needed to help these people—these norms and the Amadis—defend their souls against evil. And the worst evil of all was about to come before us. It was up to us to stop it.

My gaze began to lift, as though I expected to see Mom

and Rina hovering above me and giving me a bow of approval, although I knew they wouldn't be. We were on our own. Instead, I found a swarm of bodies soaring over the mountain, headed right for us.

Tristan! Up!

He glanced up as they flew over us. I spun back around, and everyone stopped marching as the figures dropped into the clearing in front of our group, one at a time like birds landing. But these were no birds.

They were men, yet not exactly human. They all wore black, fighting leathers on their legs, but their torsos remained bare. Strapped across their broad chests and backs were a variety of weapons—swords, machetes, daggers, and guns. And spreading out from their backs were chestnut-colored, feathered wings, as big as Tristan's and mine, but not quite as . . . beautiful. They certainly weren't Angels standing in front of us, facing our army with their wings spread wide and their powerful muscles bulging, but they weren't Demons, either.

Noah settled to the ground directly in front of Tristan and me, making my breath catch. His long, light brown hair waved over his shoulders in the breeze. His hazel eyes were filled with a fierceness I hadn't seen in him before. His fists clutched two long swords, pointed downward, toward our feet. If I hadn't known better, I'd say he was an avenging Angel, looking nearly as magnificent as Tristan.

But he wasn't an Angel. None of us were. We were only pawns.

Tristan and I both pulled out weapons and crouched into a fighting stance. We hadn't even reached the valley, and the battle was about to begin. Apparently, Lucas had sent the Summoned sons and their offspring as his front line, not caring if he lost any of them since he had the one son he needed. The Summoned were no longer confused, running away and laughing at our absurd attempts to convert them.

Judging by their challenging stances, they obviously intended to fight to the death.

And the thought first and foremost in my mind: Where did they get the wings? And why weren't they leathery, like the Demons'?

Tristan said I needed to be the one to give the order for attack, but I still couldn't bring myself to do it. Once the fighting started, this battle wouldn't end until one side was extinguished, and I already knew which side that would be. My internal war waged on—one part of me resolved on stopping Lucas from bringing Satan to Earth, and the other knowing that our attempt to do so would be the end of us all anyway. How could everyone not see that, especially the Angels?

Before I could make a decision to order a retreat or an attack, Noah and all of his men dropped to a knee and bowed their heads to me. For a moment, Tristan, my team, and I simply stood there, stunned. After recovering from the immediate shock, I opened my mind to theirs and balked at the onslaught of loyalty.

"You come to our side?" I asked, still unable to believe what I saw, what I felt. Not that the hundred or so winged men before me were enough to make a difference against Lucas's army, but the fact that they even bowed to me knocked the air out of my lungs.

"Good will win," Noah said assuredly.

I suppressed a dark chuckle. Good? The Summoned sons who'd *chosen* to go to the Daemoni? Hardly. But a stab of guilt twanged in my soul at this thought, because I'd known their souls had hope back when we cut the stones from their hearts. I'd been banking on that because it meant there would be hope for Dorian, too.

But it didn't make sense.

"We're outnumbered," I said. "You aren't enough to help us."

"We aren't. But they are." Noah pointed a finger toward the black sky with its heavy clouds that were about to let a snowstorm loose. "We fight for them, and therefore, for you."

I stared and rubbed my brow, not understanding. My sense reached out for them, and my eyes squinted as I felt their energy—all good, that of Amadis. They, too, trusted in the beings of Heaven.

"But . . . how?" I breathed. "The curse . . ."

"The curse has been broken," Noah replied matter-of-factly, his face still tilted toward the ground. "We are now on your side, our souls given to you and the Angels."

My stomach turned over on itself. "And Dorian . . . ?"

Noah didn't answer. Nobody else spoke.

"Where's Dorian?" My question was met with more silence. "Noah, get up! All of you, up. Please. Just tell me where Dorian is."

Noah rose to his feet, and the others followed in suit. He turned enough so that his back wasn't completely to me, but so he could point to the fiery pit with the tip of his sword. I followed the line of sight, and my breath caught once again.

"*Dorian!*" I screamed.

The Daemoni and the Demons in the valley erupted into cheers and battle cries as two men floated above their heads—one ensconced in a fireball and the other flying by his own power. Together, they headed for the center of the flaming pit. I couldn't sense his mind signature from here, or feel his thoughts.

"What is he doing? You said the curse was broken!"

Noah looked over his shoulder at me, his eyes dark with grief. "Dorian has broken it. But he is not released from it."

Terror gripped me. "*What?* What does that mean?"

"He's the first male born to the Amadis from both Jordan's and Cassandra's direct bloodlines," Noah explained, his voice low but nonetheless easily heard. "He's the only one ever in existence who could break the curse. He's done just that by

279

choosing to sacrifice himself by giving himself willingly, without desire for power or lust or anything else in return except for freedom of the Ames men."

"Which he is one, too," I insisted.

Noah turned back toward Lucas and Dorian who now floated above the center of the pit. "His commitment set us free. Keeps us free."

My whole body trembled, my heart beating louder than the Shaman's drums. "No. This can't be!"

I sprang into the air and flew toward the center of the valley while keeping to its outer edge, close to the mountain. My eyes took in everything, my mind searching the thoughts of the thousands of Daemoni before me. Their excitement escalated, fed by the sickest, most malevolent images that brought bile up my throat. Demons dropped from the sky, their leathery wings beating against the air a few feet above the Daemoni's heads. The darkness of black magic and evil from the pit rose and curled over my skin and feathers like a shadowy, acidic fog that made my nerves raw. I jumped when Tristan dropped in next to me.

My eyes landed on two women and two men at the far edge of the pit, directly across from us. Rene and Cruz curled their bodies around Victor and Edmund. The shifters' eyes glowed yellow like the cats they were, excitement filling them as they gazed at Lucas and Dorian with a deep hunger. Their lips curled away from their fangs, and their claws lengthened, shredding Edmund's and Victor's shirts. Victor, like all of the vamps among the Daemoni, let out his fangs, and millions of demonic eyes glowed red or yellow as they watched. Unable to contain themselves a moment longer, Rene and Cruz burst into their feline forms, and shifters everywhere transformed, too.

Roars and howls sounded around the valley, and all coherent minds concentrated on the chant of, "Do it! Do it! Bring us our lord!"

Not even Tristan had the power to silence them. Not this many at once. Tristan, Owen, and I together were still no match for Lucas and his dozens of sorcerers scattered in the crowd, thrilling for the moment to use their darkest of magic. We could only watch in horror until Tristan saw our opportunity . . . or first blood was drawn.

"Do you think Dorian and Lucas are shielded?" I asked him.

"They are," Owen said. "Too heavily for us to break."

"Tell the mages to prepare anyway. They'll have to drop it eventually, if a battle is what they really want."

Owen gave the signal.

"Shooting anything before they do will be seen as first strike," Tristan reminded me.

I nodded. I didn't even want to fight, and we certainly wouldn't be the ones to throw the first punch. But I had to accept that this was going to happen, no matter what I thought of it. I had to be prepared to give the orders I so badly did not want to give. I had to find my courage to do what needed to be done, regardless of how terrifying it was.

Someone moved in the Daemoni crowd. A sorcerer, based on the mind signature. And then a whoosh of air blew over us. A few of our people, including Blossom, cried out. Char and Owen both grunted as though taking a direct hit.

"There goes our cloak and shield," Owen ground out between clenched teeth.

And so it was about to begin. I opened my mind and pushed my way into those of my people.

Warriors! I called out to their minds. *The time has come! We must gather our courage and let our goodness and love give us power. The evil below has tried to take everything from us. They have tried to wipe out all that is good. They attempt to take away life as we know it, this world that we love. They want to destroy our very souls. We will NOT let them succeed!*

A loud wave of cheers rushed over our people, eliciting growls from the Daemoni.

Warriors! I yelled again. *We must defeat this evil here once and for all! We must take back our world! Are you willing? Will you fight with me?*

The answering roar was deafening. The emotions choked me all up again.

Then stand ready!

At once, the voices fell silent as a graveyard, and everyone's bodies tensed, coiled for action. Mages' hands turned palm out, and some wands rose in the air. The order hovered on my mind's tongue, and I knew it was only a matter of minutes, perhaps seconds, for me to give it.

Unless . . . unless there was still some way to stop Dorian.

Pretending as though he hadn't noticed the battle cries, Lucas's hand wrapped around Dorian's wrist, and he spun in the air so they both faced Tristan and me. His icy eyes locked onto mine, and his lips curled upward in a grin that made the hairs on my arms stand on end. Dorian's gaze came up to us.

Don't do this, I called out to him. *You can get away!*

"No, Mom, I can't. *This is what I want. This is what I'm meant to do.*"

No, it's not!

His eyes pleaded with me to understand, but I refused to accept his decision. I fisted my hands and yanked, trying to use my power to pull him to us.

Owen, help!

Tristan, Owen, and several mages tried to help me, but Dorian didn't budge. He blocked our power with his own.

"So glad you came to witness this, my daughter." Lucas's voice, usually icy and smooth but now low and gravelly, beastlike, easily carried to us. "Your payment for everything you've taken from me is much appreciated."

A growl rumbled in Tristan's throat, and my own echoed it.

Dorian, he's using you.

He tipped his head in a small nod. *"But I had to free the others so they could fight for you."*

My throat constricted, and tears blurred my vision. *I know. And we thank you for it. But you don't have to do this. Please, Dorian. He's opening the gates to Hell.*

The corners of his lips lifted almost imperceptibly, and his eyes hardened as they held mine. *"He's going to try. You must stop him."*

I blinked the tears away and stared at my son. At the man he had become, hovering bravely by Lucas's side.

"He's so much like you," I said to Tristan.

His large hand wrapped around mine. "No. I don't have the courage he possesses in his little finger."

"He won't forget the stupid curse and just break free."

"Of course he won't. He's our son, *ma lykita.*"

Lucas heard Tristan, threw his white-blond head back, and bellowed out a terrifying laugh. "Oh, no, you're mistaken. Dorian is no longer yours. He's *mine* now." He leveled his head, and his gaze fell on his army. "Are you ready, my children? My brethren?"

The Daemoni and the Demons roared in response. The flames in the pit jumped and grew, leaping higher as though trying to taste the sky. The evil voices fell back into their chant, only louder and faster, their feet stomping and their fists pounding the air. The Shaman's drums beat steadily. Dark magic spells soared through the air.

My eyes darted over the scene. "What is he doing? I can't read his thoughts. His mind's just full of excitement and anticipation for the power he'll have."

"I imagine Dorian has to make some kind of official declaration of his allegiance. See. There are the Ancients." Tristan nodded to the left side of the pit, where several cloaked figures stood. The Ancients. The originals. Demons themselves.

Lucas lifted his hands above his head, barely quieting his followers. "The time we have been waiting for has finally come. The soul we needed has given himself to us. After millennia of bowing to the humans and allowing the Angels and Amadis to dictate over us, we can finally be free!"

The crowd cheered.

Warriors! On my call! I bellowed silently.

Silent cheers passed through our minds. Shifters burst into their beastly selves. Vampires let their fangs protrude, and their nails lengthened into claws. Magical energy sparked over the fingertips of our mages. But still, I held back my final order.

"There has to be a way we can still stop this," I whispered to Tristan as electricity crackled across my own palm and fingers.

"Unleashing your power will only start things. Are you ready for that?"

I closed my fist before I lost control of the charge building inside.

"*I love you, Mom and Dad,*" Dorian whispered.

We love you, too, little man. Until the end of forever, I replied, my wings closing in as though they could protect my heart from the commitment in his eyes and voice.

"Let us call to our lord and welcome him!" Lucas bellowed as he turned himself and Dorian in a circle. "Let us give our lord what he needs!"

The Daemoni and the Demons let out a collective sound that made my skin crawl and lifted the hairs on the back of my neck. As the terrible, Satanic screech continued emitting from their mouths, they all turned toward us, and crouched, ready to pounce.

The noise undulated and then transformed into clearly audible words. "The blood of our enemy."

"The blood of our enemy!" Lucas confirmed, his voice echoing over the valley and against the mountains.

I sent my own silent command to our people. *Not yet. Wait for it.*

Then one of Lucas's hands waved toward Tristan and me, and his other darted out toward Dorian as though to grab him by the shoulder and show off his claim, so quick even I didn't see the blur of movement. At that millisecond in time, the world stopped. Time stopped. No, not stopped. It ceased to exist in natural terms, as some movements came in the slowest of slow motions while others flashed by.

Dorian's eyes, locked on mine, widened for the briefest fraction of a second that lasted minutes, and then tightened. His mouth, full like his father's, flattened with determination. Lucas's lips continued moving in slow, exaggerated motion, the syllables drawn out and lost on me, silenced by the whir in my ears as the most horrific feeling a mother could have slid down my spine, over my soul. My focus telescoped in, focusing entirely on Dorian, and I entered his mind, finding memories of Tristan, me, Mom, Owen, and the rest of our family flashing by in quick succession.

"*Until . . . the end,*" he whispered before his mind blacked out.

Then his head began falling to the side as a thick line of crimson stretched across his throat.

CHAPTER 23

My breath froze in my lungs. My heart toppled along with my stomach. My brain refused to translate what my eyes witnessed, because it couldn't possibly be right. Lucas couldn't have possibly slit Dorian's throat.

Could he?

No. No, no, no. It didn't make sense. I was missing something. Lucas had no reason to kill Dorian. He had every reason to keep him alive, on his side. So what the hell just happened?

These thoughts ran through my mind in a millisecond that felt like hours. Lucas's lips were still moving, his hand hadn't even reached his side yet. The blood on Dorian's throat hadn't even started dripping.

"THE BLOOD OF OUR *YOUNGEST* ENEMY." The words he'd been speaking while slicing my son's throat finally reached my ears and computed in my brain.

Jolted me into action.

"NOOOOOOO!" I screamed as I whipped my wings out. Several feathers, hard as steel, shot out of the edges, turned over, and flew like arrows toward Lucas. I wished I would have known they'd do that earlier, especially when they pierced through his shield. Before he knew what hit him, my purple ones and many of Tristan's silver and black ones peppered into Lucas's chest. His fireball disappeared, and he hung in the air, holding Dorian's slackening body and staring at us openmouthed.

Tristan and I launched ourselves toward him and Dorian, while the Daemoni and Demons fell eerily silent. For the briefest of moments, I was sure all anyone across the valley could hear was the sound of Tristan's and my wings whooshing through the air. Thoughts were confused and jumbled as each side still tried to grasp what just happened.

It had all been so quick, but I knew. And I opened my mind back up to my people waiting with bated breath.

FIGHT! I ordered.

And with another roar, shields dropped and the battle began.

As Tristan and I advanced toward the pit, the confusion and shock in Lucas's eyes cleared, and his mouth crept into a vile grin. Then he opened his hand and released Dorian. My son's body plummeted downward, into the pit of flames. And Lucas followed.

"NO!" I screamed again as I flew faster through the valley. "Dorian!"

A spell of black magic whirred toward me, but one of Owen's green streaks blocked it before it hit the shield Owen had thrown over me. I hadn't reached the edge of the pit yet when two Daemoni vampires leapt into the air and grabbed at me, dragging me downward. I spun out of their holds while releasing the guns from their holsters and kicking each vamp in the head as I did so. With perfect clarity and focus, I aimed my guns at their hearts and shot them both. They fell immediately, their hands scrabbling at the silver bullets lodged in their chests. A dark gray werewolf lunged at me, its claws catching my calf and raking through my leathers and skin as its muzzle snapped and snarled, trying to latch on to me. I trained a gun at its head and pulled the trigger. With an *arf*, it went down. Before I could push myself higher into the air, two more Daemoni blocked my way. A paw with extended talons headed for my face, but I blocked it with my forearm, ducked, and spun. With flying fists, elbows, and feet, I fought them off of me, and then shot them in the heads for good measure.

Remorse immediately tried to trickle in and slow me down, but I had to shove it away. Whether the souls had hope or not, I had to choose between my life or theirs, between my son's life or theirs. I would choose my son. I would choose good. I couldn't waste time, breath, or concern worrying about them when I had to reach Dorian and Lucas.

I rocketed myself higher into the air to avoid more Daemoni obstacles. Below me, Tristan fought off several others, but I had to leave him. I had to get to Dorian.

Thinking the air was safe was a critical mistake—Demons chased me now. One of them shot a ball of fire at me, Owen's shield around me sizzled as it was devoured, and the fireball slammed into my leg. My leathers singed upwards, but no heat burned my skin. Rather, icy needles shot into my flesh, like the freezing cold of Hell had done while I was down there. Another ball of Hellfire hit my other leg, and then a third burnt off my leather jacket, leaving me in my vest and leather pants that barely covered my butt now. When a fourth ball soared at me, I kicked it away with my combat boot. I couldn't see where it went because two Demons zoomed in on me.

Nails as long as pencils and sharpened to vicious points grasped onto my limbs and dug into my skin—one around my left wrist and the other on my right ankle. Their thin wings whooshed against the air as they flew in opposite directions, trying to rip me in two. I twisted around and shot them both. The silver bullets penetrated their thick hides and lodged into their flesh, eliciting ear-piercing screams. They dropped back for a moment, but mere bullets wouldn't kill them, and they continued to fly at me. I shot at them again, slowing them, and I swerved around other Demons as I soared toward the pit. The Demons followed, but I didn't care. As far as I was concerned, I was leading them back home.

I sped straight for the center, leaning forward to angle downward. As I headed for the flames that had swallowed my son's body, I thought, *They're in your hands now.* And as soon as those words crossed my mind, an epiphany hit me. By going after Dorian and trying to stop Lucas, I was leaving my people behind to fight the battle here. But I wasn't leaving them on their own. I felt this truth in my heart and in my soul. I knew that what they were doing—fighting for the world, for humanity, for *good*—was the right thing to do, and somehow, no matter what happened, everything would turn out right. The way it was supposed to.

The way God willed.

My faith may have only been the size of a mustard seed, but that was all I needed. That was what Sheree had been trying to remind me with her tiger mind. If that tiny amount could move mountains, then my people's faith would surely win this war. And finally, my own belief was added to it. So I did what I hadn't done in way too long.

I prayed.

Dear God, Angels, whoever's listening, I'm so sorry for losing my faith in You. I'm so sorry for being arrogant and proud and dismissing Your work around me. Please forgive me. I know only because of You, are we even alive. But my people need You. Please help them. They cannot fight this battle alone, but with You, they will find victory. I leave them in Your hands. I trust in You to protect them. To protect my son, too. And if it is Your will, I trust in You to protect me as I once again go to Hell and do as You have asked of me—stop Lucas and Satan.

With that, I tucked my wings behind me to make me more aerodynamic as I shot downward toward the flames. As I came closer, though, a clawed hand grabbed at my ankle, stopping my plunge. The Demon whipped me to the side, tossing me into the air. I twisted around and shot at its horned head while kicking my leg free. I stared it in its black eyes as I repeated my prayer aloud. It covered its pointy, bat-like ears and let out a high-pitched screech as it soared away.

I fell backwards through the air, face up as lightning streaked across the formidably dark clouds hanging low in the sky. But something else caught my attention . . . made me gasp. Before I turned to dive into the pit of flames, I gave my wings a steadying flap to hold me for just a moment longer over the pit of flames as I stared upward in awe at the glorious sight all around me. I finally saw what everyone else had known because their hearts and souls had been open to what I could not see with my eyes.

Angels.

Angels everywhere. With huge, white, feathery wings and long, flashing blades, Angels fought in the battle side by side with my people. Thousands, no, *millions* of them. Some slayed Demons while others fought with the Amadis and norms against the Daemoni. The odds had flipped over to our favor, at least two to one.

Seeing with my eyes what I had felt moments before—that my people and the norms were protected and would win this battle—I flipped over, closed my wings tightly against my back, and sailed downward, into the fire. Like forked tongues, the flames leapt and licked at me, but as I came close enough to touch them, they suddenly separated, opening into a hole that became a wide tunnel through the fire. Ahead, Lucas's and Dorian's bodies continued falling. I flew for my son.

CHAPTER 24

A thirst for blood like I hadn't felt in years tore through me. Alexis and I both shot Lucas, and our feathers sank into his chest with several satisfying thuds. But it was too little, too late. Our son's body sagged, and then it dropped from Lucas's grip, straight for the fire below them. Down, I presumed, to Satan, who waited for Dorian's blood to open the gates and free him from Hell.

The look that had been on Dorian's face at that devastating moment would haunt me until my final day. Steadfast, determined, knowing. And, I believed, expectant. Expectant that his mother and I would stop the madness Lucas intended. But we were failing our son. *I* was failing him. We'd never get to him in time.

As we soared for Dorian and Lucas falling into the fiery pit, Alexis gave the order, and the battle began. Our people sprang into action, and so did the Daemoni. Were-animals roared ferociously. Vampires hissed and growled. Claws and fangs found their marks, spells streaked through the air, and metal clanged against metal.

And the Angels fought, too.

Many brawled with the Demons, while others dropped

down to help the Amadis and the norms against the Daemoni. With the Angels fighting alongside us, we'd win this battle and this war . . . as long as we could stop Lucas. And save our son while we were at it.

The Daemoni didn't make it easy, though. They attacked both of us as we flew for the center of the fire-filled sinkhole. Powerful magic blasted into Owen's shield around me, disintegrating it on impact, which was just as well. My powers were stronger when not shielded. With a wave of my hand, I paralyzed the three vampires that attacked me, while pulling shuriken out of sheaths in the straps across my chest. I threw the stars at the bloodsuckers and were-beasts targeting Alexis, and their razor edges sliced across their throats and lodged into their chests. They dropped away, leaving only two for her to fight off so she could push ahead. With a twist of my wrist, I killed the three paralyzed vamps, as well as the other Daemoni that dared to come in my way. I'd forbidden myself from using that power since my conversion, but this was war. There was no time for combat, and their desire to be at the center of this fight said enough about the condition of their souls.

Alexis reached the center of the pit before I even crossed its outer edge, and without hesitation, she dove down through the flames. I froze for a moment as I watched my wife disappear, headed back to Hell.

I shouted profanities while throwing my power at the bodies rushing toward me.

But they didn't fall away. In an instant, dozens of Demons, immune to my powers, had appeared, hovering over the pit, blocking my way. Their oily bodies and black eyes reflected the orange and yellow of the flames. I flicked more shuriken, decapitating several, and when I exhausted my supply, I reached behind me and released the swords on my back. And I charged, swinging and arcing, dropping heads two at a time. For every Demon I slayed, however, another appeared.

I growled with frustration. Why had Alexis been able to

pass through, but they seemed intent on preventing me from doing the same? Had they not been fast enough to stop her? Had it been a mistake? Or did they purposely allow her but not me? Why— The realization struck me at the same time a Demon's claw did.

"*NO!*" I roared as I swung a silver blade through the new attacker's neck.

With renewed rage, I arced the swords furiously, side to side and back and forth, cutting my way through the pack of Demons. I *had* to reach the opening. I had to stop Alexis, or the hope for not only our son, but the entire world would be lost.

Blow after blow of the Demons' claws and weapons pounded into my body, but I pushed on. Several Angels flew down and helped me, decommissioning the evil beasts to clear a path to the opening. Through the murderous red haze clouding my vision, I was surprised to see Rina and Sophia swinging swords and decimating Demons.

"You must follow her," Rina said as she spun and slid her sword across a Demon's horn, lobbing it off. It screeched in agony. Her sword swiped again, and the creature's entire head fell. "She needs you."

Sophia decapitated another on the opposite side of me. "She must stop Lucas, but she needs your help."

"Be what she needs, Tristan," Rina added, "and she will do what needs to be done."

I threw an angry look at her. "Like Dorian needed to do?"

"She will be okay. Her faith is restored."

"And Dorian?" I snapped.

"Save him," Sophia commanded. I glanced over at her. "Bring back my daughter and grandson. They don't belong there."

We each sliced through more Demons, progressing toward the center of the pit.

"Of course," I snarled. "But you and the Angels need to do me a favor when this is over."

Sophia stabbed a Demon in the chest and swung it away, flinging it off her blade. "What?"

A black hole among the flames suddenly appeared. Angels fought off more Demons that swarmed toward me, trying to stop me before I flung myself through.

"Keep my family out of fucking Hell!" I yelled before I tucked my wings behind me and nosedived into the opening.

The aperture became a tunnel, barely large enough for my wings to spread and push me down. The fiery walls blurred all around me, streaks of orange, yellow, and white. I saw no signs of my wife, my son, or Lucas ahead, and I rumbled with anger.

"*Alexis!*" I called out with my mind, hoping hers would hear me. When no response came, I shouted out loud. "Dorian! Alexis!"

The flaming tunnel disappeared, and I soared into darkness that swallowed my yells and everything else.

I dropped into the thick blackness of a complete void.

CHAPTER 25

I rocketed downward faster than the normal rate of falling, the flames around me blurring into orange and yellow streaks, but I couldn't close the gap between Dorian and me. We passed through some realm of Hell, where no normal laws of physics applied and distance was an illusion —a real life version of the universal nightmare of running for a door that remained forever out of reach. I flicked my hands in front of me to summon Dorian's body, but he continued falling away.

The flaming tunnel gave way to a thorough blackness, much like my Hell I'd sat in for so long. I lost sight of Dorian, Lucas, and everything else, including all sense of place. But the cool air continued to rush against my skin, so I knew I still sped downward. At the precise moment I realized I could slam into a wall at any time and thought about stopping, a pinprick of light shone, growing bigger by the nanosecond. I was racing toward the lake of fire. Two flecks below grew into Dorian and Lucas, still headed that way, too. I pushed myself harder, giving my wings a few hard beats. Dorian suddenly came within arm's reach.

I opened my hand to grab his leg, but pain blasted into my

arm and shoved me to the side. Lucas's fist came around again, aiming for my head. I blocked his punch and flipped over, landing two kicks into his ribs. Taking advantage as he tumbled in the air, I shoved my hands at him, my power pushed him away, and then I dove again for Dorian. I'd barely flown a few yards when my whole body was yanked back and then hurled around, into a hard wall or pillar. Screaming pain tore through my back and torso.

"Fighting is pointless," Lucas sneered, somehow able to hold himself upright without falling. "You can't win down here."

He twisted and hurled himself down toward Dorian. I followed, able to move faster than him now, while reaching behind my shoulder to retrieve the sword strapped to my back. When I passed him, I swung my arm out. The silver blade sliced across his torso. He let out a beastly howl. With a quick stab, I plunged several inches of the sword between his ribs, and then with a kick of my foot, flung him off. He soared into the distance to where I could see him no more, and he didn't return.

I knew I couldn't have killed him so easily, but I didn't waste time wondering where he went. Maybe we got lucky, and Satan decided to eat him instead of possess him. I could only hope for such an outcome. I aimed for Dorian again as his body quickly plunged toward the lake of fire. Using my wings to push myself harder than ever, I swooped down at the last possible second and grabbed him by the wrist right before a flame swirled around his foot. With another hard thrash of my wings, I turned us back upward and flew with all my power.

Earth's surface could not be seen above. Not even the flames of the tunnel and pit. There was only blackness for as far as I could see. For all I knew, the opening had closed already, and I was zooming us toward a head-on collision with some kind of ceiling. But that was better than either of us plummeting back downward.

Dorian's mind remained blank, but I could hear and feel a faint heartbeat. The wound in his neck must have healed up quickly before he could bleed out. The faintest trace of relief slid through me, and my little bit of hope blossomed further when I sensed the mind signature soaring toward us.

"*Alexis*," Tristan yelled. "*Go! Get to the surface!* You *carry the blood of their enemy's youngest.*"

My heart stuttered. Shit. Stupid me for not realizing that sooner. But it didn't matter.

I have Dorian, I told him. *He's alive. Don't worry—we're getting out of here before Lucas comes back.*

I'd no more than thought the words when a searing pain wrapped around my ankle and spiraled upward to my bare thigh. I glanced down as a fiery tentacle, reaching from the depths of the lake of fire, tightened around my leg. Tiny needles of ice pierced through my skin and wiggled their way deeper into my flesh. Another thin finger rose from the lake, stretching upward toward Dorian and me. My wings beat frantically against the air as I tried to pull my way free. With a snap, the tentacle pitched us to the side.

I slammed into a hard surface and then was wrenched the other way. The force loosened my grip on my son, and he slipped from my hold.

"Dorian!" I screamed. "Tristan, help!"

The other tentacle wrapped around Dorian's waist and pulled him away, out of my view. The one on my leg whipped me again, smashing me into another wall. One more time, and then everything disappeared.

I was pretty sure I stayed conscious, but all of my senses went blank. The lake of fire and the glow it put off had vanished, plunking me back into that black state of mind. My leg no longer burned from the cold or the fire. I could neither smell nor hear anything, and Tristan's mind signature had disappeared. I couldn't even decide if I was flying upward, falling back down, or remaining completely still.

Satan mind-fucked me again.

"And I enjoy it so much." He didn't so much as speak the words. More like he licked them down my back as they slithered over me, serpentine and slimy, making me shudder.

But if I'd really heard or felt them, they dissipated, leaving me in complete nothingness again. No senses. No feeling. Nothing. Except . . .

Excruciating agony tore across my upper back. A scream flew out of me and didn't stop as tears filled my eyes and streaked down my face. I bucked and thrashed, trying to stop the attack, but unable to. I was pinned in place by some kind of force as pain like I'd never felt before sliced into my shoulders and down my back. My torso arched in and out and twisted side to side, but found no escape. Bones broke and my skin and flesh were shredded, drawing out scream after scream until my throat turned to sandpaper and my voice faded into silent cries.

"Can't have you flying away again, now can we?" a snaky voice asked before I blacked out from the agony.

CHAPTER 26

The relief of seeing my wife carrying my son up and away from the depths of Hell had barely washed over me when ropes of fire whipped out of the blazing lake below. Like tentacles, they looped around Alexis and Dorian and snatched them back downward. And I was still too far away to reach them. I flew as fast and as hard as I could, but by the time I emerged from the darkness, Alexis was gone.

My muscles clenched, and an inhuman roar ripped from my stomach as I looked around wildly. *Dorian*. The cord of magma carried his flaccid body across the lake of fire. I flew farther down and across, after him.

"Dorian!" I shouted, hoping to rouse him, but he didn't respond.

The tentacle whipped him to the far side of the lake and then uncoiled from his body, releasing him. He fell to the shore of black lava rock with a thud. I soared for him.

"Dorian, wake up." I landed next to him and bent down to check for vitals.

He couldn't die body and soul down here. Alexis would never forgive me. I'd never forgive myself. The second I felt a faint pulse, I sensed the other presence and sprang upward and around.

A falchion blazing with Hellfire swung toward me.

I bent backwards just in time for it to miss me and shot a ball of fire from my palm as I came back up. Lucas wielded the weapon with both hands, and with a jerk of his head, the flaming ball made a sharp turn and flew into the lake. He twisted the wide sword in the air and arced it back toward me again. I jumped out of the way and thrust my hands out to give him a hard shove of power. It had no effect on him.

"*I* have the power now." His mouth widened in a grin. "All of it is mine for the taking. *You*, as you've come to prove, are worthless."

He spun around and swung the sword. My feathers hardened into steel right before the blade carved into my left wing, and my whole body jolted as pain shot through every nerve. But my wing held. Lucas's eyes narrowed, and his lip lifted in a snarl. Although it didn't exactly feel good, he'd obviously hoped for more damage.

"You don't matter anyway," he growled, and he turned toward Dorian's prone body and swept the sword down.

I sprang in front of him and caught the width of the blade in my hands. Hellfire burned heat and ice into my palms and fingers as I gripped the falchion and yanked it free from Lucas's grip. Before the Hellfire could do permanent damage, I flipped it in the air and caught it by its grip. I swung the weapon toward Lucas.

He only laughed.

And then disappeared.

"Coward," I yelled.

He reappeared several feet away. I sprang at him, sword swinging. He jumped back another few yards. His chuckles echoed off the lava and nearby cliff walls, the sound like an aluminum can rolling over rocks.

"Come on, Seth," he taunted. "Surely you can do better.

Show me you still have it. Maybe I can find a place here for you after all."

"*Never*," I growled as I flew at him, the broad end of the sword aimed for his heart.

At the moment I thought it would plunge in, something large and looming crashed to the ground. Thick, iron bars suddenly surrounded me. Knocked the falchion out of my hands. I launched upwards but slammed into an iron ceiling. Lucas laughed as I dropped back to the ground. I charged at the bars between us. His whole body shook as his blue eyes lit up like lasers.

"A caged animal," he mused. "So fitting. Isn't that what you like, to be imprisoned under others' control? And you could have had it all. You could have had *this*."

He pounded his fist against his chest.

"As if I ever wanted to," I growled.

He snorted. "Instead, you prefer to be a caged bird with your pretty little wings."

I threw my hardened wing out at him, but he caught the released feathers in his hand. "That won't work twice."

At the same time, the razor edges of my feathers cut partially through the bars.

Lucas's eyes blazed bright red, and his head jerked as his smile dropped away. "We can't have that now."

He lifted his hand toward me, and blinding pain pierced into my head. A siren's scream accompanied it, and my hands grasped at my scalp. An invisible weight pressed onto my shoulders, forcing me downward. My knees buckled, and I groaned as I went down, all the way to my stomach. I could hear nothing. See nothing. Only feel the rough edges of lava rock scoring into my chest and the blaring pain in my head.

But even that was incomparable to the agony that ripped across my shoulder. Down my back. A blistering slice through my flesh. Throbbing pain into my shoulder blades and spine. The feeling of raw nerves exposed to the air.

Blackness overtaking me.

I came to gasping for a breath. I felt as though I hadn't breathed in days. The acrid air of Hell burned my throat and lungs, but I couldn't help gulping it in. I still couldn't see. Couldn't hear.

The ground under me quaked. I struggled to push myself up to my hands and knees. The sensation of being lifted in an elevator followed. I scrabbled to my feet and lunged forward. Iron bars caught me. I felt my way around the circle of bars, none of them damaged anymore from my wings. I was still entrapped, rising into the air in some realm of Hell.

And my wings—my shield, my weapon—were gone.

The ground stopped moving. I remained in total blackness. Total silence.

Until the screams began.

A familiar voice.

A sound I couldn't live with.

The agonized shrieks of my wife somewhere in the far distance rose into a crescendo and swirled around me.

Engulfed me.

CHAPTER 27

Alexis

ails filled my mind and ears when I regained consciousness. My own, I thought at first, but as I became more aware, I realized mine mixed with other voices. Cries of intense pain and grief assaulted me from all sides before I could even open my eyes. But peeling them apart against the seal of dried tears made no difference. I could see nothing, smell nothing, and taste nothing. I could only hear and feel the unending torment.

I'd thought the pain of my wings breaking out for the first time had been bad, but that didn't compare to the feeling in my back now. Curled into a ball over my thighs, in the same position I'd awoken, I tried to move my wings, but only felt air against raw flesh. I reached behind me with my hands, pulling my sore skin too tight to bear, and found nothing.

My wings had been severed. Removed. Amputated.

Only mangled, filleted flesh remained. My throat tightened, and tears brimmed and fell. I might have hated them at first, but they'd become a part of me. A very special part of me. A gift from the Angels. And now my beautiful, powerful wings were gone.

My quiet cries turned into sobs. The other voices joined

in, making me quickly forget my own pain as theirs flooded over me, into me. The misery of lost and damned souls here in Hell combined with the eternal misery inside of me from all the people I'd disappointed, hurt, even killed. And now more were being added to the list. My team. Everyone at The Loft. Everyone on the battlefield above. Dorian and Tristan. Their screams drilled through my soul, perforating it. And then came Stacey's and Bree's and the voices of countless other fae who I hadn't been able to save.

After a moment, I realized not all of those voices were in my head. They were in my ears. I opened my mind, searching for signatures. No Dorian or Lucas. Tristan's was gone, too, and I momentarily became distracted as I worried about what happened to him and Dorian. Had Tristan escaped? Had he been able to take Dorian with him? Or had Lucas or Satan captured them both?

"Alexis," Bree's voice called out from a distance. Except it wasn't really far away. No, it was very near, my slow brain decided.

"Bree?" I gasped as I sat up for the first time, blinking against the utter blackness. Faeries' minds had always been unreachable for me, so I hadn't sensed her. I blindly reached my hands out in the direction of her voice, but I felt nothing. "Where are you?"

"We're over here." A British accent.

"Stacey?"

Feeling disoriented by the blindness, I dropped forward, my hands landing on a bumpy, coarse surface. The same floor my knees rested on. I didn't dare try to stand up and walk in the darkness, so I crawled forward, toward their voices.

"Yes, it's me, but you can't get to us."

"Don't try, or you'll fall off the edge," Bree warned.

"Where are we?" I asked as my palm landed on said edge, my fingers folding over the sharp roughness of it. It felt like some kind of rock. I slid my hands to the side, twisting my body as I did. I bit back the pain in my back and shoulders as I felt my way around a circular surface.

"Hell," Bree deadpanned as I stretched my legs behind me to get an idea of the diameter of the circle I lay on. I'd barely extended my legs fully when the toes of my boots dropped off the edge, so not quite five feet across. I flattened myself all the way, inched forward as far as I dared, and reached my arms down, searching for a floor, or anything, beneath, but my hands only swung in the air. So I was on a circular platform, at least a few feet off the ground, but probably more.

"How high up?" I asked as I pushed myself to my feet and gingerly rose to stand. I had to stretch my arms out as a sense of vertigo waved over me.

"Don't know," Stacey replied.

"Higher than us," said her friend, Debbie. I gasped at her voice, not realizing she was here, too. "Baby Cakes and I are down here."

"All y'all are higher than us," a new voice, with a Southern twang, added. It came from the opposite side of my platform than where Bree, Stacey, Debbie, and Baby Cakes seemed to be, and somewhat below. "But we have no inklin' of just how high."

I blinked again, then squinted, but nothing came into focus. "Lisa? Is that you? Are all the fae here?"

"Me and Jessica are over here," said the faerie I remembered from Tennessee with the blue hair. Jessica was her sister. They'd been the ones who'd given us Sasha, and also who'd demanded I capture Kali's soul after they supposedly kept an eye on Owen for me. I had a feeling they'd kept certain other body parts on Owen, and they'd still lost him. But they'd also helped us during Tristan's trial, so I didn't completely dislike the sisters. "And yeah, all of us who have ever helped the Amadis or the Angels are here. Other creatures, too. Some have been stuck here for centuries and millennia!"

"Stacey told me about the fae, and I saw . . ." I trailed off, my throat going dry at the memory of Bree being captured. "You've been here this long?"

"We have no way to escape," Bree said.

"Did they . . ." I swallowed the lump that had formed in my throat. "Did they cut off your wings?"

Several sounds of horror echoed across the space.

"No! But the bars are iron," Stacey replied as though that were obvious.

"We're allergic to iron," Jessica quickly added.

"What bars?" I asked. "I don't have any. Just empty air surrounds me, I think."

Stacey let out a peep of excitement. "And you have wings!"

My eyes burned with fresh tears. "No. They're gone. Someone cut them off. With Hellfire, I assume."

All of the faeries, including many who I hadn't heard until now, gasped or whimpered, feeling my pain.

"Then we must be pretty high up," Bree concluded with resignation. "He wouldn't make it easy for you to escape."

"I don't reckon you try to jump to find out." Lisa may have intended to lighten the mood with snark, but only sadness filled her voice as it carried up to me.

A loud sound like thunder suddenly clapped and rumbled around us. The faeries squeaked, and I jumped back. I hadn't realized how close to the edge I was until the heel of my boot found no support. I held my breath as the edge under my foot crumbled away, and I strained to listen, but never heard the pieces land on anything below. I didn't know if that truly meant anything—if it gave an indication of just how far I'd fall or if it was only an illusion—but I wasn't about to take any chances.

I shuffled forward, kneeled down in what I hoped was the middle of my platform, and opened my mind, trying again to find any mind signatures. Instead, only the misery and pain of eternal suffering filled my brain. I had no idea if Tristan, Dorian, or Lucas was anywhere nearby or even alive.

"I can't find Tristan," I told the faeries, in case they cared. In case they hoped as much as I did that he was going to save us.

"Did you try your stone?" Bree asked.

"Oh!" I slipped my hand under my leather vest and pressed my fingers to the stone implanted in my skin, over my heart. It immediately warmed. "I feel him, but I don't know where."

"Maybe he'll feel you." A hint of hope laced Bree's words.

Another thunderous sound, and then the floor beneath me began shaking and moving.

I sprawled forward, grasping the rim of the platform with my hands and trying to gain purchase with my toes, but the edges crumbled away as though I'd been on sand the whole time. My heart jumped into my throat, and my stomach disappeared with the sensation of falling.

"Bree!" I yelled.

"What's happening?" she called back, her voice growing distant as I fell away from her and the rest of the faeries.

The platform continued disintegrating as I plummeted, forcing me back to my knees, and then crouching on the balls of my feet. Then it was completely gone, and I was falling with no wings to save me. My heart tried to fly out of my mouth as I screamed again.

But only a moment later, I landed with a hard thud on rocky ground.

I'd barely pushed myself to a half-crouch when the prickly feeling of something huge falling toward me shot a shiver down my spine. I dropped to my knees and covered my head. Something large shook the ground all around me as a loud clanging sound rang through the air, echoing off of distant walls. And bright light suddenly flooded over me, easily

KRISTIE COOK

piercing through the cracks of my arms and hands that covered my face.

I peeked through. Vertical lines as thick as pine-tree trunks surrounded me, blocking some of the light. Where was I? It almost looked like the fiery pit in the valley, surrounded by trees. I slowly lifted my head and blinked. The light wasn't really painfully bright, but had only seemed that way after so long in pure darkness. My eyes quickly adjusted. No, not outside. Not on Earth at all.

Still in Hell. Locked in a cell.

The iron bars surrounded me in a circle about six feet across, and a roof was overhead. The lake of fire glowed in the near distance, silhouetting a figure standing about ten yards away by a stone table. And lying perfectly still on the dais, as though dead, was my son.

"Dorian," I whispered as I ran for the bars. The skin of my palms sizzled as soon as I wrapped my hands around them, as though the bars were coated in acid. I jerked back and tried shaking off the burn while reaching out for my son's mind. *Dorian.*

His signature remained blank, but at least its current flowed in my mind and hadn't been snuffed out completely. The figure beside him, of course, was Lucas, tugging at his white goatee with one hand while studying me with icy eyes. I reached out for Tristan's mind signature, but didn't find it. The stone in my chest remained warm, though, so he must have been nearby. Hopefully waiting for the opportunity to rescue us.

Lucas sauntered a few feet closer to me, holding a dagger about ten inches long and twirling its point against his fingertip. "I thought you might want to watch. But you're not the only one."

He did a weird little dance backward as a horrendous sound clamored through the cavern. I dropped to my knees and covered my ears, hoping the cell's roof would hold against whatever fell from above. The crashing sound of metal on stone sounded several feet away from me, but when I looked, I could see nothing.

But I felt him.

Tristan!

"*Alexis.*" His lovely mental voice came with a silent sigh of relief. But then alarm filled him as he saw Dorian on the stone dais.

"Now that you two are taken care of, it really is time," Lucas said as he swaggered over to Dorian, to the far side of the table so I could easily see him. His eyes held mine as he lifted the knife over Dorian's chest.

I couldn't breathe. I couldn't hear anything but my heart pounding against my ribs, or see anything but my little boy, so vulnerable. Caught up in a world and a situation that was no fault of his own, yet here he was, about to die for it. He didn't look like my little boy anymore, his large body practically grown up as it was, but he would always be my baby. And I couldn't lose him.

Lucas's hand plunged.

"No!" I yelled, and the knife stilled, only an inch above Dorian's body. "Take me instead."

Lucas cocked his head to the side and lifted a brow. "You would do that? Sacrifice yourself for this man-child who belongs to me now? Who means nothing to the Amadis or the world above?"

I swallowed hard, trying to loosen the lump in my throat. Although he stared at me curiously, waiting for an answer, it probably didn't matter to Lucas what it was. He believed Dorian to be our youngest, which apparently meant his blood would open Earth to Satan. Perhaps letting Lucas proceed would have been the easiest and most obvious decision that would save the world. But what would he do when Dorian's blood didn't work? He'd never let me out of here alive anyway. And I couldn't let my son die, especially in vain.

But my life aside, could I let these babies I carried die in his place? They were also my children. Either way, I'd be sacrificing one of my own, perhaps two. How could a mother make such a decision?

"*Alexis, no! You're doing it again.*" Anger and fear shook Tristan's voice. "*You're jumping without thinking.*"

But that was the thing I realized in that moment I saw the knife moving toward my son's heart. What became clearer now. Blurting out my self-sacrifice wasn't my first impulsive move of the night. The moment I dove into the fiery pit after Dorian was.

The moment I'd chosen faith over logic.

And wasn't that what I'd done all those times before? I'd hurled myself into some dangerous situations without thinking of the consequences, but I'd always done them because I thought they were the *right* things to do at the time. And I believed God and the Angels protected the right thing, even if we didn't agree with the outcomes. They knew best. Every time I'd jumped in, I'd believed in God's will.

Just as I did now.

Because letting my son die for no reason was not the right thing to do. I was no god, and he was no Jesus. Dorian's sacrifice already broke the curse, but his death would not save humanity nor the Amadis or the Daemoni. I thought of the norms and my people fighting in the Earthly realm, and my heart swelled to near bursting with love for them. For my family, my friends, for those I'd never met. Even for the Daemoni, because I knew deep down that their souls couldn't all be damned. Many could still be saved, even those who'd been born and entrenched in evil. We'd seen that ourselves in the Conversion Center at The Loft with people like Molita. But this . . . what was happening right now . . . No good could come from Dorian's death.

Perhaps throwing these babies under the knife wasn't the right thing to do, either, and putting us in Dorian's place was probably the most illogical decision I would ever make. More absurd than leading my people and the norms into that battle, that's for sure. But that's what all of this was about. What would save the world. What they'd been telling me to do all along.

Choosing faith over logic. Depending on what I saw with my eyes less, and following what I felt in my heart and soul more.

Feeling this truth made the decision easy.

"Yes," I finally answered Lucas, ready to spew the words that would convince him to take me and release Dorian. But before I could tell him that Dorian was not our youngest, I was already on the table, face up. Magical, invisible bindings dug into my skin as they held me in place against the cold stone, my arms pinned against my sides and my legs tightly bound together. Only my head could move.

"*NO!*" Tristan's voice boomed across the spacious cavern, shaking the ground and everything else.

Pieces of dust fell from above, into my eyes and mouth. I sputtered them out and turned my head to see him. He banged his fists against the bars of his cell that was just like mine, producing a deafening racket. Next to him, in the cell I'd just occupied, was our son, his body lying on the ground, still motionless.

Trust me, Tristan, I said, but didn't know if he heard me over the clamor he created.

"You are no different than me." Lucas's ice-cold voice came from my other side, and I rolled my head on the hard stone table to look him in the eye.

"I'm *nothing* like you."

"Of course, you are. You sacrifice all of humanity for something that is important only to you. For some*one* important only to you."

I narrowed my eyes. "You sacrifice your own flesh and blood, your daughters and grandson, for your own benefit."

The side of his mouth lifted in a sneer as his eyes flitted to my abdomen. "Isn't that what you do, too?"

My nostrils flared, but I didn't respond.

"You're so predictable." He scratched his temple with the tip of the knife before casually pointing it at my face. "You fell for my bait so easily. I knew you'd be stupid enough to come after Dorian. *Selfish* enough to give up all of humanity to save one boy." He grinned when my eyes widened. "Oh, yes, I knew of the life you carry inside you. That *you* were the one I needed, after all. Why do you think I didn't kill you at the cabin? The boy was nothing but a decoy. You've made this so easy."

Tristan growled and rumbled and made all kinds of noise as he seemed to be trying to break through the bars.

Lucas glanced Tristan's way and rolled his eyes before bringing them back to me. "You should have come to my side when you had the chance, and none of this would be happening. You, Seth, your boy . . ." He twirled his wrist, swishing the point of the knife in the air as a gesture toward each of them. "All of you could have been together, pleasuring yourselves with everything you've ever wanted. With me, you could have had it all. And look at you now. Don't you wish you would have embraced my offer?"

As he intended, his words brought my *Ang'dora* freshly to mind, with its vision of the mountains and the valley and the lake. And the one tree, half of it covered in sparkling ice and half of it blooming with golden leaves. Half of the landscape frozen and dead, like Hell, like Lucas, who'd been beckoning me with those same empty promises. The other half warm, soft, and summery, where Mom and Rina proposed love, life, and goodness.

He snorted, as though I'd made a profound mistake. But I'd known what I was doing then, just as I did now.

"*Never*," I whispered through clenched teeth. "Never you."

"Oh, really? Are you sure about that?" he taunted. "I've

heard rumors that Katerina and . . . *others* . . . believed *you* to be a better leader for this final battle. That you would do what was right for the world." He traced the tip of the knife over my jawline, and I tensed my muscles, refusing to flinch. "But they were wrong, weren't they? You don't have it in you to choose the greater good over your own flesh and blood. Because you're too much like me."

I glared up at him, looking him in the eye again while I let out a humorless chuckle. "What you don't get, you unwitting asshole, is there doesn't have to be a choice. That's why *I'm* here and not anyone else."

He straightened up, bemusement and anger flashing in his eyes. Both hands closed over the hilt of the long knife, and he raised his fists above my chest. A warm tingling ran across my shoulders and down my back. Without breaking the lock of our eyes, I proffered a small smile.

"I'm nothing like you, you arrogant fuck. And do you know why? Do you know what sets us worlds apart? *You* do everything for greed and power. For control and everything evil. I do it for my family, yes, but also for my people, for humanity, and even for your people. Because I do it for love. I always have and always will. Choose. *LOVE!*"

His eyes tightened and clouded over with more confusion than ever. But after a moment, they cleared, and he let out a nefarious laugh. And when the knife plunged this time, I simply closed my eyes.

CHAPTER 28

My muscles froze, and my heart stopped its frantic pounding—stopped beating altogether as Alexis shared with her mind what she felt in her heart before she'd said the words aloud. My fists dropped to my sides, no longer banging and pulling at the iron bars that refused to budge. I stared at the girl, at the woman, at *my* woman, bound to the dais in front of Hell's lake of fire, the dagger hovering above her heart, held by her own father's fists. My jaw slackened with wonder, awe, and a whole dynamic of surprising emotions.

Because everything I thought I knew about the world, about life, about Heaven and Hell and everything in between, turned upside down at that very moment.

In my hundreds of years of roaming the Earth as a Daemoni warrior, I thought I'd learned all there was to learn. I thought I'd experienced everything I'd ever needed to. And then I realized that there was more, a different view, a different perspective of life and the world. A different way of living that I wanted. So I converted to the Amadis. For years, I experienced more, learned more, until I reached the point where I truly believed nothing could surprise me, let alone teach me.

Then came this girl. This woman. *My* woman. And every time I turned around, she surprised me. She taught me lessons I'd never realized I needed to know.

Most of all, she taught me love.

Only because of her did I know the joy and pain of love. I knew how to love, what it felt like to be loved. The love of a soul mate, of a child, of family and friends.

But one lesson hadn't been learned yet.

The one lesson she taught me now.

The real meaning and power of love.

Guilt for my past actions did not equate to love. Constantly trying to right all the wrongs I'd done in the past had nothing to do with love. Doing the right things for the wrong reasons was not only irrelevant to love, but spat in its face. Those were all about me.

Love was this. This girl. This woman. This beautiful creature displaying love in all its powerful glory. Showing her faith through her love for not only me, our children, our family and friends, and our people, but for everyone—good, evil, and everything between. And showing her love through her faith.

Because they belonged together, love and faith.

All this time we'd been fighting each other, her following her heart and me following my soul. Her believing in love and me in faith. And neither of us was wrong. Neither of us was right. We'd needed to bring those two powers together.

And my girl, my woman, my wife, was doing it.

Her voice rose with her conviction as she glared at Lucas. "I do it for *love*. I always have and always will choose LOVE!"

Her words, her commitment, the strength of her meaning flooded over me like a bucket of warm water. I soaked it in, understanding for the first time ever the extent of her feelings. Experiencing for the first time in my long life what she did—

an unselfish love that surpassed the easy kind and expanded to the hard stuff. Love for those who were difficult to love, who refused love, who pushed it away, who thought they were above it. For those who so many would think didn't deserve it —like me . . . like our enemies. The kind of love we were meant to have for all other souls. The kind of love we were given by the One who created love in the first place.

Love and faith—an invincible combination.

Her love flowed into mine to give us strength. My faith streamed in with hers to give us power. And that was everything we needed.

The skin on my shoulders and down my spine prickled and tingled, and I recognized the sensation. My wings exploded from my back. A roar tore out of my chest.

I would be what she needed. Until the end of forever.

CHAPTER 29

Alexis

*R*ather than pain stabbing into my chest, my back
and shoulder blades tingled again, and at the same
time the blade should have plunged into my heart, the
crunching sound of metal and a terrifying roar filled the air.
My eyes popped open to find Lucas's hands paused with the
tip of the knife pressing into my leather vest and his eyes
darting wildly. A large, dark streak came at us, and in a blur of
motion, Lucas disappeared, and the stone dais I lay on
collapsed like a house of cards. My freshly grown wings burst
free, each purple and black feather hard and sharp as a double-
edged sword. They cut through the magical bindings holding
me, and I sprang from the broken platform.

Tristan paused long enough to check on me as his own
new wings spread wide, and then he flew after Lucas. Swiping
the edges of my wings across the iron, I cut through the bars
between my son and me and sprang inside for him. I'd
planned to slip my arms under his shoulders and knees and lift
him up like I'd done so many times before, when he was little.
But one look at him, and I knew I couldn't do that. Like I'd
had to do with Tristan, I circled my arms under his, clasped

my hands together over his chest, and launched myself upward into the darkness.

"*I lost him,*" Tristan said as he soared up next to me. "*Let's just get to the Earthly realm.*"

Hold on. I need you to light up.

A flame suddenly appeared in his outstretched hand, lighting our way, and I led him upward, hoping to find the faeries. At least a dozen cells like the ones that had held us were perched at the top of narrow pillars that rose hundreds of feet above the lake of fire. I flew by each one, using my wings to cut through the iron, and Tristan followed, pushing the bars out of the faeries' way. Flying bodies with colorful, butterfly-like wings suddenly surrounded us.

"We'll free the others," Stacey said, and she, Debbie, and Baby Cakes flew off into the darkness.

My focus centered on saving my son in my arms and the babies in my belly before something worse happened, and Satan was the one who was freed. "Let's get out of here."

I shot upward with Tristan, Bree, and many other fae behind me. Half a dozen Demons swarmed in on us.

"Go, Lex!" Tristan yelled at me.

"We can take care of these," Bree confirmed.

With a glance over my shoulder, I saw that the fae could indeed. Unlike when they were attacked and picked off one-by-one, now they severely outnumbered the Demons. Holding tightly to Dorian, I jetted upward, swerving around the evil winged spirits that tried to block me. I couldn't fight with my son in my arms, but if a Demon came close enough, they received a swipe of my wings that sent their heads plummeting back to Hell, where they belonged.

Fighting continued behind me. Lucas's mind signature came back into range as he attacked Tristan, who blocked his way to me. I opened my mind to Tristan, sharing Lucas's thoughts while I continued toward the surface. But then evil slithered into my head.

"*Where are you going, Alexis?*" Satan asked, his voice clear and smooth . . . sexy and alluring. "*This is where you belong. Here, with me.*"

I paused, hesitating, drawn to his glamour. Nightmarish visions flashed in my mind—Mom's death, the norms I killed, the children on the train—and their screams filled my ears.

"*You knew you belonged here before,*" he taunted. "*Nothing has changed.*"

I gave my head a shake. *No, I was wrong then, and you're wrong now. Forgiveness has been granted.*

"Go, Alexis!" Tristan bellowed again from below me. He must have heard Satan in my mind. Lucas laughed. He must have, too. But I suddenly worried about Tristan . . . about leaving him in Hell again.

You need me, I said to him.

"*I'll be fine. My faith—and my love—are where they belong.*"

Although my stomach knotted, I continued upward, leaving him behind once again as I accelerated. I held Dorian's large body close against me as we flew through the fiery tunnel, toward the pit and the surface of the Earth. With a shaky heart, I shot us up and out.

And into chaos.

My ears rang with grunts, yells, roars, and the clanging of weapons. The odors of baby powder, sulfur, iron, and blood wafted in the air. Lightning streaked webs across the clouds above, thunder rolled overhead, and fat snowflakes glowed orange like embers as they fell. My breath came out in icy puffs in front of me. Faint little streaks slipped through Dorian's lips, too.

I landed near the rim of the pit and laid him out of the way of the warriors, then soared high into the sky to gain a view of the battle. For as far as I could see in every direction, Angels clashed with Demons in the air. On the ground, more Angels helped the norms and Amadis who fought Daemoni and Demons with human bodies. Thousands of dead and injured lay scattered about the Earth. Black, silver, and crimson stained the snow as weapons, claws, and fangs sliced through flesh and blood spurted.

I tried to find my team, my mother, and my grandmother, but it was impossible in the bedlam. To add to it, several figures shot out of the pit.

The fae came first, including Bree, Stacey, Debbie, Baby Cakes, Lisa, and Jessica. I dipped down closer as more flew out after them, followed by all kinds of supposedly mythical creatures, some whom I wasn't sure should have been freed. I dropped back down to Dorian's side in case something tried to attack him, and each time a figure emerged, I held my breath, waiting for Tristan. My chest began to tighten as I thought about him being left behind last time, unable to fight his Demons. *He defeated them. They no longer have power over him.* I tried to calm myself, but not until he came through the flames did I finally believe it.

Tristan rose from the pit, along with Lucas. They fought each other on a fiery tentacle so fat, it looked like a snake or eel. When the thing lifted itself higher and twisted, it exposed what looked like a yellow blazing eye in the orange and red magma. And I swore it searched for me, because as soon as its gaze landed on me, it zipped in my direction. Tristan and Lucas flew up in the air when it did, and they continued their hand-to-hand combat.

The snake's flame of a tongue lashed out at me, and I flattened myself over Dorian's body, keeping us protected with my wings. When it pulled back, I jumped up and shot an electric charge at it, but the power had no effect. This was a beast from Hell. My sword and guns were gone, taken when I'd been captured, leaving me with my hidden dagger and knife—both too short to reach the snake's head without my skin getting burned. I had my wings, but I couldn't leave Dorian, unconscious and helpless.

The fiery serpent charged at me again. I rose up just high enough to pull it away from Dorian, my wings hard and lifted, ready to slice into the thing. Tristan saw it charging my way, though, and abandoned his fight with Lucas. He flew over the snake, banked into a turn with his wing angled down, and severed it in half. At the same time, a green light streaked toward us, slammed into the fiery pieces, and they disintegrated into black smoke that wisped downward, into the flames. On the far side of the pit stood Owen.

I lowered to the ground to check on Dorian when someone's power blasted into me, knocking me sideways. As I tried to catch my balance, Lucas landed nearby, his hands out toward me, and wave after wave of power slammed into me like knives blazing with Hellfire. Burning cold sliced into my flesh, oozed into my blood and bones. I lifted my wings to block it and shot Amadis power back at him, but he was so strong, so dark.

Since he had no use for Dorian anymore, I took the chance and launched myself upward, drawing him away from my son. As expected, Lucas tried to follow, lifting himself several feet above the ground, his power still blasting at me. Until a white and black streak knocked into him, tackling him to the ground. Vanessa's fists pummeled Lucas's face several times, and then her head dove down before he threw her off of him with his power. He launched himself into the air, blood pouring out of the side of his head. Vanessa spit Lucas's ear to the ground. I soared after our sperm donor.

His power pushed back at me, a force that slowed me down as I flew against the resistance. Two Angels swooped at him, long swords out—no, not Angels, exactly, but Mom and Rina. Each of their blades glinted in the light of the fire as they swung toward him, carving a bloody X into Lucas's chest. He lurched backward before hanging in midair, his expression wild and confused as his power stopped blasting at me. His red eyes filled with flames when they found Mom and Rina who hovered above me now. He yelled something unintelligible as he tried to lift his hands toward them, but I could feel their power storming down at him.

I took the opportunity and sped toward him. He laughed at first, then smirked, which was followed by a cry to his people for help. Nobody came. Except Vanessa, who sprang up and grabbed him from behind, pulling him to the ground. And Tristan, who paralyzed his body. I stopped several feet in front of this man who was supposed to be my father, pausing only for a second to relish in the terror shining in his eyes.

Then I whipped my right wing out.

The feathers' edges swept across his throat.

A sound like "no" gurgled through the gash.

Then his head rolled off his shoulders and toppled, blood spurting from the stump of his neck like a fountain. Snowflakes descended into his empty, icy eyes and gaping mouth.

And everything around us fell still.

The fighting ceased. Battle cries silenced. Nobody moved so much as a finger. Everyone simply stared at Lucas's beheaded corpse.

The fountain of crimson ceased as shards of bright blue light flared from his body. They twisted together and grew into tentacle-like forms and curved upward and high above the gruesome form that had once been a man. The light gathered together, spiraling into a glowing ball that pulsed out a beat as it grew.

The blackest of all magic soared over my head, sending an eerie tingle down my spine. The ball of light absorbed it, expanded and brightened.

It throbbed one more time.

Then it whizzed toward Dorian.

"No!" I dropped to my son's side.

But I couldn't stop it. The ball circled around me and plunged into his body, and a moment later, he gasped awake, clawing at his chest. My head snapped up toward Mom and Rina.

"His *soul?*" I shrieked. "Did Lucas's soul just possess Dorian?"

Mom's blade plunged into Lucas's torso again. She twisted it around, and then yanked it out. On the silver tip was a white gauzy substance, thin and smoky—like Kali's soul when I'd removed it from her physical body.

"No, not his soul." Mom flicked the essence into the fiery pit.

The edges of the sinkhole instantly began closing in. The flames dimmed and lowered. Vanessa flung Lucas's body into it, and Tristan picked up his head by the hair and tossed it in, too. My sperm donor, body and soul, disappeared into Hell. As if being sucked down by a vacuum, thousands of evil souls in their Demon forms sailed into the pit, screeching in protest. The fire immediately extinguished, and the ground closed up.

"What was it?" I asked desperately as I turned back toward my son, my hands flitting over him, checking him for injuries. Specks of dried blood clung to his neck, but that was all.

He rolled away from me and pushed himself to his feet, drew in a deep breath, and glanced around. His resemblance to Tristan still blew me away.

"He has Lucas's power now," a cloaked figure from the side of the pit hissed. One of the Ancients. "Which means he has ours."

My poor heart stopped once again. "He . . . he has the power of Lucas *and* the Ancients? What does that mean?"

In answer, the remainder of the Daemoni roared in some kind of evil cheer. And then they attacked again. The fighting resumed.

Magic spells and powers shot from the Ancients toward

Tristan and me. We both flew at them, swooping by them, but when we thought we'd severed their heads with our wings, they disappeared into black smoke. *Cowards*, I thought as I swept around to view the battle.

Although they were severely outnumbered with the Angels helping the Amadis and the Normans, the remaining Daemoni fought with renewed vigor. More blood spilled. More bodies crumpled to the ground. I opened my mind, sharing the enemies' thoughts with our allies, while I used my own powers. Tristan paralyzed several until the Angels or Amadis could defeat them. Then his next thought came to me, and I had to stop him.

No. I shook my head, and he restrained his deadliest power. *Enough have died already. There's only one person who can stop this.*

Tristan nodded, and together, we dropped down to Dorian, landing on each side of him.

"Dorian, you can end this," I said. "You have Lucas's power. You have control over them now. Right?"

He turned his head to look down at me, and my stomach dropped at the glow in his eyes, making me gasp.

Before he could respond, a body soared through the air toward us and landed not too far away. She immediately jumped up, shaking her blond hair out of her face—Lesley. Alys's vampire friend who'd been so close to choosing conversion. She charged back the way she came, but Vanessa was faster. In a blink, Vanessa held Lesley's heart in her hand. Was her soul still safe? What had she chosen in the end? I would never know.

"Dorian, do something," I begged.

Two more bodies flew at us. Met the ground in front of us with successive thuds, both face down in the snow. Both blondes . . . and instantly recognizable.

"NO!" I screamed as I lunged at them.

Two were-cats, a cheetah and a jaguar, leapt at us, pushing

me away before landing at Dorian's feet. They crouched and bowed, then instantly transformed into their naked, human forms—Cruz and Rene.

"We brought you a gift, master," Cruz purred as Rene spit something bloody and tubular out of her mouth.

Dorian knelt down and turned the smaller body over at the same time I moved the other. My breath whooshed out of me, and my hand slammed over my mouth.

"No," I wailed as I dropped to my knees. "No, no, NO!"

I gathered Charlotte into my arms, rocking and holding her, pushing her hair out of her face. Her sapphire blue eyes held no more light. No more life. Next to me, Dorian studied Heather, a chunk of her throat and trachea ripped out.

"Dorian, stop this!" I cried. "Stop it now!"

His jaw muscle twitched as he clenched his teeth while staring at Heather's face and her bloody, battered, lifeless body. His eyes, still hard, narrowed as he stroked a finger over her cheek, blinked once, and then turned them onto Cruz and Rene. They both fell to all fours, their heads down. Dorian ignored them as he rose to his full height, nearly as tall as his father standing next to him.

Tristan clamped his hand on Dorian's shoulder. "Do the right thing, son."

A growl rumbled in Dorian's throat, and his nostrils flared as he glanced down at Tristan's hand, and then squared his shoulders, effectively shrugging his father off.

"It's over, my children." Dorian's voice was no louder than normal, but reverberated across the valley with unprecedented power. The endearment sent a shiver down my spine. "Stand down!"

The fighting stopped as suddenly as it had before, but the Daemoni, several thousand remaining on their feet compared to the hundreds of thousands before, only stood there, staring at Dorian.

"Who is with me?" Dorian asked with a command to his

voice I'd never heard before. All of the Daemoni dropped to a knee. "Then come."

My hand grabbed at his leg. "Where? Where are you going?"

He turned those hard eyes on me, a glint of red glowing in them. "Away from you."

My eyes widened. "*What?* No! It's okay. If there's hope, we can convert them. You can convince them, can't you? They'll listen to you! They can become Amadis. Like you, Dorian. You're still Amadis. You still belong with Dad and me."

"No, I'm not. I'm nothing like you. These are my people now, and I belong with them." His voice raised a notch. "*I* must take care of them. Not *you*."

He spat the last word out as though it offended him.

"Dorian—"

The red in his eyes glared brighter, and his voice came out in a near roar. "Stop trying to control me! I am not your baby anymore!"

I flinched, and a heartbeat passed between us as we gazed at each other, his eyes glowing with the power swirling within him now. More power than any of us could possibly comprehend. And not the good kind. The kind that was intoxicating, difficult to deny, too easy to embrace . . . which Dorian's mind showed he was doing now—embracing it. His body delighted in the energy charging through it.

I shook my head. "No, Dorian. Please don't do this. Be stronger than this."

"Don't worry, *mother*. I'm stronger than you could possibly imagine."

A small smirk crossed his face before he broke the lock of our eyes, turned away from me, and lifted his arms into the air. The wind gusted up, circling and whipping around us. The Daemoni corpses disintegrated into ash, picked up by the wind. The gusts lifted the bloodstained snow into a tornado that spun around us, blasting ice crystals into my face and eyes. Just as suddenly as Dorian had created it, the snow-tornado disappeared, along with the Daemoni.

And so had my son.

CHAPTER 30

The shock of everything being over and the evil ones gone hung in the air, as tangible as a suspended curtain waiting to fall. As if time stood still and the world had stopped spinning, waiting for our minds, hearts, and souls to catch up with reality. I didn't know if anyone actually breathed. I knew I didn't. Every cell of my body seemed frozen as I knelt on the ground with Char's dead body in my arms. The only movement came from the fat snowflakes that continued to fall.

Then someone in the distance let out a cheer.

Many others followed. Mages, vampires, and norms whooped and hollered, and shifters let out resounding roars and howls. Even the Angels shook their fists and weapons in the air. The sounds of everyone congratulating each other reached my ears, but so did the cries of those who'd lost loved ones.

Owen, who'd been on the far side of the pit, suddenly appeared next to me.

"As I said, Alexis, good always wins," he declared.

I slowly lifted my head to stare at him as though he'd lost his mind.

"Do we?" I choked out as a tear ran down my cheek and fell onto Char's.

His gaze dropped to the body in my arms, evidence to the contrary. His breath hitched as he drank the sight in, and the light in his eyes dimmed as his face fell. Then he crashed to his knees next to me and scooped her out of my arms, pressing his mother into his chest. His wails carried the forlorn song of the souls in Hell, breaking my heart more than it had been already. Mom dropped next to him and wrapped her arms and wings around Owen and her best friend.

I gathered the other body into my arms and held Heather, tears streaming down my cheeks as her eyes stared without seeing. Such innocence. Such loss.

"Heather?" Sonya's voice screamed from the distance, quickly approaching. "Heather, where are—No! Oh, no!"

The vampire eyed us, and I didn't want to look her in the eye, to be the bearer of such horrific news—again—but I had to. And my look was all she needed. Her jaw slackened. Her eyes widened. She streaked toward us and collapsed in front of me.

"No, Heather, oh god, no," she cried as she took her sister from me and into her own arms. She curled around the girl, her whole body trembling with sobs. I folded myself over her, covered us with my wings as Mom had done with Owen and Char, and held them both as my tears mixed with hers.

When the worst had passed, I hid my wings to find Blossom and Sheree hovering over us, their faces streaked with tears. They tried to comfort Sonya and Owen both as I stood up, swept my eyes over the corpse-littered valley, and shook my head.

"*Nobody* wins in war," I whispered.

Tristan slipped his arms around me. I leaned my head against his chest, drawing on the calming effect he had on me because my nerves were so taut, so raw. My heart so irrevocably broken. Rina and Cassandra appeared by our sides.

"No truer words have been spoken," Rina said.

Cassandra nodded. "Yes. However, on this day, good has defeated evil. We will mourn, but we may also rejoice."

Voices in the distance cheered, but everyone around me grieved.

The sounds of victory eventually succumbed to a quiet steadfastness as the Amadis began taking care of our dead, giving supernaturals and Normans alike an Amadis send-off. My heart grew heavier with each one until I thought my body couldn't possibly hold it any longer. And then came Heather. Then Charlotte . . . and I could barely form coherent thoughts let alone speak the words she deserved. She'd become my surrogate mother. My mentor. A courageous and strong warrior. I loved her so much, and she was gone.

The realization that Dorian wasn't coming back, either, sank me.

A song that sounded both mournful and uplifting at the same time came from the heavens, from the Angels. And then all but Mom and Rina disappeared, and the veil between Earth and the Otherworld was restored.

"You're staying?" I asked with the first trace of hope since killing Lucas. "For good?"

Mom frowned. "No, honey. We don't belong here."

"But we will stay for a bit longer," Rina said.

Nobody else was quite ready to leave, either, partly out of a special bond they'd all formed from fighting side-by-side, and partly because the air here was temporarily safe for them, and they wanted to make the most of being outside. Our mages transformed the Daemoni camps into more homey and comfortable accommodations for the night as the snow fell harder. A quiet celebration became louder as the night passed and hard liquor was discovered.

I, however, could not possibly join in. Neither could my team. We gathered in a large tent together and mourned our losses. Every time I looked around at the faces that meant so much to me, I couldn't believe Charlotte's was no longer there. Would never be there again. And neither was Dorian's.

Owen left first, and Vanessa followed him. Then Jax and Blossom said their good-nights, followed by Sheree.

"You don't have to leave," I told her, knowing how much she adored Char and that she had no one to mourn with.

"I'm going to find Sonya," she said from the doorway to the tent. "She's probably all alone."

I nodded my appreciation. I spent the rest of the night wrapped in Tristan's arms, my own returning his embrace. Mom and Rina took turns holding and comforting us.

"I can't believe he left," I sobbed, my chest heaving as I remembered the look in my son's eyes.

"*That* is his purpose," Rina said.

"To lead the *Daemoni*?" I cried.

"He is doing what he is meant to do," Mom said. "Something only he can. Remember what I told you."

"I didn't think you meant this!" I pressed the heels of my palms to my eyes, trying to stop the unending tears. "His soul will be lost. He won't even get to choose. The evil energy is too strong for him, too overwhelming. I saw it in his eyes. He's just a little boy! He hasn't matured enough to handle such power."

Mom stroked a hand down my back. "The power was new, honey. New to him. It will settle, and he will control it. After all of this, you must have faith that there is a reason he received that power and nobody else. Because he *is* strong enough to handle it."

Tristan swept his arms around me again and pulled me in tightly. "He is alive, Lex. He is brave, and he *is* strong. You know he is. He has too much of you in him to give in so easily. You healed the fractures in your faith and made it whole again, so embrace it and let go of what you can't control."

I swallowed the painful lump in my throat, stared at the magical ball that produced a yellow light for us, and pulled on divine strength within me. My son *was* alive. Thank the Angels for that! When I'd thought the world had ended, I would have killed for that to be true. And he wasn't trapped in Hell for eternity, which he very nearly had been. He wasn't living under Lucas's control or as a servant to Satan. His soul, at least for now, was still his own. My gratitude for that fact outweighed everything else. All I could do now was pray that he held on to it and trust God and the Angels to protect him. Hopefully, one day after everything settled, we would be reunited as a family. I could see that vision clearly, as though a premonition of what would come.

That would be my rope of hope I would hold on to for as long as necessary.

"Everything is as it should be," Rina said, before she and Mom eventually left us, too, to search for Noah.

Their reunion gave my heart a small but much-needed lift. When Cassandra had said we should rejoice that good had defeated evil, Rina and Mom must have been thinking about Noah and the rest of the Summoned and their descendants. I still hadn't fully grasped that they'd come to our side. Another victory to be celebrated. Some day.

With the evil gone, the sun finally dawned the next morning, sparkling on the freshly fallen snow that covered the spilled blood of the longest night. Owen began creating portals for everyone to return to their underground communities until we could decide how to fix Earth. We said our goodbyes with promises to officially celebrate when the time was right.

"Trevor?" I said in surprise when I turned to find a familiar werewolf in front of me. Tristan and I had just sent a couple, Rissa and Gray, whom I'd only met now, through a portal to Georgia. They must have been part of Trevor's or Sundae's packs. The tall, thin female stood by his side. "Sundae!"

"Couldn't leave without saying so long," Trevor said.

"Thank you for coming," I breathed. "Did you . . . any family . . .?"

Sundae smiled slightly and shook her head. "Gray's my brother, and you see he is fine. So are our packs. We were lucky. We're returning whole."

I blinked several times, pressing down the grief of *not* being whole, and nodded. "Where do you stay?"

"We have a safe place under the bar and shop," Sundae replied.

Trevor dropped a thick arm over her shoulders. "Why do you think I teamed up with her? This is one smart lady."

Sundae rolled her eyes. "When you live the life we do, I couldn't help but fall in with those crazy preppers, knowing doomsday would come sometime. It's big enough for both of our packs and some local norms, too."

"We'll come check it out sometime," Tristan said.

Trevor nodded. "We'll have to celebrate with a few."

"You have beer?" Tristan asked, sounding even more intrigued.

Sundae laughed. "That was gone months ago. But we got shine."

Just the thought of moonshine made me want to gag.

We finished our farewells with Trevor and Sundae, and they stepped through their portal and disappeared. The next familiar face we ran into caught me off guard, although I shouldn't have been so surprised to see him. Noah dropped his head in a bow.

"Please," I said, "you really don't have to do that."

He lifted his face and eyes to me and grinned. The first time I'd ever seen him do so. "Only showing my respect. And my allegiance."

"You and the others have more than proved that," I said. "You fought with us."

"And we will do so again," said another man who stood behind Noah, his head down.

"Let's hope we don't have to," I murmured. *Especially when my son is with our enemy.*

Noah's hand squeezed my shoulder. "Know that we are here for you."

"And where is *here*, exactly?" Tristan asked.

Noah didn't look at him, but instead gave me another bow of his head. "At our leader's beck and call."

At once, all of the Summoned spread their chestnut-colored wings and sprang into the air.

When everyone but my immediate team had left, we stood with Mom and Rina by the portal to The Loft.

"You're not coming with us." I didn't state it as a question. My chin trembled with the answer in Mom's and Rina's eyes.

"It is time," Rina confirmed.

They gave each of my council members a farewell hug. Mom and Owen held each other for a long time.

"Tell her I love her," Owen whispered, although most of us could hear him anyway. "I never said it enough."

Mom squeezed him tighter. "She knows, Owen. And I know she loves you more than she could ever say."

He pulled back and gave a small nod before averting his head and pressing his fingers to his eyes.

One by one, my team stepped through the portal until only Tristan and I remained with Mom and Rina. Since we would be flying back to The Loft, Owen closed the portal, leaving the four of us in a long-awaited peace in the valley. When I turned to Mom and Rina, I couldn't stop the tears.

"I don't want to say goodbye," I cried as my grandmother held me. "I've said it too much already."

"We will visit when allowed," Rina promised, which made me feel a tiny bit better.

Mom turned from Tristan, and I turned to her, and I threw myself at her.

"I wish you could stay." The tears flowed harder. Regardless of how infuriating she'd been, she was still my mom. "I miss you so much. And you're going to be a Mimi again."

She stroked her hand over my hair as she held me tightly. "One way or another, I will be here." She pulled back and placed her hand over my heart as her mahogany eyes met mine. "Even if it's only in here, know that I am always close, Alexis. We all are."

"It's not the same, Mom."

"I know, honey. But until we know more, that's the best I can offer."

I pulled her back against me, holding on because I knew when I let go, she'd be gone for good. In a different world, a different realm. Eventually, however, I had to release her. Well, she let go of me and stepped out of my arms, forcing me to. She placed a hand against my cheek and gave me a small smile. "Trust in the Angels, Alexis. For you. For those babies. For Dorian."

With that, they disappeared, leaving me nodding and crying at the same time.

Tristan and I flew to Hades before we headed home, hoping to plea to our son, but Hades had been deserted, as far as we could tell. The Shaman village near the main entrance had been abandoned, and the back entrance, the ice cave Vanessa and I had gone through last time, had been collapsed. There was no telling where Dorian was now. All we knew was that he didn't want to be with us.

By leaving with the Daemoni, with the harsh words he'd barked at me, I couldn't help but feel that he'd disowned us. But my hope for him didn't waver. My love for him would never falter.

We took our time flying back to the U.S. and The Loft, allowing our hearts and souls to mend somewhat before we had to jump in and face the new reality before us. When my mind didn't focus on Dorian, Charlotte, Heather, and the rest of our losses, it wandered into the future. Questions with no immediate answers circled in my brain, such as how the world would rebuild itself, who would emerge as leaders, if the countries and states would stay as they used to be, or if new boundaries would be drawn. When could I take a long, hot shower again with my man? Would we ever be able to eat fresh food? How long would it be before we could begin manufacturing again or rebuilding the power and communication networks?

"*It'll take time,*" Tristan answered my thoughts. "*The Daemoni did a lot of lasting damage. The world may never be the same again. Which probably isn't a totally terrible thing.*"

No, it wasn't. In the Before time—before the Daemoni ruled and the Demons walked the Earth—many norms believed the world could use a push of the reset button. Now, they'd been granted that wish. If only nature herself wasn't so desolate.

As we flew farther south and entered the States, we left the dirty, gray snow behind, finding the warmer weather of spring. And a surprise greeted us.

Tristan, look. Green!

Speckled against the monotone landscape of Earth were various flecks of green. I immediately dropped to the forest of bare trees to inspect. We landed on the top of a huge redwood, most of it gray and seemingly dead. Except for the one branch in front of me.

"A leaf!" I squealed as I gingerly lifted it under my hand. "An honest to god green leaf."

Liquid silver trickled down the branch toward the tree's thick trunk, and Tristan swiped his finger through the rivulet. He held it to his nose, and after inhaling, he smiled before bringing it under mine.

"It smells like Sasha," I said. "Baby powder."

My heart twanged at the thought of Sasha, who'd disappeared after the battle, which brought on thoughts of Dorian again. I hoped she was with him, protecting him from the evil of his so-called people, serving as a constant reminder of us and our love.

"My guess is Angel blood," Tristan said, bringing me back to the here and now. "And I'm thinking everywhere where there's green, Angel blood spilled."

I glanced around the forest, seeing only specks of color in the gray. Just like it had in the Otherworld, the battle for humanity must have waged all around Earth. "Their blood might heal the world, like mine."

He nodded. "It'll still take time, but at least we don't have to drain you."

I punched him lightly in the shoulder. He gave me a beautiful grin, and I couldn't help but return the smile. He was my light in the bleak world, keeping me hopeful for brighter days ahead. His gaze fell to my lips and lingered, and when his eyes lifted to mine again, my stomach dropped. In a good way. His expression smoldered with desire, igniting a low burn within me.

I backed up until I pressed against the trunk, and he advanced predatorily. He lifted his hand under my jaw, held me still as he gazed into my eyes for several pounding heartbeats before his eyes dropped to my mouth again. My lips felt dry and chapped as my breaths came shallow over them, and my tongue slid out to wet them. A low, playful growl rumbled in him before he leaned down and captured my mouth with his. His lips were firm, but soft as silk, urgent yet giving. His tongue implored my lips to part, and when they complied, it delved inside, tasting me, devouring me.

My psyche must have needed his touch, his love to become physical, because passion instantly rose. My heart sped. My belly quivered. My thighs already shook with need. And we were still only kissing, deeply, pressingly. My chest heaved, my breasts pressing against him. He moaned into my mouth, and then slowly pulled away. My lips tried to follow.

I'm not done kissing you!

He chuckled. I opened my eyes.

"Let's find somewhere a little more accommodating," he suggested.

Granted, balanced at the top of a redwood with branches blocking our wings in, this was not an opportune place. Tristan leapt off, and I followed him. He landed in a clearing next to a flowing stream. I landed in front of him. Our wings disappeared. I rushed into his arms.

As our mouths found each other again, our hands moved frantically to undress each other. I pulled his shirt over his head, and he unzipped my vest, freeing my breasts that ached with demand for his touch. I forgot about the ugly scar and being self-conscious. I needed him to touch me and love me like I'd never needed him before. His hand immediately found one breast, cupping it, fondling, pinching and pulling my nipple. My fingertips skated over his hard chest and up and down the ridges of his abs. They flexed under my touch, causing a ripple of pleasure to run through my own belly. We parted long enough to remove our boots, each of us eyeing the other, our breaths already coming in pants. I yanked down my shorts—what was left of my leathers—as he removed his.

A jolt of pleasure at seeing his naked body in all of its perfection shot through me, causing me to shudder.

His brows pinched together.

"What's wrong?" I asked.

"Are you sure about this?"

I smiled. "Absolutely!"

He glanced down at my not-quite-flat belly. "I don't . . . want to hurt them."

Now I chuckled. "You're practically a doctor. You know better than that."

He glanced down at himself, and then his gaze came back

up at me, a cocky grin on his face. "But look at this! Aren't you even a little afraid?"

Full-on laughter burst out of me. His eyes fell to my shaking breasts, and all humor left them, replaced by flagrant want. That look he gave me . . . Oh god, that look. My laughter disappeared as warmth and wetness pooled between my legs.

"Not even in the slightest," I panted before I leapt high onto him, wrapping my legs around his upper torso and my arms around his head, pressing his face into my breasts.

He grunted out a laugh-moan before his mouth became occupied, kissing and sucking its way up and over the round flesh, until he found its tight and puckered tip. His hands pressed into my back, and I leaned against them. My shoulders arched over them and my head fell back as he pulled my nipple and part of my breast into his mouth. His tongue swirled and flicked. His mouth sucked, and his teeth grazed. My hips ground against him, teasing the tip of his erection as it pressed against me. He moved his attention to my other breast, and my hands dove into his hair, my fingers curling around the locks. As his mouth worked, I whimpered and moaned, moving myself against him. Every part of my body screamed for more. My thighs clenched and quivered.

Unable to hold back a moment longer, I loosened the hold of my legs just enough so I could slide down onto him. We both gasped with the beautiful sensation.

"Lexi," he moaned against my throat as he plunged inside of me. "My sexy Lexi."

I lifted and descended, meeting his upward thrusts, relishing the strokes against the hot, swollen flesh inside me. He was my rock. My light. My love. My everything. My glorious lover making sweet, hard love to me. We rocked together, skin against skin, hearts pounding, minds opening, sensations flowing and twisting together, heightening, expanding, soaring . . . exploding.

"Lex!"

"Tristan!"

We hung there in pure, unadulterated oblivion, convulsing against each other, melding together, drawing out the bliss for as long as we could make it last. And slowly, we drifted back, our muscles trembling, grins spreading, eyes full of love and adoration.

"I love you," we both said at the same time.

"Forever," he added.

I smiled and whispered, "And always."

CHAPTER 31

5 MONTHS LATER

"CHOO-CHOO-CHOO-CHOO." Alexis pushed the air through her clenched teeth while gripping my hand in one of her fists and Vanessa's in the other. She squeezed so hard, my skin turned white, and I wished there was some way I could relieve her pain, but there wasn't. All I could do was be there for her.

When the contraction passed, Carlie's head popped up from between my wife's legs, where she sat on a low stool at the end of the bed. Alexis lay on the mattress we'd brought back from the shelter to the Caribbean room specifically for this occasion, her legs propped up on pillows. She'd insisted our babies be born here rather than in an underground bomb shelter, even if it did have the ironic name of The Loft. So Owen, Blossom, and I had been busy preparing our house in the Florida Keys, creating a protective bubble around it and cleansing the air and everything else within it.

"You're doing fine," Carlie said, giving her patient an encouraging smile. "We're getting close."

I squeezed Alexis's hand. She looked up at me with glassy eyes that quickly filled with pain.

"Argh!" Her teeth gritted as she breathed through another contraction.

"Good." Carlie's head disappeared for another moment. "You're doing great."

She didn't come up, and I peeked over Alexis's legs to see her hands moving around.

"I . . . have to . . . push," Alexis groaned.

"Whoa, whoa, whoa. Hold on," Carlie ordered.

"I can't fucking hold on!" Alexis yelled as she gripped my hand harder. Vanessa and I exchanged a look, her eyes filled with humor and her lips pressed together.

Carlie lifted her head and nodded. "Okay, go ahead. You can do this."

Alexis's torso lifted from the bed as she bore down. My arm slid to her back, supporting her as she screamed and groaned. The contraction passed, and she fell back, panting.

Carlie let out a noise of excitement. "I think . . . Yep . . ." She bent over and peered closer before letting out a little squeak. "I see a head!"

I leaned her way until the stretch lifted Alexis's arm from the bed, trying to see for myself. She released her grip on my hand.

"Go," she said between pants. "I know you want to."

Blossom rushed over and took Alexis's hand. Vanessa's arm slid under Alexis's back to brace her for the next contraction. I hesitated, not wanting to leave my wife's side.

"Go!" she barked.

"Get over here," Carlie snapped at me. "Hurry!"

I joined her at the end of the bed, and my gaze landed on the most frightening and most beautiful view I'd ever seen.

"You can do this, Lex," I said as Carlie moved to the side so I could kneel down in front of Alexis.

She came off the bed again, groaning and pushing.

"There's the crown," Carlie said excitedly. "Get ready to catch, Tristan."

I positioned my hands in preparation and listened to my wife scream in pain as our child's head emerged from her. I gently clasped it between my palms and held it still as Carlie cleaned out the nose and mouth. A few moments later, with another push, the rest of the body slid out and into my palm.

Carlie went to work immediately, but I could only stare at the tiny human.

Tears filled my eyes as Carlie lifted my hands to lay the baby onto Alexis's stomach.

Alexis lifted her head off the bed, her hair plastered to her sweaty scalp, and her mouth stretched into a tired smile. "Finally. A girl."

Carlie clamped the umbilical cord and pressed scissors into my palm. My normally calm hands shook as I cut through. Sheree took the baby to towel her off, and the little thing let loose a loud cry while she was wrapped in a blanket. Just as Sheree was about to pass her back over, Alexis bolted up, screaming again.

"Baby B!" Carlie rushed back over to the end of the bed, and I hurried to join her.

After several pushes, the head crowned, followed by the body sliding into my hands. And I was no less awestruck the second time around. Sheree and Carlie both gasped, followed by Vanessa and Blossom. My own breath caught in my lungs, and my vision blurred as I tried to blink away the tears. My whole body shook now as I cut the cord and lay the baby on Alexis's stomach, my cheek muscles aching from the grin on my face.

I hurried over to Sheree to take our crying girl, but I couldn't quite figure out how to hold her itty bitty body in my arm that suddenly felt like an ape's, too large and unwieldy to be safe.

"Like this." Sheree smiled as she settled the bundle into the crook of my arm.

Our baby quieted as soon as I held her. Her lids opened wider, and then she blinked at me.

And from that moment on, I would never be the same man.

God help anyone who so much as tried to lay a finger on her.

I sat on the bed next to Alexis as Carlie and Sheree cleaned and checked the younger twin.

"She's so beautiful," Alexis whispered as her fingertip traced over our daughter's tiny nose.

"Of course she is." I pressed my lips to her temple. "Look at her mommy."

Tears rolled over Alexis's cheeks as she looked up at me. She lifted her hand to my face, and with her thumb, wiped away my own tears.

"And not only you two," I said as Sheree brought over our other little bundle. Alexis took the first baby while I held the second. "Meet the other love of my life. What am I going to do surrounded by *three* of you?"

Alexis's eyes widened, understanding. "*Seriously?*"

"Look for yourself, if you don't trust me."

She peeked under the blanket. "Wow. Not that it matters anymore, but . . . *wow*."

As I held the baby in one arm, I slipped my other behind my wife's back and hugged her and our daughters to me. Alexis shivered under my arm.

"If only Dorian were here, everything would be perfect," she said with a sniffle.

"He is, my love. He's in our hearts. Maybe one day in our lives. Until then . . ."

She sighed and nodded. "We give praise for the blessings we have."

"Exactly. And for me, that would be you. All of you . . . you are my everything. My heart. My love. My woman. My children. My world."

CHAPTER 32

Alexis

$\mathcal{W}$hat could be sexier than a hot man holding a baby? My own Mr. Beautiful holding two babies.

Every time I walked into a room to find Tristan holding one or both of our newborns, I fell in love all over again. When he leaned in and kissed a tiny forehead, my heart melted. And when he got up with them in the middle of the night because they wanted to walk, not feed, or when he volunteered to change a dirty diaper? I absolutely died.

We'd spent the last few days since the birth on what I deemed a family honeymoon in our beach house at the Keys. We needed time to adjust to parenting newborns, and our babies needed time to acclimate to life outside the womb. We weren't alone, of course. Vanessa and Owen, Blossom and Jax, and Sheree and Carlie each took turns "guarding" us, although I knew they really wanted to spend time with the babies.

Because there was no real danger anymore. We'd won the war. The Daemoni had essentially disappeared from the face of the Earth. Along with my son. A reality I'd come to acknowledge, although not fully accept, months ago. One day,

I vowed to myself, I would get my son back. I just prayed his soul would stay intact until then.

Soon, we would be returning to The Loft, which ironically provided more creature comforts than the house here. Owen had magically created a system to give the beach house somewhat fresh water for the bathroom and cleaning diapers, but it wasn't a long-term solution. Neither was the generator running on magic. Besides, we had a lot of work ahead of us to turn the people of The Loft into a full-scale community, hopefully on Earth's surface sometime in the future.

In fact, Tristan had gone through a portal to The Loft this morning to help with preparations for the babies. So I was surprised when I padded into the Caribbean room, wearing a t-shirt and stretchy yoga pants, to find the large body standing by the open sliding doors, the sandy-brown head leaned over the bassinet the twins shared as a breeze fluttered through the sheer curtains around him.

But then my heart jumped into my throat when my mommy-exhausted brain caught up and identified the mind signature. At the same time, Vanessa suddenly appeared beside me, the rush of air she produced lifting the ends of my hair.

"I sense Daemoni," she hissed as she stepped farther into the room, her head cocked as she scrutinized the figure in the other opening.

I hurried inside and clamped my hand on her arm to stop her. My heart raced as I walked past her, closer to the bassinet and the sliding glass doors. My throat and tongue felt full of sand.

"D-Dorian?" I whispered.

The breeze settled, and the curtains fell still, hanging to each side of the doors. My son stood in front of the babies' bed, no longer a child but a grown man. He wore a midnight blue suit, as though he'd come to a business meeting, making him appear even older. His light brown hair was perfectly coifed, although . . . he had the scruff of a beard on his jaw!

My hand covered my mouth as I stared at him, tears welling. He looked up at me with hazel eyes that sparkled with gold and a small smile on his lips.

"Hi, Mom." He spoke quietly, not to wake the babies.

Although I, too, sensed Daemoni, I didn't feel as though we were in any danger. I rushed to him and threw my arms around him.

"Dorian! Oh my god!" I whispered. Tears flowed as I held onto my son, afraid to ever let go of him again. "I knew you'd come back!"

He held me for a long moment, but then stepped out of my embrace. He gazed down at the blanket-burritos before him.

"I had to come," he said as his gaze swept between the sleeping bundles. "To welcome my sisters into the world."

God, my heart. I swiped at the tears and moved to stand at his side. "Dorian, meet Brielle Sophia and Elliana Katerina."

"Which is which?"

I pointed to the one on the left. "That's Brielle." I paused, my brow furrowing for a brief moment, then pointed to the other. "That's the baby of the family, Elliana."

He chuckled quietly. "Are you sure? They look exactly the same."

"I'm their mother! Of course I'm sure." I gnawed on my lip as he looked sideways at me. I sighed, my shoulders dropping. "Okay, so we have to color code their blankets to tell them apart. The only thing different between the two is Elliana has a little birthmark on her hip. Otherwise, yes, they look exactly the same. But trust me, they're not. When they're not sleeping, they're like night and day."

My body automatically tensed when he reached a finger out to stroke each of their tiny faces. My son or not, he still exuded Daemoni energy, and my motherly protective instincts pricked. I couldn't help myself from monitoring his thoughts, although they remained pure, authentic. The babies slept through his touch, and I let go of my breath when he pulled away.

"I brought them a present," he said as he stepped backwards, onto the screened-in lanai. He produced a tiny white puppy in his hand when he returned. She jumped into my arms and slid her blue tongue over my cheek.

"Sasha," I whispered, and then I looked at Dorian and shook my head. "No, Dorian. She's yours."

"She's not. She's already been ordered to protect them. They're her masters now."

"But—"

"Mom." He sighed and then lifted his hand to my jaw. I couldn't help but lean into it. "I don't need protection. From anybody. I'm the most powerful creature on this Earth. You don't need to worry about me anymore."

I pressed my hands on his chest and pushed him outside. I slid the doors closed so we wouldn't wake the babies, but I felt Vanessa's eyes on us from inside the room.

"I do worry!" I snapped at him. "You have no idea how much your dad and I worry. What are you doing, Dorian? *Why?*"

"I'm taking care of my people, Mom. Because they're my people."

"But they're not! *We* are your people. *We* are your family! What are they doing to you?"

He shook his head, his eyes soft as he gazed at me. "Nothing. They're doing nothing to me. I'm the one in charge. *I* lead *them.*"

I blinked. I breathed. "Well then, lead them to the Amadis. They can be saved, Dorian. So can you!"

The gold in his eyes darkened with sadness. "No, they can't. Not all of them. It's too late for many. But somebody has to lead them. Somebody has to keep them in line."

I pressed my hands to my chest. "But why you? It doesn't have to be you. You don't belong there!"

His large hands encircled my small wrists, stilling me. He looked into my eyes, trying to drive home his reasoning. "It can *only* be me, Mom. If not me, then it would be Victor or Edmund. Is that what you want?"

I stared at him, unable to breathe.

"Do you want either of those two leading your adversaries who want to end you? Those who want to kill your daughters?" He released my wrists and frowned. "That's what they want to do, Mom. That's why it must be me. *I* can control them."

My throat worked to swallow what felt like a dirty sock that had suddenly lodged in it. My heart sank as his truth settled into me, into my bones. My bottom lip trembled as I fought against it, not wanting to accept it. But this was what Mom had meant. He wasn't our possession. He owned a piece of my heart, a piece of my soul, but he was his own person. And as she had said, we had to hope and pray that we'd done enough to prepare him for the world and for his role in it. That we'd given him enough love to protect his soul.

I wrapped my arms around him and tried to flood him with more love. "I'm so sorry, Dorian. So sorry it's you."

"I wish . . ." He pulled away from me, his expression still full of sadness. "It doesn't matter what I wish. This is how it is." His gaze shifted, looked through the screen and the water beyond the half-gray and half-green brush. He shook his head. "I have to go now."

My eyes widened. I didn't want to let go! "Don't you want to see your father?"

He sighed as he looked back at me. "I can't stay any longer."

He leaned in and tapped his lips to my forehead, but before I could respond, even to say goodbye, he disappeared with a pop. I caught a brief glimpse of him on the lawn before he shot into the air.

"*Love you, Mom. Until the end.*" The words whispered in my mind.

Love you, little man. No matter what.

And then he was gone for good. I wrapped my arms around myself in a hug as tears silently rolled down my cheeks.

"You know there's still hope for him," said a tiny voice from behind me.

"Yeah, I know," I said with a sigh as that same hope settled back into me.

Then I realized I didn't recognize that voice. I spun around. An unnaturally cute, young girl, early teens perhaps, with bright pink hair and clothes to match stood next to the bassinet.

I threw the sliding glass door open. Where was Vanessa?

"Who are you?" I demanded. She had no mind signature.

"I'm Pinky. Stacey's me mum." And that explained why. She was a fae. "They're so cute. I love babies. Mum sent me to see if you need help. I can watch over them, or . . ." Her eyes glinted as she looked out at the patio where Dorian had been moments ago, and a smile played on her lips. At the same time, her cheeks turned a rosy pink to match her top. "Or I can watch over Dorian. You can make him my mission."

I sensed the crush on him, which would partially explain her motivation, but I tilted my head and narrowed my eyes. "In exchange for what?"

She giggled, a musical sound, as her eyes crinkled. "You've already paid up, Alexis. The fae folk are the ones in debt. *We* owe *you.*"

I blinked several times, and then I nodded. They did owe us for freeing them. And that could be quite convenient.

"Yes," I hurried to say. "Keep a close eye on him. Make sure he stays good . . . as good as he can be."

She let out a little peep of excitement. "Thank you! I promise to watch him closely, every minute of the day and night."

With a quick peck on my cheek, she disappeared. I smiled, but then I blew out a sigh. Poor Dorian. What had I done to him?

"You're okay?" Vanessa asked from the doorway when I padded over to the bed.

I threw my arms up and let my hands smack down against my thighs. "I don't know. But I will be. Some day. For now, I guess I'm as good as I'm going to get."

Since the babies slept, I took advantage of the peace and lay down. My body rarely had time to regenerate in the last three days, constantly feeding and changing diapers between the two of them. Sasha came in and curled up on the bed next to me. I sank my fingers into her soft fur and drifted off.

When I awoke to little whimpers and fusses, Tristan was leaned over the bassinet, picking up one of our bundles—Brielle, I thought, by the sounds of her. And I knew without a doubt it was my husband this time. He looked up at me and pressed a finger to his lips before he snuck away with the crier. He'd check her diaper, but she probably wanted to eat. I'd barely lay back on the bed when Elliana awoke with a loud cry. Yep, that was definitely Elli.

I picked her up and walked outside, where Tristan sat on the patio chair holding a quiet Brielle. Her tiny fists waved in the air as he leaned his face down to snuggle against her neck. Damn. My ovaries exploded for the millionth time. How was I so lucky?

I sat down in the chair across from him, rested my ankles on his thighs and pulled the crying Elliana to my breast. She latched on hungrily. When she was done, we traded babies, and the whole time, we talked about Dorian's visit.

"I wish you could have seen him," I said. "He's changed so much already. And I guess not all for the bad."

Tristan gave me a guilty smile. "I have seen him."

I straightened up. "*What?* When?"

"A while ago, when I came here to see if we could make

this place safe for you and the babies. He stopped by, but he'd made me promise not to tell you."

I frowned. "Why?"

"He wanted to surprise you." He paused as he rearranged Brielle to burp her. "And I think he might have needed more time. He's the most powerful being in this world, possibly more than you and me combined, and the most courageous soul I know, Lex. But I'm telling you, he was scared to death to see his mom again."

My frown deepened as I considered this. And then I laughed as a sense of relief washed over me. "He's going to be okay, isn't he?"

"I think so. We will always hope. We may not like it, but he's serving his purpose. Doing what he needs to do. All we can do is love him unconditionally and be there for him when he needs us."

I nodded as my heart swelled with the love I had for all of my children. Then I chuckled again. "I guess Mom and Rina had been right all along about him. The Angels had always known."

"Which is how we know Dorian is serving his purpose. We just have to have faith that his soul will survive the tests he's being given." He paused as he gazed out at the sunset. "I fully believe he will. He's strong and brave. He'll lead them the way they need to be led while the world restores itself."

I watched the sun hovering over the distant edge of the water, casting gorgeous pink and orange strokes over the clouds and the sea's surface. And I remembered what Tristan had once told me about his love of sunsets—how they marked the close of another day that had never been promised, how they meant somewhere else in the world a new day was dawning. I smiled inside, appreciating his words more than ever.

He lifted my hand and pulled me up, out of the chair. He guided me onto the free side of his lap. With Brielle in his other arm and Elliana in mine, I leaned against his shoulder.

"This is our future," he murmured. "Our beautiful little family. They'll grow up one day, too, and fly the coop, you know."

A calming and warm sensation of peace settled over me as I melted against him, knowing that future would come, but seeing the hope in it. Hope that I'd believed in my heart not too long ago had been completely lost. Yet here we were, the future literally in our hands.

I smiled, tilted my head back, and kissed his cheek. "And then it will be just us in our empty nest. You and me together until the end of forever."

"And always. Don't forget always."

"Never," I whispered as he leaned down and pressed his mouth against mine.

*J*olted awake at the scream of my baby. No, make that both babies, crying like I'd never heard them before. Tristan sat up next to me, both of us blinking against the light of early morning, before he bolted out of bed and blurred to my side, where the bassinet sat. Both Brielle and Elliana kicked their little legs and waved their tiny fists, their faces red, almost purple as they screamed.

"What's wrong with them?" I snatched Brielle up, and Tristan picked up Elliana, but both babies continued to wail, as though something caused them intense pain.

I tried to feed them, but neither had any interest. When we lay them down to change their diapers, they only screamed harder. Their voices quickly grew hoarse as they coughed intermittently between howls. They had no tears, but I did.

"I don't know what to do," I cried as I looked at Tristan, begging that he knew, but he shook his head.

We sat on the bed, up against the headboard, trying to soothe them. Sasha bounced around frantically, also disturbed by their cries.

"Do you think it's colic?" I asked. Even if it was, I had no idea how to make them feel better. I hated this part of parenthood—the part where you wished like hell that you could take their pain away and make it your own to relieve their suffering.

"Maybe it's gas." Tristan turned Elliana over to lay on her stomach over his forearm. She immediately stopped crying as she inhaled ragged breaths and shuddered as they came out. He patted his hand on her back to burp her, but she broke into screams again. His hand froze in midair, and he let her lay there, her arms and legs dangling over his thick forearm.

I lay Brielle on her belly over my leg in a similar position, and her cries diminished into hiccups. Tristan and I looked at each other, bewildered. My heart had finally settled down when they both began screaming again, even louder than before. Their little backs quivered and arched. Their fists beat at the air. I thought I heard the sound of paper crinkling and ripping between their sobs.

Then at the exact same time, feathers sprang out of their shoulder blades.

I practically jumped out of my skin. "Oh my gosh! They have wings!"

Instantly, they both quieted, and then even cooed.

As the lavender-colored wings began to uncurl, a laugh popped out of my mouth. Relief flooded me as the girls squeaked and sighed, happy again. We turned them over and held them out in front of us, both of our mouths gaping. Their wings opened behind their backs with a wingspan of about a foot.

They both gave us a smile. Their first real smiles.

"What does it mean?" I wondered. "How . . . ?"

Tristan studied the babies, as perplexed as I was. "No. Idea."

"It means the world has changed."

The familiar voice came from outside, on the lanai. With Brielle still in my hands, I sprang from the bed and ran for the sliding door. I swished it open and grinned at the sight in front of me.

"Mom! You came!"

She smiled back at me and wrapped her arms around me, with Brielle between us. When the baby squirmed, she pulled back and took her from me. The love and joy in her eyes as she studied her granddaughter made my heart balloon.

Tristan cleared his throat from behind me, and I glanced over my shoulder at him. *Oh. Oops.* He wore nothing but boxer briefs under the sheet. I rushed over to retrieve Elliana from him, then ushered Mom outside.

"Mom, meet Brielle and Elliana. Baby girls, meet your Mimi."

"Brielle and Elliana," Mom echoed softly as she held them both.

I grimaced and squirmed. "I know the Angels gave me the name Gabriella. I did hear the whisper in my mind. But they only gave me the one name . . . and it was . . . I don't know . . . we wanted to make it ours, too. For both of them. Did you know Heather and Charlotte had the same middle name? Ann? And the girls' middle names are for you and Rina, which is tradition. I mean, for you anyway, but we didn't know . . .."

I babbled away, sounding like Blossom. Mom never tore her eyes from the girls when she finally interrupted me. "Their names are approved, Alexis."

I blew out a breath of relief.

"The Angels are very pleased." Rina's voice came from behind me, and I spun around to hug her. "Sorry I was delayed. Let me see."

She pushed past me and reached out for Elliana. I thought for a moment Mom was going to fight her with the look she gave her own mother, but she must have realized there were plenty of babies to go around.

"I'm so glad you both came to meet them," I said, clapping

my hands together under my chin. "They're beautiful, aren't they?"

"Of course they are," Rina agreed. "They are yours, yes?"

I beamed with so much pride, my heart should have exploded.

"Your wings are so tiny and adorable," Mom spoke in baby talk to Brielle.

"About that . . ." I started, and as the realization that my babies had wings slammed into me, the questions bubbled forth with no filter. "How do they have freaking wings? How on earth can we possibly hide them? I mean, they're too little to do it themselves, right? Do you know how hard it'll be to take care of them with those? What in the hell do they *mean*?"

Tristan came out at the moment my last question spewed, wearing pajama bottoms and nothing else. I promptly became distracted as my crazy hormones nearly gained control of my senses, and I came very close to kicking Mom and Rina out with the babies so I could jump his bones right there and then. I forced my eyes away from the perfection of his chest and abs to glare at Mom and Rina. They seemed to ignore me, their full attention on the babies. I knew they were cute and all, of course I did, but seriously!

"Mom? Rina?"

"You do not need these yet, little one," Rina murmured, her only answer as her hand swept over Elliana's back. The baby's wings disappeared. Mom did the same to Brielle, and Rina finally glanced up at me. "They still possess them, but they will not need them for a while. They have been hidden until the time comes."

"Thank you," I breathed as I sank into one of the chairs. Sasha trotted across the patio and jumped into my lap. "But what do they mean? What do ours mean? We're not Angels . . ."

Tristan came over to stand behind me, his hands gripping the back of my chair as he leaned on it. We'd both been dying to learn the answer. Mom and Rina, each with a cooing baby in their arms, turned to face us.

"As I said, the world has changed," Mom repeated. "It went through massive destruction, but now it is time for its rebirth."

"Satan and the Demons have been imprisoned where they belong," Rina added. "Humanity will continue for many more centuries, perhaps millennia, to come. However, there is an imbalance now, and it will take time for balance to be restored. You and your descendants will ensure that happens."

I stared at them with an arched brow. "I thought our war was over."

Mom smiled at Brielle. "It is, honey. As much as it can be. Evil and good will always be at odds. It's their very nature. It's the nature of this entire physical world and the souls that live on it. There will always be strife. There will always be the good and the bad and every shade between. And that is okay. That is how it's meant to be. You cannot have one without the other."

"Daemoni still exist and always will." I sighed. "I get that. I also get, as much as I hate it, that Dorian must be the one to lead them."

Rina nodded. "Dorian will be a good leader for them as they recover and rebuild."

"Recover and *rebuild*?" I asked in disbelief. "Why would we want that?"

"Because there is a gross imbalance," Rina said matter-of-factly as she stroked a finger over Elli's cheek.

"What?" I demanded. "Isn't that good? We finally outnumber them for once."

Tristan leaned harder on my chair. "A huge imbalance to one side, like this, leads to power struggles. The Daemoni will want to grow again, to regain their power. If Dorian doesn't allow that, they'll fight him for control. If he loses, we have Edmund or Victor or some other threat to contend with. If Dorian keeps them in control, however, growing their numbers naturally, he'll better be able to maintain his position. And once there is balance again, they will feel less threatened by us. We'll return to where we were several years ago. Co-existing while we try to help as many as they try to hurt."

"Exactly," Rina agreed.

"Hold on," I said. "Grow their numbers naturally? You mean, we *allow* them to turn norms?"

"Their shifters and mages can reproduce," Tristan reminded me. "With our numbers protecting the norms, they won't try to turn or infect any unless they stumble upon someone dying anyway. It will be a very slow growth."

Well, that made me feel a little better. We had enough to deal with in this new world. We didn't need to worry about the Daemoni, too.

"Do not become complacent, though," Rina warned. "Demons still roam this world, many in human form. They are a major threat. They must be found and sent back to Hell."

I stared at her with my mouth partly open. I'd forgotten about the Demons in human bodies, who hadn't been sucked back into Hell with the others. Frustration grew within me, making me antsy. We'd only had a few months of rest, a few months to mourn our losses and celebrate our victory, and it already sounded like they were asking us to prepare to fight again. I squirmed in my seat.

"Remember, our war is never completely over," Rina said. "However, it is not what you think. The world has changed."

They kept saying that, speaking the obvious. I only feared what hadn't changed—the unending need to fight.

"You have new members of your army," Mom said. "We have given you the Hunters to track down and defeat the Demons. The Angels have blessed them with new gifts that will help them. They can also assist with the Daemoni, if needed. The Hunters serve you, Alexis. They will serve your daughters and their children. Just as the Amadis will continue to do."

"As will the Normans," Rina announced. She didn't simply say it. She declared it.

"What does that mean?" I asked, my mind racing.

Mom tore her eyes from Brielle's face and lifted her gaze to lock onto mine. Her lips curved into a small smile. "It means you rule Earth now."

"*What?*"

Rina handed Elliana over to Mom before coming to stand before me. She dropped down to her knees to be at my eye level. "Alexis, darling, it is time."

"Time for what?"

"Time for us. For you. For thousands of years, the Normans ruled Earth with the Daemoni and the Amadis hidden in the shadows. Everything remained in balance for many centuries. But then evil began to tip the scales, and Lucas and the Daemoni began to gain control. He brought in the Rule of Demons, and that period lasted longer than we care to admit. It began long before it escalated to recent times. But that era is over. You have brought it to an end. You ask what your wings mean?"

I nodded. "Yes. Why do we have them? I mean, besides them being useful as weapons and everything. Why *wings*? They're not like yours or the Angels, so I take it that means we're not Angels. Right?"

She tilted her head as she leaned in and took my hands into hers. "Collectively, you, Tristan, your daughters, the Ames sons . . . you are, indeed, a form of Angel. The lowest form, but still in the hierarchy. You are Earth's Angels."

My breath hitched.

"You, darling, are the leader of them all."

I choked and shook my head. *She can't be serious.*

Rina nodded. "Yes, we are serious. You and your children after you and their children after them will continue to rule until Earth is reborn and rebuilt, until humanity has been fully restored, until balance has been achieved. Over the years, you will be blessed with many more Earth's Angels to assist you."

My brow shot up. More children? Was that what she meant?

"This is why your daughters before now could not be born," Mom said. "Besides Dorian, who had his own purpose, you could not have children until now. Until you ended the last era so this new phase in Earth's cycle could begin."

Rina glanced up at Tristan, then her warm gaze fell back on me. "You have not only birthed these children, but you have birthed a new time. You and Tristan, together with your people, will rebuild this world into what it is meant to be. You, along with these beautiful babies who are the next generation, have ushered in a new era on Earth—the Age of Angels."

The Age of Angels. The words echoed in my mind as I stared forward in disbelief. I had no idea what to think. We were freaking Angels! Not the heavenly kind singing hallelujah in the clouds all day long, but that was never me anyway. I was a warrior. As was my husband. As were my people and everyone else who remained on this Earth. We were not simply survivors, but fighters. Champions. All of us.

But our fight wasn't over.

In fact, it may have only just begun as we faced the challenges of building a new world, but we would persevere. We had love, and we had faith. We had humanity, and we had God's will. We had hope. With everything we had going for us, we'd not only continue to survive, but we would grow.

The Age of Angels.

The words began to take root inside me, the meaning planting itself into my soul. The future of this world lay before us, the success of it placed entirely in my hands. A prospect that was both terrifying and exciting. Daunting yet . . . *doable.* I knew in my heart and soul that we could do this. That I could do it. With Tristan by my side, I knew I could accomplish anything. Because it wouldn't just be me or the two of us, but everyone between here and God's throne, including the Creator, himself, would be backing us.

Together, we would bring in this Age of Angels.

The ultimate warrior and the fierce protector, standing side by side, hand in hand, souls bound as one. Nobody could beat us. For we were together and had already won.

Because in the end, good always wins.

Want more Soul Savers? Continue with the Age of Angels mini-series, books 8-10, now available!

Be sure to join my exclusive reader newsletter to receive bonus content, such as *Wonder: A Soul Savers Collection of Holiday Short Stories & Recipes, Genesis: A Soul Savers Novella, Prophecy of the Wolves: A Soul Savers Novella*, and more. You'll also be the first to know about new releases, sales, and special events. There's still more to come! Don't miss out!

Please consider leaving a review for *Fractured Faith* and the rest of the Soul Savers series. Just a sentence or two is greatly appreciated. It's one of the absolute best things you can do to support your favorite authors. Thank you in advance!

GLOSSARY & CAST

A.K. Emerson – Alexis's famous pen name.

Alexis Ames Knight – Amadis matriarch. Married to Tristan Knight and mother of Dorian. Youngest daughter to ever go through the Ang'dora and to become matriarch. Her bio father is the leader of the Daemoni. Known abilities include telepathy, electricity, telekinesis, super strength, speed and senses, Amadis power.

Alys – Recently converted Amadis vampire.

Amadis (uh-MAH-dees) – Secret matriarchal society that serves as the Angels' army on Earth, currently led by Alexis Ames Knight. Their purpose is to defend human souls from the Daemoni and to convert Daemoni souls to Amadis. Consist of a variety of supernatural beings.

Amadis daughters – Women of the bloodline of the original creator of the Amadis. Each daughter eventually serves as the matriarch.

Amadis power – A special power of love and light gifted to the Amadis by the Angels. The Amadis daughters receive it during the Ang'dora. Other society members are granted a lower level of power upon conversion and official acceptance into the Amadis.

Ammi – Started the London cell of AK's Angels with her sister Kristen. Turned into a vampire and converted immediately by Char and Alexis.

Andrew – The Angel who fell from Heaven and fathered Cassandra and Jordan before eventually ascending (read about it in *Genesis: A Soul Savers Novella*).

Ang'dora – Literally means "gift of the Angels" (Ang = angels, dora = Greek word for gifts). An enigmatic change all Amadis daughters go through to receive their powers and supernatural abilities. Usually happens in middle age, after the daughter has experienced major milestones of life as a human, but Alexis went through it quite early. Except for Sophia, no Amadis daughter has given birth after the Ang'dora.

Angels – Spirits of Heaven who (primarily) remain in the Otherworld. Most fight in the age-old war with Demons, battling for human souls.

Armand – French vampire on Rina's council, he oversees Amadis police force and is anti-Tristan. Killed by Daemoni.

Attair – Amadis warlock from Arabia who's on Rina's council and is anti-Tristan.

Baby Cakes – Faerie who's a friend of Bree, so she's helped Tristan and Alexis. For a price, surely.

Blossom – Alexis's best friend and council member. Amadis witch from the Daytona coven.

Bree – Tristan's birth mother. Fae.

Brielle Sophia Ames Knight – Baby daughter of Alexis and Tristan, twin to Elliana, sister to Dorian. Currently an unknown creature with wings.

Brogan – Amadis vampire, turned when the Daemoni first came out to the humans during the war. After retiring from the military, he started The Prepper's Stash House, a multi-million dollar doomsday prep company, which turned out to be a really good thing for Alexis and A.K.'s Angels, who converted him to Amadis. He's much cooler than his nephew, James.

Carlie – Alexis's human classmate during her first year at college. Now a doctor in D.C.

Cassandra – Half angel, half human who started the Amadis (read her story in *Genesis: A Soul Savers Novella*).

Chandra – Amadis were-tiger and member of the matriarch's council who oversees the region of India.

Charlotte Allbright – Amadis warlock, Owen's mother, Sophia's best friend, and overall badass aunt figure to Alexis.

Cloak – A magic spell performed by mages that hides or makes invisible its subject. Often used in conjunction with a shield.

Conversion – The process of eliminating dark or light energy and replacing it with the opposite, then indoctrinating the supernatural being into the new society. The Amadis purpose is to convert Daemoni souls before they become damned, destroyed, or forever lost. However, on occasion, Amadis members will convert to the Daemoni (e.g., Ian).

Cruz – A Daemoni were-jaguar.

Daemoni (day-MAH-nee) – Satan's servants as the Demons' army on Earth, currently led by Lucas. They turn humans to harvest their souls and build their army. The Amadis try to stop them.

Debbie – Faerie in England who helps Alexis and Tristan from time to time. Cohorts with Stacey, another faerie.

Demons – Spirits from Hell, some being angels that fell from Heaven with Satan as his followers and others being his creations. They take various physical forms, including horned and winged beasts and possessors of human meat suits.

Dorian Knight – Son of Alexis and Tristan, unknown creature but currently human. Known abilities include self-healing and flying. Converting to Daemoni?

Earth's Angels – Newly created by the Angels, on the lowest rung of the Angel hierarchy, includes Alexis, Tristan, the Summoned sons who have converted back to Amadis, as well as their offspring. Alexis leads them.

Edmund – Summoned son and member of the Daemoni. Known abilities include flashing, super strength and speed, idiocy, and being an overall douche-canoe.

Elliana Katerina Ames Knight – Baby daughter of Alexis and Tristan, twin to Brielle, sister to Dorian. Currently an unknown creature with wings.

Eris – Daemoni witch from ancient times who helped Jordan create the potion that changed everything (read about it in *Genesis: A Soul Savers Novella*).

Faeries/Fae – Little is known about the fae as they tend to stay away from human affairs, as well as those of the Amadis and Daemoni. A handful do enjoy wreaking havoc in the Earthly realm, and sometimes they may even help out. They're considered Otherworldly creatures, because their world is not exactly part of Earth. They closely guard their secrets about the Faerie realm.

Ferrer – Blacksmith mage who lives on Amadis Island.

Fertility Stone – The faerie stone Bree gave Tristan when he was a young boy, embedding it in his heart with the instructions to give it to his true mate. Only when she has possession of it can he father children. The stone also allows the holder to share their emotions so he could feel his mate's love—but also the possessor's darker emotions.

Flashing – The supernatural ability to transport to another location up to a hundred miles away (give or take) in the blink of an eye. While objects can be held or attached to the body during a flash, Tristan is the only known creature who can flash while carrying another person. While both Daemoni and Amadis can flash, it's not necessarily a natural ability for all—some creatures have to be assisted by mages.

Galina – Russian Amadis warlock and a member of the matriarch's council, she favors Tristan and Alexis.

Hades – Daemoni HQ, an underground city in the Taymyr Peninsula of Siberia.

Heather – Human girl, Dorian's babysitter and friend, daughter of Phil and sister to Sonya.

Hellfire – Direct from Hell, used by Demons, one of the few things that can scar, severely maim, and possibly kill Alexis and Tristan.

Hunters – Humans (or are they?) who know about the supernatural creatures and kill them.

Ian – Member of the Daemoni, converted from the Amadis. Known abilities include compensating for his miniscule junk by spilling secrets, causing problems with the Amadis, and ruining Alexis's life.

James – The boy Alexis punched in the nose when she was a teenager. Later became a hunter, and they met up again in D.C.

Jaxon – Were-croc from the Australian Outback who's become part of Alexis's team. Blossom's beau.

Jeana – Sorceress who tortured Alexis and Owen to learn Lucas and Kali's secret about the Norman soldiers. Mate of Merrick. Dead.

Jelani – Wizard from Africa who is one of the matriarch's council members.

Jessica – Faerie with a southern accent, calls Lisa her sister.

Jordan – Early leader of the Daemoni who sought power over all, inadvertently helping to create the Amadis (read his story in *Genesis: A Soul Savers Novella*).

Julia Acerbi – Vampire and Amadis matriarch's council member. She'd been one of Rina's closest advisors and friends.

Kali – Daemoni sorceress who took over Martin Allbright's body. Dead.

Katerina "Rina" Ames – Past matriarch of the Amadis. Known abilities included telepathy, super strength and speed, flashing, bonding souls, converting souls to Amadis, making ballgowns everyday attire. Ascended.

Kristen – Human girl who started the London branch of AK's Angels with her sister, Ammi.

Kuckaroo – Amadis village in Australia.

Lesley – Daemoni vampire. Companion of Sonya and Alys. Died in the war.

Lilith – Bree's daughter and Tristan's sister. Dead.

Lisa – Faerie with a southern accent, calls Jessica her sister.

Loft, The – Formerly The Prepper's Stash House, a massive underground nuclear bunker that had been the storehouse for the multimillion dollar doomsday prep and survival training company. Given to the Amadis by Brogan, the owner, after A.K. Angels arrived for shelter and converted him. Sarcastically renamed The Loft.

Lucas – Alexis's sperm donor and leader of the Daemoni. Often (but not always) uses the last name Emerson.

Lykora – An Angelic being that is extremely loyal and highly protective of its master. When in hidden form, looks like a small white dog, but when in defensive mode, can grow as large as necessary to protect, has a wolf head and body, tiger stripes on a white coat, and feathered wings.

Mages – The wide classification of supernatural beings that can wield magic, including witches/wizards, warlocks, and Sorcerers/sorceresses. These general sub-classifications are based on strength of power. Some may call themselves by other names, depending on the type of magic they use, preference, or other reasons (e.g., Shamans, Druids, etc.).

Martin Allbright – Powerful warlock, Charlotte's husband and Owen's father.

Merrick – Sorcerer who tortured Alexis and Owen to learn the secret about the stones that control the Norman soldiers. Jeana's mate. Dead.

Minh – Vietnamese witch, member of the matriarch's council, oversees the Asian region.

Molita – Daemoni born warlock converted to Amadis during the war.

Noah – Sophia's twin brother, Rina's son, a Summoned son with the Daemoni and controlled by Kali.

Norms/Normans – Normal humans.

Oliver Winston Chambers – Sophia's true love who was turned to a vampire then buried under a building in Charlotte, North Carolina, for a century. Dead again.

Ophelia – Witch who serves as head of staff at the Amadis matriarch's mansion.

Otherworld – Currently unknown but seems to refer to Heaven and Hell, as well as Faerie.

Owen Allbright – Warlock and Alexis's so-called protector. Also like a brother to her and Tristan's best friend. Known abilities include shielding, cloaking, magical bindings, flashing, and pushing everyone's limits.

Phillip Jones – Human wife beater, child abuser, and overall scum of the earth who drove an older orange Camaro. Heather and Sonya's father. Dead.

Portals – Magical doorways that can only be created and controlled by sorcerers/sorceresses and extremely powerful warlocks like Owen. They allow teleportation to anywhere in the world just by stepping through.

Rene – Daemoni were-cheetah who chases Alexis down in Hades.

Safe House – Homes, lodges, and other accommodations scattered around the world where Amadis can retreat to when under attack or when going through the conversion or transformation process.

Sasha – Dorian's lykora.

Satan – No explanation necessary.

Savio – Italian were-shark who was on Rina's council and was anti-Tristan.

Seth – Tristan's former name when he was Daemoni. The Daemoni still call him that.

Sheree – An Amadis were-tiger who'd been bitten and turned against her will by the Daemoni. She was Alexis's first ever conversion from Daemoni to Amadis. Now she helps with conversions of others and is a close friend to Alexis.

Shield – A magic spell performed by mages that puts a protective barrier around its subject. If the subject is not also cloaked, the subject can still be seen, so it's often used in conjunction with a cloaking spell.

Shihab – Wizard from Arabia who sat on Rina's council.

Solomon – Vampire, Katerina's partner, and Amadis council member. Known abilities include being scary AF. Dead.

Sonya – Recently turned vampire, now converted to Amadis. Heather's sister. A.K. Emerson's "biggest fan" (a/k/a stalker).

Sophia Ames (a/k/a Mom a/k/a Mimi) – Alexis's mother and Amadis daughter. Known abilities included telekinesis, summoning and manipulating water, persuading others to do as she likes, sensing the truth of a situation, super strength and speed, flashing, converting souls to Amadis. Ascended.

Sorcerers/Sorceresses – The most powerful of the mages that can boost their energy by siphoning more from the earth and everything around them. Their greed for power, narcissism, and general disdain for pretty much everyone make them loners and also not part of the Amadis.

Stacey – A faerie in England who helps Alexis and Tristan from time to time. Cohorts with Debbie.

Stefan – Warlock, council member, and Sophia's former protector. Known abilities included creating a protective shield, flashing, serving as Alexis's only father figure. Dead.

Summoned Sons – Amadis sons, twins of Amadis daughters/matriarchs, who always go to the Daemoni, as though magically summoned. Include Noah, Edmund, and Dorian.

Sundae – Alpha of the Georgia wolf pack. Trevor's mate.

Sylvie (Aunt Sylvie) – Blossom's aunt and leader of the Daytona Beach witch coven.

Teah & Teal – Human cousins who'd joined A.K.'s Angels

in Florida with Heather and Sonya. Teachers at the school in The Loft.

Trevor – Amadis werewolf and leader of the main Florida wolf pack. Sundae's mate.

Tristan Knight – Former Daemoni converted to Amadis by Sophia. Matriarch's second, best friend, and husband. Dorian's dad. Sexy AF warrior. Known abilities include shooting fire from his palm, quickly determining the best solution if he knows enough of the facts, telekinesis, paralysis, instant killing power, super-duper strength and speed, brooding with guilt, giving a girl multiple Os.

Vampires – Supernatural beings that are sustained by blood. They can also feed on fear and other emotional energy. There are vampires on both the Amadis and the Daemoni sides.

Vanessa – Formerly one of the Daemoni's star vampires recently converted to Amadis. Alexis's half-sister, Victor's twin, and Lucas's daughter. Known abilities include stirring up trouble and pissing everyone off.

Veil – The magical barrier between the Earthly realm and the Otherworld. Beings in the Otherworld can often see through the Veil to the other side, but those on Earth cannot see into the Otherworld. Well, except for those with the sight, but the talent is very rare.

Victor – Vanessa's twin brother, Alexis's half-brother, Lucas's son and Daemoni vampire who's not too bright.

Warlocks – Part of the mage classification, supernatural beings who are born with the ability to wield magic and physically endowed with strength and speed, making them excellent warriors. They are not gender specific and are on both the Amadis and Daemoni sides.

Whitby Abbey – Ancient abbey on the northeastern coast of England. The place where Dorian was found, where Alexis faced off with Lucas, and where Sophia, Rina, and Winston died.

Witches/Wizards – Part of the mage classification, supernatural beings who are born with the ability to wield magic, usually using a wand as well as spells, incantations, potions, elemental energy, etc. While they can be quite powerful, their powers and physical strengths aren't as strong as Warlocks or Sorcerers. Using the term Witch or Wizard was traditionally by gender, but really is up to each individual's preference. There are Witches and Wizards on both the Amadis and Daemoni sides.

Were-creatures/animals (a/k/a Shifters) – Supernatural beings with two combined spirits—human and animal—and they can physically shift between their two forms. There is a were-creature/shifter for nearly every predatory species on Earth, and they're on both the Amadis and the Daemoni sides.

Zombies – Reanimated corpses with deadly bites. Created by mixing necromancy magic with fatal and highly contagious viruses, such as Ebola. Lucas made them as an experiment and to provide meatsuits for the Demons he planned to let loose on Earth.

FRACTURED FAITH PLAYLIST

(Songs I listed to on repeat while writing this book)

Hello by Evanescence
Empire by Shakira
Guilty All the Same by Linkin Park
Wrong Side of Heaven by Five Finger Death Punch
Without You by Breaking Benjamin
Into the Nothing by Breaking Benjamin
All of Me by John Legend
Iridescent by Linkin Park
Until It's Gone by Linkin Park
Glory and Gore by Lorde
Battle Cry by Imagine Dragons
Conquistador by Thirty Seconds to Mars
Keys to the Kingdom by Linkin Park
Birth by Thirty Seconds to Mars
End of All Days by Thirty Seconds to Mars
Do or Die by Thirty Seconds to Mars
Your Love Is a Song by Switchfoot

Author's Note: If you've been paying attention to these playlists, you'll notice Thirty Seconds to Mars and Linkin Park show up quite a bit throughout the series. Along with Evanescence, Soul Savers might not have existed without them. When I rediscovered my love of writing, I also rediscovered my love of music. They went hand-in-hand for me. I saw 30 Seconds to Mars in concert while writing book 3. Unfortunately, I never got to see Linkin Park live, and my heart broke when I learned of Chester Bennington's death. Mental health is very real and close to my heart. It's something more of us struggle with than we likely know, including myself and much of my family. I know books can help, providing a temporary escape and distraction from harmful, unhealthy thoughts. Music helps, too. If you are one of millions who struggle with mental health, I hope you are able to get the help you need. And I hope you are able to find solace in books and music, or whatever brings you joy.

With this in mind, I'm making this series a tribute to Chester Bennington. The music and art he created spoke to my soul, and I am forever grateful for it.

ABOUT THE AUTHOR

Kristie Cook is a lifelong, award-winning writer in various genres, primarily New Adult paranormal romance and contemporary fantasy. Her internationally bestselling, award-winning Soul Savers Series includes seven books, as well as several companion novellas and short stories. Over 1.2 million Soul Savers books have been downloaded. She has also written The Book of Phoenix trilogy, a New Adult paranormal romance series. Her books have been featured in *USA Today's* HEA section, on Good Morning America, and in the Emmy's Gifting Suite.

Kristie also created, writes in, and publishes the award-winning Havenwood Falls shared world, a collaborative project with multiple series, dozens of authors, and countless stories.

Besides writing, Kristie enjoys reading, cooking, traveling, getting her hippie on, and feeding her addictions to coffee, chocolate, cheese, and her latest TV obsession. She has lived in eleven states, but currently calls Florida home.

CONNECT WITH ME ONLINE

I love to hear from and connect with readers. Please don't be shy.

Facebook Reader Group: https://www.facebook.com/ groups/KristieCook.AKAngels.KnightRiders/

Email: kristie@kristiecook.com

Author's Website & Blog: http://www.KristieCook.com

Facebook: http://www.facebook.com/AuthorKristieCook

Twitter: http://twitter.com/kristiecookauth

Goodreads: https://www.goodreads.com/KristieCook

Instagram: http://instagram.com/kristiecookauth

BookBub: https://www.bookbub.com/authors/kristie-cook

Word of mouth is very important for any author. If you enjoyed the book, please consider leaving a review, even if it's only a sentence or two. This is one of the most important and appreciated things you can do for an author.

ACKNOWLEDGMENTS

I've always said that writing the acknowledgments is harder than writing the whole novel, and with this being the last book of the series, I realize I had no idea before. I'm not sure where to even start.

Actually, I do, because first and foremost, I thank the Creator. Besides my role as mother, I had lost my sense of purpose for a while. I could see my sons growing up and wondered what I would do when they left the house. Then God blessed me with new babies, just in a different form. I'd given up on my dream of writing fiction, figuring I'd been given my writing talents for other uses, but once God gave me Alexis, then Tristan, and then their stories, I began to feel a new sense of purpose. I had no idea if these tales would go anywhere beyond friends and family—or even just myself, if I'm being honest—but I thought then that if they made a positive impact in only one person's life, I would have served my purpose. I hear every day from fans whose lives my stories have affected. There have been many times along this journey where I've nearly lost my faith, like Alexis, but I held on to it. All you need is a mustard seed. I have been so blessed in so many ways, all because He gave me this gift, these book babies, and this purpose. And most important to all of this, He gave me you.

I couldn't have done this without the support of my real-world family—my husband, Shawn, and our incredible sons, Zakary, Austin, and Nathan. They've cheered me along, suffered through empty cabinets and refrigerator, and were more than understanding of the times I had to lock myself away to get these voices out of my head. Much appreciation to the rest of my family, too—my parents, my aunts and uncles, my cousins, my grandparents, and the huge number of in-laws, who all played a role in leading me to this point in my life.

Some of the best and most surprising blessings I've received on this journey are the friendships I've formed with readers. In fact, one group, Kristie's Crew, has become a second family. Chrissi, Stacey, Julie, Debbie, Jessie, Inga, Claire, Kath, Mindy, Rissa, Christina, Heather, Lisa, and Kate —you are my sisters from other misters. Thank you for all of your support, love, and friendship.

Other amazing friends I've developed on this journey include my bestie, Brenda Pandos, my amazing P.A., Kristen Yard (who *will* be writing acknowledgements of her own one of these days), and S.T. Bende, one of the biggest-hearted and most talented people I've ever met. I seriously don't know how I would have finished this book without the three of you. I'm so proud and blessed to call you my friends.

Also, thank you to Lily Rowserein for my gorgeous new covers for the entire series, as well as to Regina Wamba and Brenda Pandos for the previous covers that were also so beautiful. Thank you so much to my betas, Chrissi, S.T., Stacey, Julie, Claire, Christina, Mindy, Inga, Jessie, and Heather, for giving me honest feedback and challenging me to do better. Also to Kristen and Jen for raking through the bloopers, oopsies, and flat-out errors.

So much appreciation to the many authors who have given

me encouragement to keep on, even when you didn't know how much of a difference you've made, including Sarra Cannon, G.P. Ching, Raine Thomas, R.K. Ryals, Rachael Wade, Lynn Rush, LK Gardner-Griffie, Beth Isaacs, Hope Collier, Eva Pohler, Mary Ting, Nely Cab, Lani Woodland, Jamie Magee, Shelly Crane, Amy Bartol, Lila Felix, Denise Grover Swank, and so many more.

Finally, I can't even come close to expressing my gratitude to you, dear reader, who have stuck with me and these characters until The End. To Kristie's Warriors (now Club KC), who do so much to share their love for this series with the world. To all of you who have emailed me and connected with me on social media, I appreciate those little messages and interactions more than you know. I pray that this story has been all you hoped for, and maybe more. I hope you close this book with a heart full of love and faith. And I hope that I'll see you again soon between the pages of my books. After all, there is so much more to come. Much love to you!

BOOKS BY KRISTIE COOK

SOUL SAVERS

Recommended Reading Order:

A Demon's Promise

An Angel's Purpose

Genesis: A Soul Savers Novella

Dangerous Devotion

Dark Power

Sacred Wrath

Unholy Torment

Fractured Faith

Age of Angels Part I: Awakened

Age of Angels Part II: Lost

Age of Angels Part III: Marked

Prophecy of the Wolves: (A Soul Savers Tie-In Novella)

Wonder: A Soul Savers Collection of Holiday Short Stories & Recipes

HAVENWOOD FALLS

Recommended Reading Order:

Forget You Not

Lose You Not

Break Me Not

The Collector: Awakening

Savage Salvation (Sin & Silk)

Sun & Moon Academy Book One: Fall Semester

Sun & Moon Academy Book Two: Fall Semester

The Winged & the Wicked (with T.V. Hahn)

Havenwood Falls Short Story Anthology 2018

Havenwood Falls Short Story Anthology 2019

Havenwood Falls Short Story Anthology 2020

BOOK OF PHOENIX

The Space Between

The Space Beyond

The Space Within

www.ingramcontent.com/pod-product-compliance
Lightning Source LLC
Chambersburg PA
CBHW030548260626
47157CB00006B/2230